DOCK

BANDIT PATH

RAVENSWOOD ARENA

KNIGHT'S PASS

CROWN ROAD

MERMAID LAGOON

THE ROAD LESS TRAVELLED

HUNTER'S TRACK

QUEEN'S WALK

Madame Bouffant, the Palm Reader

ROAMING GIANT ROUTE

Ravenswood Gift Shop

TALON AND FANG TRAIL

Eye of Newt's, the Herbalist

THE GROVE

Dear Reader,

I cannot wait for you to dive into this epic story of Ragnarök, renaissance faires, and three Valkyrie sisters who hold the fate of the nine worlds in their hands! Bryn, the hot mess and the youngest, is determined to stop it, but she'll need the help of Juniper—a half human, half giant (and possibly her half sister, too?)—as well as her crush, Wyatt, who might just be the Black Knight of lore.

Debut author Freya Finch has crafted a fun, funny, page-turning Norse thriller filled with characters who'll become as dear to your heart as they have to mine.

So in the tradition of hygge, light the fire, cozy up to the flames, and feed your soul with this heartwarming and exciting story that feels both timeless and necessary.

Who run the world after all? Girls!

xoxo

Melissa de la Cruz

MELISSA de la CRUZ STUDIO

RISE

FREYA FINCH

 MELISSA de la CRUZ STUDIO

HYPERION
Los Angeles   New York

First Edition, July 2024
10 9 8 7 6 5 4 3 2 1
FAC-004510-24109

Printed in the United States of America

This book is set in Aldus Nova Pro/Linotype; Crypton/Fontspring;
Fairfield/Adobe; Bartender/Fontspring
Designed by Phil Buchanan
Illustrations © Shutterstock

Library of Congress Cataloging-in-Publication Number: 2023945476
ISBN 978-1-368-10099-1

www.HyperionTeens.com

FOR MY BEST FRIEND AND HUSBAND, ALEX

PROLOGUE

By the light of the moon, in the frozen heart of the Iron Woods, the dead ones hunted her.

Juniper gripped the giant reindeer's fur as they crashed through the dense and unforgiving underbrush of the wild forest, fleeing from the thick smell of smoke and ash that had once been her home. Heavy, rhythmic footfalls like beating war drums sounded behind her. Unable to fight the terrified voice in her head telling her not to, she chanced a look over her shoulder.

Three quick shadows were gaining on her. Their armor caught the faint moonlight cutting through the trees and the fiery glow of their eyes. Ancient frost-covered pine trees moved at will in the Iron Woods, making the forest almost impossible to navigate, but the dead men never lost their trail.

"Don't stop until we reach the edge of the wood!" She urged the reindeer with a kick, and he huffed, skipping forward, breath steaming from his mouth.

From a pouch at her belt, she grabbed a fistful of seeds and tossed them blindly over her shoulder. Roots and vines exploded out of the ground where they landed, knocking the dead men sideways, but nothing could stop them.

Juniper's heart thrashed like a hare in a trap. "Hurry, friend!"

But the reindeer couldn't run much longer. Terror would only get them so far, and even so, it wasn't enough.

Her village hadn't stood a chance.

While the people slept, the dead ones had come from nowhere, peeling out of the forest like a silent storm. They slunk through the darkness and into the village, stamping out the communal fires with moldy boots and frostbitten feet, nothing more than a hush. The reindeer whined in their stables, but no one knew what was happening until it was too late.

Juniper had been sleeping under a pile of furs by the hearth when her grandmother ripped her out of her slumber and shoved a pouch full of seeds into her hand. At first, Juniper didn't know why she needed her magic, then she heard the screams.

"The village is under attack," her grandmother said. She was already dressed for battle, her broad chest covered in lamellar armor and padded leather.

"Who is it, Amma?" Juniper threw her moss cloak across her shoulders and grabbed her wooden staff, ready to fight.

But when she looked into her grandmother's eyes, the deep lines of the woman's face as familiar and comforting as a map, she saw confusion and terror, and that was more frightening than anything Juniper had ever known.

"It has begun," she said.

Juniper's heart hitched. "Now?"

With a strong push, Amma shoved Juniper out the door.

The horde was still nowhere to be seen. There was only the distant sounds of screams. Juniper and Amma rushed by a father as he carried his barefooted and sleepy-eyed children to a loaded cart; dogs whined and limped to safety; the smell of smoke already choked the air.

Despite the gray in her hair and the wrinkles in her face, Amma moved quickly, leading the way to the stables. Juniper had to jog to keep up, tucking her staff tightly under her arm and cinching the pouch of seeds to her belt.

"It is wrong," Amma said. "We knew this day would come, but it should not be like this. You must go to the valkyries on Midgard. They are the only ones who can help."

Fires lit up the village like midday, but smoke muted everything. Shadows moved through it. Friend or foe, Juniper couldn't tell. Everything was happening so fast.

In the stables, reindeer thrashed, wild-eyed, in their stalls. Amma led one out, and he stomped his hooves impatiently. Juniper steadied him with a gentle hand.

"But, Amma, I do not know how to get to Midgard!"

Her grandmother pulled her close and tucked a bird's feather, long and black as night, into Juniper's jerkin pocket. "Use this, a gift from your mother. It will take you there."

"My—my mother? But you said never—"

"Listen to me! You have prepared for this." Before Juniper could protest, Amma secured their family's sacred periapt inside Juniper's seed pouch then kissed her forcefully on the brow. "May he protect you. You have one week."

A thunderous boom shook the ground as one of the longhouses collapsed. Juniper's heart lodged in her throat.

All at once, reality set in.

This was her home, and it was burning.

"Amma, I cannot leave you!"

"You must. You are not safe here any longer. Get to the edge of the wood, to open sky—"

High keening screams sliced through the village. The battle raged, growing closer. Amma grasped Juniper tightly and, using her immense strength, tossed her onto the reindeer's back.

"Use the stars. Go, child!"

With a flat smack, she sent the giant reindeer galloping, whisking Juniper away. By the time Juniper turned to look, Amma had already vanished in the smoke.

All around her the dead ones pounced and hacked, gnashed and battered, destroying everything and anyone in their way. Fires blazed, sheep fled, houses crumbled. She barely had strength to hold on to the reindeer's antlers as he leaped over splintered timber and broken fences. They landed heavily near three dead ones looming over fallen bodies, swords dripping in blood.

A cry escaped her lips.

The dead men raised their heads, looking at her like wolves eyeing their prey.

Juniper galloped. They chased.

The dead would leave none alive.

Juniper and the reindeer tore out of the village gate and into the Iron Woods. No one in their right mind would dare enter the walking forest at night, but Juniper had no choice.

The darkness swallowed her.

She yanked and pulled the reindeer through the gaps in the trees as the forest shifted, dodging roots and trunks of ancient firs and pines, but the dead were at their heels.

She lobbed more seeds, more roots sprang up. They ensnared one of the dead ones, and his scream sounded like blades on a grindstone.

The other two were almost upon her. She couldn't stop, couldn't slow. The forest was a freezing, unforgiving landscape full of creatures and monsters, and everything that was dead stayed so. It was the law of nature. But nothing about this was natural.

Only dark, forbidden magic could summon draugar.

Appearing as if from thin air, a draug stepped in front of her path, his glowing ember eyes bright in the dark.

She yanked hard on the reindeer's fur, and they skidded to a stop in the dirt.

Faint moonlight caught the dead man's face. It looked like it had been eaten away by animals, exposing broken teeth and a caved-in cheekbone. His eyes glowed like smoldering hearths, without any of the warmth. What remained of his skin was blue-white, the color of a frozen bog, and his leather armor barely hung on to his skeletal frame. She could see through his rib cage.

The draug lashed out with his sword.

Juniper knew he had struck true, but terror didn't let her feel it.

She threw a handful of seeds into his face and roots sprouted in his eyes. Blinded by flowering fireweed and bilberries, he roared as Juniper kicked the reindeer into a gallop once more.

Cold air snatched the breath from her lungs, and tears swam in her vision. She shouldn't have left her grandmother to fight alone.

Before she could turn back, the trees parted, and she realized too late that the ground ahead ended.

A cliff.

Juniper yanked hard on the reindeer's antlers and he reared up, kicking. He bucked her off just before the edge, and what would have been a straight drop to a black, oily river below.

She lay in the moss, dazed, and the frightened reindeer fled without her, disappearing into the churning forest.

Juniper tasted blood. She'd bitten her tongue. Her ears rang and the world spun. She was going to be sick. Then her eyes landed on the open bag on the ground. "No!" Her seeds had spilled everywhere. Clumsily, she tried to scoop them up, but they were too small, and too many.

Half of her magic was gone.

She couldn't let it go to waste. Hand outstretched, she summoned one last spell, calling forth her magic. Her eyes glowed green as the seeds sank deep into the frozen ground and grew into twisting roots, bursting up out of the frost and weaving together like a great tapestry to create a large, impenetrable wall between herself and the draugar. With a heavy push, she guided the barrier to span from one edge of the cliff to the other.

There was no way they could reach her now.

She managed to sit up and press her back against the wall to catch her breath. Beyond the river below, inky black trees waved like tall grass in the valley and the moon was full and bright in the velvet purple sky. A cosmic branch of twinkling stars cut through the night—Yggdrasil, the sacred tree connecting the nine realms. Midgard was one of them. She had to get there. She couldn't give up now.

But pain bloomed bright and hot, stealing Juniper's breath. With trembling fingers, she pressed her hand to her side and her fingers came away warm and wet. The draug's sword had cut through her leather jerkin. How deep, she didn't know, and she was afraid to look. It took everything for her not to faint.

She swallowed the metallic taste of blood in her mouth and listened.

The trees behind her had settled, they weren't walking anymore. No whoosh of the wind, no reindeer's hoofbeats, no clang of draugar armor.

Using her staff, she managed to stand but stumbled as the world tipped beneath her. Pain mixed in with the crippling cold. If the dead didn't get her, the frost would.

With stiff fingers, she pushed her hand into her pocket and took out the black feather Amma had given her. She didn't have the faintest idea how it worked; this magic was not of this realm. She waved it like a wand, but nothing happened. Panic bubbled up her throat. What was she supposed to do?

She looked out across the waving black trees, trying to remember what her grandmother had said. The throb in her head made it difficult to focus.

A breeze tickled the back of her neck like ghostly fingers.

Fear made her blood run cold like the unfrozen river below.

Slowly, she turned.

The last draug emerged from the ground between her and the root wall, passing through dirt as easily as fog.

She screamed and leaped back, nearly falling over the cliff's edge.

His horrible orange eyes fixated on her, the grip on his decrepit sword unwavering.

He could walk through solid ground. Nothing could stop him.

She was trapped.

"This realm does not belong to you!" Her voice trembled like her hands, holding her staff in front of her.

He attacked.

With her staff, she knocked his sword back and tried to run, but he was faster.

His ice-cold hand grabbed her arm and her foot slipped, right over the edge of the cliff. She fell, taking the draug with her.

Wind howled as they plummeted toward the black river.

The draug held on like a vise.

Juniper was too scared to scream.

Her grandmother's voice came back to her, *Use the stars!*

Juniper held out the feather, reaching toward the sky.

The river was rushing up to meet her.

"Take me to Midgard!"

There was a crack of lightning, and the feather burst with blinding starlight as Yggdrasil's power surged through it.

Juniper squeezed her eyes shut.

The air bent and fractured, splitting open with a kaleidoscope of cosmic color.

With a thunderous boom, Juniper and the draug smashed through the veil separating worlds and traveled to Earth.

1

I'M SO DEAD.

All I can do is watch, my stomach in knots, as the cop knocks on my front door. There's no time to plan my escape. With a Chicago police officer flanking either side of me, it's not like I can go anywhere, so I brace myself and wait for the inevitable.

Based on the way the cops glance around, I'd say they've never had to drop someone off at a renaissance faire before. When I told them where I lived, they probably thought I was lying. I wouldn't believe me either. Every time we order out, the delivery guy quadruple checks that he's bringing four extra-large, extra-everything-except-sardine pizzas to Ravenswood Medieval Faire, and that this isn't some practical joke.

My family lives in a replica three-story sixteenth-century English town house, and are one of a few families who live in Ravenswood year-round. Like all the other buildings in the faire, our house has got wattle and daub walls, a thatched roof, and exposed wooden beams like out of a storybook. A sign for Martel Metalworks swings on iron hooks above the forge on the first floor. While we're only a little ways north of the city, when you visit, you can almost forget you're in the same time period. Ravenswood goes hard on aesthetics, that's probably why it's so popular. It's as close to the real thing as you can get. When I was growing up, most of my teachers at school would think I was being hyperbolic when I said I lived in a tourist attraction until Mom would show up for parent-teacher conferences in her gown and surcoat, smelling like iron after having made souvenir swords all day.

One of my first memories is of her in the forge, the heat of the fire stinging my eyes, as she pounded a sword into shape, sweat glistening on her high brow and dripping off her long nose. When she looked down at me and smiled, I remember thinking she was the most beautiful person in the world.

People know us as The Martels Who Live In a Theme Park, which I guess is better than The Martels Who Are Real-Life Valkyries. Some folks have several generations of firefighters or farmers in their family tree. We're just like that. The only difference is that our family shepherds the dead to Valhalla, exactly like the myths.

The best way I can describe Valhalla, as Mom described it to me, seeing as I haven't been there yet, is that it's like an arena as big as a city and made of solid gold and silver with five hundred and forty doors, each one wide enough to fit eight hundred men standing shoulder to shoulder. Folks there live just as they did on Midgard, but not everyone can get to Valhalla. It's on Asgard, the realm of the gods, run by the All-Father Odin. And it's not like Odin collects dead people like my grandpa collected baseball cards. Odin chooses the ones who die valiantly in battle so he can build an army of the strongest, toughest, bravest warriors for Ragnarök, the final war at the end of time. He calls his soldiers *einherjar*.

Even though the einherjar died in pretty gruesome ways, they live their lives like heroes in Asgard, flesh and blood, but with all the perks that come with being Odin's chosen ones. Every day they train for Ragnarök, battling each other and coming back to life—or afterlife?—until they're unbeatable. And every night they feast with their brothers and sisters in arms, partying it up and eating an immortal boar. Barbecue forever. As if that's not amazing enough, beautiful valkyries stationed in Valhalla serve the einherjar endless cups of magical healing mead to patch them up to do it all again the next day. It sounds like paradise, and it's our job to get them there.

No one else in our world knows our secret, and it needs to stay that way. For obvious reasons.

Within seconds of the knock at the front door, the sound of harried footsteps storming down the stairs can be heard, and the door flings open. Prima stands before us wearing a bath towel around her head, and an expression of absolute, pure rage.

"Really, Bryn?"

She's clearly just gotten out of the shower. It's past the faire's operating hours and the guests are long gone, so Prima has changed out of her chemise and surcoat for her University of Chicago T-shirt and bleach-stained sweatpants. She's tall, practically towering over me, and her face is sharp as a diamond. Though her stare is lethal, I force a smile.

Officer Higgins says, "Good evening. Is there a parent or guardian we can speak to?"

"Our mom, but she's..." Prima blinks, the wind taken from her sails. "She's at work."

My heart sinks.

Three days ago, Mom left on a top secret mission and never came home. When she's not training us, teaching us how to fight or how to use our magic, Mom is at the All-Father Odin's beck and call as captain of the valkyries here on Midgard. And we have no idea where she went.

Prima is only nineteen, two years older than me, but she's been looking after us since she got back from college. Her glare returns to a low simmer as her eyes fall back on me. "What did Bryn do this time?"

The cops glance at each other, as if daring the other to admit it. Finally, Officer Higgins says, "She stole our car."

"You what?" To say that Prima looks feral would be an understatement. The cops take a faltering step back as heat radiates from her eyes like a thousand laser beams. They would have no idea why they're afraid of her—they can only feel the air shimmer and shake, like being front row at Lollapalooza. We valkyries can make even the strongest warrior turn tail and run whether we mean to or not.

In an attempt to ease Prima's righteous fury, I smile and wave meekly, which is a lot harder with my wrists handcuffed in front of me. Prima's eyes widen briefly upon seeing them, and the air pulsates like a thunderclap. Her temper is tangible.

Higgins must sense that Prima is about ready to throttle me because he changes his tune, fast. "Calm down, ma'am. No need to do anything drastic."

"I am perfectly calm," Prima says, through clenched teeth. She doesn't even blink about being called *ma'am*.

Before we truly mastered keeping our powers in check, words were often thrown around about us, like *creepy* or *unsettling* or *freaky*—I was called that last one a lot in elementary school. It's hard keeping our powers under control, especially when we're mad. It can make the people around us twitchy.

Prima's gray eyes are hard as steel as she looks at me. "Is she under arrest?"

The cops glance at each other again. I can tell they don't want to be here any longer than they have to. "Not today," Officer Higgins says. "But next time, we won't let her off with just a warning."

Officer Higgins uncuffs me and I rub the feeling back into my wrists.

"Thanks for the ride, fellas," I say.

Quick as a flash, Prima grabs me by the front of my hoodie and says, "I'll take it from here, officers. Thank you." She yanks me inside the house and slams the door in their faces before I can open my big mouth again.

Prima stares at the closed door, her shoulders tense, standing still as a statue, listening as the cops retreat. The air pulses. Nuclear explosion imminent.

Maybe, if I'm quiet enough, she'll forget I'm here and I can slip away into my room and hole up until dinner. But the second I try to sneak up the stairs, there's another knock at the door. Prima whips it open so fast, I'm worried it's going to come off its hinges.

Standing on the threshold is a boy about my age in jeans and a T-shirt. A very attractive boy. He's wearing round, gold-rimmed glasses and has a flop of curly black hair. A long scar cuts down the left side of his face. When his dark eyes move from Prima to me they widen slightly, and my insides do a little twirl. Did he see me get dropped off by the police just now? He must have. Why else would he be staring at me? Mortifying.

Also, he's not alone. He's with another man, because I hear some-one else's voice from out of view. "Hi! Is everything all right? We saw the police—"

"Everything's fine," Prima says, as my face burns. The boy's still staring at me, his brows drawing together like he's trying to figure me out, which only makes him cuter. Not that it matters. He probably thinks I'm some kind of delinquent. Which, maybe I am?

"Oh, okay. Well. Sorry if we're interrupting something," says the man. "Is Kara home?"

It takes Prima a second to answer. "My mom? She's, um, out."

The boy with the glasses blinks, maybe realizing he's been staring at me, and looks at his muddy boots. I use the distraction as an opportunity to creep backward up the stairs.

"Oh, all right!" the other man says. "If you could tell her we stopped by? I'm—"

"Sure! It's just now isn't a great time," says Prima. She has a white-knuckled grip on the door, eager to end the conversation.

"I see!" the man says. "We just moved to Ravenswood, so she can visit us any—"

When I'm halfway up, the stairs betray me and creak.

"I'll pass along the message, thanks!" Prima slams the door again and rounds on me. "Brynhildr Miles Martel, don't you run away from me!" I scurry up the rest of the stairs but Prima's hot on my heels. "Have you lost your mind?"

I reach the second floor and spin around, backing up into the kitchen. The TV blares from the adjoining living room, and Prima's laptop sits open on the kitchen table, a galactic screen saver on display. The back of my knees bang into the bench near the table as the TV sings a jingle about used cars for sale. "I can explain," I say.

"Oh, you definitely will. And it better be good."

My other sister, Reagan, is nowhere to be seen. Without her as backup, I put the table between Prima and me. "It's all one big misunderstanding. You don't have to freak out, Pri."

She slams her laptop closed, hard enough that I wonder if she cracked the screen. "I am freaking out the normal amount. Do you realize how bad this is? You should be in jail right now."

"But I'm not! How about we pretend this didn't even happen? *Anyhoo*, I'm starving. When's dinner?" I notice the smoke alarm is on the table, its batteries removed. Prima in the kitchen is a recipe for chaos, like the meat loaf that had turned into a meat *brick*, or the plastic cutting board that melted to the stove, or the Grilled Cheese Incident That Shall Not Be Spoken About. Now that I think about it, there's a distinct smell of smoke in the air. "Are we ordering out again?"

"Bryn..." Prima's freckled face is turning an ugly shade of red, bordering on purple, and the dishes in the cupboard start to rattle as her temper flares.

Our fat orange tabby cat, Butternut Squash, meows and waddles over from her spot on the couch to greet me. I scoop her up and scratch her under the chin, and she starts purring immediately. "Butters, save me," I say. "Prima's gonna get fifty to life for my murder, and that'll be two fewer people to feed you! Do something!"

Jaws clenched, Prima marches to the open window overlooking the backyard and leans out. I slide up next to her to see, too, because of the commotion below. By the sound of things, my other sister, Reagan, isn't having a great night either.

"A text, James?" Her back is to me, but I can hear the tears in Reagan's voice. "You break up with me over text?"

Half-heartedly, James tries to comfort her by holding her elbows, and smiles. "It was easier that way. Think of it like a letter, but faster."

"How is that better?"

Most people know Reagan, our middle sister, as Lady Silverhand, the faire's beloved knife-throwing warrior princess, dazzling crowds with her beauty and skill. She's still wearing the belted kirtle and

15

smock costume she wears onstage. I have a feeling she and James have been fighting since her last show ended.

For the record, I never liked James. I always thought he was a pompous blowhard. But I'd rather throw myself headfirst into a pile of horse muck than tell Reagan that she has terrible taste in guys. Who cares that he's the Prince of Ravenswood? Sure he can swing a sword, but it's only for show, and James is the best at being the worst of them all. You can't go ten feet without seeing his face on a poster advertising the daily knight tournament.

"Don't cry," he says, charming smile locked and loaded. "This can be a good thing. You'll get to see new people, I'll get to see new people—" He has to raise his voice for Reagan to hear him over her caterwauls. "It's a win-win!"

Prima clears her throat and calls down, "Reagan! I need you. Come up here, please."

Reagan whirls around, fists at her sides. Dark mascara streams down her puffy round cheeks and her large gray eyes swim with more, unshed, tears. She's the prettiest one in our family, even in the midst of an emotional breakdown. "Can't you tell I'm in the middle of something?" she asks, voice wobbling.

Prima gives me a long sideways look. "I wouldn't bother you if it wasn't important."

Unfortunately, James uses the distraction as an opportunity to escape into the thicket of trees, fleeing into the faire. Coward. If I wasn't in major trouble right now, I'd chase him down and show him what happens when he breaks my sister's heart.

Reagan notices the empty spot where James used to be. She screws up her face and brings her hands up in front of her, palms facing each other. Her eyes harden and her arms shake as the air between her hands pulses with power.

In the space between her palms, a shimmering knife materializes out of nothing. The blade's edges are blurry, but growing more solid by the second. The knife shudders, as if itching to be released, but Reagan holds it back, baring her teeth in concentration. Once it's ready, she lets out a yell and throws the knife toward a poster of James stapled to a nearby oak. With a great WHOOSH, it slices through the flyer, cutting the poster in two, the bottom half of James's face fluttering to the grass. The knife dissolves into thin air.

Creating astral weapons is advanced valkyrie magic, way harder than summoning armor. She's been working on it all year since Mom first showed her how. Both she and Prima can do it. I'm still trying to get the hang of it. Being a valkyrie takes a lot of practice.

Reagan wipes her hands on her skirt, makes a satisfied *hmph*, and looks up at us. "Do you think I'll ever be happy again?"

Prima groans. "Reagan, please come inside. Your baby sister is a criminal."

Reagan wipes her runny nose on the back of her wrist and nods, heading around to the front door.

Prima ducks her head back in the house and sighs. The air around her settles somewhat as she pinches the Yggdrasil pendant hanging from her neck. Mom gave us all one when we took our valkyrie oaths. It helps us channel the power from the World Tree, like armor and weapons. Without it, it's a lot harder.

I was really little when she first showed us how she summoned her armor. Her silver pauldrons and breastplate shined with the magic of Valhalla, and her winged helm made her look like a raven, Odin's favorite animal. Right then, I wanted to do everything I could to become a valkyrie, just like her.

Prima sighs loudly. "If it's not you, then I have to deal with Reagan's drama, or I'm setting dinner on fire." She gestures to the smoke alarm on the table. "Today is the absolute worst."

The front door opens downstairs and the sound of Reagan kicking off her shoes precedes her soft footfalls up the steps. She makes a beeline for the fridge and takes out a box of leftover pizza from inside. "What's this about being a criminal? Did Bryn hop the turnstile again?" she asks.

Not fair. That only happened once, when I forgot my CTA pass and my train came early. If I'd missed it, I was going to be late for school, and I couldn't get another detention.

"Worse," says Prima.

"Trespass in the Fitzgerald estate's pool again?"

They were on vacation in Bora-Bora. They weren't using it anyway.

"Worse."

Reagan kicks the fridge door closed, baffled. "Worse?"

"I was trying to find Mom," I say.

They both stare at me. Prima puts her hands on her hips, waiting for me to continue.

To avoid their scrutiny, I focus on petting Butters, who is still happily purring away in my arms.

"I'm really worried about her," I say. "It's been too long for this to be a regular mission for Asgard. So I figured the police would have some sort of database in their car, and I could see if there was a Jane Doe or someone matching her description at a hospital or morgue. And I couldn't exactly tell them she's away on special valkyrie business, because *duh*. So I thought, instead of sitting in this house all day worrying about her, I could do something. Obviously, I didn't find her."

"So you were just in the cop car? Didn't actually steal it? Drive it around?"

"No, I didn't actually steal it. The door was unlocked. Happy?"

Prima watches me, grinding her teeth, like she's chewing on all the things she wants to say but can't. "No, for the record. I'm not happy. For the last time, Mom's not missing! She's busy!"

"But she always lets us know she's safe! Something's wrong!"

"How do you know?"

My breath hitches. Do I really want to admit that last night I had a nightmare where Mom was in trouble? Just thinking about it, I know it's stupid. But it felt so real. Even though I can't really remember the details. The second I woke up, it slipped through my memory like sand through my fingers. The only thing that stayed was dread.

"I just do," I say.

Prima whips the towel off her head and drags her fingers through her dark brown hair. She cut it short at school, coming home for the summer with a bob and bangs, a drastic change for someone like her. Her definition of adventure is reading in her room or using new highlighters in her planner. She's never done anything wrong in her life. Everything with Prima is a neat little three-ring binder, sorted and organized.

"Why do you have to make everything worse, Bryn?" asks Prima. "Everywhere you go, you cause trouble."

Reagan says, "Hey, come on, Pri. Ease up a little. No one got hurt, right?"

"That's not the point!"

"She's just looking for attention."

I hate when they talk about me like I'm not standing right here.

"She should know better," Prima says. She turns to me. "We're valkyries. We're not supposed to be running around, doing whatever we want, whenever we want, especially since Mom's working.

We're not kids anymore. Our duty is to this realm and to Yggdrasil and to our oath to Odin. Have you forgotten that?" Prima's eyes are pleading now.

Those eyes say everything she won't: *Why can't you be like us?*

As my sisters look at me, something squeezes my heart, hard enough to make my chest hurt. To tap on the glass of that particular emotional barrier is asking for a dam to break. But I smile, like it doesn't bother me.

I hold up Butters and stretch her out toward Prima, using the cartoonish voice I always use whenever speaking for our cat. "*Bwyn has learned her lesson, Pwima. She won't do it again. She pwomises.*"

Butters blinks at Prima with her blank, thoughtless, adorable face.

Our cat isn't the smartest in the world—then again she isn't actually a cat but our hamingja, the physical form of a luck spirit attached to our family. You can tell because of the luck rune in her white chest fur.

Prima's mouth twists as she stares at me hiding behind Butters. It's hard keeping a straight face when Butters looks that cute. I need all the help I can get.

"Okay. You're right, Butternut Squash," she says, folding her arms over her chest. "Bryn won't do it again, because she's grounded."

My jaw drops. "What?!"

"Grounded. The rest of summer."

"It's June!" Butters squirms out of my arms, jumps on the table, and scampers off. My luck has literally run out on me. "You can't ground me for months!"

"Yes, I can. With Mom not here, I'm in charge. You're not leaving these fairgrounds. No mall, no movies, no phone, no friends—"

"Lucky for you, I don't have any friends," I say, like it's a snappy comeback.

Prima stares at me, her face totally unreadable, but it's not news to her. It's kind of tough having regular friends. *You* try being friends with someone who has to keep their whole life a secret. It's not fun.

Prima holds out her hand, wiggling her fingers expectantly, the universal signal for *hand it over.* "Phone. Now."

I groan. The second I pull my phone out of my jeans, she swipes it out of my grasp.

"And don't even think about getting into any more trouble," she says. "Or I will escort you to the afterlife myself."

$$\bowtie$$

I kiss the bowstring to the corner of my lips, drawing my arm back, and stare down the target. The red spray paint on the hay bale stands out against the faded light. A cluster of arrows already sticks out of the bullseye. I add another.

Usually target practice in the backyard helps me calm down, but I'm still sour about Prima grounding me.

"'Or I will escort you to the afterlife myself,'" I sneer, mocking Prima's voice. I lodge another arrow into the bullseye.

Night has truly fallen. Crickets chirp in the bushes, fireflies wink among the trees, and horses neigh as squires take them back to the stables. In the distance there's a party, cheers erupting due to what I can only assume is an intense game of cornhole between staff members. Firelight from the hanging lanterns throws a warm glow across the lawn and the steady clip-clop of horses trotting down the lane makes the night feel softer. The only people roaming the streets now are our neighbors, closing up shop, sweeping the streets, or coming home from a grocery run in town.

I let loose another volley of arrows, fluidly moving from my quiver to my bowstring like plucking a harp.

I'm a good shot only because I have the best teacher. Mom passed down everything she knows to us. Being a valkyrie means being a skilled fighter, a master of all weaponry, but only one weapon truly calls to each of us. Prima chose the spear. Reagan chose knives. Obviously, I picked the bow. But I'm the only one who can't summon my weapon from nothing.

It takes a lot of practice to do what we do—the callouses on my fingers are proof enough. We train for years in preparation to bring Odin's chosen heroes to Valhalla. I still haven't been called to do it yet. I bet I wouldn't be Odin's first-round draft pick anyway.

With my quiver now empty, I walk to the target and yank the arrows out like a clump of grass. The way Prima looked at me still stings. It doesn't matter that I was trying to help find Mom—to her, I'm still an annoying problem.

Why can't you be like us?

Sure, Prima didn't say it, but she didn't have to.

Everyone knows Prima is the smart and responsible one, and Reagan is the talented and lovable one. Me? I'm just...not. I can't compete with them. Even though I kneeled at the World Tree on my ninth birthday, just like they did, wore the same crown of ash branches, carried the same distaff and mead-bearing cup, swore the same oath, I don't know how to be like them.

I force myself to take a deep breath, and close my eyes. When I open them again, I look up to find the tallest tree in Ravenswood, Yggdrasil, the World Tree, which connects all the realms.

Here on Midgard, it looks like a giant ash tree, but in the grand scheme of things, it's basically a twig holding up the world. On a clear night far from any light pollution you can see the rest of Yggdrasil too—the Milky Way.

In the middle of a place like this, no one knows how important that tree is, but it's a useful landmark at the faire. You'll never get lost in Ravenswood. All you need to do is look up.

A soft voice floats across the lawn. "Hey, Bee." It's Reagan.

"Hey," I say, taking aim at the target once more.

She watches me, tightly holding her hand-knit cardigan around herself. Only after I fire off five more arrows does she finally say, "Prima cares about you, okay?"

I roll my eyes. "Did she send you here to say that?"

"No, this is my own peacemaking mission. You two are throwing off the vibes in the house." She takes a seat on the wooden bench and pats it, summoning me. I don't argue and I collapse beside her.

"Do you want to talk about it?" she asks.

Usually I can lift my chin, swallow my feelings, and make a joke, but this time something hard and painful feels like it's crawling up my throat. I wish I could say, *I'm terrified something bad has happened to Mom and I don't know what else to do and I'm afraid of losing everyone I care about.* Instead, I say, "Nah, I'm good."

Reagan studies me for a long moment with her round gray eyes, her lips scrunched into a line, but she doesn't say anything—even though I know she wants to.

"Do *you* want to talk? About James?" I ask.

She sighs, ragged and annoyed. "Nah, I'm good."

Touché. "At least tell me he's not a transphobic dickhead, because otherwise I have to go to the hardware store real quick and buy a shovel and tarp and—"

Reagan huffs out a laugh. "No, no. Don't murder him. He's just a regular dickhead."

She leans on me, resting her ear on the top of my head, and wraps her arms around my shoulders. It's easy for people to fall in love with Reagan. She's popular, and kind, and she makes it all look so easy, even though I know it's not.

When she was five, Reagan knew she was trans, knew she was a girl. Valkyries have always been women, so when it was time for her to take her oath, she was so scared that she'd be turned away at Yggdrasil, that she wouldn't get to be a valkyrie. But Mom assured her she had nothing to worry about, that hundreds of valkyries throughout history had been just like Reagan, and they were all amazing, and she was right. Turns out the divine validating your identity is pretty awesome. I envy her in that way, for being so confident in knowing who she is. There's no question when it comes to her fate.

Fate, for us, isn't an abstract concept. We're all too familiar with the power of the three Norns: Urd, the past; Verthandi, the present; and Skuld, the future. They see everyone's fate, even the gods', weaving destiny like a tapestry. They know what has happened, what's happening right now, and what will happen. But good luck trying to find them to ask about it. They've got their hands full. My nana, a valkyrie in her day too, spent her retirement making sweaters for all of us for every Yule. It took her the whole year to make one for everybody. Imagine trying to weave a tapestry literally made of eternity and finding the time to do anything else.

When it comes to Reagan, I bet her fate is as neat and tidy as the bow she wears on the back of her head. Mine is probably a tangled mess of headphone cords shoved in a Norn's pocket, forgotten about, then thrown in the laundry spin cycle.

"I'm worried about Mom," I say.

"I know. Me too."

"So you believe me? That something's wrong?"

The crickets fill in the silence while Reagan takes a breath. "I don't know. She's probably halfway across the world dealing with some crisis," she says. "I'm always worried about her."

As captain of the valkyries on Midgard, Mom has to drop everything at a moment's notice to fly all over the world with her raven cloak to do Odin's work. He rarely leaves Asgard these days, relying on people like us to take care of things here. If it's not bringing warriors to Valhalla, it's doing one of a hundred other duties in his name, like retrieving magical weapons, finding ancient texts of wisdom, or accepting offerings on his behalf. It's a lot of work. There aren't as many valkyries as there used to be. As time went on, people either quit or died or decided not to take the oath, until it was just us. There are a few retired valkyries still puttering around, but they're ancient. No one would expect them to go on a mission.

"Mom's alone," I say. "We *should* be worried about her."

"This isn't the longest she's been gone for," Reagan says. "Mom's a pro."

Until we become fully fledged, there's no one to look out for her. I know Mom's capable, I know she can take care of herself, but at the same time, I can't shake the feeling that it's different this time. I swallow the lump in my throat and try not to think the worst. Easier said than done.

Reagan loops a clump of brown hair that fell out of my stubby ponytail and tucks it behind my ear. "Can you promise to be good? At least until Mom gets back? Please?"

I sigh. Only she can melt my heart like this. "I'll try."

She smiles, pats a beat on my knee, and stands up. "I'm heading in. Want to do a face mask with me? The avocado-honey one is calling your name."

"No, thanks. I'm going to stay out for a bit longer." I'm not in the mood to be in the same room as Prima right now.

Reagan puts her hand on the top of my head for a second before she leaves, then I'm alone again.

Instinctually, I grasp my Yggdrasil pendant and think of Mom.

I remember the day she gave it to me so clearly. It was right here in the backyard on my ninth birthday, a sacred number in our family, and it was the day I swore at the foot of Yggdrasil to uphold my duties as a valkyrie.

It was a snowstorm, but that didn't stop me from practicing for hours with my first real bow, one with arrows that had points instead of suction cups. When it started getting dark and my fingers had gone numb, she gave me my necklace, the delicate filigree of the pendant in the shape of Yggdrasil. Even though it was a far cry from her usual sword or knife, I'd recognize Mom's work anywhere. I'd never been prouder to wear anything before in my life. I let her put the cord over my head and was surprised at how heavy the pendant felt.

All I ever wanted was to be like her.

I think she knew that, because she smiled a little when she put it on me, and then something passed over her face, something I didn't quite know what to make of at the time. Looking back now, I realize she looked haunted.

Her grip tightened around my shoulders and she said, her breath misting in the cold, "Always remember, Bryn, when you aim with your heart, you can't miss. It takes courage and strength to fight, but once the arrow leaves your hand, you can't take it back. Sometimes the bravest thing you can do is choose not to shoot at all. Do you understand?"

I wasn't sure I knew what she meant, but I had the distinct feeling that she was telling me something she wished someone had told her long ago. So I nodded.

Mom's gray eyes glinted in the evening light as she looked at me for a heartbeat longer. Then the corners of her eyes crinkled and she smiled again. It was like she wanted to tell me something more but decided against it. Instead, she bopped me on the nose with her gloved finger and made me giggle.

"Just you wait, Bryn Martel," she said. "You're going to be one of the greatest valkyries yet. And I can't wait to see it."

I drop my hand from the pendant and tip my head toward the hazy orange night sky, clouded over by Chicago's light pollution.

"Yeah, right."

2

"Top o' the morning there, luvs! Would you be in'erested in these very stylish T-shirts or wee wa'er bottles on this steaming hot day? How about these Ravenswood limited edition coffee mugs? Or this talking dragon for the young 'uns." I gesture like Vanna White to various Ravenswood merchandise on the shelf behind me, giving it my all.

The guests wear identically tight smiles and their eyes dart around, as if searching for help. "We're just looking," they say, in unison. Before I can tempt them with Ravenswood-branded sunglasses, they hurry out of the gift shop and disappear into the crowd.

I fold over the counter with a heavy sigh.

The air conditioner in the window roars behind me, staving off the heat from the mid-morning sun, but the layers I have to wear for work don't help. How they did it in ye olden times, I have no idea. I'm melting.

My day started out all wrong. Because I didn't have my phone as an alarm, I overslept, and Prima woke me up at the last second, giving me barely enough time to throw on my tunic and surcoat. And, lucky me, I lost out on bathroom privileges because Reagan already had dibs, taking up the whole sink to do her stage makeup. I had to sprint across the entire park to make it to work on time.

Guests have been coming and going all morning, but I haven't sold much of anything, so I spend most of my time throwing pens like darts at the wooden sign above the door: THOU BREAK IT, THOU BUY IT. A few Ravenswood pens stick out of the soft wood.

I pick up another pen and take aim, one eye closed, lining up a shot, but something outside makes me pause.

A raven sits on the roof of the ticket booth across the lane. Its glossy black feathers gleam in the bright sunlight, and it watches the fairegoers below with clever eyes. Another raven lands next to the first, flapping its wings and shaking out its head as it settles in.

Now that I think about it, I saw quite a few on my rush to work this morning. One sat on a guidepost, another on the stage where some bards were tuning their dulcimers for Top 40 hits, more on the Ravenswood red and gold bunting in crisscrossing through the market square.

I don't want to think more of it—ravens are just animals—but I know things most people don't.

Ravens are Odin's watchers and messengers. They fly all over Midgard to report what they see back to him on Asgard. It's bad luck to kill a raven—you never know what Odin might have in mind for revenge.

The hairs on my arms stand on end and I shudder.

"Bryn."

I whip around and smile, slathering on as much charm as possible as I hide the rest of the pens behind my back. "If it isn't my favorite king, Mr. Beaumont," I say, sounding like a pirate.

Ravenswood's operational manager, Richard Beaumont, is a forty-something barrel-chested man, with a short-trimmed golden beard and a hearty dose of sun exposure on his sharp nose. When he's not in civilian clothes doing his rounds, he's dressed to the nines in a red velvet cloak and a gold-embroidered tunic, complete with a gold crown. This morning, he's sporting a pale yellow polo, having probably just come back from the country club. There is a distinct lack of smile lines on his face. "What did I say about you and your accents?"

"That I'm a naturally gifted actress and they're Oscar-worthy." At best, my accents are inconsistent, starting out cockney, then turning into Australian, and then sometimes, for truly baffling reasons, into Russian. No matter I've been practicing forever, I just can't get the hang of it.

Mr. Beaumont hums, unamused. "Leave the showmanship to your sisters. I hear you had a run-in with the police last night."

"Ah! A case of mistaken identity." Sometimes I wonder if he has eyes everywhere, like Odin.

Mr. Beaumont hums again, one of his straight eyebrows raised. While his son, James, is stupid and mean, Mr. Beaumont is smart and mean. I'm not sure which is worse. "We won't be having any more trouble from you for the rest of the season, will we?"

"No, sir! Consider me the last person you have to worry about."

Mr. Beaumont runs a finger along one of the shelves, home to plush toy dragons, checking for dust, but he won't find any. It doesn't matter that I've spent all morning arranging the display, Mr. Beaumont is always eager to chew me out for any reason. He pushes one dragon a millimeter to the left and sets off its voice box. "I'll melt your heart!" it says in an annoying cartoon guffaw. Satisfied with his contribution, Mr. Beaumont glances at me. "Critics from *Travel Expert Magazine* will be here any day now. With the King's Feast soon, we should be on high alert."

The King's Feast is an extravaganza of epic proportions. Every summer, guests are invited to dress up like nobles, dine in the great hall, and dance to English folk ballads at Ravenswood Castle. The castle isn't one of those cardboard props you might see at a country fair. No, this is the real deal, with huge towers, solid stone walls, a drawbridge, and an inner keep, even a dungeon where they do haunted tours on Halloween. On the day of the feast, lines to get in stretch out to the parking lot. It's one of the best days of the year.

Mr. Beaumont brushes invisible flecks of dirt off some Ravenswood T-shirts hanging on the rack. "The critics will look for any reason to dock points from our total score, so we must be perfect. No, better than perfect—"

"Better than perfect? Easy!"

"—exceptional. Flawless. The epitome of immersive entertainment. We'll finally receive our long overdue title of America's Best Renaissance Festival. We can't have anything, or any*one*, interfering with that." He looks down his long nose at me, like I'm a bug on his loafer.

"Right on, my liege."

"Good," he says. "I don't want to have this talk again." He begins to exit out the back where he came in, but he spins around and points a finger. "And no more accents."

I salute. Message received.

By the time he leaves, the ravens outside have gone.

⋈

When lunch rolls around and I'm practically starving, I head to the Dragon's Den Tavern, Ravenswood's largest bar and restaurant. It's kind of hard to miss, especially with the giant red dragon made of plaster snarling down at you from the roof.

At this hour, the place is already popping off. Most of the tables are packed. Barmaids flit in and out of the crowd, wielding platters full of steaming food and bubbling drink. Loud laughter carries through the room.

LED-lit chandeliers swing overhead and dozens of coats of arms hang from the ceiling, buffeted by giant ceiling fans. Rosy-cheeked people sit on benches at long tables, eating and drinking and taking a break from the sun, as they anachronistically enjoy delicious turkey legs and ye olde deep-dish pizzas. My mouth is watering by the time I get to the back of the restaurant, and I grin when I spot shiny auburn hair behind the bar.

"An ale, please, bar wench!" I call, my voice booming.

Trudy, who was leaning over an ice machine, stands up and slowly turns around, smirking at me. "Valiant effort, kiddo." She bends down to a cooler beneath the bar, brings out a freezing cold bottle of water, and hands me an apple from a basket near the till. I take both, no question. She's always giving me food on the house. Who am I to complain?

"Don't blame me for trying," I say as I tear open the water bottle and down half of it in one go. "Maybe someday it'll work."

"Them's the rules," she says. "I don't make them, but I do enforce them. If I didn't, I'd be out of a job. No offense. I kind of need this gig, at least for now."

"I know, I know," I say. "I'm mostly joking."

Trudy's teeth flash pearly white behind her bright red lipstick as she smiles, and I smile back. This is an unofficial ritual of ours, me coming to visit her, but it's one of the highlights of my day.

Trudy is older than me, probably in her late-twenties, and drop-dead gorgeous. When I first met her, I thought she was the lead singer of a rock band or an Irish princess. As a barmaid, she gets to wear a white short-sleeve chemise with a red bodice, and it shows off the colorful tattoos snaking up her arms.

She came to Ravenswood for the start of the summer season, coasting up to the staff campsite north of the fairgrounds in her Mustang. Hands down the coolest person I've ever met. It was easy to become her friend.

"Something on your mind?" she asks, inspecting me with her bright green eyes.

"No, nothing," I say. I twist the apple stem idly, making it spin.

She reaches over and presses her finger into the crease between my eyebrows. It takes me by surprise and I nearly drop the apple. "You're a bad liar."

I can't help but laugh.

"Is this about your little run-in with police?" she asks.

"You heard about that?"

"Kiddo, everyone heard about that."

Ravenswood is like a family. Everyone knows everyone, and that means everyone knows everyone's business. All small towns have the same problem. You can't so much as fart without half the faire knowing what you had for breakfast.

I sigh. What a nightmare.

"Getting in trouble sometimes means you're alive," says Trudy. "It's no big deal."

"But it is a big deal. I'm trying to help, and all I do is get in the way."

In one practiced motion, Trudy takes a strap from her wrist and ties her glossy hair in a knot at the base of her neck. She always does that when she's serious, a sign that she's listening. She told me once that being a bartender is like being a part-time psychologist. "Spill."

"I'm grounded."

"Getting brought home by the cops will do that." I love Trudy's sarcasm most of the time, but the way Prima looked at me last night still tugs at my gut.

I peel at the label on my now-empty water bottle. "It's like no matter what I do, I'm a screwup. And how can I compare to them, you know? Like, Prima got a full ride to U of C and she's so smart and responsible, and everyone loves Reagan and she's got her own show here now, and..." I trail off. Pouring my guts out doesn't feel so hard in front of her, and Trudy nods in understanding.

"Family is messy, pretty sure that's the definition in the dictionary. Comes with the territory. But family doesn't always know the real you. They're looking out for you, sure, but they'll never understand. Sometimes you gotta do your own thing with or without them."

She gets it. Not like Prima or Reagan. They are stuck in their own worlds. They don't know what it's like being their sister.

"Soon enough," Trudy says, "you'll be able to hit the road like I did. Carve your own path. It'll get better." She hands me another bottle of water. "I promise."

"Thanks, Trudy."

A couple of frat guys press up to the bar, looking ready to order a few beers. They're rowdy, laughing and pushing each other. I can tell they're going to be a handful.

"You ready to take our order or what?" one guy asks, rapping his knuckles on the bar.

Trudy flashes me an exasperated smile before she puts on another one reserved for customers. "Always ready for you, hero," she says, adding a hint of flirtation that ensures her tip jar is full. She winks at me as I slip off the bar stool and let her get back to work.

I've still got some time before my lunch break is over, so I take a lap through the faire with my water bottle and apple in hand.

Saturdays are always packed, especially during the summer, and it's slow going as I float through the sea of guests in tunics and flowing dresses while they study the faire map trying to decide if they should go to the pirate ship cruise in the lake or try their hand at axe throwing. Some guests are taking selfies in front of Ravenswood Castle and Yggdrasil, which stands beside it.

The tree is already decked out for the King's Feast, sparkling with gold bells and scarlet ribbons. You don't have to be like us to know the tree is special. The air around it hums with magic. Millions of invisible spirits called *landvaettir* have made Yggdrasil their home. They themselves aren't what make Yggdrasil special. You can find landvaettir pretty much anywhere, but they like to live in fields, or rock formations, or any tree really. You just need to listen to know they're there. If you hear the branches moving and there's no wind, you can bet it's the landvaettir saying hello. Ever since I was little, I've dropped shiny pennies or pieces of food in the tree for them. Mom used to say it was good to show kindness to your neighbors, and I took that to heart. I try to give them a treat every day. They're as much our neighbors as anyone.

I drop a penny from my pocket on the tree's roots when I pass it, and the bells on Yggdrasil's branches chime merrily.

Cheers erupt from the arena nearby. I can't resist the pull of a good show. I haven't had a chance to see this one yet, so my curiosity gets the better of me. Every season, the Ravenswood corporate heads come up with new spectacles to keep things interesting, everything from jousts to acrobatics troupes to mock battles. Right now the tiered stands are packed to the brim to watch two guys, both about my age, in full armor, swords in hand, as they prepare to face off in the fighting ring.

I lean on the wooden fence to get a better look.

Prince James beckons to the crowd, his voice booming over speakers hidden in the trees. He's got a microphone taped just below his golden hairline. High cheekbones, strong jaw, charming smile; he looks every bit like a prince from a fairy tale and he knows it. Typical. Knights are like high-school jocks. The role attracts a certain brand of personality that calls for big muscles and a bigger head.

"Fair and gentle folk, I, Prince James, ask you to bear witness to the duel. My cousin, the loathsome Black Knight, has threatened to usurp the throne."

I'm in the minority for wanting to see Prince James get his butt kicked. Only two boys, no older than ten, are with me as they scream, "Go, Black Knight! Get him!"

I take a bite of my apple. Cheers to that.

The Black Knight is new to the faire. I don't recognize him, at least at first.

I do a double take and realize he's the boy from last night, only without his glasses. He probably doesn't wear them when he's performing. I would have believed he was a totally different person if that deep scar on his face hadn't given him away.

As the Black Knight, he stands taller and paces the ring like a caged animal, looking way more intimidating now than he did standing on my doorstep. With that convincing scowl on his face, I could almost forget he's acting. He looks like something straight out of central casting. If a Hollywood producer wanted to find a stereotypical villain, they'd have to look no further, what with his black hair and dark eyes. Even his suit of armor is burnished iron. He holds his sword in well-practiced hands, warming up his wrists by swinging the weapon in circles. He stares James down beneath straight brows with stoic determination, like there isn't a whole crowd watching. It's impressive for anyone my age to be a knight.

"We must now fight to the death!" James says, his irritably convincing British accent carrying over the speakers. "Prepare yourself, fiend!"

Battle music from the speakers fills the air and James and the Black Knight throw themselves at each other, moving in a well-choreographed duel. The moves are real, but the fight is not. While the same character wins every time, the performers still need to sell it. They train a ton to fight convincingly enough for a crowd to eat it up.

People gasp as James barely blocks the Black Knight's attack. They circle each other, and James leaps in for a strike. The crowd hoots and hollers, cheering with each near miss and artful parry. The pair are fantastic showmen. It's almost like the real thing.

At one point, it looks like the Black Knight is going to win. He rushes in, his sword crashing down toward James's shoulder, but James catches him just in time. They're locked together, arms shaking, until James hooks his foot around the back of the knight's knees and pulls, and at the same time twists his wrist, making the Black Knight drop his sword.

The knight falls to his knees, defeated, in the soft dirt, and puts his arms behind his back with his head bowed, sweat dripping from his hair.

Prince James stands, breathless but smiling, and basks in the victory with his head held high. He gestures once again to the stands, brandishing both swords like trophies, and the crowd roars.

When the Black Knight speaks, everyone goes quiet, like they're holding their breath.

"I surrender," he says, his voice amplified. "The only thing I do now is beg for mercy." He puts his hands behind his back and exposes his neck, giving James an easy victory.

James lowers his swords. "A traitor to home and crown begs for his life, but I shall grant it. As Prince of Ravenswood, I uphold decency and honor!" He addresses the crowd, turning his back on the Black Knight. "Do these witnesses accept the outcome?"

A kid screams, "Look out!"

Prince James whirls around as the Black Knight pulls a knife from behind his back and makes to stab him.

The crowd gasps.

James plunges the sword through the Black Knight's chest and the stands explode. The Black Knight dies beautifully, the blade pinned between his arm and chest, falling to the ground and lying motionless in the dirt while Prince James preens for the audience.

"Justice prevails! Long live Ravenswood! Thank you, thank you!"

I clap, amused. What a show indeed.

As the crowd disperses, an announcer lists off the next performances, and I'm swallowed up by the mass of people exiting the stands. Like driftwood, I'm carried with the sea of moving bodies and spit out into the square in front of the castle. I'm about to head back to the shop when I spot the Black Knight stomping out of the arena. He's covered in dirt and doesn't look happy about it, scowling as he marches toward a huge black gelding tied to a post. He flicks his wrist, expertly unspooling the reins as the two Black Knight fans from earlier rush toward him, eagerly brandishing a notebook.

"Can we have your autograph?" one of the boys asks him.

The knight glances up, caught off guard. I don't think he expected anyone to talk to him, not when James is currently surrounded by a hoard of adoring fans, flirting and signing autographs left and right, posing for photos and kissing cheeks. The knight looks at the notebook, color rising in his face, getting redder by the second. Outside of the ring, he slouches, like he's taking up too much space.

He nods and takes the pen while the boys bounce with excitement, grinning at each other. I don't think he's used to the attention; he can barely keep eye contact. When he's done with the two signatures, the boys roar with victory. "Thanks, Mr. Black Knight!"

"Uh, please, call me Wyatt."

"Thanks, Mr. Wyatt!" the boys say as they run off.

Wyatt smiles after them and starts to lead the gelding by the reins, but he sees me across the grass. We lock eyes. His smile drops and so does my stomach.

I've been staring at him like a total creep.

The only logical thing I can do is spin on my heels and hoof it in the opposite direction, fists at my sides. I want to fall in a hole and die. Why am I such a freak? Heat spreads on my cheeks like I've been slapped and I press my cold hands against them as I head back to work. I have plenty of time to beat myself up on the way, but I stop when I hear a KRAK from above.

Dozens of ravens sit on the branches of Yggdrasil. They watch over the faire with their clever eyes, snapping their beaks impatiently as if waiting for something.

KRAK-KRAK, they say.

Park guests go about enjoying their day, none the wiser, but I'm rooted to the ground as the hair on the back of my neck stands on end. I've never seen so many in one place before.

But something spooks the ravens and they take off as one, vanishing into the bright blue sky.

3

"I'M TELLING YOU, PRI, I KNOW WHAT I SAW!"

At home that night, Prima stands at the stove, tasting a noodle from a boiling pot of pasta.

"How many ravens?" she asks me. Then she says to herself, "Why does it taste sweet? Did I mix up the sugar and salt again?" She frowns at the water.

There are more important things than dinner right now. I can barely stand still, it's like I've got ants crawling all over me. "I don't know! I didn't count them."

"I can make this work, I think," she mutters, not listening.

I dance out of the way as Prima hauls the pot to the sink, pouring the pasta into the colander. Steam burns her hands and she drops the pot with a tremendous crash, sending boiling hot water into the air. Prima is good at a lot of things—getting a full ride to University of Chicago to study literature, captaining her varsity volleyball team all the way to state champs, managing the store in Mom's absence. But a chef, she is not.

She sucks a burned knuckle and turns to me. "What were you saying?"

"Ravens!"

From her seat at the table, Reagan looks up from painting her nails a deep shade of crimson and says, "Not to be that person, Bee, but in case you forgot, we live in *Ravens*-wood. They're all over the place. It's not exactly like seeing a unicorn."

"I'm serious," I say. "I got this weird feeling, like when a storm is coming."

"It's probably nothing," says Prima.

"Yeah," Reagan adds. "Ravens are animals, after all. Could be perfectly normal."

I fling my arms wide. "We're valkyries! When is anything perfectly normal?"

"Are you sure they were ravens? Could they have been crows?" Reagan asks.

I know she's trying to be helpful, but I want to tear my hair out.

Prima sighs, fed up. "Did you see any other omen?"

"No, but what if it wasn't Odin? What if it was Mom?"

"If you're trying to get out of being grounded, I swear—"

"I'm not! What if Mom is in trouble and she's trying to tell us?"

"Mom's fine," Prima says, slowly, as if I didn't hear the three million times she's already said it. "She's working!"

I put my hands on my head and groan. "When Mom left, she got a message from a raven with a note tied to its leg."

"Normal valkyrie stuff. What about it?"

"What if she's stuck somewhere and sending ravens is the only way she can talk to us? Something is weird! I don't like it!"

With a wave of her hand, Prima brushes me aside and pulls bowls from the cupboard.

"Why would you think I'd lie about something like this?" I ask, pleading.

Reagan and Prima share a glance and it makes my blood boil.

Of course, I'm just the annoying baby sister, what do I know?

"Believe me or not," I say, throwing my hands up as I head for the door. "I don't care." But I really do care. I don't know why I said that. I care so much, it almost hurts.

⋈

Usually when I'm doing target practice, I can calm down, but it's not working this time. No matter how many bullseyes I hit, I can't seem to relax.

Fighting with Prima is a dumb thing to be hung up on, and I know it shouldn't bother me, but it does. The thing about being a valkyrie is you know an omen when you see one, and when it comes to omens, there's no better culprit than the raven god himself: Odin, the highest seated god in Asgard. The All-Father is notorious for his obsession with wisdom and knowledge. I've never met him, but Mom says she hardly ever sees the gods either. They're too busy living their immortal lives in Asgard to bother with the everyday of humanity. But I wouldn't put it past Odin to pull a fast one now and then.

In all fairness, I really do try to convince myself what I saw today was just a coincidence. Seeing a bunch of ravens at once isn't inherently a sign of doom. They're animals, and hungry ones too, probably looking to steal a french fry out of an unsuspecting guest's hand. I read somewhere that a group of ravens is called an *unkindness*. Sort of setting them up for failure on the popularity score, but who am I to say? It's probably Odin's idea of a joke.

Still ... It can't be a coincidence, can it?

Ravens, Odin, valkyries, it's all one package deal.

And no matter what I do, I guess I can't escape being reminded of my sisters. If they're ravens, then I'm a magpie. The same, but different.

KRAK-KRAK.

Out of the night sky, a raven descends toward me, swooping up sharply before landing perfectly on the bench nearby. Only one. Better than an unkindness, at least.

"Orders from Asgard?" I ask, tipping my chin. I check its leg for a message, but there's nothing there.

The raven hops toward me. It's kind of cute.

"Are you looking for my mom, too?" I ask the raven. Its beady eyes look at me blankly. "Join the club. She's not here."

The raven tilts its head to the side, seemingly confused.

"You wouldn't happen to know where she is, would you?" I ask.

Rrah, the raven croaks.

"I'll take that as a no." I spin around, plop onto the bench next to the raven, and sigh. With my phone confiscated, I've resorted to talking to birds. Great start to my summer.

With its beak, the raven picks at the drawstring on my hoodie.

"I don't have any snacks," I say, gently shooing it away. "You might have better luck at the Dragon's Den Tavern. They throw out all the uneaten french fries about now."

Rrah.

It's clear, the raven isn't going anywhere.

I sigh again. "Listen. You don't want me. My older sisters are inside, they're more qualified to handle whatever it is anyway."

At first I think it's a trick of the firelight from the lamps, but the longer I look at the raven, the more I'm sure that one of its eyes is glowing, getting brighter, as it stares at me.

I can't look away, even though I want to. It's like I'm being pulled forward, drawn in by razor-sharp talons.

"What is—?" I start to say, then there's a rush of wings and I'm pitched into raven-black darkness.

I'm standing on solid ground, but it's different than the soft grass of my backyard. I think it's stone, but I can't see anything. Everything is quiet, but I can tell I'm standing in a wide-open space. The air feels bigger somehow.

Am I dead? What happened?

I'm still holding my bow, but it's taking a long time for my eyes to adjust.

I find my voice. "Hello?"

Slowly, shapes start to take form in the dark.

I'm standing in a vast hall, so big I can't see the ends of it. I'm a long way from my backyard. As far as I can tell, the hall is empty, even the raven is gone. Oak tables and benches stretch for miles around, disappearing into a haze of fog. Unlit braziers and half-melted candles loom like statues in the dark.

The ceiling is made of wooden shields thatched together, shrouded by the ghost of a million stars, swirling in galaxies and nebulas of pastel purples, blues, and pinks like a cloud indoors.

I know this place, even though I've never been here before.

Valhalla, Odin's hall in Asgard.

How did I get to another realm? Last I checked, I either need to cross the rainbow bridge of Bifröst, or use a raven cloak to travel to Asgard. I must be missing a few pages from my valkyrie-in-training guidebook.

"Hello!" I call again, louder. No one answers.

So I walk.

The hall is totally wrecked. Mead horns litter the floor, some benches are knocked on their side or split in half, plates and cutlery lie smashed and they crack underfoot. The air has an odd, metallic smell to it that I can't quite place.

Where is everyone? There should be millions of einherjar feasting and drinking here, recovering from a day of training, but it's like they got up and left suddenly, no time to clean.

I grip my bow tightly to my chest, ignoring the growing anxiety bubbling beneath my rib cage.

A snowflake floats in front of me. I hold out my hand to catch it, but it doesn't melt. It's not snow. Ash?

None of this is right. This isn't at all what I expected. I imagined Valhalla was like a frat house where the party never ends. This? This is wrong.

"Valkyries? Odin?"

No one's home.

A drumline hammers out a beat in my chest, and I keep walking. As I go, more ash falls from above, littering down from the nebula ceiling. A soft, gray dusting of it becomes a layer so deep that it seeps into my high-tops. Ash turns my brown hair gray and gathers in the hood of my sweatshirt. I pull my collar up to cover my mouth and nose to keep from choking.

For what feels like forever, I carve a lonely trail through the empty hall, until a shadow takes shape through the ash storm.

A gigantic throne sits in the middle of the hall next to a massive tree that glitters like starlight, its trunk as wide as a barn. Yggdrasil. Thousands upon thousands of weapons stick out of the World Tree— spears, swords, and axes embedded deep within the bark, waiting to be pulled out.

No one sits on the throne.

The closer I get, the worse my stomach twists and the skin on the back of my neck tightens.

I'm not alone.

"Who's there?" No matter how hard I squint, it's almost impossible to see through the ash. It's falling thick and heavy now, like a blizzard. But then something moves.

Heavy paws thump on the floor and a hulking mass of black fur rises up behind the throne.

A giant wolf.

The wolf growls, deep and gravelly. It's so loud, it shakes the floor. Sharp fangs catch the muted light and eyes blazing with fire flash in the dark, leveling down on me.

Training kicks in. I nock an arrow and let loose. But before it can hit the wolf, the arrow makes a popping noise and evaporates into a cloud of ash. Frantic, I let loose another arrow, and it turns to ash, too. Before I can try again, my bow crumbles to dust in my fingers.

Heart racing, I rush to the tree and grab one of the swords stuck in it. But when I pull on the hilt, it doesn't budge. I brace a foot against the trunk and try again, but it's stuck like cement. I try a knife, and then a spear, but it's no use. I'm not worthy to wield any of them.

The wolf circles me, shoulders low, hackles raised. It's easily as big as a city bus. It peers down at me, making my blood freeze.

I can't move.

This has to be a nightmare.

The wolf's breath is hot on my skin. It smells like death, decay, and blood. A cavernous voice echoes in my head, and I know it's the wolf speaking.

Time's up, little valkyrie.

Molten orange eyes appear in front of me, and all I see is fire.

KRAK-KRAK. The raven's cry snaps me out of it.

The next thing I know, I'm in my backyard again, shivering like I've been standing in a snowstorm for hours. No time has passed, but what I saw was too real. I leap to my feet, scanning my yard for the wolf. The ash is gone from my hair, my bow is back in my hand, and I'm home. Everything is normal.

Who am I kidding? Nothing about any of this is normal. Mom never said anything about ravens making us see visions.

"What was that?" I ask, rounding on the raven.

Infuriatingly, the raven only looks at me. Then, with a flap of its wings, it takes off toward the trees.

"Hey! Wait!" I'm running after it before I realize what I'm doing.

When I crash out of the copse of trees and onto Charlemagne Lane, I catch a glimpse of the raven flying down the street leading toward the castle. "Come back!" But the raven is too far ahead.

By the time I get to the square, I've lost it. There's no sign of the bird in the tree, or on the castle, or on any of the bunting lines canopying the square. All the nearby shops are dark, shut down for the night, and the square is totally empty. None of my neighbors are around, not even to walk their dog.

Ravenswood Castle stands tall, lit by the spotlights from below, dark and silent. Next to it, as usual, stands Yggdrasil, calm and sturdy, as it's been for thousands of years. Its green leaves flutter in the soft breeze coming off Lake Michigan, gently shushing me like Mom did when I had nightmares as a kid.

And like those nightmares, whatever the raven showed me wasn't real. Right?

I press my hand to Yggdrasil's trunk and take a second to catch my breath. The bark is cool, the feel of it assuring beneath my palm, even though my stomach twists into a knot.

All I want to do is run home and tell Mom what I saw. If it was a vision of the future, or whatever... She's had more experience with ravens, she would know what to do.

The next best thing is to tell Prima or Reagan, but even then, would they believe me? *I hardly believe me.*

Rrah-rrah-rrah, the raven calls from above, invisible in the branches of Yggdrasil. It sounds like it's laughing.

"I'm starting to think you're having fun messing with me," I say, irritated.

The raven doesn't answer. Yggdrasil's branches sway, making the bells ring loudly, a cacophony of noise.

But then I realize, none of the other trees in the square are moving. It's not the wind.

My heart skips. Something is coming.

I clutch my bow tighter, bracing myself.

The raven squawks out a warning.

The tree shakes like it's in the middle of a storm. It's like the land-vaettir are trying to warn me.

Is the wolf here already?

Before I can do anything, I'm blinded by a prismatic burst of light. Bright dots dance in my vision, and I blink to clear them, ready to fight.

Instead of the wolf, two people appear out of thin air and collapse in the street, a tangle of arms and legs.

One of them is a girl. She kicks out, sending the other sprawling back, and scrambles on the ground to get away. She's clutching a staff but struggles to get to her feet.

The other one is a man. Slowly, he stands, not in a rush. He's tall, and rail thin, and—with a lurch—I realize he's wielding a rusty sword. It glints in the lamplight.

This isn't a fight in the arena between two actors. This isn't pretend.

The girl's head snaps up when she notices me. Her eyes are wide, terrified.

That guy is going to hurt her.

"Run!" she screams.

I do. Right at them.

4

"Hey, stop!" I shout, rushing in.

The guy ignores me as he raises his sword, ready to strike the girl on the ground.

Before he can do anything, I grab his arm and whirl him around. "Hey! What are you do—AUGH!"

One thing is immediately obvious: this guy is dead. Like *dead*-dead. Like, freak of nature in all meaning of the term, dead.

His face doesn't have lips, or a nose, and half of one of his cheeks is missing. He's more of a skull at this point. It looks like he's been gnawed on by animals, revealing bone and sinew. What's left of his skin is cold and shriveled and it's mottled blue and white, like frostbite. The smell of earth and decay overwhelms me. The worst are his eyes—they glow orange like the setting sun.

Fully decked out in tarnished leather armor, rusty chain mail, and a corroded helmet, he's ready for battle.

I snatch my hand away, wiping the feeling of dead guy on my hoodie. A laugh escapes me, nervous and high, as he takes a step toward his new target—me.

"Sorry, I didn't mean to scream. . . ." I swallow a lump of fear in my throat, walking backward, my palm sweaty against my bow. "I've never met a zombie before."

He hisses like a snake as he comes closer.

"Ha, yeah totally," I say.

Rearing back, the zombie whips his sword at me just as I slam my hand to my necklace.

With a burst of light, astral armor materializes around my body. Silver breastplate, vambraces, chain mail, winged helm—all of it magically melting over my clothes in the blink of an eye.

As my armor solidifies, the sword hits me in the chest, knocking me back twenty feet and into the wooden fence near the castle. Splinters fly everywhere.

The girl screams. To her, it would have only been a second. She must have thought I was a goner. If not for my armor, I would have been.

The dead guy is stupidly strong for a pile of bones. If he's surprised that I'm still alive, he doesn't show it. I doubt there's much going on in that empty skull to begin with.

I get to my feet and draw an arrow from the quiver on my back. "Drop the sword," I say, staring him down. I sound a lot more confident than I feel.

He rushes me, sword up.

I let loose one-two-three arrows in quick succession. Each stick in his padded leather armor, but he doesn't slow down. In a second, he's on me, cutting and slicing for my neck.

I duck and dodge out of the way, but he's wicked fast. I need space.

I leap to the side and take aim.

My arrow hits the side of his jaw.

Like a Frisbee, the lower half of his face goes flying, disappearing into the dark. A black tongue dangles from his gaping mouth like a bloated worm.

He goes, "*GAHHH!*"

I go, "Gah!"

Fury in his eyes, he roars at me, his tongue waggling.

I think he's going to come after me again, but instead the ground opens up underneath him, and he starts to sink, like he's in quicksand.

"Do not let him escape!" the girl cries. She shoves her fist into a leather pouch and throws a handful of seeds at the zombie's feet. Roots spring up from the ground, wrapping around his body like ropes.

Magic. She's got magic.

The zombie struggles to break free, chopping at the roots with his sword. He's halfway in the ground, melting into the dirt.

I draw another arrow, aiming for his eye, and let fly.

The shaft makes an odd twanging noise as the arrow lodges in the back of his helmet, pierced through his brain, or rather where his brain should be. The glow in his other eye fades, and he crumbles into a pile of dirt. When he does, a cloud of silvery-white smoke rises and disappears into the air.

All that's left of him are my arrows, and his armor and sword. And, as the girl lowers her hand, the magic roots shrivel up and wither away.

A chill rakes through me and my whole body shudders. You'd think a valkyrie would be prepped to deal with dead folks, but there's a first for everything. I've never seen anything like that before.

The girl looks exhausted, but she stands, using her staff as a crutch. She winces, pressing her hand to her side.

"Are you okay?" I ask, as my armor fades and I'm back to being plain ole me.

"A valkyrie," she gasps. "I ... I found you." A softness passes over her face and she wavers as her eyes roll back. She crumples to the ground, hard.

I rush to her and find her leather vest is covered in blood. Her head lolls to the side and when her hair falls away, I see she has slightly pointed ears.

"No way...." I say, shocked. "You're an elf?" As if this isn't the weirdest day already.

She cries in pain.

The square is still empty, not another person in sight. But no way can I leave her here.

There's only one place we can go, even if it's the last place I want to be.

$$\bowtie$$

I help the elf girl walk all the way home. I've got one of her arms thrown over my shoulder, and she holds on to her staff with the other. She's barely conscious, drifting in and out.

"This is Midgard?" she asks, dazed. She stares at the castle, then at the tournament ring, then at the swinging dragon boat ride. "How peculiar." I take it she doesn't have theme parks where she comes from.

"Almost there. You're going to be okay," I say as my house comes into view.

The upper floors are lit up, but the shop downstairs is still dark. I use my foot to open the door and bring her inside. Prima has already shut down the forge for the night, but its embers give off just enough light to see by. I help the girl sit on a wooden chair by the forge near a row of swords on display and set her staff down by my bow and quiver.

When she sits, she clenches her teeth. ᵀ can't tell how bad she's hurt, but I know it's not good.

"I'll be right back," I say. "Sit tight, don't move. I've got just the thing."

She nods, her lips as pale as her hair. I'm glad she can trust me this much.

Quick and quietly as I can, I sneak upstairs and poke my head around the corner.

Reagan is sitting on the couch hand-sewing her dress for the King's Feast. Butters naps blissfully across her shoulders while Netflix blares on TV. Prima is in the kitchen, her back to me, leg bouncing, as she sits in front of her laptop at the table. They're too distracted to realize I'm there. It's a feeling I'm all too familiar with. If I'm not making trouble, I'm invisible.

I should tell them about the elf girl, about the zombie, about the vision of the wolf.

But something stops me.

As I watch the back of Prima's head, my mouth tastes bitter.

Prima's wrong. I haven't forgotten my oath. I can prove I'm not always making trouble. I can be a valkyrie, just like them.

I set my jaw. I can do this alone. I don't need anyone's help.

My eyes flick to the stoneware jug next to the microwave, barely in arm's reach. They'll never notice it's gone.

Without a sound, I loop my finger through the jug's handle and slink back downstairs.

The elf is exactly where I left her but jolts when she sees me. She's jumpy. Anyone would be, especially after nearly being hacked to pieces by a monster movie extra.

When I uncork the jug, the sweet, floral smell of honey fills the air. I hand it to her.

"What is this?" she asks, taking it tentatively. I can't quite place her accent. It almost sounds like she's a fairy-tale princess from Appalachia.

I turn on a work lamp on the counter, giving us more light. "Mead. From Valhalla."

That's all the explanation she needs, apparently. She tips the jug back and takes a swig. As she does, the blood on her vest vanishes and the gash in her side closes up. The magical mead stitches her skin back together, good as new. Valkyries in Valhalla have an almost never-ending supply of the stuff, but here on Midgard we need to import it. It doesn't make us immortal, but it does make life easier.

When I was young, I was always falling out of trees or crashing on my bike or trying to do archery trick shots on my skateboard. Every bump, bruise, scrape, or broken bone, the mead has patched right up.

"You're lucky we had some. We're almost out," I say, as I kneel on the floor in front of her. Since Mom left, we haven't been able to refill our supply. Without a raven cloak, we can't travel to Asgard. "You'll have a pretty cool scar though."

She hands the jug back to me. There's some still left, but I can tell the mead's working. Color returns to her cheeks and she lets out a sigh of relief. Except for her pointy ears, she looks human and about my age. Her eyes are a deep, mossy green, the same as her moss-covered cloak, and her braided hair is white as snow. I don't mean to stare, but I've never met an elf before. People from the various realms rarely commingle.

Her relief is short lived as panic replaces it. "I must warn you. There is no time—"

"Breathe. We killed—uh, re-killed?—that guy. You're safe. I'm Bryn. What's your name?"

"Juniper. Juniper of the Iron Forest in Utgard. I was sent to find you."

"Utgard? As in, Jotunheim?"

She nods.

Jotunheim is a realm on the outskirts of the universe. Although it's connected to Yggdrasil, like all other realms, it's a forbidden world of enchanted forests, and monsters, and . . . "You're a giant?" I feel stupid for asking.

"I am half-giant, actually," she says.

"Cool." I'm impressed. That explains the seed magic. I want to ask her a million things. "So how did you get here? Traveling realms is superhard."

"Indeed. If not for this." From a pocket in her vest, she holds out a sleek black feather.

I stare, open-mouthed, as she hands it to me. I'd know it anywhere. "From a valkyrie's raven cloak?"

"It was a gift from my mother when I was born."

"I didn't know Jotunheim had any valkyries."

"It does not. That is why I had to come to Midgard. I assure you, I would not be here if it was not of the utmost importance." Her eyes harden, determined. "Where is Kara? I must speak with her."

"She's not here. She's . . . missing."

"Missing?" Juniper says, stunned. "Where did she go?"

"Million-dollar question. But how do you know my mom's name?"

Juniper takes a breath, steadying her gaze on me. "She is my mother as well."

My ears ring like I've been bonked over the head by that zombie. "Oh," I say.

Questions race in my head but trip at the finish line. I can't form a single coherent thought.

I don't think she's lying, because looking at Juniper now, it's obvious. It's not one feature in particular, but I can see Mom, like that painting made of dots at the Art Institute of Chicago: The whole thing comes together the longer I stare at her.

All this time, I thought it was only the four of us—me, Reagan, Prima, and Mom. Even though Dad was gone, Mom never dated anyone else. We were enough. Weren't we?

Memories with her rush through my head at a million miles an hour. Lounging on the couch for "manicure and movie" nights, and hand-sewing my wicked witch Halloween costume, and helping me with baking soda volcano science projects, and singing to Dolly Parton songs while making birthday cupcakes, and training me how to shoot a bow long into a winter night, even as an infamous Chicago blizzard approached.

I don't have the mental bandwidth to do the math on how or when Mom had a kid in another realm, let alone a secret one. Besides, giants are supposed to be sworn enemies of the gods in Asgard and, by proxy, valkyries.

Did Mom really have a secret love child with someone across enemy lines? Does Prima know? Or Reagan?

Why would she keep a secret from me?

All I can do is sit back on my heels and stare.

Juniper asks, carefully. "Are you well? Do you need to regorge?"

My lips are dry as I say, "I'm fine, but quick question: Is my brain leaking out of my ears? No? Okay, good. Give me a second."

I can't think, but the raven feather is cool and smooth under my fingers, and the touch of it grounds me. I'm finally able to take a breath.

Okay. One thing at a time.

"Raven cloaks let valkyries fly anywhere, to any realm, at any time. But a single feather only has enough magic for a one way trip, activated with starlight," I say. Even I can tell it's been spent. It's just a regular feather now.

"You are a valkyrie, are you not?"

"No, I am. I'm just not . . . graduated. I haven't passed my final test."

Juniper gives me a blank look.

"I still need to bring someone to Valhalla," I admit. If Juniper is disappointed, she doesn't make it obvious. I bet she was expecting a real valkyrie, and instead all she gets is me. "So without a raven cloak, I don't have a way to get you home."

"I cannot go home," Juniper says. "Draugar, like the one you saw, destroyed it. If the prophecy is true, it is only the beginning."

Her eyes shine in the soft light and my stomach plummets.

A raven cries somewhere outside.

The wolf's voice comes back to me. *Time's up, little valkyrie.*

I know what Juniper is going to say before she says it.

"Ragnarök is coming."

5

"RAGNARÖK?" PRIMA ASKS SHARPLY. "WHAT DO YOU MEAN Ragnarök is coming?"

My sister looms over Juniper with the sort of expression that's directed at me most of the time, one that says you-better-explain-yourself-right-now-or-else. A Prima specialty. Juniper sits on the couch with her hands pinned between her thighs, looking like a kid in detention.

I know, I said I could do this on my own, but when Juniper told me that the end of the world was coming, I needed backup. I brought her upstairs to meet Prima and Reagan, who hadn't even noticed us coming in until I cleared my throat and introduced her.

Juniper told them everything she told me, including the fact that she's our half sister, and they handled it about as well as I expected. Meaning, not very well at all.

Reagan holds Butternut Squash close to her chest, staring at Juniper with her round eyes even rounder. "How do you know Ragnarök is coming?" Her voice goes up an octave when she asks.

"A battalion of draugar attacked my village. I barely escaped."

"I fought one," I say.

Prima rounds on me now. "Fought one?"

"Zombie-looking dude. One of them hitched a ride with Juniper when she used this." I hand her the raven feather but Prima freezes. Instead, Reagan takes it. She inspects it with a keen eye, her face pale.

"The magic's been used up," Reagan says, confirming what I felt earlier. Juniper's stuck here. Reagan stares at her, wide-eyed. "Feathers from a raven cloak don't just fall out. Mom had to have given this to you."

Prima says, "Start over from the beginning. What happened?"

"I live in a village deep within the Iron Woods of Utgard, on the outer rim of Jotunheim, with my grandmother," she says. "Our village is small, and we were not prepared for an attack. Most of us are not warriors. The only dangers we face are from raiders or hungry beasts, but this was . . ." Juniper shakes her head. "This was different."

"What are draugar, exactly?"

"Hel-walkers, the dead risen again. A draug can move through solid ground, does not need to rest, or eat, or find shelter from the cold. An unstoppable army to match Odin's."

"Who's controlling them?" I ask. I try to ignore the shiver that runs down my spine. Fighting one draug was scary enough, but fighting a whole army? I don't want to think about it. "Someone has to be, right? A dead guy can't just decide to get up and walk around on his own."

I look to my sisters for some encouragement, but all I get from them are stony stares.

"Only death magic can control them," Juniper says. "It is why I have to find Kara."

"Why didn't our mom take you to Midgard?" Reagan asks. "Why did she leave you there in Jotunheim?"

"I was hoping she could tell me," Juniper says. She rubs her hands together between her legs, like she doesn't know what to do with them. "But she is one of the only people who could help us. A valkyrie."

"Well, she's not here," Prima says.

"I understand. That is why I must help you find her. To save my village, to kill the draugar, to stop Ragnarök."

"Okay, slow down," Prima says. "We still don't know it's Ragnarök."

Juniper shifts, like she's eager to get started. "My grandmother said that it was all wrong. This is not how Ragnarök is supposed to start. I know that first there must come a never-ending winter, then the sun turns black, and the stars fall as fire burns the sky, and Heimdall blows his horn, making all nine worlds quake—"

Reagan interrupts. "But none of that is happening. No Filmbulwinter, no eclipse, no earthquake. Nothing."

Yet, I think, and then wish I hadn't.

"What else could it be but Ragnarök?" Juniper asks. "My grandmother would not send me here if it was not true!"

My stomach is in knots. It's like I'm walking into a test I didn't study for, even though, objectively, I have been studying for Ragnarök my entire life. I never felt ready, and especially not now.

Mom told us about the Prophecy of the Völva—the *Völuspá*—an ancient poem by an unnamed witch with the ability to see the future. The witch told Odin about the imminent fall of the gods—the Aesir and the Vanir—against the armies of the underworld in Hel and the giants in Jotunheim, about the destruction of all the realms, and about Odin's own death fighting the great wolf Fenrir.

Fenrir's father, the spurned trickster god Loki, will escape prison and sail on a ship made of fingernails to lead an army of the dead and monsters against Asgard. The Hel-walkers will bring with them Fimbulwinter, a never-ending blizzard. Civil wars will break out across all the realms. And in the chaos, the wolf Fenrir will break his chains and kill Odin, and the fire giant Surtr will burn down Yggdrasil.

It'll be an age of axe and wolf. Gods against giants. Families torn apart. The big showdown. Even Odin can't stop it.

It's the whole reason why Odin built his army of einherjar at Valhalla in the first place. He wanted the best fighting chance he could get to prove the witch wrong.

If Odin is scared of Ragnarök, all of us should be.

Juniper goes on to say, "I believe the dead are marching through Jotunheim, and soon they will be in Midgard, to meet the gods in their final battle."

"Makes sense, I think, but..." I don't want to believe Ragnarök is coming, but not believing in something doesn't make it not true.

"It *doesn't* make sense," Reagan says. "The prophecy says everything is supposed to be sequential. Why would the prophecy change?"

"Maybe someone is changing it, changing fate," I say.

Everyone looks at me like I sprouted a third eye. All I can do is shrug. "Mom always said that fate isn't laid out like we think, right? That it's the choices we make that can shape the future. Even Odin wants to change his own fate. So what if someone's decided to take the future into their own hands? Someone like Loki?"

Prima, though, is always a skeptic. She likes rules. She likes order. So what she says next doesn't surprise me in the slightest. "We don't know for sure that it's Ragnarök. Without other elements of the prophecy, and no proof, we're jumping to conclusions."

I roll my eyes. "Do we really want to wait around and see?"

Prima huffs loudly through her nose. "Family meeting. Now." She drags me by the back of my hoodie and Reagan by her arm to the kitchen, leaving Juniper to sit on the couch with a curious Butternut Squash beside her. Juniper sits frozen, as if she's afraid that our cat might turn into a vicious monster. I don't think there are a lot of cats where she comes from.

"Great. This is just . . . *great.*" When Prima's flustered, she's not the most eloquent.

I can't tell which one is more shocking, the fact that we have a half sister or that the end of the world is approaching. It's a real one-two punch.

"Do you believe her?" Reagan asks Prima as she anxiously fiddles with the ends of her hair.

Prima shakes her head, and says, "It doesn't add up."

I fling my arm out. "I fought a draug. What's not to add? One plus one equals trouble."

"Look, I believe you on that part, but I don't believe the whole 'it's Ragnarök' thing." Prima's voice is low as she recites the passage from the prophecy. "'Axe-time, sword-time, shields are sundered. Wind-time, wolf-time, ere the world falls.' The prophecy is like a play-by-play. Everything is laid out in a specific order. We don't have all the facts."

The skin on the back of my neck tightens at the mention of wolf-time.

Time's up, little valkyrie.

I suppress the shudder. No way what I saw was real. Prophecy is one thing, but a vision is another. I couldn't have seen the wolf Fenrir in Valhalla. Still, I want to mention it, but Reagan and Prima are already talking at light speed about eclipses, and volcanic eruptions, and general end-of-times chaos. It's like I'm not even here.

"Could she really be our half sister?" Reagan asks, switching topics. "I mean, that's such a weird thing to lie about."

"I wish Mom were here," Prima says. She drags her fingers through her hair, then folds her arms over her chest and takes a deep breath.

I glance at the closed door to Mom's room, just off the living room, as an idea pops into my head. "We could use Mom's scrying kit to find her."

Prima rounds on me. "Absolutely not."

"Why?"

She starts counting on her fingers, in her classic Prima way. "One, it's in Mom's trunk, which is, A, locked, and, B, her private stuff. And two, scrying is advanced valkyrie seidr. You have no idea what you'd be messing with."

"Even I don't use seidr," Reagan says.

Seidr is one of the oldest forms of magic, passed from Odin and his wife, Frigg. A person can use it for astral projection, or to summon and control spirits, even see the future, but it's not for the faint of heart. It can make a person lose their mind if they're not careful, foaming at the mouth and writhing on the floor as their blood boils with magic. Just like anything, it takes practice, but Mom's hesitant to teach us, even if valkyries have been doing it for thousands of years.

I've seen Mom use it only once, when she didn't think we were around. We'd been outside playing Valhalla (with Prima being the valkyrie, Reagan being the einherjar, and me being the monster because I was always the monster for some reason), and I had come back inside because I was sick of being the troll, when I saw Mom kneeling on the floor in her bedroom. She was putting white tiles into a bowl of water and humming under her breath. The air was thick with the power in her voice. She didn't notice me, and I sneaked away before she knew I was watching. I could tell it was private, but I still don't know what she was using it for.

"I know seidr is dangerous, but we're running out of options here," I say. "This is the end of the world we're talking about. If seidr can help us find her, we should use it. She'll know what's going on. If this really is Ragnarök we're up against, shouldn't we use everything we have now?"

Prima shakes her head, frowning. "No. Not an option. It's too dangerous. We don't have to resort to that yet."

"What if Mom's disappearance has something to do with Ragnarök?"

"It's not Ragnarök!" Prima snaps, eyes blazing. "There has to be another reason...."

Reagan holds up her hands, slicing the thick air pulsing between us. "Everybody, chill. We can figure this out."

I let out a huff and know it's no use fighting, not with Juniper here. "Fine. If you're not going to listen to me, what are we going to do about Juniper? She said her home was destroyed. She's got nowhere else to go." I can't imagine what that must be like. One day, your house just...gone.

Prima drags her hand through her hair again but doesn't answer me. She studies Juniper and then glances at Reagan. I can tell in that one look that I don't like what I see.

"No," I snap. "You're not throwing her out."

"You trust her?"

"I do, yeah," I say, lifting my chin.

"She's a giant."

"So? Giants are people, too." Like Midgard, Asgard and Jotunheim have regular people living there. It's the gods' universe, we just live in it. "None of this is her fault."

Prima glances at Reagan, who shrugs, at a loss for words.

I'm putting my foot down on this. Prima and Reagan can be skeptics all they want, but I'm not like them. "If you kick her out, I'm leaving, too."

"We don't know anything about her," Prima hisses. "For all we know, she could be the one who's controlling the draugar somehow. This could be a trap."

"Mom gave her a feather from her cloak for a reason. She's family."

"She's not. If she was, why wouldn't Mom tell us about her?"

"Give me a break," I say. "She looks just like Mom!" The picture frames on the walls start to shake as my temper flares. "Since when have you become so cold-blooded?"

Prima pinches her lips between her teeth, glaring at me. The water glass on the table vibrates like it's *Jurassic Park*.

Reagan throws out her arms between the two of us again. "Please. Enough."

Prima and I break eye contact and the picture frames stop moving. The glass of water settles back down. I chew away at the inside of my cheek to calm myself, but all I taste is bitterness. If there's one hill I'll die on, it's this. Prima seems to know that too, but all she does is take a shuddering breath and run her hand through her hair again.

"Pri, I know you're scared," Reagan says. "You too, Bee. *All* of us are scared. But we have to help each other, right? We have to stick together."

She bobs her head at Prima, who huffs in response. "Juniper is going to stick out like a sore thumb at the faire."

I almost laugh. "Are you joking? She'll blend in with all the other people who walk around dressed up like fairies and elves. No one will even notice she has pointy ears. In fact, people might ask her where they can buy some."

"And she can borrow some of my old dresses," Reagan says. "Come on, Pri. Are you really so heartless?"

Prima rolls her eyes and throws up her hands. No one is immune to Reagan's persuasion.

I push by Prima and Reagan and go back to Juniper, scooping up Butternut Squash—who has taken an interest in Juniper's moss cloak, sniffing it, tail up—in one move. Juniper hasn't moved an inch, and she looks like she could use the rescue.

"Who's your dad?" I ask. "Is there a way you can talk to him? See if anyone from Utgard can contact you? Tell them you're okay?"

Juniper frowns, twisting her mouth in a way that makes me think she's upset she can't give me the answer I want. "I never met him," she says. "I only have my grandmother." At the mention of her grandma, Juniper's eyes go glassy. I think she might cry, but she takes a breath and straightens her shoulders. "She sent me here to find help, but we must act quickly. If I do not return in a week, they will believe I've been captured."

"What? Why?"

"You are Odin's vanguard. Giants distrust the valkyries. My people . . . if they still live, they could have fled to a neighboring village . . . but if my people have reason to believe I have been taken hostage, they will not hesitate to act."

"Are you a princess or something?"

"My grandmother is a Ring-Breaker."

"A what?"

Reagan speaks up, "It means something like chieftain, or ruler. The ruler breaks off pieces of their jewelry and gives it to their loyal followers."

"How do you know that?" I ask.

"*Beowulf.* I did a dramatic reading of the poem for one of my theater classes."

"I am a valuable hostage," Juniper says. "My grandmother sent me here to get help. I am her last hope. She is strong and I have to believe she is still alive. I do not want to fail her."

"You won't," I say. I hand Butternut Squash over to Reagan. Beside her, Prima is wearing a permanent frown. I speak to Juniper but I give Prima a pointed look. "You're not a hostage, but you can stay with us if you want."

Prima's left eye twitches.

Juniper doesn't seem to notice. "I cannot impose—"

"It's no biggie. I've got plenty of space in my room. It'll be like a sleepover."

"A sleepover? Over what?"

"No, not—that's just what it's called." I can't help but smile. "It's a thing friends do together."

"Oh!" Juniper's face brightens. "Friends."

Prima's eye twitches again and she spins around, mumbling something about finding blankets.

Reagan bounces Butternut Squash in her arms and gives Juniper a soft smile. "We'll find a way to get you home to your grandmother," she says. "But in the meantime, you make yourself comfortable."

⋈

"It's not much but ..." I say, opening the door to my bedroom. It's a mess.

My room is in the attic. It's tiny compared to Prima and Reagan's, but it's cozy, especially during the winter. I used to share a room with them, but we all complained about space, so I moved up here. I've really made it my own, with posters and messy bookshelves and fairy lights crisscrossing the ceiling. I even made a map of the CTA to look like it was from Middle Earth and taped it to the door. My bed is wedged under the sloped ceiling and Butters leaps onto it, claiming a spot for herself.

Juniper takes a cautious step inside, taking everything in. She has to maneuver over piles of my dirty clothes. I kick them into the corner where I put my bow next to my skateboard.

"Are all homes on Midgard illuminated by magic?" Her eyes go to the fairy lights.

"You mean electricity?" I'm about to make a joke, but on second thought realize maybe electricity really is a kind of magic. "Uh, I guess!"

"It is wonderful," she says, turning to me. She sounds genuine, but I think she's being polite.

"If I knew someone was coming, I would have cleaned. I don't have many friends over."

I didn't mean to say that last part out loud. Luckily, Juniper doesn't linger on it. "Thank you. For saving me, too. I do not know what I would have done if you had not been there."

I wave her off. "Don't worry about it."

We both fall quiet. I'm not sure what else to say. Juniper clasps her hands in front of her, looking around my room with her lips sucked in. This is awkward when it doesn't have to be. I'm not really sure what else I can do besides the bare minimum.

"You're probably totally wiped," I say. "I'll show you where the shower is and you can get cleaned up."

By the time she gets out and comes back upstairs, her hair tied up in a knot, dressed in a Ravenswood T-shirt and a pair of Prima's old volleyball shorts, looking like any other kid on Midgard save for the ears, Butters is already curled up among the blankets.

When Juniper sees her she takes a slight step backward. "This creature is . . . friendly?"

"Oh, Butters is harmless. You can pet her if you want."

Juniper looks at me like I've just asked her to jump off a cliff. Butters turns up the cuteness dial to eleven and curls onto her back, looking up at Juniper with big orange eyes. No one can resist those wiles.

Slowly, Juniper reaches out and puts her hand on Butters's head. Butters grabs her with her paws and shoves her head harder into Juniper's palm, closing her eyes.

"See? She likes you already," I say as I arrange the pillows on the floor.

Juniper smiles as she scratches Butters behind the ears, relaxing a little. "She is vibrating."

"Purring. I think she has a new favorite." Butters is a good judge of character. Prima and Reagan still need work. I add, "Besides, you're family."

With a sad smile, Juniper says, "I am sorry I could not have told you another way. I did not know I had sisters either. Not before tonight."

"Then I'm pretty sure we can go down in history as having the craziest family reunion ever."

Juniper fiddles with the hem of her T-shirt. "My grandmother is very protective. I wish..." She doesn't finish her sentence. She looks down at Butters, and I can tell she's trying to keep it together.

"Hey," I say, changing the subject. "You're exhausted. Take my bed."

Juniper jolts up straight. "I cannot! You are doing too much."

I'm already on the floor with a bunch of pillows and blankets Prima found in the closet. "You went through enough. You deserve it." I don't let Juniper put up any more of a fight as I pull up the blanket and lie down on the high-pile rug. "Too late. I'm already cozy. Night!"

Juniper sighs and climbs into bed. I turn off the lamp and unplug the fairy lights.

The dark is full of the sound of crickets chirping, of Butters's contented purring, and of Juniper's shallow breathing. She must be exhausted, but I can tell she's wide awake. I don't blame her. If I got transported to another realm after escaping from a zombie apocalypse and spent the night in a stranger's house, I'd have a hard time falling asleep, too.

I hold my Yggdrasil pendant.

So much is happening so fast and I can barely keep up, like I'm running on a treadmill on full speed and any second I'm going to face-plant.

When I try to close my eyes, all I see are the orange eyes of that draug. And my heart pounds so hard, I swear it's trying to break out of my chest. That vision. Could it be coming true?

"Um, Bryn?" Juniper's voice is soft in the dark.

"Yeah?"

"Would it be tolerable to keep some of the magic lights on?"

"You read my mind."

I plug in the fairy lights, and eventually, fall asleep.

6

SUNLIGHT CUTS ACROSS MY EYES, AND I BLINK THEM OPEN, blearily, wondering who the hell turned on a car headlight directly on my eyeballs, before everything that happened yesterday comes rushing back.

A shadow moves near the window, and I start awake, only to realize it's just Juniper kneeling by the windowsill, braiding her hair near my pathetic, dying Boston fern. She smiles when she notices I'm up.

I manage to prop myself on my elbows. My back is stiff, and I instantly regret every decision I've ever made in my life leading up to this moment. "Morning," I say groggily.

"Good morning!" Juniper says.

"You look chipper," I say. "Did you sleep okay?"

"Indeed! I am renewed and refreshed, ready to take on the day. My grandmother always says, 'Rare falls the prey to sleeping wolves.'"

"Your grandma sounds like a spunky lady," I say, rubbing the sleep from my eyes.

"She is!" Juniper says, brightly. "The same cannot be said about this poor thing though." She gestures with her chin toward the dying Boston fern, its swordlike leaves a rusty yellow color. It's supposed to be the easiest plant to take care of indoors, but I somehow found a way to kill it. What can I say? I'm talented like that.

Juniper twists her wrist expertly as she finishes the last of her braids, then inches on her knees toward the fern and hovers her hands over the dying leaves. When she does, her eyes glow and the plant changes in an instant. It perks up, like it's just been watered, and stretches its now-green leaves toward the sun beaming through the window. Already, it looks way happier.

I know Juniper has plant magic, but it's still amazing to watch her do it.

"There!" she says, then smiles at me. "All better."

Unlike me, she is definitely a morning person.

$$\bowtie$$

Reagan left a couple clothing options for Juniper to wear on the stairs, but by the time I realized Juniper had put everything on—tank top, flannel shirt, denim overalls, floral skirt, and all—it was too late. Even though she looks like she got into a fight with a thrift store clothing rack, she pulls it off. At least her clothes will distract from her ears.

Together, we head downstairs and find the kitchen is empty, dirty bowls already piled in the sink. A pang of annoyance jolts through me. Prima and Reagan were the ones who were suspicious of Juniper, and yet they didn't bother to come check on us to see if we were alive. The only one around is Butternut Squash, who sits on the back of the couch, watching birds out the window. Her tail flicks excitedly and she chitters as a goldfinch flaps up to the glass and then disappears from view.

"Help yourself to whatever you want," I say to Juniper, gesturing to the fridge. But when Juniper opens the door, she finds it miserably empty. All that's inside is a jar of pickles, the last dredges of a jug of milk, and a mostly empty bottle of ketchup. Someone needs to go grocery shopping.

"That is quite all right," Juniper says, closing the door. "I would rather we start looking for Mother. What happened the last time you saw her?"

"We were sitting on the balcony together." I gesture to the door off the kitchen. My chest aches when I think about how normal it was. "I was changing the string on my bow and she was reading when a raven came with a message tied to its leg. Mom said she'd be back later, kissed me on the head, and left."

Juniper scrunches one corner of her mouth in thought. "And you do not know what the message said?"

"Official valkyrie business. Top secret. So I don't know."

Juniper scans the kitchen, as if she'll find a note or something Mom left behind. "Did she go to another realm perhaps?"

"Doubt it. Her work is here on Midgard. Without that message, we're just guessing." My eyes go to her bedroom door. "But there's one place we haven't checked yet . . ." With Prima and Reagan gone, there's no one here to stop us.

Mom's room is bright in the morning sunlight filtering through the lace curtains. Her bed is piled high with quilts, the book she was reading the night before she left lies open and facedown on the bed-side table, and some jewelry rests on top of her dresser. It's like she left a couple minutes ago and will be back any second.

When Juniper looks around, her face falls. "This is where she sleeps?"

"Yeah," I say, watching Juniper carefully.

She runs a hand along the carved wood of the four poster, her gaze distant. I bet if I walked into my estranged mother's bedroom for the first time, I'd be thinking about too much to speak, too.

As we look around, there's nothing here that's an obvious clue where Mom went or what she was doing before she left, like a map or a note. The only interesting thing in the room is the trunk at the foot of the bed. It's an antique, handed down for generations, from one valkyrie to the next. When I run my hands over the lid, I can feel the braided knots carved into the wood and the runes lining the edges. It smells like cedar and mothballs.

When I try to lift the lid, I find it's locked.

I expected this. "Hold on," I say, and rush back up to my room. When I come back down, I show Juniper what I grabbed. "Lockpicks," I say.

"Lockpicks? Are you a thief?"

I kneel in front of Mom's trunk. "I wouldn't go that far."

Lockpicking is kind of like doing a puzzle, a problem to solve. When I first got into the hobby, I would sit out on the porch with Mom on hot summer nights while she'd read and I'd pick the same padlock over and over, getting faster every time. I used to think it was a pretty useless skill, something for my hands to do, like Reagan and her knitting—I never thought I would actually use it.

"I wouldn't do it unless I had to," I tell Juniper.

Juniper looks unconvinced, but doesn't stop me as I slip the wrench in the lock and then the hook. I feel the pins give and I twist the wrench. The trunk pops open.

Folded neatly in one half of the trunk should be Mom's raven cloak, but of course it's missing. She would have taken it with her on her mission. Next to the empty space are three of the cloak's raven feathers, lying on a sheepskin pillow.

"Just like the one you had," I say. One for each of us.

"Can we use them to find her?" Juniper asks.

I shake my head. "One way trip, remember? A feather from her cloak can only be used once. We'd need to know where she is first. Don't want to be stranded somewhere without a way home. You could use one of these to get back to Utgard though." I point to the new set.

"Not without Mother. I cannot fail Amma...." Juniper works her lip with her teeth, thinking. "Can you go to Asgard to ask if anyone knows where she is?"

"The only one who'd know where Mom went is Odin, and he's not going to take an audience with me."

"Why?"

"I'm not a real valkyrie yet. I'm not worthy." I don't mean to sound self-deprecating; it's a fact. "Besides, Mom's work is on Midgard. She has to be here, somewhere. And if Ragnarök really is coming, I don't want to leave."

Gently, I take the pillow of raven feathers out and set it on the floor beside me, then move Mom's jewelry boxes, her wedding photo album, and short top boxes packed full of printed photographs of all of us as kids.

Juniper picks up one of the boxes and opens it, pulling out a random photo to look at.

"Is this you?" she asks. She turns it around to show me. It's of a dark-haired man holding a baby above his head like a trophy, both he and the baby grinning so wide, it's the first thing you see.

"Prima," I say. "With my dad."

"Where is he?"

"He's dead."

Juniper's face falls again. "Oh, I am sorry."

"Don't worry. He died when Mom was still pregnant with me. Never even met him." I always try to sound casual about it, but deep down it twinges. I'm a little jealous of Prima and Reagan. At least they have pictures with him.

Juniper looks back at the photo. "How did it happen?"

"Car crash," I say, busying my hands with sorting through the rest of Mom's stuff. "Drunk driver was going the wrong way down the highway and...Not exactly Odin's definition of a warrior's death, huh?"

Juniper goes quiet for a moment as she looks at my dad's face. "Did he know about valkyries?"

"Of course. I don't know a whole lot more though. Mom doesn't like to talk about him, and I don't like to ask." The idea that Mom had Juniper secretly in another realm with another person makes my insides twist. How? When? Juniper seems about my age—or does time move differently on Utgard? And why would Mom keep it a secret from us? What if it was before Dad died? What if Mom and Dad didn't have the romantic but ultimately tragic fairy tale I grew up believing? I have so many questions, but I'd feel rude for asking any of them, so for once I keep my mouth shut.

Juniper doesn't say anything either as she puts the photo back in the box, closes the lid, and sets the box on Mom's bed. And then my stomach twists again when I realize Juniper doesn't even *have* photos of herself as a baby.

"I am sorry for prying," she murmurs.

"Don't be. We're both curious."

One corner of her mouth lifts up.

At the very bottom of Mom's trunk, I find a black velvet pouch. It clicks like a bag of Scrabble tiles when I pick it up.

"Is that...?" Juniper starts to ask.

"Mom's seidr kit," I say.

"Are you certain you want to be touching that?" She sounds like I've picked up a ticking time bomb.

Using seidr is tempting. I could use it to find Mom, but it's dangerous. Prima wasn't lying when she said so earlier. Mom used to tell us horror stories of people who died using seidr magic they weren't trained to use. That kind of power isn't something to play with.

As if on cue, Juniper's stomach growls and she looks at me, apologetically. That settles it. I put everything back in the trunk, including the seidr and the raven feathers, and close the lid.

"Lucky for you," I say brightly, "I have the day off from work. Let's get out of here, grab some food, and I can show you around, introduce you to some folks, make you feel at home while we figure out what to do next."

Juniper smiles, shoulders relaxing. "That sounds lovely."

⋈

Outside, the day is bright and the morning clear. I feel a million times better the second the sunlight hits my face. All this talk about the dead walking and dark magic is bumming me out. Juniper grips her staff close in hand, skipping beside me, still barefoot, to catch up.

My neighbors are out and about, getting ready for the day, opening their windows and letting in the fresh morning air. No one so much as glances twice at Juniper as we walk together down Shilling Street toward Talon and Fang Trail, following the scent of food drifting on the wind. I point out different shops and stalls as we go, doing my best to help her get to know Ravenswood. I should probably get her a map from guest services.

Juniper takes in everything with wide eyes. "So this is a . . . what did you call it, a 'theme' park?"

"Yeah. People come here for fun, a way to escape the real world."

Ravenswood is all I've ever known. While most of my classmates grew up with white picket fences and a mowed lawn, I grew up with performance stages and an archery range. Some people might think it's weird, but it's home.

My stomach drops when I think about draugar attacking Madame Bouffant, the palm reader, or Bob at Bob's Bits & Baubles with his handmade glass jewelry, or Smokey Joe and his fireworks shop. I take a breath, and remind myself I won't let anything bad happen.

"The rest of Midgard doesn't look like this," I say. "Not by a long shot."

"How peculiar," Juniper says, her gaze lingering on the spinning barrel ride as employees power it on for some test runs. Her face lights up and she looks at me. "Before I forget, I was hoping to acquire some more seeds. For my magic. I cannot create vegetation from nothing. If I have any hope of standing against the draugar, I need to prepare."

"How does your magic work exactly? You control plants?"

"Yes," she says, a little breathless, she's so excited to talk about it. "Make them grow, will them to move, sometimes talk to them—"

"Talk?" I say, turning the corner onto Talon and Fang Trail. We pass by a band of bards as they tune their dulcimers and mandolins just as I catch a whiff of sausage and cinnamon rolls coming from the Dragon's Den. "You actually talk to plants?"

"Oh yes! That is one of the only ways to truly understand them. A vital part of my magic stems—heh, *stems*—from communication. I encourage growth. Bring the best out of them. However, I must first introduce myself to the seeds before I can properly use any spell to fight draugar."

"Well, there's seeds everywhere," I say, gesturing around to the tree-covered path and flowers in window boxes. "Take your pick.

Hopefully we won't be encountering any draugar though. Mom will come back and stop all this."

"Yes," Juniper says, raising her staff. "I am sure we will find her!"

"Is that used in your magic, too?" I ask, gesturing to her staff.

"Oh! No. This is for more direct magic." She mimes bonking herself in the head and smiles.

I'm glad, despite everything, she has a sense of humor. I like it.

In the Dragon's Den, Trudy and the head chef are chatting at the bar, and her eyebrows shoot up when she spots us.

"Hey, Bryn!" she says, breaking into a smile. "Keeping out of trouble? We were just talking about your mom. Haven't seen her in a while."

"Oh, she's working," I say, defaulting to the usual story. "Out of town for a bit."

"Out of town?" Trudy asks. "She has another job?"

"You know how it is."

The chef bobs his head, then he lumbers off to the kitchen. Trudy accepts the answer with a shrug and tells us to sit anywhere. Juniper and I take the end of one of the long tables.

"You are . . . in trouble?" Juniper asks.

"Huh?"

"Trudy said so."

I wave my hand like I'm dissipating smoke. "It's a long story."

"You get in trouble a lot?"

"Some people say it's one of the few things I'm good at."

After a minute, Trudy comes over and stands with her hands on her hips. "So, you coming to the barbecue tonight?" she says to me, smiling, then she looks at Juniper. "Bringing your friend?"

"Trudy, this is Juniper. Juniper, Trudy. Juniper is visiting from abroad, and I'm showing her the sights. I figure we'll start with the good stuff. Get her a real taste of the Midwest."

"Then you've come to the right place! I like your hair," she says to Juniper. "It's really cool."

Juniper's hairstyle starts off as a French braid up top and then breaks into three parts, one braid down her back, the other two over each shoulder. The tips of her pointed ears go pink when she blushes. "Thank you! Everyone in my village wears their hair like this. The individual threads weave and wind their way like lines of time, and while they may separate and go their own way, they always come back together again. It is one of the strongest shapes in all nine realms."

"Ah," Trudy says, a bewildered smile stuck on her face. It's obvious Trudy thinks Juniper is really into fantasy role-play. "Cool."

I break the awkward silence. "One of everything from the menu, please, Trudy."

Trudy tears her eyes away from Juniper to smile at me. "The works. You got it." She glances at Juniper one last time before she leaves to put the order in.

Juniper leans over the table and asks, "The works?"

"Cheese curds, elephant ears, jalapeño poppers . . . You'll see."

Juniper says with doubt in her voice, "You invented half of those words."

"I swear, I didn't."

Juniper makes a face, and her eyes go to the exposed rafters overhead. "This is a strange place."

"Just wait till you get out into the real world. You're going to lose your mind when you see a skyscraper."

"A sky-*what*?"

⋈

After we eat our fill of greasy breakfast, we take some jalapeño poppers to go and we make a lap around the faire.

"These poppers, as you say, are delicious!" Juniper says, eating what I think might be her fifteenth one in a row.

"Can't stop Ragnarök on an empty stomach," I say, ducking out of the way of a group photo in front of the Brews Brothers' Tavern.

Ravenswood is well and truly packed now. The two of us can barely walk side by side down Avalon Way without getting separated by groups of families with strollers or people huddling over a map in the middle of the street. Screams of joy come from the drop tower and the swing ride, and hawkers shout "Ice *crrr*-eam!" and "Doughnuts! Getcher doughnuts!" It's a lot for Juniper, whose head seems to be on a swivel. She's handling everything surprisingly well though. I'll let the jalapeño poppers take all the credit.

"So you believe me?" she asks. "About Ragnarök?"

I nod. "Yeah. That draug... Definitely not normal. I hate to admit it though, but Prima's a little right. We can't know for sure, not without Mom. But once we find her, she can get you back to Utgard and stop whatever is happening there from spreading."

Juniper nods, reassured. "Thank you. With the aid of the valkyries, we stand a fighting chance."

I shush her gently, and lower my voice. "About that... See, no one here knows that valkyries are real. So if you could keep it down—"

"What do you mean? Why not? You are protectors of the realm and Midgard's last hope. The bards should be singing tales of your heroism, not—whatever this is!" She points at a woman playing a Taylor Swift cover on the hurdy-gurdy. The woman looks somewhat offended, so I push us on.

"Valkyries and magic, not really a thing these days."

Juniper balks, scraping her thumb clean on her front teeth. "Not a thing? Magic is all around us! A gift from Yggdrasil itself! If we have any hope of defending ourselves against the armies of Hel, we must use all resources at our disposal!"

"Times change. The old ways still exist, but it's harder to find. People forget." We turn on Crown Road past the archery range, and I have an idea. "You know what? Come over here. I want to show you something."

When we get to the castle square, I can't help but check if the draug's armor and sword are still around. Knowing how Ravenswood operates, it's been swept up as garbage long ago. Finding armor on the ground is not surprising in a place like this, but nothing from the fight is left.

There's just enough time before the daily court procession for us to cut across the already crowded street and pop out the other side near the castle's drawbridge. Lots of people stand waiting for the parade of actors escorting Prince James through the fairgrounds. It's a huge hit, especially with the people who want to ogle James up close.

Juniper's mood visibly brightens when she sees Yggdrasil near the drawbridge. "Oh! Look at you! You are beautiful." Juniper beams up at the branches. "Your roots run deep. So long as you stand, there is still hope."

I touch her shoulder and say, "I want you to meet my friends. Landvaettir. This is Juniper."

The bells on the branches chime even though there's no wind.

Juniper's jaw drops. "How fortunate!"

"What do you mean?"

"Landvaettir! They are luck deities."

"You have them on Utgard?"

"Oh yes! Amma says that if they like you, they bless you with good luck!"

"Well then, I think I need all the luck I can get," I say as I pull out a couple pennies from my pocket. I toss one into a knot at the base of the tree and hand the other penny to Juniper and she does the same.

The bells let me know the landvaettir are happy.

When the branches shake, something drops. It helicopters down, falling right into Juniper's outstretched hands. "A seed!"

"They don't fall from Yggdrasil too often," I say, impressed. "The landvaettir must really like you."

"I will cherish it forever!" Juniper says, eyes welling up.

Cheers erupt. The procession's started.

Standard-bearers hold red and gold flags high as forty people walk or ride on horseback down Crown Road to the beat of a handful of frame drums and the tune of a couple flutes.

At the front, King Beaumont sits atop a gilded palanquin, his voice booming as big as his smile as he greets guests. Following him, you can't miss Prince James, waving and beaming his trademark smile from atop his golden horse, winking to the adoring crowd. Next come the queen's ladies, all wearing delicately embroidered silk gowns, their heads veiled as they walk like they're floating. I even spot Reagan blowing kisses to the crowd surrounded by a handful of her performing knives.

Someone else catches my eye, though, at the back of the procession. Wyatt, the Black Knight.

He sits atop his horse, his black armor and the horse's black coat gleaming in the bright sunlight. His face is stony, solidly downcast, his dark curls lightly thumping against his forehead. But that's not what catches my eye.

The cheers seem to fade away as my heart drains into my stomach. It's like someone's dimmed the lights and put the world on mute.

No one else seems to notice the halo of golden light surrounding Wyatt's head.

I don't know how I know it, I just do.

His halo shimmers and gleams with the light of Valhalla.

Odin has chosen his newest einherjar.

But first, Wyatt has to die.

7

"Hello! I am Juniper of the Iron Woods. It is very nice to meet you," Juniper says to the acorn in her palm. In typical behavior for acorns, it doesn't respond, but she adds it to the pile gathered in her skirt anyway. The seed she got from Yggdrasil sits in a glass charm on a string around her neck while she gathers more acorns.

The sun has already set, and the staff barbecue is well underway. At the start of every summer, corporate throws a big party for staff to celebrate the high season. All the full-timers, part-time workers, and other vendors and performers on their ren faire circuit come together at the seasonal staff campsite on the north site of the park to dance around a huge bonfire; eat heaps of slow-roast meats, corn on the cob, and coleslaw; play epic rounds of cornhole or horseshoes; and dance to non-medieval music. Think of it like a block party. It's a great way to meet new folks as well as catch up with familiar faces. It's usually one of my favorite nights, but I'm not in a particularly festive mood.

While Juniper busies herself searching for seeds to replenish her magic supply, I keep an eye on Wyatt. My stomach churns as I peer at him from the shadows around an RV.

There's no other explanation for what I'm seeing. I may be good at physics—that being the only subject in school I'm actually passing—and I know that light can reflect in weird ways and make you see things that aren't there but . . . This isn't a trick of the light. Wyatt is going to be Odin's newest einherjar.

Wyatt stands apart from the other actors, shoulders slumped, one hand in the front pocket of his jeans and the other holding a red Solo cup. He's wearing his round, gold-rim glasses again and a white T-shirt. Civilian clothes. He looks like every other kid I go to school with. In other words, he looks normal. Except for the golden halo still shining around his head. Sometimes it glows brighter, rhythmically, like a heartbeat or a ticking clock, and every time it does, my heart feels like it's going to burst out of my chest, *Alien*-style.

Wyatt's a lot different outside of the arena. Sometimes I forget the performers at Ravenswood are just actors, and not really knights. His face is stony, his brows lowered as he takes in everything around him with a serious frown. He doesn't seem to be having a particularly good time either, not like James—the center of attention—surrounded by a cadre of other actors near the bonfire, talking and laughing loud enough that it carries all the way over to me lurking in the shadows.

It's like I'm touching a live wire. I'm so jittery, my bones might vibrate out of my body, but at the same time I'm paralyzed with dread. How can Wyatt die in battle, here at Ravenswood? Is it related to Fenrir in my vision? Is he going to die in Ragnarök?

None of this makes any sense, and I don't know what to do. Neither Prima nor Reagan have been called to bring anyone to Valhalla yet. Why do I have to go first? Mom should be here. She always said she would help us when we were called. It feels wrong that I have to do it without her. All of it feels wrong.

Wyatt's just a kid. It shouldn't be like this. Why does Odin want him anyway? Wouldn't he be better off claiming a grown man for his army? Wyatt's my age, and I barely know what I'm doing half the time, so how can he be any different? Why is his time up? Why him at all? And for what? Why's he so special? Special enough that he has to die for it?

I knew this day would come, and yet now that Wyatt's fate is right in front of me, I don't know what to do. I know what I *should* do, but . . .

It's not fair. None of it.

"Who are you staring at?" Reagan asks. I nearly jump out of my skin. I was so busy watching Wyatt, I didn't hear her come up behind me.

"No one."

"No?" Reagan's eyes scan the people around the bonfire. I hold my breath, waiting for her to spot Wyatt's light, but Reagan's eyes snag on James as he laughs. She takes a deep breath and sighs. Obviously seeing him is rubbing up against some raw nerves, but Reagan's too poised to let it get to her.

Can she not see Wyatt's halo? He's all I can look at.

Reagan glances over her shoulder at Juniper, who's still collecting acorns, and smiles. "Glad to see someone is getting use out of my ever-expanding wardrobe," she says, noting the eclectic outfit Juniper borrowed. Juniper is deep in conversation with an acorn and doesn't notice us.

"Where's Prima?" I ask. I don't take my eyes off Wyatt.

"Home. And no, Mom's not there yet. I can tell you were going to ask." She's right, I was. All I want is for Mom to be here right now to talk some sense into me.

I'm going to explode. I have to say something. I have to know. "Hey, you wouldn't happen to . . . see anything weird, would you?"

Reagan scrunches her nose and furrows her brow, trying to follow my line of sight. "No?" She says it like a question, as if that itself needs an answer.

"Just wondering," I say, trying and failing to hide my disappointment. She can't see Wyatt's halo. That means this is definitely *my* task, he is *my* einherjar to deliver. Alone. I was chosen for this, just as much as he is, and it makes my stomach sink.

"You look sick," says Reagan. "You didn't have any of Madame Bouffant's punch, did you? That stuff's, like, all Malört."

I shake my head. I'm afraid if I talk, I might puke.

If I tell Reagan that Wyatt's been chosen, she'll tell me it's a blessing. She'll say it's for a reason, for the greater good, that it's an honor to be chosen. But that's the thing—I don't want to take Wyatt to Valhalla. I don't want him to die. Period. I can't tell her he's been chosen. If I do, it becomes too real.

It's then that James notices us—notices Reagan, rather—and perks up.

Reagan's breath hitches and her hand darts out and latches on mine. She murmurs out of the corner of her mouth, "Quick, pretend like you said something funny."

"Huh?"

Reagan throws back her head and lets out a high, staccato laugh, fake as I've ever heard. The people around the bonfire stare at us. Even Wyatt looks at us over the rim of his Solo cup as he takes a sip. It occurs to me way too late that Reagan's trying to make James jealous, make it seem like she's over him. "You're cracking me up, Bryn!" Reagan slaps me on the arm, turns, and walks toward Madame Bouffant's punch bowl, leaving me exposed.

Mostly everyone goes back to their conversations, including James, and I have to wonder if Reagan's plan to look cool and collected worked or not. But Wyatt's still staring at me. His dark eyes latch on to mine, and all my blood drains out of me.

Meticulously, Wyatt drags his eyes back to the party, and the halo around him shimmers like candlelight. He has no idea he's going to die.

"Hello!" Juniper's voice makes me jump. She's talking to another acorn in her hand. "My name is Juniper of the Iron Woods—"

By the time I turn to look at Wyatt again, his spot on the grass is vacant.

He's gone. I just barely catch the glow of his halo as he weaves his way through the crowd. He moves fast, like he's just remembered he left the stove on.

I can't let him out of my sight. If anything happens to him . . . I don't even want to think about it. I tell Juniper I'll be right back, dart out from behind the RV, and shuffle across the grass, moving quickly but as quietly as possible past James and his retinue and around the pavilion, following the telltale glow of Wyatt's halo.

I emerge into a small outcropping of tiny homes on trailers, but there's no sign of Wyatt. He's gone. I've lost him.

If I didn't know any better, I'd think he gave me the slip.

I can't sleep.

If I had to put money on it, I'd say I spent the whole night tossing and turning on my spot on the floor. Hours go by, and I can't stop my mind from racing. I try to get comfortable, pull my blanket over my head, count sheep, but sleep never comes, because every time I close my eyes, I see Wyatt shining in Valhalla's light.

I bury my head in my pillow in an attempt to blot out his face from my memory, but I can't seem to shake him. It's like that light burned a hole through my mind's eye.

All I can do is lie here and watch the moonlight crawl its way across my bedroom wall. I stare up at the poster of Bigfoot wearing a T-shirt that reads HAVE YOU SEEN MY ALIEN WIFE? hanging near my bed, the corner peeling, and try to ignore the squirming rat king of anxiety in my gut.

"Amma..." Juniper talks in her sleep, curled up on my bed. She's breathing quick, and her hand twitches. She's having a nightmare. But after a moment, she settles back down, her breath evening out. She's only just escaped one battle, and now another one might be coming our way, and I have no idea how to stop it.

What am I supposed to do?

It's no use trying to sleep anymore. I have to get out of here, clear my head.

Quietly as I can, I crawl out of my nest of blankets, grab my bow leaning against the wall, and slide the cracked window farther open. The night is warm and the crickets are chirping up a storm. I watch Juniper, waiting for her to shift, but she doesn't even twitch.

I duck out the window, the bow and quiver slung across my back, and climb down the ivy-covered trellis propped up on the side of the house. I've done it so many times, I can climb down with my eyes closed.

The second my foot hits the ground, I feel better, and now that I'm standing here I feel silly. What did I expect? A draug to leap out at me from behind every bush or around every corner?

The pressed dirt is cool under my bare feet as I head east, toward the castle. Without my phone, I have no idea what time it is, but it's so early even the landscapers haven't arrived yet to mow the grass or tend to the gardens. I know it's still a long time until anyone will miss me or care that I'm taking a stroll in my jammies. The sky is only a dusty gray and the air is crisp and cool against my sweaty skin. At least now I can breathe.

It doesn't feel like a battle is looming. I half-expected ten thousand orcs gathering at the gates by now. Cue the lightning, cue the rain, cue the music. But no. Everything is quiet and calm. The birds haven't been woken up yet. So much for the dramatics.

If there's an army on its way, it's taking an awful long time to get here.

The square is dark and empty, as usual. All that's here is the wooden stage, newly set up for the King's Feast, with huge speaker towers standing like hulking statues, and a black-and-white cat that is licking itself underneath a pretzel stand. The opposite of ominous.

I plop down at the foot of Yggdrasil.

"He's not really going to die, right?" I ask, tipping my head up to face the branches. I know the landvaettir won't respond, but it helps to say it out loud. Doing that at least makes me feel less crazy.

From behind me, the sound of footsteps is getting closer.

I leap to my feet, an arrow drawn back.

Juniper freezes, staring at me with wide, scared eyes. Over Reagan's old silk pajamas, she's wearing her moss cloak, her staff clutched tightly in one hand. "Apologies," she says.

I lower the bow, and let out a puff of breath. "Sorry, I thought you were—" I stop myself from saying it, because saying it makes it too real.

"You thought I was a draug?"

I swallow my heartbeat in my throat and nod.

"I heard you leave," she says. "Is everything all right?"

I plaster on a smile and wave her off. "Yeah! No worries. Go back to bed. Everything is coolio here." I wince. At least Juniper doesn't know how lame the word *coolio* is.

Juniper comes closer to me, looking up at the tree. She presses her palm against the trunk and pats it affectionately, like petting Butters. The leaves above rustle in the breeze. "Would you like to talk about it?"

I smile, but it's stiff. "Talk about what?"

Juniper may be new to this world, but she wasn't born yesterday. "You have been acting strangely. Did the jalapeño poppers upset your stomach?"

"Ha! No, not that." I take a seat again, pressing my back up against the tree, and Juniper kneels beside me. She places her staff in front of her folded legs and gently lays her hands in her lap. "Just a bad dream, is all."

"I had a bad dream, too," she says.

"What about?"

Juniper thinks about it for a moment, chewing on her lower lip. "I dreamed of the day Mother left me with Amma in Utgard."

"You remember it?"

Juniper shakes her head. "I do not. Amma says I was safer with her. I was too young to remember. But in my dream, Mother was walking away from me, but I couldn't run after her. I sank into the ground, and I couldn't move. And when I called out to Amma to help me, she didn't come, because the village was on fire."

"I'm sorry," I say. "I mean it."

Juniper bows her head and sweeps her hand across the grass, like she's smoothing out wrinkles in a shirt. "It's as if my dream is coming true. When I search for Mother, she only gets farther from me."

"We'll find her," I say. "She can't be *nowhere*. We won't give up."

When Juniper looks at me, she lets out a breath, like she's finally got a weight off her chest.

It's my turn to share with the class.

"I saw something today," I say. "A sign. From Odin."

Juniper shifts to sit on her butt, staring at me with round eyes. "When did this happen?"

"When we were here earlier," I say, nodding to the now-empty square. "Odin chose someone to go to Valhalla."

Juniper leans in, fully invested now. "Who?"

"His name is Wyatt. He works here as a knight. I don't really know him though. He just moved here. He's . . . going to die soon."

Juniper blinks a few times, no doubt running through the same questions that have been keeping me up all night.

"And this wasn't even the first time I had a vision," I say. "Before you got here, I saw a wolf sitting on Odin's throne in Valhalla."

The color from Juniper's cheeks drains away. I don't mean to scare her, but I want to be as honest as I can. For whatever reason, I can talk to Juniper better than I can talk to my other sisters.

"But then you showed up," I say, "and I haven't told anyone about any of this yet."

Juniper looks disturbed. "This wolf . . . You saw Fenrir, the wolf destined to kill Odin in Ragnarök?"

"It can't be, can it? I'm not even sure what I saw was real. Valhalla empty, ash falling like snow. That would mean Valhalla is ruined. But that can't be true, not if I saw a sign from Odin a couple hours ago, unless it . . ." I want to say *hasn't happened yet*, but even I can't wrap my head around the idea that I had a vision of the future.

Juniper doesn't say anything. She looks awfully pale, even in the lights coming off the castle, but she must be thinking it, too.

I shake my head. "I know I'm supposed to follow orders. I'm a valkyrie, it's my job to bring Odin's chosen soldiers to Valhalla. . . ." I lick my lips, my mouth is dry. "But I don't want Wyatt to die. I don't want anyone to die, especially if I can help it."

Juniper stares at me. But I don't see any judgment in her eyes, or that she'd run off and tell on me to Prima or Reagan. But she doesn't look like she's sorry for me either, and in a way I can appreciate it.

"I'm probably the worst valkyrie ever," I say, smiling, despite myself.

"No," she says. "Not at all. What are you going to do?"

That's the question I've been asking myself all night. I'd hoped I'd find some sort of answer, or some guidance, but . . . I'm alone. "I don't know," I say.

Juniper tips her head back to look up at Yggdrasil and sighs, but then her expression changes and she stands up.

"What's up?" I ask as she steps to the tree.

She traces her hand on Yggdrasil's trunk, then jolts like she's been electrocuted. "Oh!" She gasps, holding her hand tight to her chest.

"Are you okay? What is it?"

"It's . . . Yggdrasil! It's speaking to me!"

My jaw drops. "What?"

She looks at me with a spark in her eyes, and if that were me, I'd be freaked out hearing the universe talk. But she laughs. "Yes! It is a tree, is it not?" Eagerly, she puts her hand back on the trunk.

I can barely sit still. I move toward her on my knees. "What's it saying?"

Juniper closes her eyes and focuses. Between the slit of her lids, I can see her eyes are glowing green. "No words. It does not use speech like we do. It is a . . . feeling, but it is more than that. It sounds like the Iron Woods. Alive."

I don't understand, but I don't have to.

"Slain-chooser . . ." she says. "It is saying a slain-chooser was here."

My heart practically bursts out of my chest. "A valkyrie! Mom!"

Juniper frowns, her brow furrowed in concentration, but already my mind is running wild.

"Right after she got the raven-message, she must have come here. Why though? Can you ask what Mom was doing here?"

"It does not say." Juniper's frown deepens. When she looks at me, her eyes glow like a neon sign. "Something is wrong."

The moment she says it, the branches overhead start to sway, just like that day when Juniper crossed realms.

I'm on my feet, scanning the square. It's like I've been dunked in an ice bath, my blood runs cold. "More draugar?"

Yggdrasil is shaking so badly now, I'm worried the tree will fall on us. But all at once, it stops. Juniper drops her hand from the tree, gasping for breath. She holds the glass vial around her neck like a lifeline.

"What was that?" I ask.

My answer comes as the ground shakes, like an earthquake.

Boom.

Boom.

Boom.

If I didn't know any better, I'd say it's like..."Footsteps?"

Juniper grabs her staff. "Getting closer."

A roar rumbles like thunder from the southeast, coming from the lake behind the castle. By the sound of it, whatever can do that is huge.

Juniper and I lock eyes as we both realize the same thing at the same time.

A monster is here.

8

JUNIPER AND I TAKE OFF TOGETHER DOWN KNIGHT'S PASS,
rounding the arena, and sprint toward the docks. Juniper follows me
as I leap over a low fence and cut through the park at breakneck speed.

More roars come from behind the trees leading to the beach. I don't
hesitate as I hurl myself through the dark, taking a shortcut through
the thick line of trees separating the faire from the lake. Sticks and
small stones scrape up the bottom of my bare feet, but I can't care
about it now. I don't even think to warn Prima or Reagan.

The closer we get to the lake, the louder the roars are.

Boom. Boom. Boom. Whatever it is, it's coming.

My lungs are burning by the time I skid to a stop in the sand at the
beach. I can't quite believe what I'm seeing. In the lake, a giant shape
is slowly rising from the water, walking with huge lumbering steps
to shore. Easily two stories tall, bald-headed, cracked gray skin like
old Play-Doh, it's not of this realm.

It takes a few beats for me to process, but Juniper knows what it
is immediately.

"A cave troll!" She sounds just as surprised as I am.

Arms the size of tree trunks, the troll moves slowly, dragging its knuckles in the sand. It's naked, but that doesn't mean much when it looks like a week-old scab woke up and chose violence. It snarls and snorts lake water out of its shovel-sized nostrils, then shakes its head as if dazed. Blinking bulbous black eyes, the cave troll looks around, before finally noticing us.

It pulls back its lips revealing craggy teeth, sharp as slate.

All I can do is freeze. "Don't move," I say. "Maybe it plays by T. rex rules."

"I do not know what that means," Juniper hisses at me, though it's worth noting she doesn't move either.

There's no time to explain.

The cave troll huffs, snarls, and then roars at us, spittle flying everywhere.

So much for that.

I nock an arrow and aim right for its face.

Perfect shot, but the arrow bounces off the troll's cheek. Its skin is strong as cement.

My arrows won't work.

The troll lifts a gigantic fist and raises it above its head. All I can do is jump out of the way as the troll's fist slams into the beach like a hammer, making sand fly everywhere.

Some gets in my eyes, and I blink through tears as Juniper stuffs her hand into her pouch and throws an acorn at the troll. When the seed hits the ground, it sprouts. Roots burst out of the sand, snaking up the troll's arms and holding it like anchors.

But the troll is too strong. It roars and wrenches itself free, snapping the roots like toothpicks.

I manage to scramble to my feet just before the troll comes for me again, slamming its fists down, pounding the ground like a toddler throwing an epic tantrum. Sand rains down on me and gets in my eyes, and I'm blind for a second, a second I can't afford to lose, but I can't open my eyes. They sting like crazy.

Tears blur my vision, and all I see are shadows.

I can only guess where to go as I juke and dodge, blinking furiously, to get away from this big, dark shape lunging for me. Every time the troll smashes the ground, it's like the world is going to split in two. I can barely stand upright as the ground tips beneath me.

My eyes clear just as the troll lets out a howl of frustration and grabs a huge piece of driftwood from the shore. It's a fallen tree, the trunk as long as a car, and the troll lifts it easily over its head like a club.

"Bryn!" Juniper hurls an acorn at my feet. Roots sprout out of the ground, surrounding me in a dome of plants just before the troll swings down.

"Thanks!" I say, as the roots shake with the force of the blow. It's holding, for now.

We're running out of time. Someone will hear the noise and come running, and I don't know how to talk my way out of this one. There has to be more I can do. This troll has to have a weakness.

I put my hand to my pendant and my valkyrie armor appears in a flash of light, and I get another arrow from my quiver. I'm so lucky I didn't leave my bow at home.

When I dive out from behind the roots, I take aim, lining up the shot, and shout to get its attention.

"Hey, you!"

The troll snarls at me and I let loose, the arrow flying right for one of its eyes, but the troll turns at the last moment, and the arrow ricochets off the side of its head uselessly.

"What, are you bored already?" I taunt.

The troll either ignores me or doesn't understand what I said. It takes lumbering steps across the beach, heading for the faire.

"Where is it going?" Juniper asks.

"Doesn't matter! Stop it!"

The troll drags the driftwood behind like a child's toy, grunting as it walks. It's slow, but every step it takes is easily ten feet across. Juniper and I have to run to keep up.

Juniper summons more roots, lassoing the troll by the wrists and the neck. As she uses her magic, her eyes glow green, commanding the plants to grow like crazy. She grits her teeth and pushes down, making the roots slither back into the sand, anchoring the troll again.

The troll thrashes wildly, roaring and trying to yank free.

I take another shot at its eye, but it swipes its hand, knocking the arrow out of the air before it has a chance to do much of anything.

"Does this thing have any weaknesses?" I call out.

"Sunlight!" Juniper shouts back, holding her staff out toward the roots. "Cave trolls cannot survive in sunlight!"

The sky is a dusty pink. The sun's coming. If we can just keep the troll busy for fifteen minutes—

The troll's three-toed feet dig into the soft sand, straining against the roots. It roars and gnashes its craggy teeth and flexes its huge muscles, and the roots snap.

The troll is loose and it's coming for me. It winds up for a heavy swing with the driftwood and roars at me, and I let loose another arrow, aiming for its mouth. With a small *dink!*, the arrow bounces off one of its huge teeth.

I don't have any time to dodge out of the way.

Juniper screams. "Bryn!"

The troll swings the log with a giant roar.

It hits me, full force, right in the chest. My armor catches the brunt of it and dissipates, the energy spent, but the blow knocks me clear across the beach.

I eat sand as I skid to a stop near the dock.

I can't breathe. My lungs won't work. The wind got knocked out of me.

Juniper screams again, but the troll is coming right for me.

Another voice shouts across the beach. "Hey!"

Both the troll and I turn to see, and even though my eyes swim with tears, I'd recognize him anywhere.

Standing at the tree line, dressed in athletic shorts and a T-shirt, is Wyatt.

In his hand is a sword. He must have grabbed one from the arena when he heard the fight.

Valhalla's light shines brightly around his dark curls, getting brighter by the second.

Suddenly, it all makes sense. *This* is the battle.

This is how it's supposed to end for him.

"No." I think I say it out loud. I'm not sure.

He shouldn't be here. He *can't* be here.

Wyatt takes in everything, from the troll, to me, to Juniper, and a hard look settles on his face. His eyes darken as he charges in, sword raised.

The troll doesn't have the processing power to understand what's going on.

It doesn't react as Wyatt slides in the sand, slicing the troll's ankle with the sword, but the steel only sparks against its hide.

Wyatt realizes his mistake too late.

The troll raises its fist and pummels Wyatt sideways.

Like a rag doll, Wyatt flies across the lake. His limp body skips like a stone across the surface, before he slows near the dock and sinks below the water.

He doesn't come back up.

The troll huffs, satisfied, and continues walking toward the faire.

Juniper takes off after it, but I can't tear my eyes away from where Wyatt disappeared. The world is collapsing around me.

This is all my fault.

I scramble to my feet and sprint toward the dock, ignoring Juniper screaming my name. The water is black, except for the soft glow coming from below.

Wyatt is dying.

My bare feet pound the wooden dock before I jump and dive in after him.

9

THE WATER IS COLD. IT STEALS THE AIR FROM MY LUNGS like another punch to the chest.

My brain turns to static as my muscles seize up. It's dark, it's freezing. I blink my eyes open to see a glow coming from below me.

I swim down.

The deeper I go, the more the water presses on me from all sides, making my head feel like a can of pop ready to explode. It gets harder to swim. No matter how hard I pull myself down, I'm fighting something more powerful than I am.

My heart thunders in my head, but I keep going. I can't turn back. I'm almost there. The light is getting brighter.

In it, there's a silhouette.

Wyatt.

His eyes are closed, his arms drifting above his head as he sinks.

The light around him is only getting stronger, pulsing like the rhythm of drums, but then I realize I actually hear them.

Valhalla. It calls to him.

His destiny is to serve his afterlife in the halls of Odin, to sit among others who have fought bravely in battle, to await the final days of Ragnarök and fight the enemies of Asgard.

His destiny is to die.

Like an old song I once sang by heart, I know what I have to do. I have one mission, and one mission only: Valhalla needs an army. I must deliver.

The second I grab Wyatt's wrist and pull him close, the light around him shines with a rainbow of color and when I blink, the light turns into a portal.

A rainbow bridge of celestial light stretches behind him. The Bifröst, leading to Asgard. The city of the gods gleams golden in the distance.

All I have to do is take him there. Easy as that.

Peace washes over me. It's odd, knowing it's that simple. Laughable, really. This whole time, I was so worried, and for what? All Wyatt needs is a little push. Bring him to the shining halls of Odin, and his destiny will be complete. The Norns have seen his fate, have already stitched his life thread into the great tapestry of time. All he has to do is die.

The golden light fills my vision. It's all-consuming. I'm drowning in it. His brothers and sisters are waiting for him. The drums of Asgard pulse through the water, pulse through my veins.

My armor rematerializes around me, all on its own, as the power of Asgard surges through my body.

I am a valkyrie....

But I don't let Wyatt go.

My lungs burn. My head pounds. My muscles scream at me to do something. Deliver him to Valhalla! End this! Fulfill your duty!

I squeeze my arms tighter around Wyatt's body and rip him away from the light.

A voice in my head screams at me to turn around, but I kick us up toward the surface.

The drums of Valhalla get louder, as if calling him back.

Voices follow me, chanting with the drums in a language I don't know. I ignore them.

The farther I take him, the fainter Valhalla's light becomes.

I kick hard, but my legs are like rubber. We're not getting anywhere. Fast. I need air.

My chest is going to explode, but I hold Wyatt close.

Everything is getting dark.

I can't take it anymore—

I kick one more time and my head breaks the surface.

I cough and sputter and gag as I haul Wyatt up with me. His head lolls to the side, resting on my shoulder. He's so heavy, and I sink under again, swallowing nasty lake water, but I manage to get him above the surface just enough.

"I've got you."

Sounds of the battle seem so far away, Juniper and the troll still at it. I need to get us to shore.

The sky is starting to grow more pink as I float on my back, keeping Wyatt's face above the water, until I get solid ground under me where I can drag him the rest of the way.

He's as heavy as a sack of potatoes, and he slumps on the wet sand as I drop him.

"Wyatt." I kneel at his side and shake him.

Blood runs from his hairline and mixes with the dirty lake water on his skin.

I brush the dark wet hair away from his face and hold his cheeks. He's so cold, but he doesn't move.

He's not breathing.

"No, no, no. Wyatt, come on."

Nothing. I check his pulse. It's barely there.

I didn't save him then only for him to die now.

I take off my helm just as my armor fades and lean down to help him breathe—but Wyatt coughs and lake water spurts out of his mouth.

Relief washes over me. All I can do is sit back on my heels and watch as he heaves up more water. He rolls onto his front, each cough racks his whole body, and he curls up into himself, fisting the sand, and shakes his head.

"You're okay," I say, breathless.

Wyatt shakes his head again. His back arches with each ragged breath he takes.

"You..." he rasps. Under a curtain of wet hair, I see his eyes. His face is tight and his lips are curled back in pain. "Get..." He's not looking too good.

"Take it easy. You almost drowned."

"Get...away..."

"Huh?"

It's then that I *really* notice his eyes. I don't think they were glowing before, like amber in sunlight.

With a wild scream, Wyatt rises to his knees and mist envelopes him entirely. I fall over as the mist washes over me, too.

When it clears, standing in Wyatt's place is a huge grizzly bear, easily as big as an SUV. Brown fur, round ears, wet nose, the whole nine yards.

The bear's eyes are level with mine, and it looks right at me.

It takes me a second to find my voice again. "Wyatt?"

The bear's amber gaze shifts to the battle happening between Juniper and the troll. It rises up on its hind legs and roars so loud, I cover my ears.

In one move, the bear leaps over me, and charges after the troll.

10

ONE WORD REPEATS OVER AND OVER IN MY HEAD: *bear, bear, bear.*

It takes a few seconds for my brain to restart. Nearby, my bow and quiver lie on the sand where I dropped them before diving in after Wyatt. I grab my stuff and bolt to my feet.

Juniper stands, left in the wake of the bear chasing the troll, stunned, staring after them. "What happened?"

I don't slow down as I run past. "That's him! That's Wyatt!"

"What?!" Juniper chases after me as we follow the sounds of a fight through the troll-shaped hole in the trees.

I can't expand on the statement. I'm having a hard enough time believing what I just saw. One second he's dying, the next he's a bear. I don't know what else to say.

We burst back out of the trees and into the faire just in time to see Bear-Wyatt leap at the troll, tackling it from behind. The troll trips and falls forward, collapsing into the tournament arena with a tremendous boom as part of the wooden fence crumbles underneath them.

Wyatt crawls on top of the troll's back, his claws digging into its rocklike hide as he wrestles the troll to the dirt. It's a more even fight now as Wyatt bites wherever he can. He clamps down hard on the troll's shoulder with ginormous teeth, and the troll roars in fury.

The troll manages to get its feet under itself again and stands with Wyatt still hanging on with all his strength as he digs his claws and teeth in, like a big bear backpack.

Together, they stumble through the empty tournament arena, knocking over racks of swords and shields. Wyatt's huge paws barely break the troll's skin, but the troll isn't happy about it anyway.

The troll swings its arms, trying to grab Wyatt, but it can't get a hold of him at the right angle. It's too stupid to think of another way to get Wyatt off its back, so it does the only other thing it can do—smash.

The troll jumps up, tucks its legs in, and falls backward, crushing Wyatt underneath it.

The ground trembles, but Wyatt still doesn't let go.

The troll tries it again, and this time Wyatt roars in pain and goes limp. The troll then grabs Wyatt around the neck and throws him across the arena.

As he lands, his body digs up a long trench, but Wyatt manages to roll onto his paws, burying them deep in the dirt to stop himself from crashing into the stands. He roars, flashing his giant teeth.

Meanwhile, the troll turns and continues making its way toward the square. It pushes through the bunting hanging overhead, breaking them as easily as walking through spiderwebs.

Wyatt charges again and grabs the troll by the arm, but the troll shakes him off. It doesn't even slow down. It's on a mission to get somewhere.

It clomps out of the arena, shrugging off Wyatt's attacks, and heads into the castle square. Wyatt barrels forward like a speeding train, and smashes into the troll's side, making it stumble and topple a nearby tower of speakers set up for the feast and sending up a shower of sparks. But it ignores Wyatt as if it's got one thing and one thing only on its mind.

The tree stands at the other side of the square, and the troll is heading directly toward it.

"Oh shit. It's going for Yggdrasil."

Juniper shouts, "We must protect it! Do not let the troll damage it! It could sever Midgard from other realms!"

"So how do we stop it?" I'm starting to run out of arrows. Not like they're doing much good anyway.

"I do not know! I have never faced one before! Cave trolls are from the deepest hollows of Jotunheim. They live underground, hardly ever leaving their territory. If we can just make it to sunrise!"

Wyatt isn't giving up. He rises on his hind legs and swipes at the troll's head, punching and scratching with his giant claws. The troll grabs Wyatt by the throat and smashes him to the ground. He's slow to get up.

Juniper's eyes glow green as she calls forth the power of plants. Roots snake out of the ground and wrap around the troll's ankles and wrists. That slows it down enough for us to catch up. Her hands shake as she holds out her staff, commanding the roots to her will.

The troll grunts as it strains against them, but it won't be enough to stop it.

We're running out of options and I'm less than useless. I look up at the sky, at the still pink haze of dawn. *Come on, sun!* We just need a few more minutes.

I look around for anything that might help, and my eyes land on the microphone system set up for the King's Feast. Speakers all around the square, hidden in trees.

"I have an idea!" I call out to Juniper. "Hold on!"

"I am holding!"

She's not going to last much longer.

I sprint for the wooden stage, hurtling past the troll on the ground. It tries to grab me with fingers the size of snowboards, but Wyatt stops it.

He charges in for the troll again, grabbing the troll's arm with his massive jaws and yanking it down to the ground. Juniper commands more roots to help. Her hands shake as she raises her staff and a sweat breaks out on her forehead.

I jump up onstage and grab the microphone, but it's not turned on. I fumble for the switch.

The troll bellows and pulls. The roots snap and Juniper collapses, exhausted.

The troll's massive fist connects with the wide side of Wyatt's body and he rolls across the square, sliding in the dirt like a snowplow. Wyatt rises on unsteady paws and shakes the dirt from his head, dazed. I'm running out of time.

My hands are so sweaty, I almost drop the microphone.

The troll's back on its feet again.

Finally, I feel the switch and flip it. Feedback whines through the speakers in the square.

The troll is almost at the tree.

I press my lips to the cold metal of the microphone and make a low, guttural grunt, imitating the troll's own noises.

The troll stumbles to a stop and looks around, baffled. My voice is coming from every direction, flowing out of all the speakers.

"What are you doing?" Juniper cries.

I turn away from the microphone. "Something stupid!" Then I press my mouth to the microphone again, growling and grunting my heart out.

All I can do is hope I sound like the most seductive cave troll I possibly can. *Come and get it, ya big hunk.*

The troll spins around, confused, looking for the source of the sound. Even from here, I can tell its brain is working on overdrive to figure out what's going on.

It steps away from the tree, swinging its giant bald head from side to side, searching.

Yes! It's working! I don't stop. *Hey there, handsome!* I hope I'm saying.

The troll's eyes land on me, and it snarls.

My plan may have worked a little too well.

Now I've just made the troll mad.

It rushes me, fist raised, and I leap to safety just before the stage explodes in a shower of splinters and nails. The troll follows me as I run in the opposite direction of the tree. Its footsteps thunder behind me, getting closer and closer. The sun can't get here any faster? I try to run up Charlemagne Lane as quick as I can, but the troll has other ideas. It slams its fist into the ground, the force of it making me trip and land hard in the dirt.

I roll over, scrambling back, and the troll is on top of me.

"Bryn!" Juniper cries.

The troll raises its arms and swings down. I duck my head and roll, and the troll misses me by inches.

The troll tries again, slamming down with its fists, and I roll the other way.

I can't get up.

The troll raises its door-sized fists one last time. Snarling, baring its teeth, ready to smash me into a bloody pulp. It looks even more horrible in the rising morning light.

I duck, covering my head, waiting for the inevitable, then sunlight bursts through the trees.

When the troll lets out a horrified roar I look up.

Everywhere the sunlight touches, the troll's skin turns from a doughy gray into a hard, cracked stone.

It stares at its hands as its fingers cement together like chiseled rock. When it looks up at the golden sky it howls as half of its face turns to stone, too. Furious, it tries one last time to smash me.

Morning brightens the whole square just as it brings its stony fists down and sunlight melts over its body.

The troll turns completely to stone, and its fist stops, inches from my face.

Like a statue, it looms above me. Its mouth is still open, its face stuck in permanent fury, its arm lowering in a blow that will never hit.

I scramble out from underneath it, breathing heavy.

The troll stares right through me, its eyes now made of solid rock.

Juniper slowly gets to her feet, panting, and Wyatt stumbles as he walks toward me. He lets out a whine, swaying on his feet, before he collapses and bursts into a cloud of mist. Lying in the bear's place is Wyatt the human, fully clothed, unconscious, and bloody.

The square is almost totally destroyed. The stage is hardly more than a pile of splinters, the speakers are a sparking, smoldering mess, the arena torn apart.

It occurs to me just how bad this all looks.

"We have to get out of here," I tell Juniper.

Juniper hoists one of Wyatt's arms over her shoulder, and I grab his other arm, and we lift him. As we carry him like a scarecrow between us, his chin drops to his chest and his sneakers drag in the dirt. I squeeze Wyatt's wrist tighter, feeling his pulse under my fingers.

"Let's get him back to the house," I say, and Juniper nods.

Past her, I think I see a person watching us from around the castle and my stomach flips. Someone must have heard the fight and came to see what was going on. But when I do a double take, whoever it was is gone. In fact, I'm not sure anyone was ever there in the first place. I'm honestly surprised there isn't a huge crowd.

Wyatt moans. He's bleeding pretty badly. I hold him tighter and together we flee the scene.

11

I messed up. Big-time.

Seeing Wyatt in the full light of morning, passed out on my bedroom floor among my dirty clothes, really puts everything into perspective. I denied a god—no, not just a god, the All-Father—his claim.

Literally, the entire point of being a valkyrie is to bring chosen soldiers to Valhalla, and I can't even get that right.

It's official. I am the godsdamn worst valkyrie ever.

I'm so tired, and my whole body aches. Fighting that troll was the hardest thing I've ever done. All the hits I took start to catch up to me, and my chest is one huge bruise. The only thing I have energy to do is to sit next to Wyatt and stare.

Wyatt's eyes are closed as his chest slowly rises and falls with every breath he takes. His mess of dark curls clings to his forehead, caked in dried blood from the gash somewhere in his hairline. With his face turned to me, I can see the deep scar running from the bottom of his left eye to the corner of his mouth. His hands make loose fists as they rest against his flat stomach. His shirt and athletic shorts are filthy, still clinging to his body with lake water. He's dressed for a morning run, probably heard the noise and came to help.

My stomach drops as I remember the way the troll knocked him into the lake and how I couldn't do anything but watch. I shake my head to clear the memory, and force myself to take a breath.

He's alive. I saved him.

How much does he know? Does he remember what happened? Does he know I almost took him to Valhalla? Does he know he can turn into a bear? I can't stop rolling the same questions through my head, like marbles clattering together. This whole time I thought I had things figured out, and now this... I didn't know anyone like him could still exist. Can he turn into other animals?

The jug of healing mead appears in my line of sight, snapping me back to reality.

"I found it," Juniper says. She gestures with the jug and I take it.

"Thanks. Did Prima or Reagan give you any trouble?"

"No. No one saw me. I believe Prima is in the shop, and I heard Reagan in the washroom, singing about how she is stronger and how her loneliness is not killing her no more?" She says it like a question, as if she isn't sure what to make of it.

I almost laugh. I don't have to guess. Reagan is no doubt blaring a post-breakup playlist in the shower before work. She's had her fair share of heartbreak, but this breakup with James must be particularly brutal if she's singing to Britney Spears.

"Ah yes," I say. "It's an ancient battle cry passed down from a powerful enchantress."

Juniper stares at me. "I fear that you are teasing me."

"I would never!" Even *I'm* not immune to the power of Britney Spears.

I uncork the jug and the smell of floral mead washes over me. From the sound of it though, I can tell there's only enough for one more person.

"Are we sure you want to use the last of it?" Juniper asks as she sits next to me, voicing my own doubt. "What if someone needs it later?"

Like Mom? I shake my head, punting the thought from my brain. Mom's not hurt. I have to believe that. Wyatt is in front of me now, hurt and in need. I squeeze the jug tightly.

"We'll burn that bridge when we get to it," I say.

Juniper watches as I put the jug to Wyatt's lips and pour the mead into his mouth. Just like when I first met Juniper, it only takes a second for the blood to disappear from Wyatt's head. But he's still out cold. The mead will take some time to wake him up, so all we can do now is wait.

"Okay," I say, taking a moment to process what just happened. "So how about we address the bear in the room?"

Juniper totally misses my joke. "You said there was no magic on Midgard."

"I didn't know about this," I say, gesturing to him. "He must be a berserker. But . . . I've never met one before."

"Berserker?"

"Odin's favorite warrior. Mom used to tell us stories about them. They would go literally berserk, getting so angry they'd turn into bears. They'd be almost unstoppable on the battlefield. Not even fire or iron could bring them down. But I thought they all had died."

Juniper nods, everything coming together. "I would imagine that is why Odin called him to Valhalla. A berserker in his ranks would be invaluable."

"Ugh. Don't remind me."

Juniper chews on her lip. "I am sorry." She ducks her head, then looks up at me from under her pale eyebrows. "But you have to admit, I do not imagine the All-Father will be too pleased about this."

"Okay, I know! I messed up. I just . . ." I trail off, staring at Wyatt lying in front of me. How many people in his life would miss him if he died? His parents, siblings, friends, crushes... The people who love him most wouldn't get to see him again, probably. They'd never know what happened.

Valhalla or not, he'd be gone.

I made a choice. I changed his fate. Just like my namesake.

My sisters and I were named after valkyries who came before us, a tradition that's been passed down for ages. I was named after arguably the most famous one, Brunhild. The legend goes that she disobeyed Odin, choosing to save a king who Odin wanted dead. As punishment, Odin stripped Brunhild of her valkyrie power and put a sleeping spell on her. Eventually, she was rescued by a dashing hero, a classic princess in a tower situation. Normally, this is where you'd think the story is over, but you'd be wrong. Brunhild didn't get a happily ever after. Her life was full of betrayal, and deception, and misfortune, and then she stabbed herself and died. The end. Great story, I know.

But if Odin cursed Brunhild for disobeying him then, what will he do to me now?

It's all I can think about as I stare at Wyatt, and when I do, everything is crystal clear. He's alive, and that's what matters.

"Odin can be mad at me all he wants," I say. "I'm not sorry."

Juniper wrings her hands, watching me carefully. Her voice is soft when she says, "That was extremely clever, what you did with the troll."

I can tell she's trying to make me feel better and I wave her off. "You and Wyatt did most of the work. I was pretty useless."

"You were not! It could have been much worse. You thought quickly. If you had not been there, who knows what would have happened."

A chill rakes down my spine. "It would have destroyed—"

Before I can finish, Wyatt's eyes snap open and he lurches up into a sitting position, making both Juniper and me jump back.

"What happe—" Wyatt pants, looking around wildly. He squints, narrowing his eyes, and then from a pocket in his shorts he pulls out his glasses. Miraculously, they're still intact, if a little crooked. "Where am I?" he asks.

"My bedroom," I say, heart still pounding. "But *shh*. Keep quiet or my sisters will hear."

He stares at me and blinks a few times, processing. From under his butt, he pulls one of my dirty socks—custom ones with Butternut Squash's face on them—then drops it back on the floor. It's taking him a second to understand.

Once I get talking, I can't stop. "Sorry, I didn't know where else to take you. You were pretty beat-up. I'm Bryn. We met earlier. Well, we didn't really *meet*-meet. You and your dad, I think, came here asking about my mom the other day, and—oh!—I saw you after your show that one time. You probably don't remember. But I work here, too. Not like you though. I'm nobody." My chest hitches when I try to take a breath. I can't help it, my adrenaline is through the roof. I jerk my head toward Juniper. "This is Juniper. She's cool."

Juniper gives him a small wave and he looks at her with the same wide-eyed stare he gave me, probably trying to figure out if he's dreaming or not.

I try to handle my next question as tactfully as I can. "How much do you remember about this morning?"

Wyatt shakes his head slightly, like he's trying to clear it. "I got up to go for a run when I heard this noise.... There was a monster." He scrunches up his face and puts a hand to his head, and then he looks up at me with a start. "Did you see me...?"

I wave my hands frantically. "See what? That you can turn into a bear? No big deal, I see stuff like that all the time. Not weird to me at all."

Wyatt swallows thickly, his cheeks turning red, as his expression morphs into abject mortification.

"Bryn!" a voice calls from outside the door, followed by footsteps coming up the narrow stairs.

"Shit. Prima."

In the time it takes for me and Juniper to look at the door, Wyatt makes a break for the window. "Wait—" I whisper, but he's already slipped his wide shoulders through the window and is climbing down the trellis just as the door bursts open.

Prima stands with her hand on the knob, eyes fixated on us, her brows drawn together.

"What are you doing?" she asks, suspiciously. She looks me over, scanning my clothes. I only now notice that I'm covered in dirt and sand and soaking wet. "Were you outside?"

Thinking fast, I say, "Yeah! Got a quick workout in!" I flex a non-existent bicep for her. Prima's gaze turns to Juniper, who stiffens like she's been turned into a wooden board.

"Yes!" Juniper says, eyes round, smile tight. "Work outside. Outside work." She glances at my arm. "With muscles?"

She's terrible at lying. Prima must be able to see it, but she just says, flatly, "Breakfast."

The only meal that's edible in the house these days is breakfast. Cold cereal and muffins bought from the bakery.

I try to take my time eating, pretending like everything is fine, but I'm moving so slow my cornflakes have already gone soggy. I'm still shaking. Everything happened so fast. I could have easily been crushed like a bug by the troll, but here I am, pretending like everything is normal.

Reagan scrolls through her phone, her hair already dried, curled, and pinned for her morning show, while Butternut Squash sits on her lap like a sphinx. She asks Prima to pass the orange juice. Without looking up, Prima slides the jug toward her like a bartender at a saloon and keeps flipping through the Ravenswood Faire bulletin, picking at the top of her blueberry muffin with her fingers. Normally I'd tease her about being old, because she's reading a newspaper and wearing her glasses, but I know that if I speak, I'll let something slip, so I shove cereal into my mouth to occupy it.

Juniper piles spoonfuls of cereal into her mouth too, her cheeks puffed out like a chipmunk's. She glances at Prima and Reagan, as if anxiously waiting for them to say something, too The hand not holding a spoon is clenched into a shaking fist. I realize I am clenching my fist too, and I put my hand in my lap, hiding it from view. I didn't sleep at all last night. Neither, it would seem, did Prima. She's got dark circles under her eyes, and she yawns loudly.

Neither of my sisters act like they know a troll magically appeared in Ravenswood this morning.

Didn't anyone hear the fight? It was chaos, someone *had* to have heard it. Besides the person I thought I saw, no one came running to see what was happening. If I didn't feel like a walking bruise and Juniper didn't look like a ghost, I might have convinced myself it was all a dream. How could it be possible that no one heard?

Juniper and I have an entire conversation in the language of eyebrows.

Should we tell them what happened? Juniper seems to say.

No way! I answer back with a slight head shake.

Why?

I clench my jaw and shake my head again. If my sisters find out that I have anything to do with the troll, I won't just be grounded for the rest of summer, I'll probably be locked in the attic until I'm fifty.

What should we do? Juniper asks, purely with her eyebrows and her pinched lips.

I clear my throat. Neither Prima nor Reagan looks up.

"Did you two have a good night's rest?" I ask.

"Why? Did I miss Ragnarök already?" Prima asks dryly, not looking up from the paper.

I screw up my face and I'm about to snap back at her when Reagan cuts in.

"I saw you looking at that cute boy at the barbecue last night," Reagan says.

I nearly choke on my cereal. "Wyatt? It's not what you think."

"Wyatt! That's his name. He's new, right?" Reagan asks. "Just moved here full-time? The Black Knight?" She turns to Juniper, as if she'll help, but Juniper stares at her with eyes as round as her cereal bowl.

"He's no one," I say.

Reagan smiles like she knows better, but she doesn't even know the half of it.

"Shut up! Besides, what happened to me being grounded?" I ask, scrambling for literally any excuse not to talk about this. "No fun allowed, remember?"

Juniper gives me a look but I shake my head, implying that I'll explain later.

"You're allowed to have fun," Reagan says. "Right, Prima?" Prima doesn't answer as she washes her dishes in the sink. "You can't keep yourself cooped up all summer."

I regret trying to strike up conversation. Any second I'm going to blab about what happened. "Everything's cool. Juniper and I have been hanging out. Staying out of trouble. Chillin'."

Juniper nods her head vigorously. "Oh! Yes! I love hanging and . . . chilling?" Her cheeks go pink, and she has a hard time looking Reagan in the eye. She's an awful liar.

"Good!" Reagan says. "If you need anything, let us know."

"I was hoping to acquire more seeds, if you know any place I can get some."

"Seeds?"

"I use seeds for my magic. I collected some yesterday, but I used them all fighting the tro—"

Before she can say the word *troll*, I slam my hands down on the table, making the spoons and bowls clatter.

Everyone stares at me, and I put on a strained smile. "Killed a fly."

Reagan's mouth hangs open, her tongue jabbing the inside of her cheek. "Oh-*kay*. Well, Juniper, you can take any more clothes you want from my closet."

"Yes, thank you," Juniper says. She looks like she wants to crawl into the troll's cave.

"I'm heading to work," Prima says, glancing at her phone. She's tired of the conversation, which is a relief. "You should too," she adds to me, then tips her chin at Juniper. "And go find her some seeds. Or whatever."

12

WE CAN'T GET OUT OF THE HOUSE ANY FASTER. I THROW ON my chemise and surcoat as quickly as I can, Juniper grabs her staff, and the both of us bolt into the bright summer morning.

"I am terribly sorry," Juniper says. "I almost told them what happened. I am not good at lying."

"It's okay." I rake my fingers through my hair, pulling it into a messy ponytail as I lead the way toward the castle. "We just gotta stay cool."

"Cool," Juniper repeats, building confidence. "Frosty. Frozen. Cool. That I can do. So, what is 'grounded'?"

"Grounded is when you're in trouble and can't go anywhere."

"I see. In Utgard, we call it *rooted*. Once, when I was young, I drank all of Amma's linden flower cordial but I lied and told her I did no such thing. But I was so nervous, I vomited it all up on the floor. She rooted me for a week. So, you are 'grounded' because you did something wrong?"

"I tried to find Mom."

Juniper furrows her brow. "How is that bad?"

"I did something stupid and it got me nowhere. Look, the point is,

I'm in enough trouble with Prima and Reagan. I can't be getting into any more of it."

"The troll? You had nothing to do with why it came here."

"Not just that. Saving Wyatt, too. Better keep our mouths shut until I can figure this out."

Juniper nods firmly. "You can trust me. Wait. Where are you going? Is your shop not the other way?"

"It is." I'm halfway down the lane, heading toward the castle. "First I want to check something."

The square looks so much worse in proper daylight. People have already beaten us here. Clusters of staff and performers mingle around, murmuring and wondering what happened while Mr. Beaumont stands with the lead security officer and an engineer, taking note of the damage.

Left over from Wyatt and the troll's fight, huge grooves in the dirt—the size of truck tires—carve up the square, the wooden stage looks like it was karate-chopped in half, the arena like it was trashed by a rowdy crowd after a huge win.

The troll is even uglier now that I have time to study it. It stands frozen exactly where we left it, fists in mid-swing. But I swear, its eyes follow me when I move.

Fortunately, Yggdrasil is untouched. It sways gently in the breeze, the bells on the branches serving as a delightful reminder that it still stands.

"You don't think the troll will come back to life when the sun sets, do you?" I whisper out of the corner of my mouth.

"Probably not," Juniper says, shrugging. "Hopefully not."

I trust her to know more about these kinds of things than I do. "Trolls are dumb, right? Not a whole lot going on up in that skull."

"Correct. Trolls are known for reacting, rather than acting. Anyone foolish or unlucky enough to stumble into their den meets a gruesome fate. They do not have hunting instincts—rather, they wait for their victims to come to them."

"So why would it know to attack the tree?" I ask.

Juniper pauses. Her eyes go up toward the branches. "Yes. Curious," she says.

"And how could it cross realms in the first place? If you say they're from Jotunheim, how did it get here?"

"Perhaps it was an accident?"

"I'm starting to believe nothing is an accident these days."

"You don't think...Ragnarök?" Juniper's voice rises an octave, and I shush her.

"It's the end of all worlds, right? What if the divide between realms is getting thin? What if it's only the start?"

Juniper looks as worried as I feel.

"Come on," I say, tipping my head. "Last night you said the tree told you Mom had been here. Let's have a look around, see what she might have been up to."

With everyone distracted by the new troll statue in the square, Juniper and I go around Yggdrasil, looking for any clues. Everything looks normal. I'm not sure what I'm looking for exactly. Maybe ash from a fire, or a sword in the trunk, or something similar to my vision of Fenrir on Odin's throne.

Juniper puts her hand on the trunk and furrows her brow. She closes her eyes and tilts her head, as if confused. "The tree says there is a...hole?"

"Not what I expected it to say, to be honest."

Juniper clarifies, pointing up. "There is a knot in the tree, above."

I look up, but all I see is more tree. "I don't know what you want me to do with this information."

"It is saying something is there. Maybe you should find it."

Who am I to dismiss what the World Tree is saying?

I tie my skirts to my belt and take a running leap, scrambling up the trunk. I grab on to one of the lowest hanging branches and haul myself up. The bells on the branches ring out, like laughter. At least the landvaettir are having a good time. I haven't climbed this tree in years, but it's like riding a bicycle, and it comes back to me the higher I climb.

I search for a knot in the bark, and after a minute, find it wedged in a fork between two branches about fifteen feet up.

But the knot is a small hole, just big enough for me to fit my fist through.

I feel queasy. "Don't tell me I have to stick my hand in there." I can imagine a million different things at home inside, none of them magical. Bugs, spiders, an owl with a grudge. "I'd like to keep all of my fingers, please."

"It is okay," Juniper says. "Just do it!"

Easy for her to say. I hold my breath, stick my hand in the tree, and brace myself, waiting for fangs to pierce my skin, but instead I find something soft and light. Fabric?

When I pull it out, I see it's a crumpled piece of parchment. "Huh."

"What did you find?"

I hop down from the tree and land beside Juniper, but before I can hand it to her, a voice barks across the square.

"You!" Mr. Beaumont points a finger right at me, making everyone stare.

I point a finger at myself and glance around.

"Bryn Martel," he says. "My office. Now."

Mr. Beaumont's office is at the top of the castle, up a stone spiral staircase, with large glass windows that give an almost three-sixty view of the faire. To the west are the tree-covered lanes of Ravenswood, swarming with guests. To the east is Lake Michigan, where a few speedboats are already cruising on the murky blue water and the Ravenswood pirate ship for skyline tours of Chicago is just setting sail.

Juniper and I each sit on a box chair in front of his giant carved desk. Mr. Beaumont has really leaned into the whole medieval aesthetic, even here in his office, save for his computer and monitor setup. His desk phone even looks like a dragon's claw. My fingers practically itch to hold the paper I found in Yggdrasil. I had to shove it in my pocket tied under my surcoat so no one would see.

Mr. Beaumont types angrily on his keyboard, frowning at the screen, and doesn't say anything for a long moment. I wonder if he forgot we were here.

Juniper and I glance at each other, and she looks like she's going to puke up linden berry cordial if she opens her mouth.

I break the silence. "Mr. Beaumont, if this is about climbing the tree, I'm sorry. I just wanted a better look. What happened last night?"

I really play up the innocent onlooker aspect.

"I figured you would tell me." He finishes typing, stabbing the final keys harder than necessary, then slides the keyboard away from himself so he can lean forward, his hands steepled in front of his golden goatee. "Where did that troll come from?"

"I don't know what you mean."

"Where did the troll come from?" he asks again.

"Why do you think I have anything to do with it?"

"I don't remember you being at the staff barbecue last night."

"I was, though! You just didn't see me." Probably because I was stalking Wyatt like a creep all night. "Ask James, he'll tell you."

"So then you didn't see who brought that statue here? Tore up my landscape? Demolished half the arena?"

"No idea," I say.

Mr. Beaumont presses his lips into a thin, frustrated line and he stares at me, trying to suss out if I'm lying.

"Did you check the security cameras?" I ask. I'm guessing not, or we'd be having a very different conversation.

Mr. Beaumont sighs at that. "First thing. But the cameras were malfunctioning. They stopped just before midnight. They've been acting up since the start of the season."

Weird. I glance at Juniper, who is staring firmly at the floor. She's keeping it together at least.

Mr. Beaumont sighs again, stands up, and moves to the windows overlooking the faire.

"Can't go one week without something going wrong," he says, staring at the guests below. "If it's not one thing, it's another. First, the front gate tells me there's a printing error on the faire map. Then they tell me Eye of Newt's was broken into last night. Then the Dragon's Den tells me they're running out of jalapeño poppers."

Under her breath, Juniper gasps. "No!"

"Now, the lead carpenter tells me it will take days to repair the arena. The sound engineer doesn't know when we can get another set of speakers to replace the damaged ones. And the groundskeeper is throwing a huge fit about the state of the grass. What a disaster."

"Crazier things have happened," I say.

"What will the guests think when they come here? They'll see a mess, that's what. I try to make Ravenswood the epitome of perfection. And look what I have to show for it. The critics will be here any day!"

My eyes land on a picture framed on the desk. It's of Mr. Beaumont, grinning, with Ravenswood's owner, a much smaller, white-mustachioed elderly man named Mr. Langbard. Mr. Langbard is this eccentric billionaire who bankrolled the faire in the 1980s. He's mostly hands-off, so he hired Mr. Beaumont to run the faire while he continued doing his eccentric billionaire things elsewhere.

In the photo, Mr. Beaumont is cheesing for the camera, shaking Mr. Langbard's hand so fast it's blurry.

"How do you know Mr. Langbard hasn't arranged a special gift for the King's Feast?" I ask.

Mr. Beaumont immediately turns around at the name. Now *that* seems like something he hasn't thought about.

I try not to smile. I should get an Oscar. I'm acting my ass off. "It's the only reasonable conclusion, right? Maybe Mr. Langbard commissioned some artist to carve this statue, commemorating your event?"

Mr. Beaumont frowns. "What about the arena?"

"Probably the movers driving a truck, getting careless. Otherwise, what, the troll walked in here all on its own?" I laugh boisterously.

Juniper makes a little squeak.

I kick her foot and she jolts.

Mr. Beaumont's gaze slides to her. "Who are you again?"

She opens her mouth to speak, but she looks gray.

I come to her rescue. "This is my . . . Juniper. She's visiting from out of town."

Mr. Beaumont takes in her unusual outfit and lack of shoes and goes *hmm*. He doesn't even question her ears.

Outside one of the windows, I can hear people have already gathered around the "new attraction." From my vantage, I spot a few kids dangling from the troll's arm like it's the monkey bars, and one kid has claimed a seat on its shoulder. Another kid wears what suspiciously looks like the draug's old rusty helmet.

I point out the window. "There! It's already popular with the guests," I say. "By this time next week, people will be coming just to see it."

By now, the parchment I found in the tree is practically burning a hole through my pocket. I want to get out of here as soon as possible to get a better look at it.

As expected, Mr. Beaumont looks intrigued. "The troll statue? Popular?"

"You could hold a contest. Enter to win a chance to name him. I bet people would pay for a shot."

At the word *pay*, Mr. Beaumont leans forward. "Interesting." He strokes his short beard thoughtfully. A new moneymaking opportunity will make him look good with Mr. Langbard. "You may be right. The movers have been known to leave a mess...." He sigh, and nods. "Oh well. As I always say, the show must go on."

I'm practically squirming to get out of here, but Mr. Beaumont isn't done with me yet.

"But if I find out this was your idea of a practical joke, or if you're behind this in some way..."

"I'm the last person you have to worry about, my liege!"

Mr. Beaumont looks at me for a long moment, then at Juniper, then back at me. "Don't you have the gift shop to get to? What are you doing here? Get to work." He waves his hand in a kingly fashion.

I close the office door behind us and Juniper and I hurry down the stone steps, trying not to be too obvious in our relief.

"Now I *really* hope that troll doesn't come back to life when the sun sets," I say.

⋈

Finally, at the gift shop, we have a moment of peace and quiet to check out the parchment. I shutter the door behind us when we get inside so no one can spy.

"How do you lie so easily?" Juniper asks, breathless.

"I didn't lie!" When she gives me a look, I add, "Mostly! The less Mr. Beaumont suspects, the better. He can't know what's really going on."

"Even so, you are too good at it."

"We all have our special talents."

I fish the piece of parchment out of my pocket. It's soft, almost like sheepskin, and it's covered in hundreds of runes, the ink smeared and barely legible. It just looks like a huge paragraph of strange letters.

What would Mom be doing with something like this?

"I can't read it," I say.

"May I?" Juniper asks, holding out her hand.

I give it to her and she looks it over.

"It might be garbage," I say.

"No! It is not garbage," she says. "It is Asgardian."

"For real? How do you know that?"

"Jotunnish and Asgardian have similar runes. I recognize some of them here."

"So what does it say?"

Juniper taps her knuckle on her lower lip in thought. It's something Mom always does when she's thinking. It occurs to me now just how similar they are, and Juniper doesn't even know it.

"I cannot translate it now," Juniper says. "It will take some time to study."

I drag my fingers through my hair, pulling it out of its ponytail. "Okay, so then why would Mom put Asgardian runes in Yggdrasil?"

"Amma says Yggdrasil has latent magical energy that can work as a kind of..." Juniper waves her hands, searching for the right word. "Amplifier."

"Like a hotspot," I say. Juniper gives me a confused look and I add, "Ravenswood has Wi-Fi hotspots all over so people can get on the internet."

Juniper blinks a few times. "Okay. I do not know what that means, but you seem confident. So yes, with the right attunement, any spell can harness the power of the World Tree and amplify its effect."

"To do what, exactly?"

Juniper glances at the runes and puffs out her cheeks, guessing. "To protect it?"

"Makes sense...." I look around the gift shop, as if it might give me some answers, but I doubt I'm going to find any among the Ravenswood T-shirts.

"Perhaps Mother sensed what was to come," says Juniper. She doesn't have to spell it out.

I force myself to take a breath. "There's one person we can still get answers from."

"Who?"

"Wyatt."

"The berserker boy?"

"He's the only other person who saw what happened last night. And he's obviously magical. I have to find out what else he knows."

13

YOU'D THINK TRACKING DOWN A BOY WHO CAN TURN INTO a bear would be a lot easier than this.

While Juniper heads back home to get started on the runes, I go to the arena after work to find Wyatt, but the only people around are the carpenters rebuilding it. All performances on the main stage have been canceled, much to the disappointment and frustration of guests, but the other stages throughout the faire are still operational, so some of the smaller acts get some much needed attention. While it's good that James doesn't get to hog the spotlight, it makes the job of finding Wyatt ten times harder.

Since he's new to Ravenswood, I have no idea where he might be. I go to the seasonal staff campsite where the barbecue was, but he's not there. I poke my head into shops and restaurants. I even go to the beach, where you can still see distinct troll footprints in the sand. But Wyatt is nowhere to be found.

By the time I get to the south stage, where the fire-eaters are wrapping up their performance, I have lost count of how many people I've asked about him. "About this tall," I say on repeat, hovering my hand way over my head. "Dark, curly hair. The Black Knight. Big scar."

"Oh yeah. Wyatt Osborn," Freddie, one of the fire-eaters, says finally.

Wyatt Osborn. For some reason hearing his full name makes my chest tight. "You know him?"

"Yeah, his uncle's a legend." Freddie burps and beats his chest with his fist. Eating fire all day might really give a person indigestion.

"Do you know where he would be?"

"The stables. His uncle's the new stable master."

"Thank you!" I hike up my skirts and follow the one good lead I've had all afternoon.

$$\bowtie$$

The stables are kept to the south side of the faire, tucked away from the eyes of prying guests in a small clearing of oak trees, but the musky stench of horses is harder to hide. I follow my nose to come upon a large, red, wooden barn with a few trucks parked in the shade of trees out front.

A place like Ravenswood relies on skilled trainers to keep and care for all the horses on-site. I remember vaguely that there was a new stable master hired, but it never occurred to me that Wyatt would be related to him.

In a fenced yard, a horse eats some grass and doesn't even glance at me as I approach the open double doors to the barn. Hay covers the cement floor, muffling my footsteps as I walk down the aisle of stalls, looking into each one. Leather saddles sit perched on racks, smelling like fresh polish, and a few horses stick their heads out of their stalls to check me out.

"Hello?" I call.

A nearby horse chuffs at me.

"You seen Wyatt?" I ask.

The horse continues chomping on a bag of oats, but no one else is around, not until a middle-aged man using a wheelchair moves out from one of the stalls at the far end of the building.

He takes me in with a curious look as he comes closer. "Can I help you?"

"Yeah, sorry, I'm looking for Wyatt. I was told he might be here."

The man lifts his chin, amused. He's got the unmistakable twang of a Yooper accent, no doubt a Michigander. "He took Gamgee for a ride in the forest preserve. Should be back any minute now. He expecting you?"

"Uh . . ." I say. I try to gauge the situation. I figure I'll stick with the basics. "I'm Bryn. I work here. My family runs Martel Metalworks. Wyatt and I met . . . earlier."

"Martel," the man says. He takes a longer look at me. "Well, I'll be. You look just like Miles."

My stomach lurches. "You knew my dad?"

He laughs heartily and slaps the arm of his wheelchair. "Ages and ages ago. Good man. Was the best farrier I ever knew. Grew up with him too, believe it or not." His smile drops. "Sorry about your loss though. I miss him every day. How's your mom? My nephew and I stopped by the other night, but she wasn't around."

"Right! It was you with Wyatt!" I recognize his voice now. "You're not his dad."

"Yeah, nope. Just his uncle." He smiles. "I realize now our timing wasn't the best. But we needed to see Kara. Is she back yet?"

"Uh . . ." My smile falls a little. It always twinges to lie, especially to people who don't deserve it. "Actually, she's not. But soon! I'll let her know, Mister, uh . . ."

"Stan. Stanley Evans." He holds out his hand and we shake. His palms are rough and dry, stained with leather polish, but strong. "Pleasure."

"Same." I try to find the right words to not set off any alarm bells. "Was my mom expecting you? Just, she didn't mention any old friends turning up."

"She wasn't. But I know how busy she can get." He smiles. "You know, if you or your sisters need anything, don't hesitate to come over. Been pretty hectic here keeping the horses, especially since the start of the season, but don't take that as an excuse not to visit. Stop by any time, play a few rounds of cards. Maybe Kara will finally let me win at euchre. Ope, I think I hear my nephew. . . ." Stan points to the double doors, where I can hear the unmistakable sound of a horse clopping up the pavement. "He must be back."

I start heading toward the sound. "I should get going. It was nice meeting you, Stan!"

He waves before heading back to his work.

I can't remember the last time I met someone who knew my father. I hate to cut the talk so short. I'd love to know more about my dad in the good ole days, but if I don't catch Wyatt now, it might be too late.

I hurry out through the barn doors. The sun is already setting, casting the trees in a soft red glow, but there's no sign of Wyatt.

Instead, there's someone else.

James Beaumont.

He sees me and his eyes widen. "Bryn!"

I drop my head back and groan.

James rushes toward me, leaving his white horse to drink from a trough of water near the doors. He props his Ray-Bans on top of his gelled hair. He's wearing the deepest V-neck on a T-shirt I've ever seen.

"Ugh," I say, rolling my eyes. Honestly, if I was in a better mood, I wouldn't be so openly hostile, but given who it is, can you blame me? I didn't even know he knew my name. "What do you want?"

"You have to help me," he says. "I made a huge mistake. With your sister."

"No shit, Sherlock. You dumped her."

"I know, I'm—I screwed up. I don't know what I was thinking."

"Thinking? You?" I gasp.

"I just need your help, okay?"

"Why?"

"I need to win Reagan back."

I blink a few times. Did I clean my ears out this morning? "What?"

"I have to make it up to her. You're her sister, you know her best. You have to help me win her back."

I shake my head and wave him off. "No, no way."

He steps in front of me, palms pressed together. "Please. I'm begging you."

"Dude, you broke her heart. Singing-to-Britney-Spears-in-the-shower levels of broke her heart."

James takes his sunglasses off his head and runs his fingers through his blond hair, flustered. The gel makes his hair stand up, even when he pulls his hand away.

"I was stupid. Other people told me I needed to move on. But that was all noise. I should have listened to my heart," he says. "Reagan is the best thing that's ever happened to me, and I won't forgive myself for not trying to make it up to her."

I used to think James didn't even know I existed, and I'm pretty sure this is the longest conversation we've ever had. But he looks so pathetic, I actually believe him. It doesn't make it right what he did, but he looks genuinely upset.

Over James's shoulder, something catches my eye. Coming down the forest trail is Wyatt, riding his black gelding to a trot as they enter the field. Wyatt looks happy, a big grin on his face, as he pats his horse's neck. But when his eyes land on the two of us—me, in particular—his smile drops. He pulls on the reins slightly. The horse lifts its head, dancing backward, and just before I can call out to him, Wyatt and his horse disappear into the woods again.

James turns around just in time to see them leave.

"Great," I say. "Look what you did." It's not James's fault, but it feels good to blame someone.

James looks at me, eyebrows scrunched. "What do you need Wyatt for?"

"It's personal," I say.

"*Ohh.*" James smiles at me like he just learned a secret.

I flash him a dangerous look and the air crackles between us.

James holds up his hands defensively. "Okay, okay. Relax. Jeez, you really are Reagan's sister. . . ."

I take a calming breath and stare at the spot of woods where Wyatt disappeared. It's obvious, he wants nothing to do with me. Or he wants to pretend like this morning never happened. Either way, I think he hates me. Why else would he avoid me like that?

"I can bring him to you," James says. Then his smile widens. "But I need you to help me with Reagan first."

I roll my eyes again. If I could roll them any farther, I would be able to see my brain. "Has anyone told you how much you suck?"

He ignores me. "Listen, Wyatt and I work together. I kill him every day. We talk all the time. I can at least get you two in the same vicinity. Take my offer or leave it. Help me win Reagan back and I'll get you to Wyatt."

I absolutely hate this. But what other choice do I have?

I groan. "Fine."

James clenches his fist in victory.

"You know Reagan," I say. "She's a big romantic and loves those cheesy romance movies. Use those for inspiration. Sing her a song, write her a poem, whatever. Just show her how much you care. That'll at least get you in the door."

"Yeah, okay. I like where your head's at."

I hold up a finger. "But you have to say you're sorry. And you have to mean it."

14

"Do you think he will come?" Juniper asks. She's crouched near an oak, knees tucked up to her chest as she coaxes roots out of the ground. The roots snake up, reaching for her outstretched fingers with tiny tendrils.

"James said he would," I say. Though I'm starting to doubt if I should take James's word for anything. It's half past seven and the heat of the sun has let up somewhat in the small clearing of trees near the stables, but still Wyatt is a no-show. I barely had time to tell Juniper to come with me. I found her at Yggdrasil, eyes glowing, talking with the tree. She said she'd figured out a way for Yggdrasil to tell her if any more trouble was coming, so that's good, at least.

"Why are you nervous?" Juniper asks, twirling her finger around the roots, which follow her fingertip like a cat playing with a laser.

"I'm not nervous," I say.

"Yes, you are." Juniper's eyes go to my hands.

I notice I've been wringing them without even realizing it. I break them apart and hide them behind my back. "I'm not."

Juniper gives me a small smile and goes back to playing with the roots.

I don't know why I'm like this. My stomach hurts, and I can't stand still, and my palms are clammy. I'm not sure what I want to say to Wyatt, or how he'll react, or what he knows. I have so many questions, but I don't know where to start.

"Okay," I say, "maybe I'm nervous."

Juniper smiles and turns to look at me, about to say something, when she jumps to her feet. "Bryn!"

Before I can react, something hard and sharp presses against my lower back. My whole body goes rigid. Immediately, I think of a number of ways a draug can put a knife through my spine. I wait for the killing blow, but he speaks.

"What do you want from me?" It's Wyatt.

Juniper has her hands up, ready to use magic, but I hold mine out, calming her down. "It's okay." I say to Wyatt, "We just wanted to ask some questions."

Wyatt doesn't say anything. I feel the heat of him at my back, but I don't dare to turn around. All I see is Juniper, her face hard.

"You were following me at the barbecue," Wyatt says.

So he did see me. "Guilty. But that was because . . ."

"Because what?"

I don't have a good answer for him, so I smile. "Can we start over?"

Wyatt is silent. Juniper lowers her hands and her eyes dart from me to Wyatt, her brows drawn up.

But the pressure on my back lifts and Wyatt steps away, allowing me to turn.

In the fading evening light, I finally see him and my stomach executes a confusing little flip. Like yesterday at the barbecue, he's in civilian clothes. Jeans and a T-shirt, wearing his glasses again. In one hand, he's holding a book. He'd been using that as his "knife."

"What were you planning to do with that?" I ask, pointing to the book.

Wyatt's eyes flick to it but he doesn't answer. He looks back and forth between me and Juniper, his whole body tense, like he's about to run. Or fight. "Look, if you're the scarred man, just tell me. I'm sick of playing these games with you. You win, okay?"

"Scarred man? No. We're— Who's the scarred man?"

Wyatt looks between the two of us again, as if he's waiting for something. "You're not . . ." He drags his teeth against his bottom lip and screws up his face. "Who are you?"

"I'm Bryn. Bryn Martel."

"And I am Juniper of the Iron Woods."

"No, I remember that. I mean, *what* are you? You're not like everyone else."

"I'm a valkyrie."

"A—a valkyrie?" He looks at me, chest heaving.

I put my hand to my necklace and my armor shimmers into place for a moment before I let it fade away. The color rises in Wyatt's cheeks and he stares at me with round eyes.

Then he looks at Juniper. "And you?"

She holds up her hands and says, "I am not a valkyrie. I am just a mage."

"*Just* a mage," Wyatt repeats, shocked.

"Oh! And half-giant."

"Giant?"

I say, "You sound surprised, for someone who can turn into a bear."

Wyatt folds his arms over his chest and slumps his shoulders as his cheek twitches. "I didn't think there was anyone else like me."

Welcome to the club. We're more alike than I realized and my heart thumps hard against my ribs. I know what we need. "Are you hungry?" I ask.

The Dragon's Den is ready to close by the time we get there, but Trudy squeezes our orders into the kitchen last minute. The crickets and fireflies are out and the air is balmy as we sit on a picnic table in the outdoor seating area.

The last meal I had was breakfast, so I stuff myself with curly chili cheese fries while Juniper digs into her jalapeño poppers like they're about to spoil if she doesn't eat them right this second. Wyatt got a bottle of water and a slice of pepperoni pizza, the crust of which he picks at first. He leaves most of it untouched.

"What you saw me do," he says, "just pretend it never happened. It's safer for all of us."

"What do you mean?" Juniper asks, mouth full.

"Monsters have a way of finding me." Wyatt's dark eyebrows scrunch together. He keeps looking around, like he's waiting for something to happen. But it's just us out here. Finally, he says, "If we have to move because of me, I—I can't do that to my uncle again. I just can't."

"So the bear thing," I say. "That's not the first time that's happened to you?"

Wyatt shakes his head.

"Can you turn into any other animal?"

"No." He looks pained. "Please don't tell anyone."

"We won't. I wouldn't be thrilled for people to find out I'm a valkyrie either."

"And I am not even from this realm!" Juniper turns her palms up. "So we can keep secrets."

"Does your uncle know about your power?" I ask.

Wyatt nods, stiffly. "Yeah, but he doesn't have powers. When I finally got the nerve to tell him, he did his best to help, but...I haven't lost control like that in a really long time. I'm...embarrassed." He lowers his head.

"Are you kidding?" I lean back, shocked. "You're incredible!"

Wyatt's eyes shine when he looks at me. "Uh, thanks." He slides his glasses back up his nose.

Juniper asks, "But what does the scarred man have to do with this?"

"I'm not sure," he says. "The only thing I know is when things in my life go wrong, he's usually the one behind it."

"Like what?" I ask.

Wyatt's eyes turn down and he tears off a piece of crust but doesn't eat it. "Monsters follow me. Hunt me. Huge boars with glowing gold eyes, goats that want to lick all the salt out of my body, a giant snake that ate its own tail and rolled down the street chasing me one night. And the scarred man watches, like he's seeing what'll happen next. My uncle and I, we try to stay on the move, but the scarred man always finds us."

"Yikes." That sounds terrifying. "So you heard the troll and just thought it was like any other day."

Wyatt nods again.

"What does this scarred guy look like?"

"When he's himself, he's tall, thin, with these scars around his lips, like his mouth's been stitched together. But he can look like anyone. I think it's fun for him."

My blood runs cold. I know that description anywhere. Mom's told me his story hundreds of times. "Loki."

Juniper gasps, covering her mouth.

Wyatt looks back and forth between us. "Wait, hold on. Loki, as in Norse god Loki? As in trickster god Loki?"

"Yeah."

Wyatt screws up his face, confused. "I thought he was a guy with a horned helmet."

"No, that's in movies. The real Loki isn't as flashy. He got his lips sewn shut by a couple of dwarfs who were sick and tired of his tricks. He tried to weasel his way out of a deal and they wanted to be sure he couldn't fool anyone again."

"But what would Loki want with you?" Juniper asks Wyatt.

He shrugs, baffled. He's taking everything in stride, but I can tell he's dealing with a lot right now. His head might explode.

I answer for him. "Maybe Loki wanted to see if he can push Wyatt's buttons, try to get him to transform, test his limits. See what a berserker can do."

Wyatt's dark brows rise at the word *berserker*.

"You didn't know?"

"I didn't know it had a name," he says.

"Have you seen Loki since you arrived in Ravenswood?" Juniper asks.

He shakes his head and he's about to say something, but I interrupt him.

"I saw someone that morning, after the troll fight," I say, as my stomach drops. "At least I think I did. Someone was watching us."

The color leaches from Wyatt's face.

"Why did you not say anything?" asks Juniper.

"I thought I was amped up on adrenaline. Seeing things. Besides, Wyatt needed help so I wasn't thinking straight." I glance at him and he drops his gaze to the table. "It was Loki," I say. "It had to be."

"So, if the pattern is the same with Wyatt, then Loki brought the troll here?" Juniper asks. A hard look crosses her face when she turns to me. "Perhaps this is all part of his plan for Ragnarök."

"Wait, wait, wait," Wyatt says, head snapping up. "Slow down. Ragnarök?"

Juniper and I take turns filling him in on the prophecy, telling him everything we know so far, explaining as best we can about the draugar in Utgard, and Yggdrasil, and the destiny of the gods.

"So what does Loki have to do with Ragnarök?" Wyatt asks.

"According to the legend, before all this, Loki tricks the blind god Hodr into shooting Baldr, the invincible, with a mistletoe arrow—his one weakness," I explain. "Baldr dies and the gods in Asgard throw Loki out, chaining him up underground to be tortured forever. At Ragnarök though, Loki breaks out of his chains and turns against Asgard, leading monsters and an army of the dead."

"Draugar," Juniper whispers.

"And his son, the giant wolf Fenrir, will kill Odin. It all makes sense. Loki broke out of his chains, chased you all around the country, and now he's here. For the finishing act."

Wyatt taps his glasses back up his nose again and asks, "But what happens to Loki in Ragnarök?"

"He dies. The god Heimdall kills him."

"Then why would he want to start a war he knows he can't win?"

"Maybe because he can make sure the gods still lose."

No one speaks. It's like we've run out of words to say.

Wyatt just stares at me, a hard look in his eyes that doesn't seem directed at me. He looks tired, and I realize he's been dealing with monsters a lot longer than I have. Ragnarök is a lot to put on someone. He takes off his glasses and rubs his eyes. I don't blame him in the slightest for wanting to sit this one out.

"Okay," he says, after a moment. He puts his glasses back on and levels his shoulders. "What do we do next?"

"You're going to help us?" I ask.

"If Loki's been sending monsters after me my whole life to test my powers or whatever, it's time I show him what I can do. I'm not going to sit around and wait for Ragnarök to happen."

A smile spreads on my face as warmth fills my chest. "Okay," I say. "Cool. First up, we find Loki. You said he likes to hang around and watch his work unfold. Loki will be close by. Front row seat."

"How do we find him?" Juniper asks.

Wyatt sweeps his arm wide. "That's what I was about to say. He can look like anyone, anything. One time, he was a spider making a web over my bed. He's good at hiding."

That does complicate things. A shape-shifter, especially a clever one like Loki, would be almost impossible to find.

I turn to Juniper. "Any ideas?"

"We could try to trap him," Juniper says. "After he killed Baldr, Loki fled Asgard and turned into a salmon to hide on Midgard, but the gods found him and attempted to capture him with a fishing net. When he tried to escape again, Thor snatched him from the water and locked Loki away. Maybe we can craft something similar, some kind of net to capture him or at least draw him out."

I chew on my thumbnail. "Maybe those runes we found in Yggdrasil can help. If Mom put them there, maybe she didn't get to finish whatever she started."

Wyatt must sense that something's off. "What's wrong? Is your mom okay?"

"She's missing," I say. "At first I thought it was just an ordinary mission from Asgard, but if Loki's here, if he's escaped..." A bubble of emotion wells up in my throat and it makes it hard to talk. "She's the valkyrie captain of Midgard, so Loki could have done something to her. She's the only one who poses a real threat. If we find Loki, we find my mom."

Wyatt's gaze is steady with mine, making me feel more seen than ever, like he understands completely.

"Then we must translate the runes as quickly as possible!" Juniper leaps up from the table, doubles back to take her food to go, then hustles toward home.

She rushes by Trudy, who looks confused. "You better not be dining and dashing," she says to me, hands on her hips.

"Put it on Prima's tab," I say and give her a tip.

While Juniper rushes ahead, Wyatt and I walk down the lamplit street.

"So, uh," he says, palming the back of his neck, "sorry about the, uh... book thing."

I smile. "No biggie. You thought I was Loki. If I were you, I'd probably do the same thing."

Wyatt winces. "Still. I... I'm sorry."

"You're forgiven," I say, leaning in. "What was it by the way?"

"The book?" When I nod, he pulls it out of his pocket. "My sketchbook."

I laugh so loud he jumps.

"Am I really that bad?" He thumbs through the pages.

"No! Sorry! I just didn't expect... I thought knights weren't the artsy type."

"I wouldn't call it art. It's how I keep track of the monsters. Kind of like a journal. So when something finally gets me..." He trails off and tucks the sketchbook in his back pocket. "Sorry. For the longest time I thought I was losing my mind. Journaling's the only thing I could think to do."

His life sounds like a nightmare. "Can I see?"

Wyatt looks like I just asked him to strip nude, and I realize too late how personal of a request that is. But to my surprise, Wyatt takes the sketchbook out again and hands it to me.

The pages are full of drawings and handwritten journal entries. From the dates, I can tell this has been happening for years. I don't linger on anything too long, just enough to skim the pictures. There's a sketch of a long-haired person in water, their eyes just above the surface; another of a screaming man covered in seaweed; another of a little girl perched on a chimney, ready to pounce. They give me the chills, even though they're just drawings.

"You're good," I say, and hand the sketchbook back. "Like, scary good. You fought all these?"

"Yeah. And . . . thanks."

We walk in silence a little longer, neither of us seemingly knowing what to say. For once, I'm tongue-tied. I scramble for something to fill the silence. "Do you live here? I mean, here, like full-time here, or, like, at the staff campsite?" Smooth.

"Full-time. I moved in to the stable apartment with my uncle. For the horses. He wants me to have more stability. He used to live here, said it was the safest place for us. Though with Ragnarök and all, I'm not sure how realistic that is."

"I don't know. We might make a pretty good team. Loki doesn't know what he's gotten himself into. I think we're full of surprises."

Wyatt tilts his head. "The microphone trick? Not bad."

"You remember that?"

"How could I forget?"

I don't know why my face feels so hot. Before I know it, we're at my house. The lights on the upper floor are on.

"This is me," I say, gesturing to the door.

"I know," he says, bashfully.

"Right, you've been here before." I didn't even realize Wyatt had walked me all the way home, and Juniper's already gone inside. It's just the two of us, alone, and yet I want to find a reason not to go in.

"Why were you here, by the way? Your uncle mentioned he wanted to talk to my mom. Could it have something to do with being a berserker? Do you think he wanted a valkyrie's help?"

"He didn't say. Honestly, I don't think he believed in magic until I told him about what was happening. Your mom and he are old friends, so I think he wanted me to feel like I belonged here, like I could call Ravenswood home, too."

"That's sweet."

"Yeah..."

We fall into another awkward silence. Wyatt tucks his hands into his pockets and bows his head, and I can't help but run my fingers through my hair to give my hands something to do. Wyatt's not at all what I thought he'd be. Not just as a knight, or a berserker for that matter. But why won't my heart stop hammering?

"Do you want me to walk back to the stables with you? Make sure no more monsters are waiting to ambush you?"

Wyatt shakes his head. "I'll be okay. I know my way around a fight."

"Right," I say. "Well, if you see Loki, you know where to find help."

Wyatt drags his teeth on his lower lip thoughtfully, looking at me. "Here, maybe it'll help you remember from last night."

He turns to a blank page in his sketchbook, takes a pencil from the binding, and begins to draw. In a few seconds, he's done and rips out the page to give to me. It's a sketch of Loki, the scarred man—lanky, scraggly hair, gaunt eyes, and the distinct shape of stitches across his mouth. Nightmare fuel.

"Is that the person you saw when the troll attacked?" Wyatt asks.

"Maybe? It was too quick and they were far away. Sorry." I move to give it back to him.

He shakes his head. "Keep it."

I look back at the drawing and admire his work, even if the subject material is less than comforting. "You know, I think you've figured out Loki's weakness," I say, glancing up, and Wyatt gives me a curious look. I tap on the page. "He might be terrified of needles."

"Funny," he says, his lips curling.

"Not my best joke."

"Then I need to hear more to know for sure."

I grin back and when we part ways, I realize that's the first time I've seen Wyatt smile all evening.

15

JUNIPER MUST HAVE BEEN WAITING FOR ME NEAR THE DOOR, because she practically jumps out of the shadows, making all the weird giddiness that turned my knees to goo disappear. "What were you two talking about?" she asks, grinning.

"Uh, nothing."

"Nothing?" Her eyes go to Wyatt's sketch in my hand and I give it to her. She looks at the drawing of Loki and frowns.

"Not what you were expecting? We have work to do," I say, and lead the way up the stairs.

In the living room, Reagan is sitting on the couch—curled up under a blanket with Butters on her lap—reading a piece of paper. When she hears us, she quickly crumples up the page and tosses it across the room, where it lands perfectly in the trash basket in the kitchen. Another perk of being a valkyrie—we have really good aim.

"Hey, you two!" she says, casually.

"What was that?" I ask.

Reagan shakes her head. "Bills."

"Are you sure?" I ask, a smirk forming. Now I know how Juniper felt. I wait a second, and then another, and before she can move, I beat

Reagan to the trash can and snatch up the paper. I unfurl it and read it out loud as Reagan tries and fails to grab it.

"'O Reagan. Your eyes are the color of rocks, I keep the memory of them in a safety deposit box.' Good grief." Then I see the name at the bottom. "Is this a love poem from James?"

"Maybe." She pulls my ponytail, making me yelp, and tries to grab the paper.

I hold the poem out for Juniper, and she snatches it just as Reagan yanks on my elbow and I bodycheck her, blocking her from Juniper.

Juniper reads another line. "'Your hair is soft as silk, you're sweet like condensed milk.' This is truly awful."

"Quit it!" Reagan jukes, spins around me, and snatches the love poem from Juniper's grasp. This time she tears it into pieces. "I know it's awful," she says. "He can say sorry all he wants, but I won't take him back."

"You're saying bad poetry isn't the key to winning your heart?" I joke.

Reagan gives me a withering look. "I'm so over James Beaumont."

A tapping sound comes from the window in the living room. A raven is perched on the windowsill behind the couch, rapping its beak on the glass. Butternut Squash spots it and crouches, ready to pounce, ears flat and butt wiggling. Reagan rushes forward, scooping Butters into her arms, and opens the window.

"Did you find her?" Reagan asks, breathless.

The raven tilts its head and answers with a *rrah*. Reagan's shoulders drop and I take that as a no.

"You're looking for Mom?" I ask.

Reagan nods and tells the raven, "You need to keep searching."

The raven clacks its beak and blinks its beady eyes at her. Butters does her best to escape Reagan's arms.

"Nowhere? What do you mean? She can't be nowhere. You checked all of Midgard? For sure?"

The raven goes *rrah* again and puffs out the feathers on its neck. It's getting annoyed that Reagan is questioning its abilities.

"What about the other realms? Have you tried Asgard? Alfheim with the elves? Svartalfheim with the dwarves? Maybe she's off-world for some reason."

The raven croaks.

"What do you mean you can't?"

Juniper rushes forward, hopeful, speaking to the bird. "Can you get a message to Jotunheim for me? To Utgard?"

"Ravens aren't allowed in Jotunheim," Reagan says with a shake of her head. "It was part of a treaty with Odin. The giants didn't want him spying on them."

"What if Mom is there?" I ask.

"She can't be."

The raven seems to be getting impatient with our conversation and turns to go.

"Just keep looking, please!" Reagan calls after it as it flies off into the night.

For a second, Reagan stares after it, her eyebrows drawn in concern, and I break the silence. "So what made you change your mind?"

Reagan sets a thoroughly defeated Butters back down on the couch. "You know that troll statue?" she says. "Something isn't right about it. I know everyone's saying it's new set decoration but . . . I just want to make sure Mom is safe."

Juniper looks at me, eyebrows raised expectantly, like she wants me to tell the truth, when Prima comes in, bringing with her the smell of iron.

Prima takes her wimple off her head and tosses it on the laundry basket next to the washer. She must have just shut down the forge for the night.

"Where have you two been?" Prima asks, scuffing her fingers through her hair.

"Out," I say.

Juniper just nods enthusiastically.

I would have told Reagan about the troll, but with Prima here, my motivation fizzles. A part of me is still sore. Knowing Prima, she'd ground me even more if she found out I fought the troll without them. She'd find some way to blame me somehow.

"Any leads from the hospitals?" Reagan asks Prima.

"No. No one matching her description. I would have told you if I heard..."

"You're looking for Mom, too?" I ask.

Prima chews on the inside of her cheek, annoyed, and glances at Reagan before saying, "It's been too long. Something's up."

I throw my hands in the air. "Oh, so when I say it, it's bullshit. But when you sense trouble, you take it seriously."

"Bryn, don't start." Prima is unbuttoning her bodice, not looking at me. She slips off her surcoat and heads to her room in her sports bra and shorts. "I don't want you two staying out late," she says. "Be home by ten from now on."

I scoff and take Juniper by the hand. "We're going to bed," I say, making sure my footsteps are extra loud as we go upstairs.

The dream starts like this: I'm in the woods, kissing Wyatt.

His hands are all over me, warm and solid, and my skin rushes as his fingers grip the small of my back. Heat spreads inside of me, and I want this more than anything.

I hold on to him, afraid that if I let go, this moment will end.

His lips slide along mine, and his breath tickles my cheek. I grip the back of his head, twisting my fingers in his soft hair, and I smile against his mouth.

I never thought I could be this happy. So *this* is what heaven feels like.

"Wyatt," I whisper, and I pull back to look at him.

But when I do, I scream.

It's not Wyatt—it's a draug, his face rotting off his skull.

He reaches toward me with bony fingers and I run.

I have to get away.

Draugar are chasing me.

I sprint, as hard as I can, until I'm standing in the castle square in the shadow of Yggdrasil. The tree is taller than ever before, and the high noon sun blazes overhead. But the moon passes over it, swallowing it whole, until all that's left is a cold, silver ring of fire.

A horn blast rumbles through the sky, blowing any clouds away, and a low growl of a voice echoes around me.

Time's up, little valkyrie.

The wolf's eyes watch me from between the roots of Yggdrasil, poison green and hungry.

But a draug's hand bursts out of the ground and grabs my ankle, pulling me down.

I sink into the dirt. I try to scramble out, but I can't.

Runes flood my mind, flashing in front of my eyes one after the other, as furious as a blizzard. I try to fight, but I can't. I can't do anything. And the ground swallows me up.

It's an unusually slow day at the gift shop, especially for the summer, but maybe if I wasn't so caught up in replaying the dream over and over, I might have noticed the dark gray clouds looming overhead and the distinct smell of rain in the air. What few guests there are outside walk around in colorful plastic ponchos and keep looking up, expecting the worst.

I can't help but expect the worst, too. That dream stuck with me long after I woke up. Sometimes I swear I feel a skeletal hand on my ankle before I remember it was only a dream.

It takes me a second to realize Juniper's been saying my name for a while.

"Yeah?"

I turn to see her leaning on the cash counter, the parchment spread out, with a Ravenswood snow globe acting as a paperweight. She's been studying the runes we found in Yggdrasil all day while I've had to work.

"I was saying," she says, pointing to the runes, "this sequence here is a *kulning*, a summoning call, one similar to the kinds we use to call our cattle home. It is truly fascinating how alike Asgardian is to Jotunnish. I never thought we could have similar structures."

"Crazy," I say. I don't mean to sound dismissive, but my brain is elsewhere while my body has been dusting nonexistent cobwebs off a stack of princess crowns for ten minutes straight.

Juniper rambles on as I pick up a dragon plushie, accidentally setting off the voice box—"Ignite the day!"—and nest it back in the tower with the others, setting off their voice boxes, too. I only realize Juniper's stopped talking because the tenor of her voice goes up, like she asked a question.

My brain rewinds, scrubbing through the last few seconds. "Right, you think it was used to summon the troll."

"Precisely. The amplification of Yggdrasil served as a . . . What did you call it? A hotspot? To bring the troll from Jotunheim. I doubt that Mother was the one who put this in Yggdrasil. I need to study more to be sure, but . . . this may be Loki's doing." Juniper studies me carefully. "Are you feeling well?"

"Yeah!"

Juniper straightens up, propping herself on the counter, not buying it. "Is this about Mother?"

I don't answer.

"Is it about Wyatt?"

"What? No." Remembering what it was like to kiss him, even if it was only a dream, makes my cheeks hot. I turn away so Juniper can't see. If anyone found out about that part of my dream, I'm pretty sure I'd die on the spot.

"You are fond of him, are you not?"

I whip around. "No!"

Juniper's eyes shine and she grins. "Is that true?"

My chest tightens and I try to find the words to explain. "I don't! I . . . don't exactly have the best track record when it comes to that stuff."

"How so?"

I've had crushes on a few people before, guys and girls, but I've never had a relationship. How can I do that when I barely have any friends? Besides, the first time he saw me was when I got dropped off by the cops. Who would like me after that? I shrug in response.

Juniper watches me carefully, like she's analyzing the runes, but she sighs and traces her finger along the edge of the parchment.

"Well, Wyatt seems to be a good person. I trust him." Then she pauses. "Why did you not tell him that he was to go to Valhalla?"

I busy myself by reorganizing the postcard display. "I didn't think it was the right time."

"Do you intend to ever tell him?"

"I don't know." My gut twists painfully as I imagine the conversation. I'll bet being told *you're supposed to have died* might not go over well.

Maybe if we don't talk about it, the problem will go away. It's always worked for me in the past.

"If Loki is after him," Juniper says, "Loki could be trying to interrupt Odin's plans as well, using Wyatt as a pawn in his own game. Wyatt may be in more danger now, even greater than before, and he should be aware."

Fantastic.

Juniper smooths out the parchment and takes a breath. "Until I can fully translate the text, we can only guess. I was wondering, do you have a book depository of some sort? A place you keep books and records?"

"A library, no. But we have a bookshop in the faire. It might have some stuff on runes, if you want a look."

"That would be wonderful," she says brightly, just as the bell over the front door chimes. I turn, putting on my best customer-service grin, expecting to greet a guest, but my smile quickly drops like an anvil.

"Wyatt!" Juniper says, cheerfully. "Good afternoon!"

"Hey!" Wyatt smiles at her, and when he looks at me, I can't help but remember that dream. Were his lips always that full-looking? His cheekbones always that defined? His eyes always that warm?

He's in a T-shirt and jeans, his usual casual wear, and he pushes up his glasses with his knuckle. "What's up?" he asks.

"We were just talking about you!" Juniper says, turning to me brightly, and I'm too late to shush her. Would it be too obvious if I threw myself over the counter and clamped my hand over her mouth?

Brows drawn, Wyatt looks at me too, and suddenly, I feel very exposed.

I'm getting the impression that Juniper's doe-eyed naivete is her own brand of TNT. Harmless-looking at first, until it explodes in my face.

"Juniper's just joking," I say. "She thinks the monsters are being controlled by Asgardian runes made by Loki. Did you fight James today?"

"No, the arena's still under construction. I just got back from a ride with Gamgee, wanted to see y—see if you needed any help."

"Any more monsters?"

Wyatt shakes his head, and palms the back of his neck.

Juniper doesn't let up. "Wyatt, you and Bryn have so much in common. Berserkers and valkyries. Warriors! Chosen warriors, you might say. There is so much you can talk about."

I laugh a little too loudly. "Ha-ha! Classic giant humor for you. Right, Juniper?" Juniper grins at me and I'm starting to think she's adjusting to being my sister too easily.

But Wyatt's look of amusement shifts when he clears his throat and casts his eyes down to the parchment in front of us. I try to ignore the fact that my insides want to shrivel up into a dry husk. I don't know how I wanted him to react, but it wasn't that.

"So . . . the runes then," he says. "What do we do next?"

Juniper is too cheery for this. "We are going to the bookstore! Would you like to join us?"

"Sure. Is that okay?" He asks that last part of me.

I can only manage a nod, and Wyatt's eyes linger on me for a heart-beat too long before he turns away and heads to the door.

While his back is to us, Juniper leans in to me and whispers, "You can thank me later!"

I hiss back, "Not if I kill you first!"

The moment we step outside, my eyes go to the sky. The clouds are dark gray, threatening rain, and I'm about to go back in to borrow a Ravenswood umbrella when Wyatt asks, "Is it...snowing?"

If he hadn't said anything, I might have thought I was imagining it. But it's actually snowing. In June.

A gentle flurry drifts lazily on the wind. I hold out my hand to catch a snowflake and it melts in my palm. This isn't like the ash I saw raining down in Valhalla.

A few flakes catch in Wyatt's dark hair. Guests all around us gasp as they see what's happening. We may live in the Midwest, famous for its unpredictable weather, but snow in summer? That's...It can't be.

"Fimbulwinter," Juniper whispers, staring at the sky. The never-ending winter before Ragnarök.

A freezing gust of wind sweeps down the lane, making everyone shout in surprise. It's so strong, it knocks over A-frame signs and upturns trash cans. The cold bites at my skin and I duck for cover.

But just as quickly as it started, it stops. The snowflakes dancing in the air melt as the summer heat pushes back in like a sigh, and not one single flake remains.

I hold my breath, waiting, but everything goes back to normal. The rain clouds continue to swirl overhead and everyone around us goes back to their day, unbothered.

"Maybe it's climate change?" I say, trying to find a reasonable explanation.

Wyatt scuffs his fingers through his hair, getting rid of any leftover snow. "How is climate change any better than Ragnarök?"

Juniper looks at me, worried, and then at the sky again. She's at a loss for words.

"But the snow stopped," I say. "If Fimbulwinter really was here, it wouldn't have. Either that, or whatever Loki's doing is throwing off the balance of nature. Changing fate might do that."

Wyatt and Juniper glance at each other, and I think they silently agree with me.

"Come on," I say, leading the way to the bookstore. "Let's find some runes."

⋈

In Ravenswood, the only bookstore is a small cottage nested in the fairy-tale district on Roaming Giant Route near the Mermaid Lagoon. With gray shingles, green trim, white stucco walls, and a hand-painted sign above the entrance, Pagebound Books looks like a magical house whisked out of the pages of a storybook and into the real world.

Inside, it's cool and cramped, packed full of shelves upon shelves of every kind of book I can imagine. Fiction, nonfiction, bestsellers, rare books. It's such a tight fit, it's almost impossible for two people to walk down the aisle. Light has a hard time filtering through, and there's a fine layer of dust lingering in the air. Everything smells like old paper.

I used to spend a lot of my time here, especially when I was little. The elderly couple who owned the store used to let me sit here for hours, curled up in one of the aisles, to read until my butt fell asleep and I had to waddle home after closing time. Growing up, books were my only friends for a while. But the couple retired last year, moving back to Ohio to spend more time with their grandkids, and I haven't been here in a long time, so I'm not sure who runs the place now.

Juniper goes first, neck craning to look at all the titles. I move to follow, but Wyatt and I bump shoulders.

"Oh, sorry. Please." He gestures to let me through.

"No, you first," I say, at the same time.

We move, taking simultaneous steps forward, and we bump into each other again. Wyatt laughs nervously and steps back, hands up, as he makes sure I go ahead of him.

"Thanks," I say. I can feel him walking behind me and it's like I'm too big for my body as I think about how close he is. I can smell his deodorant.

I'm rescued from my thoughts as we emerge at the counter near the back of the store. High stacks of books block most of the view, and I don't think anyone is here.

"Shall we ask for help?" Juniper asks us.

Wyatt and I both shrug. I'm not sure if we're going to find anything useful, but it's worth a shot.

Juniper turns back to the counter and practically leaps sky high.

An old lady, probably the oldest lady I've ever seen in my life, appears as if out of nowhere behind the counter. She's got scraggly gray hair, loose waves coming out of a long messy braid, and deep, defined wrinkles. She doesn't smile at us, instead choosing to stare with the bluest eyes. If I ever imagined what a witch looked like, she's it.

The most disconcerting part is that she's staring at us with an intense, flat expression.

"H-hello!" Juniper stammers, gathering her wits. "We are searching for a book."

The old lady doesn't say anything. She just stares at Juniper with those blue eyes and waits.

Juniper looks over her shoulder at us, as if asking for help, and I nudge her aside. She has to play Twister to move around a stack of books on the floor just waiting to topple over.

"Hi!" I say to the woman, using my best customer-service voice. "Sorry to bother you. We're doing a project for school and wanted to read about runes. Magical runes, specifically. Do you have anything like that?"

It's like the old lady's eyes are piercing right into my soul, but slowly, she turns and disappears into a back room. I glance at Wyatt and Juniper and they both give me baffled looks.

Normally shopkeepers, like other cast members, maintain a persona when selling their goods. It helps create the ambience of the faire. Others take it to the extreme, staying in character almost all the time. This lady is in that camp.

After a moment, the old lady reappears again, as silently as before, carrying a stack of books so high it hides her face. She slams it down on the counter and dust blasts in my face. "That was fast," I say, and try not to cough so as not to be rude, eyes watering. There must be thirty books here.

I hand the top one to Juniper, who lets out an "*Oof*," it's that heavy. She props it on her knee as she opens it to peek inside. "Perfect," she says, smiling.

The book doesn't have a title, let alone a price tag. None of them do. They almost look handmade.

"Um," I say to the woman. "How much?"

She peers around the tower of books and holds out her hand, palm up, fingers gently curled. Her knuckles look like knobs in a tree.

"I'm Bryn. I live here. Martel Metalworks? Can I get a staff discount?" The old lady continues to hold out her hand, waiting for payment. "How about a loan?" Nothing. Okay, I can admire staying in character, but does she want a sale or not?

"I got it," says Wyatt. He fishes out a hundred from his pocket and holds it out. Sheesh. I guess playing the villain in the big arena pays well. The woman almost snatches it out of his hand before she disappears once more into the back of the store.

Outside, we reconvene near Mermaid Lagoon, each of us carrying ten books. The sky above us still looks like rain, but at least there's no snow.

"That was..." Wyatt says, glancing back at the bookstore.

"Creepy? Off-putting? Bizarre?" I offer.

"I was going to say *unique*."

"You're nicer than I am. I owe you, by the way."

"Don't mention it. It's not the first time I've spent too much money at a bookstore." Wyatt turns away, looking out across the street as fairegoers pass, but I don't miss the smile making his cheek twitch.

Juniper hefts the stack in her arms. "I have a lot of reading to do."

"We all do," I say.

Wyatt's gaze lands on the front door of Pagebound. "Think this place really has books in Asgardian?"

I know what he's getting at. "Could she be Loki?"

Wyatt frowns but shrugs. "I don't want to be paranoid."

"It's kept you alive this long."

"It's not the healthiest worldview."

Juniper chimes in. "If that woman is Loki, why help us?"

"Loki is the god of mischief," I say. "For all we know, he could be leading us down the wrong path, pushing us in the wrong direction. Getting in our heads."

With a sigh, Wyatt glances at Juniper lifting the books. "Do you think this will help?"

"It is worth the effort. Even if it leads nowhere, we know who to watch for."

"Okay, then let's get started," I say, looking at Pagebound again. A shadow moves at the window, and I can't help but feel like we're being watched.

16

THE SWORD SLICES MY GUT AND I DOUBLE OVER, CLUTCHING myself.

I drop to my knees....

I'm dying....

I have so many regrets....

I reach out my hand for one last goodbye, close my eyes, and then fall to the dirt.

Wyatt steps next to me. "Now you know the Gutbuster Whirlwind."

"Weird, the name doesn't give it away," I say dryly, spitting some dirt off my lips. "You do this every day?"

"Every day. Did I actually hurt you?"

"No, but I died pretty convincingly, didn't I?"

"Like you were born for it."

He extends his hand and pulls me to my feet. I dust off the dirt on my skirt, and he uses the front of his T-shirt to wipe the sweat off his face.

The sun is almost down by now. We've spent the whole afternoon with Juniper, using the empty, still-under-construction arena as our home base while we scour through the books from Pagebound. Most of mine weren't helpful—a lot of New Age hippie stuff that even I know isn't anywhere close to Asgardian. Wyatt didn't have much luck either, but Juniper wasn't giving up. Even when we came back with dinner, Juniper hadn't moved from the stands. She barely looked up from the pages of the books as she put one jalapeño popper in her mouth after another.

While we wait for Juniper and the sky starts to darken, Wyatt teaches me different choreographed sequences he uses during his performances. He and James rehearse these for hours, practicing so much, it almost becomes second nature. In its own way, it's kind of like a dance, only sometimes it ends with one of us dying in a beautiful display of angst and sorrow.

"You're not too bad with a sword," he says. "Your mom taught you that, too?"

"What she could. My favorite is still the bow. You're not bad with a sword either."

"I don't know, it's hard to explain. Whenever I pick up a weapon it's like I just know how to use it. Like I've been using it for a hundred years."

I'm not sure if that's a berserker thing or a future einherjar thing, and my stomach tumbles like a Slinky down the stairs. "Must come in handy being Ravenswood's most reviled knave," I say, trying to keep it casual.

Wyatt grins then shows me another sequence they use for a big battle scene. It's a showstopper for sure, involving fifty or so actors all fighting at once until there's one person standing. Unlike the scripted set pieces, there's a different winner each time, so the audience is left guessing. They use special names for their choreography.

This one's called the Twister.

"Good," Wyatt says, catching my sword easily, as planned. "You're a natural."

I snarl at him. "The Black Knight thinks 'e can distract me wiv compliments?"

Wyatt screws up his face. "What accent is that?"

"Hey! Don't break character!"

Wyatt can't hide his smile as we slip into a rhythm, swinging swords, jumping over barrels, and doing somersaults; it's too much fun and even I can't stop myself from laughing. It reminds me of all the times Prima, Reagan, and I used to play pirates, leaping on living room furniture so as not to fall in the water (step on the floor) and counting how many times we could hit each other with swords (wooden kitchen spoons).

When it's time for me to disarm him and I spin toward him—the Twister, as it were—I find myself nestled at his side, his sword in my hand now.

Cue applause.

I'm breathless as I stay there, tucked under his arm, and beam up at him. And when I see he's smiling back, something behind my sternum stirs, a warmth that makes it suddenly hard to breathe. I dislodge myself from his side to take a victory lap around him.

"And the crowd goes wild!" Cupping my hands around my mouth, I make cheering noises. "See? They love me! They really love me!" I pretend to cry and wave to my adoring fans. Juniper's nose is buried too deep in her book to notice, but Wyatt claps and bows.

I'm about to ask him for a rematch when the first drop hits me. The sky is a dark gray, swirling with rain clouds, and it finally fulfills on its promise and opens up.

Wyatt and I run to take shelter under one of the awnings as the rain falls, and the ground turns to mud in seconds. It squelches into my shoes and I slip just before catching myself on the fence.

"You okay?" Wyatt asks, moving to help me.

I'm still laughing as I straighten up. "Isn't rain the best? I'll take it over snow any day." I breathe deep, taking in the fresh air with relief, and notice Wyatt is watching me, just before he looks away.

He nods toward Juniper. "Should we get her?"

She's safe and dry under the overhang in the stands as she flips the pages of her book. "The rain won't last long," I say. "Hey, thanks for coming with us today."

"It was fun. Even though I barely helped."

"You provided the jalapeño poppers. It's an important job."

Wyatt's smile is nice, even when he bows his head and aims it toward the ground.

In the square, the last stragglers run for cover from the rain, shielding their heads with umbrellas and purses. The work crew in charge of hanging the bunting for the King's Feast climb down from their ladders and head into the castle to wait it out. At least the heat of the day fades and leaves the air smelling fresh and crisp, and my breath mists in front of me.

"So," I say, leaning on the fence. "How's it feel being Ravenswood's villain?"

Wyatt wipes the fog off his glasses with his shirt, puts them back on, and folds his arms over his chest. "It's not so bad. It has its moments. Some people actually think *I'm* a bad guy though. Once, a woman dumped a slushy over my head and said 'That's for Prince James!'"

"Are you serious?"

Wyatt nods, smiling bashfully. "I didn't know I was that good of an actor for someone to hate me in real life."

I throw back my head and laugh. "That's nuts!"

"I know. My armor still smells like strawberries. I can't scrub it out."

That makes me laugh again. It's not really funny, but it's easy laughing when Wyatt's around. I like that he laughs, too.

"How'd you get started doing this though?" I ask. "Who thinks, 'I'm gonna be a Black Knight when I grow up'?"

"My uncle was one for decades. I kinda picked up the mantle after he had to retire."

I think about the fact that his uncle uses a wheelchair. "Is it rude if I ask what happened?"

"It's not rude. He doesn't mind talking about it. He fell off a horse during a show and broke his back."

"Oh."

"Yeah, he almost quit for good, but he loves it too much. He started his own jousting troupe and now he takes care of the horses, trains them, rescues them. I owe him everything. When I'm eighteen, hopefully he'll let me joust."

"Your parents aren't worried you'll fall off a horse?"

Wyatt scrunches his nose and shakes his head. "They're, uh . . . not really in the picture."

I pinch my lips together, knowing I've walked up to one of Wyatt's walls. One thing I've noticed is that he's secretive about some things, plays his cards close to his chest, and I kind of get it. We're alike in that way. But I've got enough sense to back off a topic when I know it's a touchy one.

"What's your favorite part of being a Black Knight?" I ask.

"Every show there's always someone rooting for me to win. Usually kids. I think they see themselves in me, like they see this outsider who tries to get what he wants, even if in the end, he fails. It's cathartic, I think."

"I get it. I love villains," I say.

"Really?"

"Yeah! They're hot, too."

Wyatt scrunches his eyebrows together, and he stares at me.

I realize what I said and my breath catches in my throat. Does he think I'm talking about him? I mean, objectively, yes—he is attractive. I have eyes. But heat rushes up my face because I don't know when to keep my mouth shut.

"Hot?" Wyatt's cheeks are red.

I glance away and tuck my hair behind my ear. "Generally speaking."

"Right. Well, I could never be the hero in Ravenswood."

"Why?"

He points to the scar on his face. "Corporate said I was too scary for kids. But it's more fun playing the heel anyway."

Like wrestling, there's the heel—the character everyone is supposed to hate. And the face—like James, the one you're supposed to root for.

"Well, I think you'd make an excellent face," I say, still blushing.

He pauses for a moment, then says, "What about you? Why did you decide to become a valkyrie?"

"I guess the same reasons you said. It's been my whole life since I can remember. My mom, my sisters, my mom's mom, and hers, and, you get it... It's really easy wanting to be like them." I shift a little against the fence. "Maybe I could have chosen to have a normal life, but where's the fun in that?"

"Having a normal life might not be the worst thing in the world."

"I bet changing into a bear isn't all it's cracked up to be."

Wyatt lifts a shoulder. "I've learned to control it, but if I'm hurt or angry..." I remember the lake. He knew it was happening and couldn't stop it. He might have been afraid he was going to hurt me. "Not really something I'm proud of."

"Can you do it at will?"

He nods. "Only as a last resort. You saw me. I'm kind of useless after."

"Do you know what's happening when you go berserk?"

"Yeah, but I don't like using my power. It makes me feel..." He trails off, eyes on the raindrops in the puddles, like he's searching for the right word, but he says, "It makes me *feel*. Angry. Scared. Everything is dialed up. Sensory overload. And when I lose control, it's like that's all I am. And I don't want it to be."

We fall silent again. I want to tell him I get it, but then again I'm not sure I do. Sure, I've lost my temper loads of times before, but nothing like what he's gone through.

"It's just scary, especially being alone." Wyatt puts his prop sword in a barrel with the others and I hand him mine. Guess playtime is over.

"You're not alone anymore," I say.

Wyatt glances at me through his slowly fogging glasses and opens his mouth, as if he's about to say something.

"Friends!" Juniper's voice makes both of us jump. She vaults over the railing to the stands and lands under the awning with us, beaming excitedly as she holds out a black, leather-bound book. "I have discovered something I—" Her eyes go to the rain, as if she's noticing it for the first time. "Is that...?"

"Rain?" I ask.

Juniper shoves the book into Wyatt's arms as she reaches a hand out, catching some of the droplets in her palm.

"It does not rain in Utgard," she whispers. "It is too cold."

Wyatt and I glance at each other, neither of us knowing quite what to say. It never occurred to me that she'd never seen rain before, it's so common here. "Well?" I say to her. "It won't bite."

Juniper looks at me, then smiles before she darts out from the awning, straight into the arena. She tips her head back, flinching a little as the rain pelts her cheeks. Her bare feet squelch in the mud, and she laughs, flinging her arms wide and spinning in circles like a little kid.

I'm happy for her, but also at the same time kind of sad. If she'd grown up with us, she would have been here to make mud pies and splash in puddles so deep they sloshed into our boots and then come home to drink Mom's hot chocolate.... I just wish I knew why that didn't happen.

I turn back to Wyatt. "I know finding Loki is the most important thing, but—"

Wisps of Wyatt's hair are standing straight up, like someone's hovering a staticky balloon over his head.

When I was twelve, I'd been climbing a tree just outside the house when a thunderstorm rolled in. I remember how green the sky looked and how still everything got right before I felt all the hair on my body stand straight up. I practically fell out of the tree getting down, seconds before the tree exploded in a bright flash of lightning.

It feels just like that now, the air electric, full, ready to burst.

"What?" he asks, seeing the look on my face.

I shove his chest and jump on top of him just as the air explodes. CRRRRACK.

The whole world goes white. My ears ring. It's like the sky split open.

It takes a second for Wyatt's surprised face to melt out from behind the colorful spots in my eyes.

"Are you okay?" I ask. My voice sounds muffled to me, like I'm talking through water. But he looks up at me, eyes wide, and nods.

"Are you?" His hands come up, squeezing my arms.

"Yeah." I manage to pull myself off him and help him to his feet and I'm about to ask Juniper if she's okay when I see her, lying in the mud, her moss cloak smoldering.

17

"JUNIPER!"

I run, tearing across the arena, but someone beats me to her. James comes sprinting out of the castle and lands at her side.

I get there just as he turns her over.

She's not moving—

She's not breathing—

Her eyes are closed.

James leans over her, saying something I can't hear because my blood is roaring in my ears. I can't move. I'm frozen. I don't know what to do.

James locks his hands over her chest and starts compressions.

I try to go to her, but Wyatt comes up behind me, holding me back. It's all happening so fast, and at the same time, so slow. Wyatt's mouth is moving, but I can't hear what he's saying. All I can focus on is Juniper's limp hand.

She's dead. Juniper is dead.

James looks at us, teeth clenched, and leans over Juniper again.

This can't be real. This can't be happening.

I can't breathe. My body is numb.

I move toward Juniper again, but Wyatt still doesn't let me go. His grip on me is strong, but I try to break free until—

Juniper's eyes fly open and she gasps. James stops what he's doing and leans back as she coughs and sits up.

Wyatt's grip on me loosens and I throw myself on her. "Juniper!" I cry and bury my face in her shoulder as I stifle a sob.

"Bryn?" she asks, her voice small.

"Careful," says James as he watches us. Rain drips down his relieved face.

"What happened?"

"You're okay. Just take a second to breathe." James looks to Wyatt. "Help me get her home." Wyatt doesn't hesitate. He drops Juniper's book in the mud and helps her stand. Together, they walk her out of the arena and I grab the book and follow.

⋈

"What happened?" Reagan shrieks when we burst into the living room. She'd been sitting on the couch knitting.

"Juniper got hit by lightning," I say, as Wyatt and James carry her to the couch.

"WHAT!"

Reagan clears the couch as quickly as she can, throwing pillows and skeins of yarn across the room, before Juniper lowers herself down. She's covered in mud, and rain, and there's a distinct smell of singed hair floating around her. Butters flees from the couch and scampers for safety under the kitchen table.

"Take it easy," James says, kneeling on the floor in front of Juniper. "Do you remember who you are? Who I am?"

"Bad poet," Juniper says, dazed.

Concerned, James looks at all of us. "She needs to go to a hospital."

"No!" everyone says in unison.

"Why?"

No one answers right away but James throws up his hands, defeated. "Okay, jeez. I'm only trying to help."

"I am all right," Juniper says, and rubs her chest. "I am just sore."

"I thought it was only a rainstorm," I say, panicked. "I didn't know—"

Wyatt turns to me, his voice reassuring. "It was a freak accident. It's not your fault."

Try telling my heart that. It's still going warp speed. I clutch the book tightly and try to calm down.

Reagan goes to James and pulls him to his feet. "What are you doing here? You should leave."

"He saved her life," I say.

Reagan's jaw drops and she stares at him. It's as if this is the first selfless thing he's ever done. James levels his shoulders and gestures to Juniper. "I saw the strike and my lifeguard training kicked in."

"James . . ." she says.

For once, James looks like he doesn't want any credit for being a hero. He clears his throat and heads for the door. "Take her to the hospital. She really should get checked out."

He gives Juniper one last look, then he leaves and the room falls silent.

Reagan rushes to the kitchen to get Juniper some water and Wyatt sits with her. I, on the other hand, can't sit still. I pace the living room, gnawing on my thumbnail.

What if it wasn't a freak accident? What are the odds of that happening? One in a million? It can't be a coincidence, can it? What if it was meant for Wyatt? What if the gods are angry that he's not in Valhalla? What if it was him they were aiming for and missed, hitting

Juniper instead? Have I put a target on Wyatt's back and almost got Juniper killed because of it? What if this is Odin's revenge?

I taste copper. My fingernail must be bleeding.

As I pass Juniper, she reaches up and grabs my arm, pulling my fingers away from my teeth.

"I am all right," she says, locking eyes with me. "Truly."

But a bubble of guilt has already moved into my throat—it should start paying rent. Reagan comes back with a glass of water and hands it to Juniper. "The mead, it's gone," Reagan says. "Bryn, have you seen it?"

I clam up, fists at my sides. I'm so stressed, I blurt out, "I used it all."

"What? When?"

I glance at Wyatt, who watches me, waiting for me to take the lead. I try to think of a lie, some excuse, but I can't. It's Reagan. "Remember your hunch about the troll? Yeah, well . . . that was us."

Reagan looks at me, then Wyatt and Juniper, then back at me. "You mean, he knows . . ." She points at Wyatt and I nod. Confusion passes over her face, and she looks at Wyatt for a long few moments before she says to me, "Talk."

So I do. I tell her about the troll, the runes we found in Yggdrasil, the shady figure I saw watching us. Conveniently, I leave out the part where Wyatt was chosen for Valhalla. That's something she doesn't need to know. I'll keep that secret forever if I have to. Reagan takes everything in, looking with each passing minute like we're taking turns slapping her. When I'm done, I'm exhausted, like I've been carrying that secret with me like a ten-ton weight on my back.

"Why didn't you tell us there was trouble?" Reagan finally asks, brows furrowed and face red.

"I tried. Or don't you remember?"

Reagan blanches and bites her lip. She draws her cardigan tighter around herself and asks, "Even so, how'd you stop the troll? That thing tore up the whole square like a monster truck rally."

I glance at Wyatt. I don't want to put him on the spot, and he asked us not to tell anyone about his powers. But his jaw is set, and he looks at me with grim determination.

"I'm a berserker," Wyatt finally says.

Reagan stares at him, like she's hoping he'll say "Psych!" but when he doesn't, she jerks her head back and blinks hard, hand up. "Okay, you're throwing a lot at me and I need a second."

"Welcome to the party. Wyatt, Juniper, and I have been looking for ways to stop Loki."

Juniper grunts and shifts on the couch. She winces and lies back. "I was attempting to translate the runes we found in Yggdrasil. Most of the books were nonsense, but this one . . ." She points to the book in my hand and I give it to her.

When she opens it, inside are hundreds of pages of hand-drawn runes, scrawled in a cramped handwriting, like the person who wrote it was afraid that if they didn't get everything down on the page right that second, the idea would be lost forever.

"That's Asgardian," Reagan says, stunned.

"Can you read it?" I ask.

Reagan shakes her head. "No, only Mom can. But that looks like seidr. I've seen Mom use it a ton."

My ears burn. I look at the runes too and I'm reminded of the runes in my dream, flooding my mind, too fast and too many for me to remember. I can't be seeing the future, can I?

My gaze goes to Mom's room. "We could use Mom's seidr to figure it out. Use a spell to translate it."

"No, Bryn," Reagan says, eyes flashing. "How many times do you need to hear it? Seidr is too dangerous."

"That doesn't seem to stop Loki."

"He's a god. You're not."

"It would make all our lives easier, wouldn't it?" I say, and roll my eyes, but Reagan either doesn't notice or pretends not to see.

I take the book from Juniper, who looks about ready to keel over, and I flip through the pages, idly skimming them. It looks like the ravings of someone losing their grip on reality. "We think the runes we found in the tree are . . . what'd you call it, Juniper, a kulning?" I ask Juniper, but Reagan nods.

"A kulning is a summoning spell." Of course, Reagan would know. "What are you doing messing with kulnings?"

"We're not. Like I said, we found it." I flip another page and pause.

"What's wrong?" Wyatt asks.

I turn the book to show them. "A page is torn out. Juniper, do you still have the runes we found?"

Juniper winces as she reaches into her pocket and pulls out the parchment. I take it to the coffee table and spread it out, lining up the edges. The tears in the book are a perfect match to the page.

It's like all the oxygen's been sucked out of the room.

"Okay," I say. "That's one mystery solved."

Wyatt asks, "Are there any more pages torn out?"

I flip through and my stomach fills up with acid. "Two. Two more."

Juniper looks gray, and everyone else looks uneasy. Any moment, more monsters could be in Ravenswood, at Loki's command.

My voice sounds thick. "It's obvious. Loki had this book and placed the kulning in Yggdrasil."

"And I bet he's missing the book," says Wyatt, still staring at the page. "But why do *we* have it now? Why not keep it?"

It doesn't feel good that Reagan looks worried. "Who else knows you have it?" she asks.

"The woman who runs Pagebound sold it to us." I slam the book shut. "We have to talk to her."

"It might be too dangerous," Wyatt says. "If she's Loki, she could be expecting us. It could be a trap."

Reagan massages her temples and takes a breath. "We're moving at lightning speed here.... Sorry." Juniper waves her off. "Take a second, slow down. We need to be smart about this."

"We need to do something, now!" I say, and my voice cracks, and I realize just how unhinged I sound. I take a shuddering breath and hold it.

Reagan approaches me, hands out, and takes mine into hers. "Look at me." I do, and it makes me want to cry, but I can't. Not in front of people. My lungs burn as I keep holding my breath.

Reagan's eyes are soft, and she even smiles. "Everyone is okay. We are okay."

I bite the insides of my cheeks and force myself to breathe. I admit, it helps. My body stops shaking and Reagan smiles as my shoulders relax.

It's not valkyrie magic. It's just Reagan.

"Better?" she asks.

I nod.

"Okay," she says, and lets go of my hands. "When you first found the kulning, why did you think Mom had put it there?"

Juniper speaks up from the couch. "When I communed with Yggdrasil, it said the slain-chooser had been there. A valkyrie. We thought she might have put it in the tree."

Reagan taps her knuckle on her chin. "Mom uses fjötra to protect the faire. She harnesses Yggdrasil's power to stop outside threats from crossing its roots. She might have reinforced it before she left."

I practically jump. "Of course! Fjötra!"

Wyatt looks confused. "What is that?"

"Fetter magic, you know, to bind and restrain. Valkyries have used fjötra on the battlefield for centuries so the enemy side can't fight back, slows them down, traps them just like shackles."

"Like a net!" Juniper says.

"Which we can use in reverse. Stop things from coming in," I say.

"An invisible force field," says Wyatt.

"Exactly. The dwarves made something similar when they made Gleipnir, the chains that imprisoned Fenrir so he couldn't kill Odin. Fjötra is supposed to be unbreakable too, if done right." I look at Reagan. "Come on, it's a better option than seidr, right?"

"Do you know how to do it?" Wyatt asks me, hopeful.

"No..." I admit. That's the one fault in my plan. I look to Reagan for help, but she sounds unsure.

"I've only seen Mom do it once. But... if a troll got in, the fjötra might be weakened somehow. I might be able to figure out how to bolster it, but I can't do it alone."

"So you're helping us?" I ask.

Reagan takes in a deep breath. The rain batters the window and the wind's picked up now, making the tree tap on the glass, like a raven. Reagan flattens her lips. "Tomorrow."

After Wyatt goes home, Reagan starts making tea and Juniper goes to shower. Prima comes back carrying grocery bags. Her hair is soaked and she scowls like a wet cat as she shakes off the rain and drops the grocery bags on the table.

"Juniper got struck by lightning today," Reagan says, stirring the pot on the stove.

Prima's eyes harden. "You're kidding." When she sees neither of us are having a laugh, she asks, "Is she all right?"

"She's fine," I say, stooped over the mug of chai Reagan made for me. "She should buy a lottery ticket."

Prima sniffs and slips off her raincoat. "What are you making?" she asks Reagan.

"Something to help her sleep. You could check on her," Reagan says. "See if she needs anything."

Prima stiffens. "Later. I bet she needs to rest. I'm beat. I've been looking for Mom all day. I'm going to bed, too."

Reagan and I share a look, but don't say anything, as Prima heads to her room.

A few minutes later, I bring Reagan's potion to Juniper upstairs. I half-expected her to be asleep, but I find her awake, lying on her back in bed, with Butters perched on her chest.

"You okay?" I ask.

Juniper smiles. "Yes. I am still sore, but I am feeling much better. Thank you."

"This should help even more." I hand her the mug and she sits up, making Butters scuttle away.

She takes a whiff of the tea and winces. "What is this?"

"Mostly tea. But I think to help you sleep Reagan added a bunch of cough syrup." Juniper makes a face at the smell and I can't help but laugh. "Yeah, she's not the best cook either. On second thought, maybe don't drink it."

"It was very nice of her."

"That's Reagan for you," I say as I settle on my spot on the rug.

Juniper puts the tea on the floor and watches the steam rising from it for a few minutes. The rain taps against the window—it hasn't let up since it started. Normally I love falling asleep to the sound of rain, but today I'm not sure it'll help.

"Do you think a person is destined to be good or bad?"

Juniper's question takes me off guard. "I don't think so," I say. "What kind of bad are we talking about though? Are we talking, like, serial killer bad or like ... doesn't tip at least twenty percent bad?"

Juniper just hums and doesn't answer.

"What's up?"

Butters returns to the bed and starts making biscuits in the blanket before curling up at Juniper's feet. Juniper reaches out and scratches her between the ears, making Butters purr so loudly it almost drowns out the rain. "I was thinking. Earlier, you mentioned Fenrir, the wolf, about his destiny to kill Odin."

"Yeah?"

"I was just thinking about how they did it. Why they did it. To stop him, Odin locked Fenrir up deep in a cave so the prophecy would never happen. He had the dwarves create Gleipnir, the unbreakable bonds, made of the roots of mountains and the breath of fish, chaining him up forever. But Fenrir never did anything wrong, and still, he was punished for it."

Being a giant, Juniper might have a different perspective on the story, one I never really thought about all that much before.

Thinking about it now, it is pretty messed up. Fenrir's crime was being born. When I was younger, I used to believe Odin had to do it for a reason, for the greater good. Now though, I'm not so sure. How much choice does someone have if everyone else thinks their destiny is already written? If he's not actually done anything bad yet, who's to say he ever will?

I roll back into my makeshift bed on the floor and stare at the ceiling. Technically I did a bad thing saving Wyatt. I was disobedient. And any second, I could get punished for it. Unlike Fenrir, I got to make a choice, so I have no one else to blame but myself. The scary part is, it doesn't feel like I did a bad thing at all, saving Wyatt.

I don't know how to answer Juniper's question, about destiny. I'm not that wise. I just know, if I were locked up for something I didn't do, I'd hold a grudge, too.

I turn to Juniper. "Mom says fate is the choices we make. All we can do is try to do good anyway. Just because."

Juniper doesn't say anything more, and neither do I, as I'm finally dragged to sleep.

18

"WELL?" I ask REAGAN, WHEN WE MEET UNDER THE TREE by Mermaid Lagoon.

"Closed."

"Closed?"

"For the King's Feast," Reagan says. "There's a sign."

I glance at Pagebound. It looks hardly any different closed than it does open, with its darkened windows. There aren't any shadows moving inside at least. My stomach doesn't settle though. Two pages are missing from the book, and now that our prime suspect is conveniently missing, I can't help but imagine every worst-case scenario.

"Think it's a coincidence?" I ask.

"It's the King's Feast. Tons of people take the day off." Reagan starts making her way down the street, joining the other guests, as we head toward the castle. The morning is bright and humid, and raindrops still sparkle on the trees, making them look like they're made of diamonds.

We let Juniper sleep in this morning while we went to Pagebound, looking for any more info about the book we found. I haven't let it out of my sight since last night, keeping it tucked in my backpack.

Even though the rain let up sometime during the night, the ground is still muddy as Reagan and I go to check on Yggdrasil. Most other stores that are open are packed with people buying costumes to wear tonight or playing carnival games set up in lieu of the arena entertainment or pre-gaming with themed drinks like Dragon Blood Ale and King's Apple Wine.

With all these extra people around, I can't help but look for Loki. This is the perfect place to hide.

I know Wyatt says it's not the healthiest worldview, to be wary of strangers and expect the worst in people, but after what happened yesterday, I'm waiting for the next disaster to strike. Without Mom, we're scrambling for answers. I wish I could soak in the excitement charging the air, but instead I'm looking at every face. Loki has to be around here somewhere. I just know it.

Once we reach the shade of Yggdrasil, with its branches decorated with red ribbons and gold bells, Reagan glances at her phone.

"Perfect," she says. "I've got an hour before I need to get ready."

"Ready for what?"

"The feast," Reagan says, like it's the most obvious thing in the world. "You're coming, right?"

"I don't know. . . ." Can you blame me? Going to a party is the last thing I want to do right now. "Let's just do this, okay?" I heft the backpack on my shoulder and glance around.

Everyone, as usual in Ravenswood, is having a good time and taking selfies with the new troll statue nearby, and not a soul notices when Reagan claps her hands and rubs them together before planting them firmly on Yggdrasil. The air around her shimmers for a second and runes appear on Yggdrasil's bark, running up and down the trunk, glowing gold for a moment before fading. Reagan looks to the sky, and points. "Looks like Mom's fjötra was refreshed recently."

"What are you looking at?" I ask. All I see is bright blue sky and fluffy white clouds.

"Look." Reagan takes my hand and transfers some of her power to me. My Yggdrasil pendant hums. I blink as the whole sky lights up gold with an intricate network of lines, like those string games we used to play, the lines crisscrossing and intersecting into a dome overhead. It looks like it stretches across the whole faire, invisible to everyone else.

"Mom did this?" I ask.

Reagan nods. "Like I said, Mom's a pro. She never leaves Ravenswood unprotected."

Magic comes so naturally to Reagan, I'm almost envious. She's way more prepared for being a valkyrie than I am. Mom must know that, too. She's always showing my sisters advanced techniques. She knows they can handle it. Not me.

Reagan should have been the first one to bring someone to Valhalla. She wouldn't have screwed it up. But my stomach churns and I know that if Reagan had seen the light and heard the drums, Wyatt would be dead right now.

"The fjötra is strong. But like a coat of paint, sometimes it needs touch-ups." Reagan draws her finger across the sky, pointing to a fracture in the dome, in the direction of the beach, where the troll came from.

"And that'll stop any more monsters from coming through?"

"In theory!"

We make our way from the square toward the beach, winding down the sun-dappled lane and into the woods. Debris from the fight has mostly been cleared away, but you can still see where the troll scraped against the trees.

"So, why aren't you going to the feast?" Reagan asks. "It's your favorite night of the year."

I shrug. "Slipped my mind."

Reagan looks at me, dubiously. "I know, things are crazy right now. But you really could use a break. Besides, I know for a fact that dancing with a beautiful person always makes the world a little less awful."

"Huh?"

Reagan raises a single perfectly shaped eyebrow. "You and a certain tall, dark, knighted individual..."

"Wyatt?"

Reagan laughs. "Come on, it's obvious. You two have a thing."

"We don't."

She laughs again. She's always been the romantic one, teasing her friends about what cute couples they would make and gossiping about who's dating who in Ravenswood. Maybe that's why she likes those dating reality shows so much—love is like a spectator sport for her.

I sigh. "I'm just scared, all right?"

"Why? He seems to like you."

My insides do a somersault. "Really?"

"I saw the way he looked at you last night."

I shift the bag on my shoulder. Wyatt and I have gotten closer recently, but that's because we're working together. I like being around him, but at the same time I'm constantly thinking about how he was supposed to die and that kind of puts a dampener on things. I lick my lips, and feelings I've tried so hard to bottle up come spilling out of me like puke. "What if I'm cursed? What if *we're* cursed?"

Reagan furrows her brow. "What are you talking about?"

"We're valkyries. The whole point of our existence surrounds death, right? What if I'm destined to hurt anyone I ever care about?"

"Don't be dramatic."

"Oh, coming from you?" Her eyes flash but I ignore her. "First, Dad dies before I ever get to meet him. Next, Mom goes missing. Now Juniper…"

"But Juniper is fine," Reagan says. "Nobody got hurt."

"Yeah, not this time."

Ever since I could understand what grief was, I knew Mom carried hers like a baby. When Dad died, it stayed with her. She could put it down sometimes, or shift it from one arm to the other so she could do what she needed to do to get through the day, but that grief was always there. Some days it was harder to carry, others it was easier, but that pain never left.

I can't imagine what it must be like to lose someone. No, I *don't want to* imagine what it must be like. It hurts to think about it, so I won't. At the end of the day, maybe it's better to never love, so you can't lose.

What if the people who come into our lives are doomed? Wyatt was supposed to die, and it was only after he came near me.

"Have you been getting sleep?" Reagan asks.

"Not really. I keep having…nightmares." I didn't mean to say it—it just slipped out.

Reagan sighs. "You and Prima are so alike, honestly."

"What's Prima got to do with this?"

"Maybe if you two talked to each other, you'd know."

Talking to Prima is one of the last things I want to do. If there's a competition for World's Best Grudge-Holder, I win.

"You two act like you need to control everything all the time," says Reagan.

"I'm not like Prima. She's type A and a perfectionist and a worry-wart."

"Okay, kettle."

That comment short-circuits my brain, and I can't come up with a comeback. I sputter and scoff, and Reagan looks all too pleased with herself.

I decide to change the subject. "What's with her anyway? She's so weird around Juniper."

"It's taking her a little longer to adjust. I mean, finding out we have a long-lost sister is a big deal. Can you blame her?"

Kind of, yeah.

We reach the edge of the trees where a few people have set up picnic blankets on the beach, and the Ravenswood pirate ship floats on the horizon.

Reagan points out a tree. I wouldn't have noticed it at first if it wasn't for the gap in the fjötra. Glowing runes run up and down the tree, but the bark looks like it was stripped off, breaking some of the symbols.

"They're like fence posts," Reagan explains. "This one must have been damaged in a storm."

"How do we fix it?"

"Here, help me." Reagan brings me to the tree and has me stand with her, my hand in hers. She closes her eyes and immediately the air between us comes alive, like someone turned on an amplifier before they hit a chord on an electric guitar. My necklace thrums against my chest; Reagan's does, too.

"What do I do?" I ask.

"Picture what you want to do. Just like summoning your armor, or summoning your weapon, shape it in your mind's eye."

"Summoning armor is easy."

Reagan shushes me, eyes still closed. "Focus. I can't do this alone. The fjötra is about creating something with purpose."

I take a breath and close my eyes and imagine the fjötra taking shape in my other hand. Reagan's hand grows warm in mine as Yggdrasil's power flows between us, charged like an electric current.

"You want to hinder creatures who intend to do us harm. What does that look like?"

A troll comes to mind, big and ugly and mean, and then I remember Juniper's roots and how they wrapped around its body, holding it back, and the fjötra seems to respond to that. The air around us gets more solid, smells earthier. My fjötra becomes roots, deep in the earth, branches reaching for the sky.

"Then," Reagan says, "set your intention." Reagan places her hand on the bark and so do I. Our prints glow brightly for a moment and then fade as the runes of the fjötra stitch back together and the gap in the ward disappears.

The air between us goes back to normal and a weight lifts off my shoulders.

"We did it! Now no more trolls can get through!" Reagan smiles, and I admit, I feel a little bit better. It's like we're patching holes in a sinking ship, and for once the water level isn't rising.

Reagan throws her arm over me and pulls me in as we walk back home. "Do me a favor, at least. Come to the feast tonight. Let yourself relax a little. The fjötra is up, the faire is protected. You need to take a break."

I sigh. She's never going to drop it. "Okay, fine. But I'm going to complain the whole time."

Reagan's eyes sparkle. "I know you will."

When we come home, we find Juniper already in the kitchen, attempting to make tea but having a tough time figuring out how to use the stove. From a spot on the counter, Butters supervises. Juniper perks up when she sees us, smiling wide.

"You look better," I say.

"I feel better!" She moves to the table and picks up a folded piece of paper. "This was delivered for you, Reagan."

Reagan's face goes pale and she snatches the paper out of Juniper's hand. She reads it quickly, her brows pinching together with each line, and then she tears it up and crushes it into a ball.

"Let me guess," I say, "another love poem from James."

Reagan raises her chin and huffs. "Never mind about the feast. I'm not going."

"Is it because James will be there?"

Reagan scrunches her nose, but doesn't answer. "You two go. I'm not in the mood."

Whatever James said in the poem, it's not working out for him. Guess my advice wasn't so great after all. I swing the backpack off my shoulder and hand it to her.

"If you're not going, would you at least keep this safe?"

"Sure. Maybe I can look it over and see if I can find anything else. Keep my mind occupied elsewhere." Reagan scoops up Butters from the counter and coos at her, saying she's a naughty girl who isn't allowed to sit there, and goes to her room.

Just then, Prima comes up the stairs, talking on the phone. She's still dressed for the day, bringing with her the smell of steel and fire from being in the forge.

"Yes, I understand, I..." She barely acknowledges us as she comes into the kitchen, fills a mason jar of water, and takes a sip. "I know, I've been on hold for two hours already, I— No, I know, I understand."

She looks at us, her hand tight around the jar, and frowns. "I haven't filed a police report, no, I . . . Yes, no, I understand it's protocol but I was wondering if you could make an exception. . . . No, that's fine, anything would be helpful." Prima presses her phone to her shoulder and says to us, "Why are you just standing there?"

"Is it illegal or something?" I ask. "Is that about Mom?"

"The morgue. Seeing if they have anyone matching her description."

I freeze, and Juniper goes pale. She's talking to the morgue. About our mother.

"Are you going to the feast?" She says this as if everything is normal.

"I guess," I say, shaken.

"Good, we need someone to make an appearance."

I don't understand how she could be so chill right now. "What happened to me being grounded?" I ask stonily. "Curfew?"

Prima looks at me, eyes hard, and then she looks at Juniper and her gaze softens a little. "It's fine," she says. Either she feels sorry for us, or she's trying to make nice. She asks Juniper, "You doing okay?"

"Oh yes! Much better!" Juniper says, forcing cheer.

"Good." Prima sounds stiff, like she's being held at gunpoint saying it. Is she really still distrustful of Juniper? After everything that's happened? "Bryn, when I was grocery shopping earlier, I got you some Sour Patch Kids. I know it's your favorite so . . . Juniper, I didn't know what you liked, so I got you some chocolate." Her eyes go to Juniper and then back to me. "I left the bag on your bed."

Is this some sort of olive branch? I can't help but wonder if it was Reagan's idea so that I would forgive Prima for the way she's been treating us. I fold my arms over my chest. Her half-baked attempt at an apology won't work on me. "I don't want it."

"Okay, then throw it out."

Juniper looks between us like she's watching a tennis match, but doesn't say anything.

"Maybe I will." My mouth is already starting to water though just thinking about eating some, but I pretend like it's not.

Prima makes a face, then lifts the phone back to her ear. "Yes, I'm still here. . . . No one? That's a . . . Thank you. Yes, I'll call there. Oh, you'll give me their number?" Still on the phone, Prima disappears back downstairs.

"Guess it's just you and me," I tell Juniper.

"Is a morgue what I think it is?" she asks.

"Let's not think about that now. No news is good news, right?"

She smiles, but her heart's not in it. I think it's going to be good for both of us to have a break.

As we head upstairs to get ready for the feast, Juniper asks, "What is a sour patch and why are there children involved? And what is chocolate?"

The lowered drawbridge is already packed full of people lining up to get into the castle. Spotlights light the gray stone, covered in red banners, and oil lanterns light the path, casting Yggdrasil in a soft warm glow. Music from hidden speakers in the trees beckon everyone forward, adding an excited buzz to the night. The stone troll stands frozen, as always, decked out in party favors and strings of paper, as if it too is joining in on the festivities.

"I really am feeling much better," Juniper says. She is lucky—either that, or giants are built differently. She's practically skipping as we head down the lane to the feast. "You and Reagan have done an exceptional job protecting the faire. Now all we have to do is find Mother, who is *not* in the morgue."

"Right. And find Loki," I say, hiking up my skirts so the hem doesn't drag in the mud. It's one of Reagan's dresses, and I'd hate to ruin it. It's a white linen bliaut, a gown that goes all the way to my toes, with long white sleeves embroidered with golden leaves trailing out at my elbows. A golden belt cinches my waist. I'll be the first to admit that it would look way better on Reagan, but it was the only formal dress in the house that I could find in time.

Juniper's in one of Reagan's old gowns, too. It's a baby blue, crushed velvet kirtle. As a special touch, Juniper wears a flower crown out of roses she grew herself. She looks like she should be standing in the middle of a lake and bestowing magical swords on people.

The bells hanging on Yggdrasil ring out in the still air. I imagine even the landvaettir aren't immune to the excitement of tonight.

Inside, the party is going full swing.

The great hall is a thing of beauty, truly. Wood floors, giant candle-chandeliers, stone walls covered in real antique tapestries of medieval stories. A buffet lines the back wall, full of roast meats, grilled veg-etables, and cupcakes and candies piled like a mountain on a tiered display. A chocolate fountain bubbles in the corner near the stage, where the bards are playing a medieval cover of "Take On Me."

People crowd the dance floor and surrounding tables, laughing and talking and eating, dressed in their best medieval costumes—flowing skirts, and embroidered capes and silks. The way the crowd moves, it reminds me of a nerdier Lollapalooza. And I *love* it.

Normally, this would be my favorite night of the year. I always look forward to it. But tonight, my anxiety sits high and tight in my gut.

Loki could be in this room.

"What's wrong?" Juniper asks. "Do you see anything?"

"Nothing," I say.

I force myself to breathe, and remember what Reagan told me. I should only worry about the things I can control. I'm not going to be like Prima, a control freak. We did a good job with the fjötra. That should be enough.

"This is wonderful!" Juniper looks like a kid in a candy store. "I shall find the jalapeño poppers."

Juniper disappears, quick as a shadow, into the crowd.

There must be at least four hundred people here. Everyone's laughing, having a good time, and I desperately want to enjoy the night with them.

Mr. Beaumont schmoozes with some folks I recognize from corporate. He stands near the stage, dressed to the nines in his red and gold king's doublet. A gaggle of fans surround James near the buffet table, charm radiating off him like an oil spill. Wyatt's uncle Stan sits at the end of one of the long tables, laughing with some other stable hands and smashing their tankards together in cheers.

My scalp tingles, like when Mom used to brush my hair, sending a chill down my spine. Someone is watching me.

The old woman from Pagebound stands in the middle of the dance floor, hunched over, clutching a knobby wooden cane. She glares in my direction, those bright blue eyes locked on me.

"Having a good time?"

Trudy's question makes me jump. She slides up next to me, arms folded across her chest with a chill smile on her face. Her velvet green gown looks dynamite with her auburn hair. "So much better than the other feasts I've been to. Where are your sisters? I'd hoped to see them today."

"They're busy." I try to find the bookseller again. "Did you see that lady?"

"Who?" Trudy looks where I'm pointing, but she's too late. The bookseller is gone.

My pulse pounds in my head. "Sorry, I gotta go," I say, and rush into the crowd.

It's a sea of bodies, and now I know what salmon feel like swimming upstream. Just short of elbowing my way through, I weave toward the dance floor. The old lady has to be around here somewhere.

I squeeze out of a tight group of people and emerge in a small clearing near the edge of the dance floor.

There stands Wyatt wearing a black long-sleeved doublet with silver trim, the slits in the elbows revealing his white tunic underneath. No glasses today. He takes a sip from his drink and does a double take when he sees me. His raised eyebrows lower as he takes in the look on my face.

"I saw that lady again, from the bookstore," I explain, hurrying over to him. "She was just here."

Wyatt's eyes dart around, squinting. "Where'd she go?"

"I don't know. I . . ." Trying to say it out loud makes me doubt everything. Am I being paranoid? The old woman was literally just standing there. Doing nothing. Everywhere I look, it's just people having a good time. "You didn't see her?"

"I don't have my glasses," he says, sounding frustrated with himself. "Do you think she's Loki?"

"It's weird, right? She keeps appearing and disappearing, like a trickster god would." I take a deep breath. I've been playing this all wrong. I need to relax, or at least pretend to. "Come on," I say as I take his hand and lead him onto the dance floor.

Wyatt barely has time to put down his drink. "What are we doing?"

"Blending in," I say. "Rule number one of being a valkyrie: Don't draw attention to yourself. If Loki's here, we can't let him know we're onto him."

"Got it," Wyatt says.

We join the dancers just as a new song is about to begin. This time, it's a traditional country line dancing song. Most people who don't know it exit the floor, but the ones who grew up with this type of thing stay.

I try not to be suspicious as I join the line of women. I look for any trouble out of the edges of my vision while couples line up facing one another. Most guests surround us with eager smiles, phones and cameras out, an opportunity to see a show up close. There's still no sign of the old lady, but I try to stay chill.

In front of me, Wyatt stands rigidly on the men's side, the opposite of chill. His eyes dart around as a deep flush spreads on his face. He looks like he's swallowed something that's trying to crawl back up his throat as the music starts.

"Are you okay?" I ask, keeping my voice low, as I step toward him with my line.

"I'm fine," Wyatt says. But he doesn't seem fine. He's doing everything in his power not to look at me as I stop in front of him and curtsy. He must be really freaked out that Loki might be here.

"All we have to do is play it cool," I say, stepping back with the others. "Quit being suspicious."

Wyatt nods stiffly, steps toward me with his line, and bows.

When he gets close, I notice his shoulders are tight, his back rigid. It's like he's being moved by invisible strings, and I laugh.

"Relax," I say. "We're not in danger. Not yet anyway."

"No, right. Of course, I just . . ." He still won't look at me. His eyes go to the ceiling and I see the color rising in his cheeks. "You look, uh, very nice tonight," he says.

I snort. "This is Reagan's dress. It wasn't my idea."

"You didn't want to be here for the feast?"

We spin, clasp each other at the elbows and walk with our lines.

"No," I say. "I have other things to worry about."

"Sometimes it's nice having a little distraction."

Wyatt spins and bows. I curtsy in response, and step toward him. Wyatt swallows and his Adam's apple jumps behind his high collar.

"You look very nice tonight, too," I say.

He finally looks at me, his eyes bright, and my heart betrays me and does a little jig in my chest.

No one's ever looked at me like that before, and I don't quite know how to react. I want to make a joke, I want to defuse the situation, maybe set something on fire to cause a distraction, but another part of me wants him to keep looking at me, because all of a sudden I'm not so exposed. Not when he's looking. Not when he's here.

"Thanks," he says. And when he smiles, his whole face lights up.

Now *I'm* the one who can't look at *him*. I duck my head low as he takes my hand, and we walk in a line, hands raised above our heads. Where his skin touches mine feels electric.

I've never felt like this before, and I don't know how to process. It's exhilarating, and scary, and nerve-racking.

His hands are calloused and dry against mine, but they're warm and fit nicely. Every time we part, it's like my hands can't wait to find his again.

The room spins, and my head feels light.

The tempo of the music matches the rhythm of my heart.

All of a sudden, I don't want this song to end.

But it does.

I'm standing face-to-face with Wyatt. He's flushed, and his eyes are bright, and his shoulders relax as he looks at me.

I don't even hear the people clapping.

My cheeks hurt. I can't stop smiling. And neither can he.
But something on the ground catches my eye.
It's a metal tube, rolling on the floor toward us.
It stops between our feet.
And then it explodes.

19

A CLOUD OF RED SMOKE FILLS MY LUNGS. MY EARS RING.
I can't see a thing. I'm coughing, blinded, as people scream around
me. Tears swim in my vision. I can barely open my eyes.

As the ringing in my ears fades, it takes me a second to realize
what happened.

It was just a smoke bomb.

I cough, waving my hand in my face, but it only makes things
worse.

People around us gasp and gag, bumping into one another as they
try to get away, but no one seems to be hurt.

"Wya—?" I choke on more smoke as I throw my hands out, searching. "Wyatt?"

He doesn't answer, but he's coughing heavily nearby. I can just
barely make out his shadow through the smoke.

"Wyatt?" I blink a few times to see him standing but curled in on
himself, one arm stretched out toward me, another folded across his
chest. "Are you okay?" I ask.

Wyatt coughs and shakes his head. He doesn't answer me.

I try to get closer, but he waves his hand for me to get back. Drool rolls out of his mouth as he gasps for air, and he squeezes his eyes shut.

"Wyatt?" I say again.

Heavily, he drops to his hands and knees, then his eyes snap open, glowing a bright amber.

"Shit."

Wyatt disappears in a white cloud and a bear rises out of the mist. People close to us scream.

I can't move. I can't think.

As the haze dissipates, Wyatt stands up on his back legs, towering over us.

People run for the doors.

Thick foam rolls from Wyatt's mouth, and there's a wild look in his eye. This is different from the first time I saw him change.

People scramble for cover, but those outside the smoke cloud don't understand. The ones who do crash over the buffet table, trip in the water fountain, and knock one another to the ground in their attempts to get away. It's chaos.

"Bryn!" Juniper appears at my side, coughing and covering her mouth and nose with her hand. "What happened?"

Wyatt barks, his head swinging back and forth, like he's looking for something to attack. It's terrifying.

"I don't know! It all happened so fast! There was a smoke bomb—"

Wyatt lands back on all fours with a massive crash that rocks the floor like an earthquake. Mostly everyone is gone, except for us.

I have to help him.

"Wyatt!" I scream, but he doesn't seem to hear me.

He huffs, flaring his snout, and shakes his head like he's trying to snap out of it.

Juniper bends down and grabs the small silver cylinder. "This?"

Wyatt roars, clawing his eyes and mouth. It's as if he's desperately trying to get something out of his eyes. Blindly, he charges in our direction. I dive into Juniper and knock her aside as Wyatt misses us and crashes headfirst into the buffet table, sending roast meat flying.

"The smoke did this to him!" I say, helping Juniper to her feet.

"Security!" Mr. Beaumont screams from the stairs, waving his arms and panicking.

Wyatt, drawn by the noise and movement, rushes him, but Mr. Beaumont flees up the spiral staircase, screaming.

Before security can get here, Wyatt bolts for the back doors and crashes into the side hall. Servers scream and drop their trays full of hors d'oeuvres as they run into the bathroom for safety, and Wyatt gallops in the opposite direction, scraping against the walls and knocking sconces and picture frames to the floor.

"We can't let anyone catch him!" I yell at Juniper, who's sprinting behind me.

Wyatt reaches the end of the hallway, slipping on the red rug lining the floor, and crashes into an information kiosk at the end. Glass shatters and rains down on him, but he shakes it off and turns the corner.

"Wyatt! It's okay! It's okay! Stay calm!" I don't know if he understands me or not, but I need to try.

The explosion must have triggered him somehow. He's truly gone berserk.

He charges down the back hallway, spooking caterers with silver platters as they duck for cover behind kitchen doors. With a roar of frustration, Wyatt bursts through the emergency exit, blasting through the metal like it's paper, and runs into the night.

"He's heading for the gardens!" I shout.

"Good!" Juniper snatches up a handful of rosebuds at the door and throws them behind us. Roots explode from the ground, snaking up to close the door and seal it shut. No one is going to follow us, at least. It gives us time.

"Wyatt!" I call.

He's easy to track, even in the dark, he's making so much noise. He tears through the garden paths and knocks over hedges, desperately trying to get away. I don't know how else to calm him down.

We're not just gaining on him though, he's slowing down. I find him stumbling in a small rose garden, walled off with tall hedges, centered by a cherub fountain and iron benches. With a soft moan, Wyatt collapses in the shadow of a large willow tree.

He tries to get back up, but his legs give out and he falls flat once more, grunting and groaning, foam bubbling from his mouth. His eyes roll wildly in his head, and he whines in pain.

"Hey, Wyatt," I say, calmly.

"Bryn, wait." Juniper sounds scared. I don't blame her.

"It's fine. He has to know he's not alone." Slowly, I approach, hand out. "Hey. It's okay. Everything's fine."

He huffs. I forgot how big he gets as a bear. Instinct locks up my knees, and I suddenly remember why our ancestors learned real quick to be afraid of big animals. But this is Wyatt.

"You're not going to swipe at me, are you?" I ask.

He scowls and exhales, making his jowls flap like he's blowing a raspberry. It'd be funny any other time. But he doesn't make a move to hurt me. He puddles on the ground, arms and legs sprawled around him.

In the distance, people are in an uproar, yelling and calling for one another. I can just make out the echoes of a voice reverberating on the emergency speaker system.

"Attention, everyone. Please remain calm. Return to your vehicles or place of residence immediately. Attention, everyone..."

We only have so much time left until someone comes looking.

Wyatt moans and a cloud of mist envelops him. When it clears, Wyatt is human again, struggling to get up. I rush for him and kneel at his side.

"You're okay." I take his hand, and brush aside the curls hiding his face as he lifts his head to look at me. His eyes are bloodshot, his skin pale, but relief melts across his face.

"Bryn."

That's when I see movement near the tree behind him.

A person is standing there, watching us. Blond hair, wide and shocked blue eyes, his red and gold silk tunic catching the light of the moon.

James Beaumont.

And he's holding a piece of paper covered in Asgardian runes.

20

In a fury, I'm on my feet and rush James.

I grab him by the front of his tunic and pin him up against the tree. He yelps in surprise.

"What did you do to him?" I barely get the words out through gritted teeth.

"What did *I* do to him?" he asks, his voice going up an octave. "What did *you* do to him? How did you make Wyatt a . . . a bear?!"

He looks between me and Juniper and Wyatt on the ground behind me.

I clamp my hand over his mouth, his breathing hot and wet against my palm. "Don't." I doubt people can hear us out here, but I don't want to risk it.

James shakes his head and I let go of his mouth.

"What are you doing?" I ask.

"I was just sitting out here! I heard this loud noise and before I know it—" He flails his arm, summing up his experience as eloquently as expected. *"This!"*

"What did you do to him?" I ask again.

"I don't know what you're talking about!"

I glare at him. James is an actor, but he's not *that* good of an actor. He looks really freaked out, and I doubt that it'd be that easy to fake. I look down at the paper in his hand and snatch it out of his grasp. "Gimme that," I say.

I hold it out behind me and Juniper takes it.

"What were you doing out here?" I ask James. "Where were you when the bomb went off?"

"Bomb?"

"Answer the question."

"I was waiting for someone!"

"Who?"

"Reagan."

"Why would Reagan meet you out here?"

James takes a breath. "I wrote her a letter. Like you told me to. I said to meet me so I could make it up to her for all the shit I put her through."

"You wrote her this?" I ask, gesturing to the paper in Juniper's hands.

"What? No!"

I look over my shoulder as Wyatt sits up with Juniper's help and holds his head in his hands. I want to go to him, but I'm torn. I want to punch James just as much as I want to be next to Wyatt.

I turn back to James, teeth clenched. "Talk."

"I wrote Reagan a letter, apologizing for everything, telling her to meet me so we could get back together. I was waiting for her when you showed up. Now"—he shoves my hands away and straightens his tunic—"let go of me."

"Why do you have this?" Juniper asks, holding up the parchment.

"I found it!"

"Where?"

"Over there." He points to the cherub fountain burbling nearby. "When I was waiting, I saw this hooded figure hurrying through the gardens. I thought it was Reagan, so I called out to her, but whoever it was ignored me and ran away. They left this behind. Like I said, I thought it was Reagan with my letter."

Juniper hands me the paper, her face gray. "It's an Asgardian kulning. Just like before."

She's right. I recognize some of the same runes as the paper we found in Yggdrasil. "James must have spooked Loki before he could put it in the tree."

Wyatt stays on the ground, one hand holding his head. "What happened? I didn't hurt anyone, did I?"

James stares at Wyatt, slack-jawed. "You're a bear, dude."

Something in me snaps and I bull-rush James, finger in his face. "If you tell anyone about this, I will personally . . ." I try to think of all the things I can threaten him with, but I can't settle on any single one. I just clench my fist open and closed, struggling to find the words.

James shrinks away from me, pressing himself back up against the tree. Message received, I think.

"I'm not done with you yet. Don't move," I say.

At least James is smart enough to listen.

I kneel next to Wyatt. "Are you okay to stand up?"

Wyatt looks at me and nods. I give him my hand and help him to his feet. My fingers feel awfully cold when he lets go.

"Odd," Juniper says. She's holding the smoke bomb now, inspecting it in the moonlight. She sniffs it and rubs her fingers together, then holds the cylinder out to me. "Here. Smell."

"I got a full face of it," I say.

Wyatt takes a small step back, hands up, avoiding it.

"It smells like mushroom," she says. "There's a red powder on the casing."

"Mushroom?" I try to think of a reason why a smoke bomb would be made out of mushrooms, until something clicks. "Berserkers in the old days used to take magic mushrooms before battle. It would trigger their rage, make them literally go berserk. But I thought they all went extinct with berserkers. Someone must have known what would happen to you. Why else use it?"

Wyatt stares at me. "You're saying someone drugged me?"

"Not sure what else to call it. But..." I can barely wrap my head around it. "Who else knows about your power? Besides us? Besides Loki?"

"My uncle, and my dad, but he's...No one else."

"Then Loki's our only suspect." Another thought turns my stomach into ice. "What if Loki set off the smoke bomb as a distraction to put the runes in Yggdrasil?"

"That is certainly possible," says Juniper.

I hate to admit it, but that's what I would have done.

James shrieks, breaking the silence, "He's a *BEAR!*"

In one fluid move, Juniper snatches a rosebud from its stem and throws it at James. The buds grow into thorny vines and wrap around him like an anaconda, cinching his arms and legs together. He lets out a startled "Not the face! Not the face!" as the thorns threaten to prick his cheek.

I round on him. "Shut up!"

James clamps his mouth shut and nods vigorously. Juniper lowers her hand and the vines recede. James lets out a gasp of relief.

Wyatt drops onto a nearby bench, raking his fingers through his hair. "I'm sorry. I didn't mean to lose control like that."

"It wasn't your fault," I say, turning back to him.

Wyatt lowers his head, but I can see his pulse bouncing in his jaw. He looks pale in the moonlight, but at least he seems a lot better than before. Whatever it was, it didn't last long, but the guilt remains. Something hollows out my stomach, and I swallow a lump in my throat. I know the feeling.

"You do not think anyone saw, do you?" Juniper asks.

I shake my head. "No. Too much smoke. As far as anyone might guess, a regular bear got into the castle, maybe looking for food."

"Well, that's reassuring," says James. "A grizzly bear in Chicago."

I'm too tired to snap at him. "Wyatt, are you okay?"

Wyatt looks up at me, swallowing thickly, and nods. "Yeah. My head hurts, but yeah."

That's a relief at least.

James can't help himself. "I'm glad we cleared all that up but—Loki? Runes? Asgard? What the hell are you all talking about?"

I glance at my friends, searching for answers, but they look equally stumped. If we tell him everything, it's one more problem we have to deal with. But then again, he's seen too much.

James Beaumont is one of the absolute last people I want to trust, but do I really have any other choice?

"Ravenswood is in danger," I say.

James takes a few curious steps toward us. "What do you mean 'in danger'?"

"Someone is sending monsters here. Magical, dangerous monsters to start Ragnarök. It's our job to stop it."

The color drains from James's face. "Monsters . . . The troll statue. Is that real?"

He looks at Wyatt for confirmation. Wyatt just nods.

It's as if a million things occur to James at once and he freezes for a moment before he claps his hands once, loudly. "Ha! I knew the troll was real!" He grins, practically bouncing on his feet. "But if Ravenswood is in danger, that means Reagan is in danger. I can't do nothing. I want to help."

"You?" I laugh.

"I may not be able to turn into a bear, or use magic plants to do whatever, but you need me. You do!" he says, when I snort with doubt. "No one else can cover this up for you like I can. My dad will listen to anything I tell him. I can help."

Based on the way Juniper and Wyatt look at me, they know he's right. James Beaumont is the closest thing we have to an ally, and I can't believe he's our only option. But if anyone can sway a crowd, it's him.

Juniper is the first to speak. "He could tell everyone otherwise and make a bigger mess. Having him as an ally may help rather than hurt."

"We could use all the help we can get," Wyatt adds.

I have to give it to him, James did save Juniper. He may be a douche when it comes to dumping Reagan, but he's not entirely useless. If Reagan finds out that he knows our secret, she might never forgive me, but I'm not sure what other choice we have. I cross my arms over my chest. "Fine, whatever. But don't make me regret it."

Juniper waves the smoke bomb around. "Now all we must do is learn where Loki discovered this mushroom."

"Can I see?" James holds out his hand.

She gives it to him, and he looks it over, rolling it between his fingers like he thinks he's Sherlock Holmes. I'm not sure what a person like him will be able to figure out. I doubt he's the type to ace biology tests. He takes a sniff of it and hums. "Earthy, red chalk-like residue, mushroom for sure, and you said it was a smoke bomb?"

"Yes." Juniper nods. "The texture, the smell. Reminds me of home. But I do not know the name."

James taps the metal cylinder in his palm. "Eye of Newt's, the herbalist's shop. They have teas and dried mushrooms and stuff. They might be able to tell you more."

"Wait." Only now do I remember Mr. Beaumont mentioning that Eye of Newt's had been broken into, but I was too busy thinking about so many other things in his office, it completely passed me by. "Eye of Newt's was robbed the same night the troll showed up. What if it was Loki? What if the troll was a distraction, too?"

"Whatever. All I know is what's in front of me," he says and tosses the cylinder to me. "Ask for red-eyed agaricus. White cap, red spots, normally found near birch trees in subarctic climates. That's the only type I know that leaves a red residue like that."

"Huh. How do you know all this?" I ask.

"Studying. I'm getting my degree from Cornell in mycology. You're looking at the next Alexander Fleming. What do you think I do all day? Sword fight?"

Okay, so maybe I had this guy all wrong. He's still a jerk though. I don't want to give him too much credit. Even Wyatt seems surprised that James is actually being helpful, and he catches my eye and tips his head to the side, impressed.

"It is not a bad idea," Juniper says. "A new clue."

"See?" James flashes his perfectly straight teeth. "I'm full of surprises."

Already, blue and red lights illuminate the dark sky. The cops are here. Probably the media, too. We can't stay here too much longer.

I grab James by the arm and push him toward the lights.

"You're not done yet. Go give them a story," I say, "and don't make me regret trusting you."

21

THE NEXT MORNING BEFORE WORK, JUNIPER AND I VISIT Eye of Newt's Herb and Tea Shop. It's a quaint building, made of brown stones and painted wood, blending in with the forest as if it grew out of the trees itself. Windows with diagonal iron muntins are thrown open wide, letting in the balmy morning air onto brown jars and bottles full of dried herbs sitting on wooden shelves, ready to be mixed and matched to make teas and custom incense. The place always smells like a bag of potpourri. My head swims with all the smells, scrambling my mind—which is still churning from what happened last night.

After I sent James off to deal with the general public, Wyatt's uncle Stan showed up in the garden and took Wyatt home. I haven't seen or heard from Wyatt yet this morning, but I don't blame him if he wants to sleep in. I would, too. Knowing that someone out there wants to poison him is as good a reason as any. I've slept in for a lot less.

Luckily, the rest of the faire is behaving like it's business as usual. Animal control is on the case. James was even on Channel 7 news, spinning the incident for the reporter like it was a promotional event.

It's still early though, so Eye of Newt's is empty when Juniper and I step in.

The store is usually run by a guy named Newt (really), but today his son, Danny, is the one behind the counter. Danny is our age, only a year behind me at school, and lanky, with messy brown hair. Today he's wearing a tie-dye T-shirt and board shorts. But because he's got headphones on, he doesn't hear us come up to the counter. He sways to the music as he labels a new blend of herbal tea called Blueberry Enigma.

He turns around and starts, then takes off his headphones, smiling bashfully. "Oh. It's just you, Bryn." His eyes dart to Juniper, then back to me. "You're not going to tell Mr. Beaumont I was listening to music while working, are you?"

I wave my hand. "No way, secret's safe. Listen, I heard you were robbed a few nights ago."

He looks surprised that I know about it. "Well, yeah. Not the first time it's happened. Nobody was hurt though."

"Can you tell us about it?"

"Sure, I came in to open, found the door lock smashed and some of our drawers empty. Nothing major."

"What was stolen? Cash?"

"No, actually. That's the weird part. Just some herbs, a couple bags of our dried mushroom mix, some garlic braids, even took some incense."

"That reminds me. . . . I've been looking for this one mushroom, leaves a red residue. Red-eyed something?"

"Agaricus," Juniper says. "Red-eyed agaricus."

Danny shifts his weight from one hip to the other. "Yeah, I mean, no. We do have that, or rather, we did. All of it was stolen. We're totally out."

"Ah, bummer," I say, despite anxiety tasting sour on the back of my tongue. Loki could make Wyatt go berserk again. "Where'd you get it?"

"I don't know. My dad goes to those specialty herb conferences every year. Maybe he got it from there. We don't get it that often. Unlike its poisonous cousins, it's really great in soups though."

"I love soup!" Juniper says, in earnest.

"Me too!" Danny says, smiling.

"What about if you smoke it? Like, inhale it?" I ask, getting back to the task at hand.

Danny stares at me, bewildered. "I've never heard of anyone doing that."

"But what if someone did?"

Still flummoxed, Danny lifts a shoulder. "I mean, some other mushrooms can give you a bad trip, and that's only if you eat them. But smoking a red-eyed agaricus? I don't think it would do anything. Maybe in rare cases, it could mess you up, but I don't know. I'm not into that kind of stuff. Don't worry, I'm not gonna snitch. You do you."

I can't help but wonder if maybe because Wyatt is a berserker, that's why he was the only one affected by the mushroom's smoke. Everyone else was fine. That would mean it was definitely a targeted attack. But the way Danny is looking at me, asking about smoking mushrooms, he must think I'm the juvenile delinquent everyone probably says I am, so I just smile, innocently as I can.

"That sucks it was stolen though!" I say. "They're really rare, right?"

"Yeah, I think so. Up there with morels. Only people who really know what they're doing can spot them. They don't grow around here. The mountains, I think, cold places."

"Do you have any idea who might want to steal it? Maybe security cameras caught them?"

"Security cameras aren't working, not since the start of the season. Mr. Beaumont says they'll be up soon, but I don't know."

I sigh. It's a dead end.

"I've got some other mushrooms if you're interested! Or you, um...?" Danny says. He glances at Juniper, and then back at me.

"This is Juniper," I say. She's distracted by the aromatherapy dream pillows and looks up when I say her name.

"Ah! Yes! That's me!"

Danny's face is practically luminescent, he's blushing so hard. "Would you like some mushrooms?"

What's going on here is more obvious than a highway billboard. "We're good," I say. We're at another dead end, and I'm eager to check on Wyatt.

"How about some tea? I blended it myself," he says, gesturing to the Blueberry Enigma. "Or maybe you'd be interested in seed bombs?"

Juniper perks up. "Seed *bombs*?"

From under the counter, Danny holds up a small clay ball rolled in seeds. "Yeah, I make them by hand. Black-eyed Susan, prairie ironweed, anise hyssop... Native wildflowers for a little guerrilla gardening. Mr. Beaumont hates it when I throw them in the picnic areas."

Juniper squeals like someone handed her a teacup pig as Danny gives her one of the balls. "*This* is magnificent." A million ideas light up her eyes. "A more compact seed cluster for maximum power!"

Danny has no idea that he's giving her actual ammunition. He leans against the counter, raising a flirtatious eyebrow. "So, you like... nature?"

While Danny flirts, I take a lap around the shop to try to clear my head. If Ragnarök is his endgame, why is Loki messing around, stealing mushrooms? Just to make Wyatt transform, so he can have easy access to Yggdrasil? Is it because he wanted to ruin the party and do what he does best, and cause chaos? But why go through all the trouble of stealing from the shop and risk getting caught? None of this makes sense.

I drag my hands down my face and scrub my eyes as I refocus. There has to be something we're missing.

Before I can think of what, my eyes snag on a small table near the door displaying a few locally sourced bee products, like wax candles, honey, and beeswax lotion. I remember how calloused and dry Wyatt's hands were when we danced last night, and then my stomach clenches when I remember how awful he looked after, how guilty he must have felt even though going berserk wasn't his fault. I don't want him to think I'm mad at him or anything.

Before I can talk myself out of it, I pick up a bottle of the beeswax lotion and bring it back to the counter.

Danny is already packing a paper bag full of seed bombs for Juniper. "It's on the house," he tells her. "One nature lover to the next."

Juniper's smile is huge. "Thank you."

"So are you in town for long or...?"

Before Juniper can answer, a horse's muzzle appears at the window behind Danny. Its nostrils flare as it sniffs, hot breath steaming on the glass, and it then nudges the window open a little more, pushing the rest of its head through. The horse is reddish-brown with a braided gold bridle and it doesn't seem bothered by us in the slightest as it looks around the shop with impassive brown eyes.

Both Juniper and I stare as the horse opens its mouth, revealing large straight teeth etched with runes, and chomps down on a vase of blue hydrangeas near the window, snapping the stems in half.

Danny is too busy wrapping up more seed bombs for Juniper to notice.

"Um..." I say, but I'm having a hard time articulating the fact that a giant horse with runes carved in its teeth is snacking on his flowers. The absurdity is making it difficult.

The horse stretches its neck, straining to reach a bundle of dried lavender hanging upside down on the wall. It snags the end of it with its teeth and drags the flower into its mouth, chewing lazily before spitting it out.

Danny moves to turn around, but I slam the beeswax lotion on the counter, hard enough it rattles the bottles. Danny stares at me, bewildered.

"I would like to purchase this, please!"

The horse continues to search for anything else it can get its teeth on, but gives up once there's nothing left to eat and disappears from the window and out of sight.

⋈

The moment we leave Eye of Newt's, we make a break for the back of the store, running as fast as we can to catch up to the horse.

"That wasn't a regular horse, right?" I ask, breathless, as we cut through the trees.

"I do not believe so!"

In the soft dirt I spot several hoofprints leading away from the herbalist's and deeper into the trees. How many horses are there?

All of a sudden, Juniper grabs my wrist and yanks me down behind a bush.

"What is it?" I whisper.

She points through a break in the trees. "There."

A little ways ahead, I see it. The horse's back is turned to us as he uses one of his hooves to dig at some exposed tree roots. If I had to guess, I'd say he was searching for more food. The only problem is, I now realize why there were so many hoofprints in the dirt.

I count, and then recount, like maybe my eyes went crossed and I'm seeing double. It's not a horse. "It's a sleipnir."

"One of Odin's chargers?" Juniper gasps.

I nod, licking my dry lips. My heart is racing like it's got eight legs, too. "Sleipnir can run over land, air, and sea, galloping on waves of thunder. Mom used to tell us stories about them. When they run, they make a rainbow, creating the Bifröst bridge to Asgard. With a sleipnir, you don't need a raven cloak to travel realms."

"Did Loki steal it and bring it here?"

"I don't think Loki needed a sleipnir to get to Midgard. But they spend most of their time in Odin's stables. . . ." My stomach clenches when I remember one little detail. "Waiting for Ragnarök."

He turns around, sniffing the ground, and I see that he's hurt. Blood is smeared down one of his front legs tucked up toward his chest. Any second, he's going to notice us. We can't risk him running away, so I quietly step out from behind the bushes. Juniper moves to grab me but misses.

The sleipnir jolts with a start and makes to run but squeals when he puts weight on the bad leg. He rises up and kicks toward me. Huge hooves, each etched with runes, come inches from my head, and I duck so as not to get clobbered.

"Whoa," I say. "Easy."

"Watch out!" Juniper cries, but I ignore her.

"It's okay," I say.

The sleipnir slams down with his front legs and stares at me with wild eyes, ears pinned back.

"I'm not going to hurt you," I say. I pull out a granola bar from my surcoat pocket, one I had planned to eat later. "Here."

The sleipnir looks at the Chewy Granola Bar in my hand and then back at me, a bewildered expression on his face. His ears perk up, and he takes one step toward me, pauses again, and then takes another step, before he snatches the snack from my hand. The front of his rune-carved teeth nick the skin on my palm, but it doesn't hurt.

While he chews, he stares at me but doesn't move. I'm tempted to reach out and touch him, but I'm afraid he'll bolt. My knees are Jell-O.

Juniper emerges from her hiding place and comes over to stand just behind me. "I do not like this, Bryn. Not one bit. How did this creature get through the fjötra?"

"I don't know. The fjötra is supposed to protect against monsters that want to hurt us, so I guess it tracks. I don't think he's dangerous."

Juniper narrows her eyes. She asks him, "Where is Loki?"

The sleipnir looks at her, ears flattening, and stamps his hooves. Juniper backs up. "I do not believe he likes me."

I step more in front of her, hands out. "It's okay! We're cool. We can help you," I say to the sleipnir. "You just have to trust us—trust me. Can you do that?"

The sleipnir turns his eyes on me, going very still. He's huge, bigger than any horse I've seen before, and I've seen my fair share here at Ravenswood. Even compared to Wyatt's gelding, Gamgee, sleipnir are massive. No wonder Odin would want an army of them.

I hold out my hand, showing him I'm not a threat, but he shakes his head and stares me down.

"I know," I say. "I wouldn't trust me either. But you can trust the person I'm taking you to."

Juniper asks, "Who?"

"Wyatt. He'll know how to help."

"That is halfway across the faire!"

"Then we'll have to be really good at making sure no one sees."

Juniper lets out a low moan. "I hope you know what you are doing."

The sleipnir doesn't seem all that spooked now, especially after my

Chewy Bar. He must be starving. Who knows how long he's been wandering for?

Slowly, the sleipnir nudges my palm with his snout. It's warm and wet, and I rub it like I would Butternut Squash's head. He seems to like that.

"That's my secret," I say. "I never know what I'm doing."

Thanks to some quick thinking on my part (and the fact that someone left their laundry out to dry on the line), we walk the sleipnir under the cover of a large bedsheet all the way to the stables.

We hear Wyatt and James before we see them. They're standing in the aisle and their raised voices carry through the barn. Wyatt's back is to us. He's dressed in his usual T-shirt and jeans, but James is in full armor.

"—don't care that you can turn into a bear, dude. You could have said something!" James says. "I thought we were friends!"

"We're not friends."

James looks hurt. "Of course we are!"

"No, we're not." The back of Wyatt's neck is red. "Because not even the friends I had knew about my . . ." He trails off, gesturing vaguely, like he can't even say it.

James frowns, jamming his finger down to make a point. "We're friends now, and as your friend I'm telling you, you can't quit! Who's going to be my Black Knight? We're partners! The arena just got rebuilt and you're abandoning me?"

Wyatt shakes his head.

I can tell they're having a moment, but what choice do I have? I can't come back later. I have really great timing. "I hate to interrupt . . ." I say, leading the sleipnir inside.

James and Wyatt look at us, both of them stony-faced.

"We need your help," I say, and pull the sheet off the sleipnir's back. "He's hurt."

James yelps and leaps for cover behind Wyatt. Wyatt's eyes get big, staring awestruck. Gamgee sticks his head over the stall door to get a look, too.

"What is that?" James shrieks.

"A sleipnir," I say. "One of Odin's horses from Asgard. Named Chewy—like a granola bar. We have to call him something."

"W-wow," Wyatt stammers. "This is unreal." He snaps into gear as he moves to a nearby cabinet and fetches a bag of oat cakes. He tosses a cake to Chewy, who catches it midair and gobbles it up.

"A sleipnir?" James balks, going pale. "Okay! That's enough weirdness for me today, thank you!" No one stops him as he scurries out of the stables, rattling like a tin can as he goes.

I tell Wyatt the same thing I told Juniper, about what a sleipnir is and what it can do, and Wyatt's eyes shine with awe. He really loves horses, no wonder he's not afraid.

"This is amazing," Wyatt says, nudging his glasses up with his knuckle. He gives Chewy another oat cake and kneels down to inspect his bloody leg. He looks up at Chewy. "Mind if I . . . ?"

Wyatt's politeness seems to go a long way, because Chewy extends his leg to Wyatt, like he's at the nail salon, letting him take a look. After a moment, Wyatt gently sets it down, then turns to us. "Well, he's not running anywhere with his leg like that. It might be broken. We'll have to run some X-rays to be sure, but . . ." He steps back and tosses Chewy another cake. Gamgee snorts from his stall, apparently jealous, and Wyatt gives him a cake, too.

"Can you help him?" I ask.

Wyatt shrugs. "I mean, we can try. I've never treated a sleipnir before."

"Can't be too different, can it?"

Wyatt shrugs again. It's nice seeing him back on his feet after what happened last night.

"You look good," I say, then cough when I realize I need to finish the thought. "Better than last I saw you. You feeling better?"

Wyatt tears his gaze away from Chewy and smiles at me. "Uh, yeah. Thanks."

From a safe distance, Juniper watches us. I think she's still afraid of Chewy. "Are you truly ceasing to be the Black Knight?" she asks.

Wyatt looks at her then at the hay-strewn floor. "I'm a liability. I can't have what happened last night happen again." He fetches the first aid kit to clean the blood off Chewy's leg, and pulls on some latex gloves. He sits on a small wooden stool while Chewy looks right at home getting pampered.

I glance at Juniper. As long as Loki's running around Ravenswood, Wyatt's in danger. She presses her lips together and nods, no doubt thinking the same thing.

"We went to Eye of Newt's," I say. "That's where we found Chewy. Loki stole their whole stock of aga-whatever—"

"Red-eyed agaricus," Juniper and Wyatt say at the same time.

"Right. That's what I said. Loki stole their whole stock, and he may have more of it. It might be a good idea if you lay low for a while, Wyatt, at least until we can stop him." Then I add, "I'm sorry."

Wyatt doesn't look up from Chewy's leg, his jaw set. "It's okay. It's for the best." He nudges his glasses up his nose with the back of his wrist. "You stopped the monsters coming from outside, but what about the one already insi—"

"If you say you're a monster, I'm going to bite you until you take it back."

Wyatt's eyes flick up to me and a ghost of a smile twitches his lips before it falls again. "I could have hurt someone."

"But you didn't."

That doesn't seem good enough for him, and it makes my chest hurt.

"I am curious. How do you know how to care for horses?" Juniper asks.

Wyatt nudges his glasses up again, seemingly thankful for the change of topic. "It takes a lot of work running the stables, so I help my uncle with everything. We do what we can. I want to be a vet though, when I'm older. So I can do more." He gives Chewy a smile. "Ravenswood has some of the best medical facilities in the country though. Chewy'll be safe here. We can get him what he needs."

"Good," I say. "I'm glad you were the first person I thought of."

Wyatt's eyebrows rise slightly, but he quickly looks away and shifts on his stool. "Of course," he says with a stiff nod. Was it something I said?

While he may be awkward, he's different with animals. I watch Wyatt's gloved hands as they delicately sweep across Chewy's leg. "Doesn't look infected," he says. "But we can't risk it."

Wyatt wipes it with antiseptic pads and Chewy doesn't seem bothered by it at all. Wyatt's hands move with confidence, and my own hand burns thinking about his in mine. I need to think about literally anything else.

"I think Loki brought Chewy here."

"How come?"

"Do you know how sleipnir were created?"

"No. I'd love for you to tell me though."

For some reason that makes my face hot, but I ignore it as I tell him the story Mom once told me. "When peace came between the Vanir and the Aesir—the once-feuding gods who would come together later to create Asgard after the war—Asgard needed a wall to protect against the giants."

Juniper sighs at that, but I keep going.

"One day, a stranger arrived with his horse, Svadilfari, and told Odin he could build the wall for him in exchange for the sun, the moon, and Odin's wife, Frigg. The gods thought the stranger demanded too much, but they desperately wanted the wall, so they said he could have his reward if he completed the task in one season. The stranger agreed, but only if he could have Svadilfari's help. Loki said it was a good trade because he knew it was impossible to complete the wall in time, and he convinced Odin to take the deal. Better to have a half-complete wall than no wall at all."

Wyatt's hands stop momentarily at the mention of Loki before he keeps wrapping the gauze.

"But the gods didn't know that Svadilfari was superstrong, helping to build the wall faster than anyone expected. The stranger was going to win and the gods blamed Loki for making Odin take the deal. So, to get out of trouble, Loki transformed himself into a beautiful mare and seduced Svadilfari, making Svadilfari chase him long enough to miss the deadline. Later, Loki became pregnant with Svadilfari's foal and gave birth to the first sleipnir. Odin claimed the sleipnir as his prize for Loki's bad advice and gifted them to the valkyries. They've lived in Asgard ever since, waiting for Ragnarök."

Wyatt finishes wrapping Chewy's leg and secures it. He stands up and pats Chewy on the neck. "Your grandpa sounds like a real handful," Wyatt says to him.

Chewy blows out his lips and stomps one of his good hooves.

"So Loki stole Chewy and rode him here?"

Juniper says, "Even the Aesir cannot cross the Bifröst without one."

"Loki has a strong connection with them," I say. "It makes sense."

A playful look crosses Wyatt's face and he leans in to the sleipnir. "You're not secretly Loki, are you?" Chewy looks indignant at that and flips his mane. Wyatt smiles. "Just checking." He takes Chewy by the reins. "Let's get you an X-ray."

"Hey," I say, stopping him. He looks at me, eyebrows raised and expectant. "For what it's worth, I had a nice time last night. All things considered."

Wyatt blushes and clears his throat, looking at Chewy again. "Yeah. Me too."

Seeing him blush makes it feel like I'm full of bees. I clear my throat. I don't know what to do with my hands, so I clasp them and then unclasp them, put them on the stall door, then shove them behind my back. Super casual.

I stammer out, "I, uh, was thinking of—thought you might— Hmm. I got you this." I pull out the bottle of beeswax lotion from my pocket and gesture with it. "It's no biggie. Just a little something. For your hands."

Wyatt gently takes it from me, eyes softening. "Really?"

"Yeah," I say. Awkward. I turn and take Juniper by the elbow. "Well, we're going to, uh, go."

"Right. Yeah. Me too." Wyatt pushes his glasses up and bows his head.

"Thanks for, uh, everything."

"Yes, thank you, Wyatt!" Juniper says.

"Yeah, no—no problem."

I back up, watching him, but Wyatt's head is down. I think I forgot how to be a functioning person. "Okay. Bye, Chewy!" I turn and run before I have a chance to look like a bigger idiot.

22

THE SUN HAS ALREADY SET BY THE TIME WE MAKE IT TO THE Dragon's Den, but the night is calm and quiet, and the fireflies have started to come out. Lanterns glow around the outdoor dining area, attracting moths, and laughter from the Dragon's Den spills out into the warm air. I'm lost in thought when Juniper asks, "Do you like him?"

I lift my head off the picnic table. She doesn't need to clarify who *him* is. "Wyatt's cool."

Juniper rests her chin on her fists and sighs. She's hardly touched her jalapeño poppers. "Yes, but do you like him?"

"I guess. It's . . . complicated."

"Are you making it complicated or is it actually?"

"I don't make things complicated."

Juniper makes a noncommittal noise. "Will you tell him about Valhalla?"

"I don't know."

"Will you ever?"

"I don't know."

"It was good that you brought the sleipnir to him. He is a kind person."

"I think so, too." When I remember the way our hands touched at the feast, my insides get all warm and gooey like s'mores. Cozy. Like home.

But Loki is here somewhere. And that fact alone makes everything not so perfect.

"What of your—our sisters?" Juniper asks. "Shall we tell them about the sleipnir?"

"I guess. But unless Chewy can conjure the Bifröst so we can take him home, I'm not sure what we can do with him. And we still don't know where Mom is, and we're no closer to finding Loki. Everything is such a mess." I hold my head in my hands, digging my fingers in my hair.

"We must work together."

"We are."

"All of us?"

I look at her, waiting.

Juniper says, softly, "'A pine tree alone on a hill, once part of a forest but the forest is gone, has no bark or needles to shelter it.' That's what my Amma says."

"What does it mean?"

"If you have no one to support you, you do not have anything. Why are you hesitant to talk to Reagan, or Prima?"

Something in me snaps. It's small, like a hair tie around my wrist, but it hurts.

I tried with Prima. I really did. Reagan is always easier to talk to. But Prima? She's stubborn, and aloof, and a know-it-all. And after a while, why would I keep trying to get through to her? She's doing her own thing finding Mom and I'm doing mine to stop Ragnarök.

The last thing I need is a lecture on getting along. "Can we talk about something else?"

"Sure. Apologies."

Before I can say I'm sorry too, she turns toward the sound of footsteps padding in the soft grass, heading in our direction.

"Hey," Wyatt says.

I sit bolt upright as he takes a seat at our table next to Juniper. "Chewy okay?" I ask.

"All good. He's got a mild sprain, but nothing's broken. And the cut in his leg is pretty shallow. He's resting in the stall next to Gamgee. I think Gamgee is excited for a new friend."

I can't decide if Wyatt looks better in the T-shirt he's wearing now or his suit of armor. I shove a chip full of guac in my mouth and avert my gaze.

Juniper mouths at me: *Tell him.*

I shake my head and swallow. A sharp edge of chip scrapes my throat as it goes down and I take a long chug of my drink.

But Wyatt isn't stupid. He notices something going on, and he looks between the two of us. "What's up?"

"Nothing," I say.

Trudy saves the moment by appearing, to check on us. She smiles as she walks over.

"How're we doing? The poppers no good?" she asks Juniper. "I had the kitchen fire them special for you."

Juniper shrugs, apologetic. "I am not hungry."

"You feeling okay, Juniper?" Wyatt asks.

She nods and tries to smile, but I can tell she's bothered. I think she might be homesick, especially after talking about her grandma. She drops her eyes to the table and crosses her arms in front of her as Trudy clears her area.

"No problem," says Trudy. "You know where they'll be. Can I get you anything, sir knight?"

Wyatt smiles and says, "No, thanks."

Trudy winks. "Okay, let me know if you change your mind."

"We'll be heading out soon," I say. "Prima's tab again."

"You got it. Be safe getting home, okay?"

Before I can assure her we'll be fine, something makes me pause. "Why do you say that?"

Trudy glances around, lips pursed and brow furrowed. I don't think she expected me to actually ask. "I've just been seeing a shady person lately. Gives me the creeps."

Wyatt braces his hands on the table. "What did they look like?"

Trudy looks surprised for a moment, then says, "I'm not really sure. Weird vibes. They were lurking in the shadows over by the castle earlier."

"By the tree?" I'm on my feet.

"Yeah, I guess, but—"

"The third page!" I take off, sprinting for Yggdrasil.

Wyatt gives me a boost and I pull myself up the tree, climbing toward the knot where we found the first page.

"Be careful!" Reagan calls from below. She stands with Wyatt and Juniper, the book from Pagebound clutched to her chest. While Wyatt followed me to the tree, Juniper went home to get Reagan. There was no time to lose. Any second Ravenswood will be swarming with monsters.

"Juniper," I call down, "I thought you said Yggdrasil would tell you if there was trouble."

"I did, but it is not so simple, I—" Juniper fiddles with the glass charm holding Yggdrasil's seed still around her neck, nervously glancing around. "Are we certain about this? What if Trudy was mistaken?"

"There's no harm in checking," Wyatt says.

I haul myself up to the branch below the knot and shove my hand in the trunk like before. Instead of the soft vellum, I touch something different, making me flinch back at first. It's cold and hard, the opposite of paper. When I take it out, it's surprisingly light and I hold it to the moonlight. It's a silver bracelet, the twisted metal shaped like a U. Runes are etched into the surface, and on each end is a wolf's head, snarling at the other.

A shiver runs down my spine. I can barely say it. "Fenrir."

"What?" Reagan calls.

I climb down and hold it out to her. "A bracelet."

"It's an arm ring," Reagan says, taking it, with raised eyebrows.

"Arm ring, bracelet, same diff."

"Big diff," Reagan says.

"Whatever it is, it's Fenrir."

Wyatt's eyes go big. "Fenrir? Isn't he supposed to be chained up?"

"Loki placed it here to call him to Ravenswood." Everyone stares at me. "It makes sense, doesn't it? The dream I had, the vision from the raven. It all leads back to Fenrir."

Juniper looks like she's going to puke.

Reagan shakes her head and sputters. "Wait—dream? Raven vision? What?"

I didn't mean for her to find out this way. I shift and fold my arms over my chest. "You wouldn't have believed me. Prima pretty much said so, back when I saw all those ravens. One of them gave me a vision—Fenrir on Odin's throne."

Reagan's gray eyes are hard with fear, and she looks back at the

arm ring and then at Juniper and Wyatt. Wyatt has his hands inter-
locked on the top of his head and Juniper looks as pale as she did the
night I met her.

"Loki is setting Fenrir free," I say. "That's how it goes down. It's
how it'll always go down."

"What did you see in your dream?" Reagan asks.

"Draugar swarming Ravenswood, a solar eclipse, and a giant wolf.
It said 'Time's up.' It all adds up."

Juniper leans so hard on her staff, she looks like she'll keel over.

"Don't worry," I tell her. "We got it before it could do any damage."

She nods, but she doesn't look any better.

Wyatt looks troubled. He chews on his lip, then says, "He's changing things."

"What?" I ask.

"He's changing things. Loki. His MO. Before, he used the pages of
that book. Now he's using a silver arm ring? Why?"

"Does it matter?"

Wyatt furrows his brow but doesn't have an answer. I'm just
relieved we got to it first.

"Reagan, is the fjötra still up?"

Reagan tucks the book under her arm and puts her hand on the
tree. She looks skyward, then says, "Yes."

Relief floods through me. We foiled Loki's plan again.

"So now what do we do with it?" Wyatt asks, looking at the arm
ring in Reagan's hand.

"Destroy it," I say. "The One Ring style."

Juniper lunges forward, gasping. "No!" She looks at all of us with
wide eyes and wrings her hands around her staff. "What if there is
valuable information we can glean from it?"

"Juniper's right," says Reagan. She holds it up to me. "You know who else should hear about this."

⋈

We find Prima in her and Reagan's bedroom, the drawers of her dresser pulled out and her volleyball bag open on her bed. It looks like she's packing.

"Are you going somewhere?" I ask, standing in the doorway.

She stuffs a couple of socks with some other clothes into her bag and zips it shut, then looks up at me, Reagan, and Juniper. Wyatt went home to check on Chewy. I sort of wish he was here. Him being around makes me feel better.

When she sees us, Prima's expression is flat—tired—and she sighs. "Good. You're back. I'm going to see Muriel."

"Muriel? The retired valkyrie?" Reagan asks.

I remember Muriel coming to visit us when I was really little. She's one of the last remaining valkyries on Midgard outside our family, though she hung up her shield a long time ago. She lives in Florida, like a normal grandma.

"She can help us find Mom." Prima throws the backpack over her shoulder.

Reagan steps past me into the room before she can leave. "We found this in Yggdrasil." She puts the arm ring in Prima's hand.

"What is this?"

"It's from Fenrir," I say. "We think Loki is using it to call him here to Midgard."

Juniper holds the glass vial with Yggdrasil's seed tightly in her fist, looking queasy. I don't blame her. It's like Loki is playing 5D chess and we're playing checkers.

"And?" she says.

I throw my arms wide. "*And*, it's proof about Ragnarök!"

Prima scoffs.

"There's a sleipnir in the stables right now. We found it earlier. What more proof do you need? Ragnarök is here. Whether you like it or not."

"And what? You're going to fight, Bryn? You're not ready for it. You haven't even learned to control your weapons yet."

That hurts deep, and she knows it.

Reagan puts the Asgardian book down on Prima's bed. "Bryn and I reinforced the fjötra around Ravenswood, but without Mom, I'm not sure how long it will last."

"Then that's why I'm going to see Muriel. We need to find Mom. I can't keep calling hospitals or morgues."

"We *need* to use seidr to find her," I say.

The air around Prima's head warps like the asphalt in summer. "No. End of story."

"How are we supposed to match up against Loki and Fenrir and the armies of Hel if we're not using every tool we have?"

Prima huffs loudly through her nose. "How do you know it's Fenrir?"

I blink. "It's obvious."

"It could also be Odin's wolves." She points to the two heads on the arm ring. "Geri and Freki."

Along with ravens, wolves are Odin's favorite animal. He feeds them scraps off the table in Valhalla. They are loyal protectors.

Reagan looks at me, realization creeping across her face. "It's possible Mom put it there, and you didn't notice the first time you checked."

My face burns. I know it wasn't there before, but I can't prove it.

That seems like a good enough reason for Prima though, and she hands the arm ring back to Reagan.

"Reagan, you're in charge. I'll be back in a few days. If I leave now, I can make it to Muriel's retirement home in two days."

"But she's like . . . a billion years old!" I say.

"She's still a valkyrie. She'll know what to do."

"You can't leave! Have you tried calling her?"

"She's, like you said, a billion years old. Trudy's letting me borrow her car, so I won't be gone long."

"But—"

"Reagan. Call me if there's anything, news or whatever."

Reagan nods. Juniper picks up the Asgardian book from Prima's bed and clutches it tightly to her chest. She hasn't said a word this whole time.

Prima pushes past me. "You're out of your depth, Bryn. You have no idea what you're doing. Let me handle this."

⋈

The following day, I'm dead on my feet. I chug energy drinks to stay functional, but I know I look rough. I feel like I haven't slept in weeks.

Last night, Juniper cried in bed. She tried to keep quiet, but I could hear her hiccuping every so often and sniffling into her pillow until she eventually fell asleep, only to call out to Amma in her nightmares. It kept me up, but I don't blame her. For hours, I laid there with my bow next to my pillow, my eyes peeled open and staring at the ceiling, listening for howling wolves to cut through the night. Only until the sun rose did I manage to sleep a couple hours before work, but that triggered my own nightmares. Berserkers, and blood, and snow. I should have never gone to sleep at all.

We're running out of time. Juniper said if she doesn't get back to Utgard soon, the giants will think she's been captured, and it'll be grounds for war, and Prima talking to Muriel will be for nothing. Ragnarök or not, war is war.

But it's hard to imagine a war is coming when guests keep filtering in and out of the gift shop, happy and carefree while buying souvenirs and T-shirts, asking me if I had any Prince James action figures for sale.

After coming home to change and finding Juniper and Reagan going over the spellbook together and eating yet another box of pizza (I never thought I'd be so sick of something like pizza), Juniper and I head to the stables later in the evening to meet Wyatt. We see Chewy trotting laps around the fenced field with his injured leg wrapped up in gauze.

"He's looking better!" I say to Wyatt, who watches from the fence. "Great job."

"I barely did anything," he says brightly.

"Don't be so modest."

Wyatt asks, "Any luck with the arm ring?"

I shake my head. I'm not in the mood to talk about it. Prima's words still ring in my ears.

Juniper steps up to the fence, peering at Chewy with cautious, wide eyes. "Hello, friend?"

Chewy throws his head and ignores her, instead coming to me and nudging my shoulder. I rub his nose and he leans into my touch.

"He hates me," Juniper says.

"That's not true," says Wyatt. "He's just independent."

"I am half-giant. The sleipnir are warhorses, trained to be wary of enemies of Asgard."

"You're not an enemy of Asgard," I say.

"To him, I am."

"You just have to speak the same language. And Chewy's language is food. Food always gets me on someone's good side." I hand her some oat cakes hanging from a nearby sack.

Juniper hefts them warily, and Chewy gives her a sidelong glance. He looks away from her, then back at the oat cakes in her hand, then looks away once more as if he's debating whether or not to trust her. Then, succumbing to temptation, Chewy snags one of the oat cakes from Juniper's hand and crunches on it loudly.

Juniper finally smiles, but it falls again. "I must find a way to contact Utgard."

"Maybe Chewy can get you there. He can cross between Asgard and Midgard. Who's to say he can't get to Utgard, too? You could pop over and tell them you're fine in person, then come back."

Juniper's eyebrows shoot up. "Will it work?"

"I'm not sure anyone's tried. Would sleipnir be welcome in Jotunheim?" I give Chewy a solid pat on the neck.

Juniper shrugs. "I do not know."

"How does he go between Asgard and Midgard anyway?" Wyatt asks.

"When a sleipnir runs through the sky, he kicks up a storm and it makes a rainbow, The Bifröst, a bridge between worlds. I don't think it'd be too different to get to Jotunheim. But it's just a theory.... How about we take him for a test ride? I bet he's itching to stretch his legs, too. Aren't you, Chewy?"

He lifts his injured leg, like a pointer dog, and gestures toward the gate. It's as clear a sign as any that he wants to go for a run.

"By ride, you mean fly," Wyatt says, amazed.

I nod, grinning.

Juniper takes a step back and shakes her head. "No, thank you. I prefer my steeds to keep all four hooves on the ground, where there is dirt, and roots, and safety." Her eyes dart to Chewy. "Besides, I am not sure Chewy will let me."

Chewy rears his head back and snorts, proving her point. Taking oat cakes from a giant must be one thing; giving her a ride is another.

"Okay then," I say. "I'll do it myself."

I have to stand on a stack of wooden feed boxes to reach the stirrup before I can pull myself onto Chewy's saddle. I can't help but imagine what it must be like riding one of these into battle. If I was on the other side, I'm sure I'd run screaming in the opposite direction. I scratch Chewy's neck, and he pushes his head toward me, enjoying the attention.

Wyatt folds his arms over his chest. "You're going to Jotunheim? Alone?"

"Just testing his limits. Let's see if he can even make the trip, or if it even works."

Wyatt looks worried.

"I promise. I won't go too far. There and back."

"Why am I having a hard time believing you? See, you get this look in your eyes—" He points two fingers at his own. "Devious."

I smile. Am I that obvious? Fighting with Prima is making me antsy, more than I thought. Something stirs in me, and I remember what Juniper said, about the lone tree on a hill, and the part of me that wants to be alone is a lot weaker than the part that doesn't. "Fine. Come with me then, if you're so worried."

He scrunches up his face, debating himself.

"Just a quick lap in the clouds. Haven't you always wanted to ride a flying horse?"

Chewy stomps impatiently, ready to go.

"Come on," I say and hold out my hand to Wyatt. "Trust me?"

Wyatt looks up at me, dragging his teeth over his bottom lip. He knocks his glasses up his nose, then grabs my hand, and I help haul him up behind me. He settles in at my back and I'm suddenly very aware of how close he is. He seems to realize it too, because he adjusts himself so his chest just barely meets my back. That's somehow worse. I try not to focus on it as I take Chewy's reins.

"How do you feel, buddy?"

"I'm okay," Wyatt says.

"I was talking to Chewy."

"Right."

Juniper opens the gate for us and Chewy heads toward it at a trot. Nice and easy.

"I think now is a good time to tell you I'm afraid of hei—" Wyatt can't even finish his sentence as Chewy takes off at a full gallop. Wyatt barely has time to grip me tight around my torso—otherwise he'd fall right off the back—as Chewy charges through the dirt path winding through the woods toward the lake.

The path is dark, but Chewy doesn't seem to care as he hauls onward. Light emanates from below us as his hooves spark with lightning. Every time they strike the ground, it looks like sparklers on the Fourth of July.

Wyatt relaxes his grip on me after a moment. I can feel his breath on my neck as he lets out a small laugh. Chewy is fast, like we're sitting on top of a race car. The world blurs and tears fill my eyes as the wind hits them. Chewy seems to be enjoying himself, too. He raises his head and shakes out his mane, like he's finally free.

We break out of the woods and hit the beach. The sun has only just set, but Lake Michigan is pitch-black at this hour, the water like ink.

Chewy careers us down the beach, kicking up sand, and sending a shock of cold through me as the wind kicks up.

The beach turns back in toward the woods, but Chewy doesn't seem to slow down.

He's heading right for the water's edge.

"Bryn," Wyatt cautions.

I snap Chewy's reins, and Wyatt buries his face against me as sparks in Chewy's hooves shine bright, then Chewy tears across the water, running over the waves like solid ground.

There's a nighttime skyline tour boat, and we pass by it in a blink— no doubt leaving anyone who saw us with a few questions and a vow to stop at the fifth tequila shot—we're so fast.

My eyes water but my heart thunders with excitement as Chewy takes us across the lake, leaping over cresting waves like they're nothing, taking us farther across the water until Ravenswood is a strip of lights on the horizon, far from prying eyes.

"Up, Chewy!" I cry. "To Jotunheim!"

The wind drowns out Wyatt's scream when Chewy takes a running leap and launches us into the air. Storm clouds gather under his hooves, and Wyatt chants something over and over into my back, like a prayer.

This high up, Chicago looks like a sheet of Christmas lights—the farther Chewy climbs, the dimmer the lights get.

He takes us up through a cloud, pitching us into total darkness until he bursts through the top.

A million stars explode from the night, stretching across the deep black sky, swirling with dust and gas so vast and so endless, I forget to breathe.

All around us, stars twinkle and shine. The bright cloud of the Milky Way cuts through the night. Auroras in green and purple roll like waves over it all.

It's the entire universe, right here.

I'm about to tell Chewy to take us higher when I realize he's slowing down. He comes to a stop on a cloud, standing on it like solid ground.

"You okay, bud?" I ask, petting Chewy's side.

He snorts and the sparks under his hooves go out.

"No go?"

Chewy huffs and I lean over to see him raising his bad leg. It must hurt too much. He can't run to any realm on his own. Like Juniper, Chewy's stuck on Midgard.

"I pushed you too hard," I say. "I'm sorry."

We'll have to find some other way to contact Utgard.

I give Chewy a moment to rest and turn to look at Wyatt. "Hey," I say.

Wyatt's muttering to himself. "We're on a cloud—"

"Wyatt."

"How are we breathing right now? It's not scientifically possible—"

"Wyatt!"

"What!" Wyatt unburies his face from my back and his jaw drops.

"It's Yggdrasil. Holding up the universe."

Wyatt's grip on me loosens. He's forgotten about his fear of heights for a moment as the view completely overwhelms him. I catch the look in his eye, and it can only be described as ashtonishment.

Growing up so close to Chicago, I've only seen the night sky as a hazy orange. Now it's so bright with starlight, it's hard to believe this is what we've been missing.

"Whoa," he says.

Whoa is right.

Everything is so quiet, and so peaceful. I suddenly feel very small, and in a way, it's kind of comforting. My problems don't seem so big anymore.

"I've never seen it in person before," Wyatt says, his voice soft. "Sometimes I forget stars even exist."

"It's hard to look up when we've got so many problems down below."

Wyatt makes a strangled noise and says, "*Below*. Don't remind me."

"Wow." I can feel him shaking. "You weren't kidding. You really are afraid of heights."

"I'm trying to expand my horizons. Literally."

"You're not going to bear out on me while we're up here, are you?"

"Not if I can help it."

"Chewy wouldn't let anything bad happen to us, would you?" I scratch him on the neck and Chewy makes a satisfied whickering noise. I look at Wyatt again, admiring the way the starlight softens his face and glints off his glasses. "Why did you come with me if you were afraid of heights?"

"I didn't want you to be alone," he says.

"You really didn't have to."

"No, but I wanted to."

I am thankful for the dim light. He can't make out the heat rising on my face.

"It's not really heights I'm afraid of. More of a fear of falling. You're not scared?" Wyatt asks.

"Not so much anymore." He's still got a hold of me, one hand planted securely on the small of my back. It makes me feel safe.

He nudges his glasses back up his nose as he looks to the sky again. When he does, I catch a whiff of something familiar. Beeswax? Is he using the lotion I got him? My heart skips.

I study him for a long moment before I look back up at the stars.

I have a million things I want to say to Wyatt right now, but the words get tangled on their way to my tongue, and I end up biting the inside of my cheek for the attempt. Watching Wyatt staring up at the stars while we're alone, where it's so peaceful, like we're the only two people left in the universe, makes me realize that this is exactly what I want, but I can't imagine how I'm supposed to say it without sounding completely unhinged.

Because what if he doesn't feel the same way about me? What if I ruin our friendship?

Why would he like me, anyway?

Maybe this is enough. I'm okay with enough.

Wyatt takes a chance and looks down. Chicago is a splotch of lights below us, the lake a sea of black. It's a long way down.

Wyatt swallows loudly and closes his eyes. "I shouldn't have done that. Distract me."

"Okay. With what?"

"I don't know. Something."

I smile. "Sure, how about other things I'm scared of? Let's see. Animatronics... Spiders... Window air-conditioning units."

That last one makes him laugh. "Really?"

"I'm afraid they'll fall out and crush me!"

"Okay, valid."

My distraction seems to be working. Wyatt's grip has let up a little on my hoodie. "Your turn," I say. "What are you afraid of?"

"Going berserk." He answers it so quickly, it's like it slipped out. Immediately, I'm sorry I asked, as he glances at me then away just as fast and clears his throat, like he's ashamed. He shifts slightly and adds, "What happened at the feast was my worst nightmare. I've worked really hard to control it, but it gets harder when my adrenaline's up. I don't do well on planes or subways, because I'm so afraid I'll change on accident. I can't risk it. Imagine being trapped in a tin can with a bear. Even driving freaks me out.... If I can walk somewhere, I will."

"So roller coasters are off the table?"

"I know, I'm boring."

"I didn't say that." I go quiet for a second, then ask, "So you're not afraid of performing in front of thousands of people every day?"

"Doing that is easy. When I'm in character, for once I know what to say, what to do. I can lose myself in being the Black Knight."

I don't know what to say to that, so I don't say anything.

"At the party though, I lost control. I wasn't me anymore. It was like something else had taken over, and it was terrifying. And now Loki can turn me into a weapon any time he wants. And I don't know if the next time he does, I'll be able to fight it like I did. I just don't want to hurt anyone I care about." Wyatt looks at me for a brief second, then takes a deep breath and draws his eyes skyward. "It's funny," he says. "I used to want to be an astronaut when I was a kid. Totally obsessed with space. That was before I knew I was a berserker though. This is the closest I'll ever get. So . . . thanks."

My face gets hot when I smile. I know I should tell him about Valhalla, but I can't. Especially not now. This moment's actually kind of nice, and I don't want to ruin it.

"So there's other realms out there?" he asks, tipping his head to the Milky Way.

"Yep. But if Loki has his way, there won't be for long. Come on," I say, nudging Chewy. "Let's go home."

Wyatt puts his arms around me again, and it makes my stomach do a little somersault, but I blame it on Chewy as he leaps from the cloud.

Wyatt's arms are warm and reassuring around me, even as our butts rise out of the saddle when Chewy nosedives right for the waves coming up to meet us. At the last second, Chewy levels us out and glides into a solid gallop over the lake. We're riding faster than the wind.

The strip of lights that is Ravenswood starts to widen on the horizon, and I have half an instinct to pull up on the reins and slow Chewy down just so I can spend a minute longer out here with Wyatt, but I'm not fast enough. Chewy has us back on solid ground.

Wyatt can't leap off Chewy's back any quicker and lands on the dirt, letting out a relieved sigh. "Actually, that wasn't too bad," he says.

I'm about to say something to him, anything, but I'm stopped short when we hear the screams coming from the woods.

23

I GRAB WYATT'S OUTSTRETCHED HAND AND HAUL HIM BACK onto Chewy's saddle before kicking us into a gallop again.

We crash through the trees, following the screams, but when we get there, Chewy rises up on his hind legs and kicks, terrified.

In the woods, Juniper is fighting for her life against a troop of draugar. Just like the one I fought. Only there's more, at least a dozen.

Decked out in rotting armor, chain mail, and helmets, and armed with swords and axes and knives, they move so fast through the trees that the only way I can track them is by the orange glow of their eyes. Seeing their lipless grins and skeletal faces makes my blood run cold.

Juniper throws seed bombs. They explode in bright pops of colorful light like fireworks as thick roots burst out of the dirt. There are too many draugar though. They dodge out of the way, juking and weaving through the roots like running backs, charging her.

She lobs a rosebud right into the closest draug's face and the red flowers blossom like a mask over its eyes and mouth. Its muffled howls go quiet when she squeezes her fist and thorny vines crush his head.

When she sees us, she cries, "Help me!"

Wyatt is the first to leap into action. He jumps off Chewy's back, not waiting a second longer, and rushes toward the closest draug. The draug slashes down with a hatchet at Wyatt's head, but Wyatt dodges, grabs the handle, and elbows the draug in the chest. If it had guts, it would be wheezing, but the draug seems unfazed. It gnashes its teeth at Wyatt as Wyatt twists the hatchet out of its hands.

Like a batter, he winds up and swings, knocking the draug's helmet off its skull. It roars at him, black tongue out, and Wyatt swings again. This time the draug grabs the axe and stops him, grinning toothily in Wyatt's face.

Wyatt shrinks away from the smell of rot, grits his teeth, and smashes his forehead into the draug's nose-hole. It stumbles back, clutching its face, as Wyatt kills it with a final swing. Silver mist explodes out of the draug as it turns to dust.

Wyatt spins around. "Are these—"

"Yeah!" I answer.

Chewy rears up and kicks a draug in the chest with one of his hooves, sending the draug stumbling to the ground, where Juniper lashes it in a cage of thorns.

I roll off Chewy's back and nearly get chopped in half by a draug, coming for my neck. I dodge out of the way, bending like limp spaghetti noodles to avoid getting hit.

I reach for my necklace to summon my armor, but the draug whips its hand out and clutches my wrist, stopping me right before I can. Its bony fingers are so cold and its hold on me is as solid as ice.

I stare at the draug, it stares back, grinning at me with its nasty skeleton face.

Does it know what I was going to do? Is this thing...smart?

I wind my wrist, breaking its hold on me, and elbow it in the chest, then pull its helmet off its head.

The draug screams like grinding metal as it slashes with its sword, but I duck at the last second and its sword wedges deep into a tree behind me. The draug tries to wrench it free, but it's stuck.

I come up and punch it in the side of the head, smashing its face into the trunk. Silver mist washes all over me as the draug dies.

"What happened?" I ask Juniper as I try to pull the draug's sword out of the tree. It's really stuck in there, and I can't get a good grip. My palms are too sweaty. It won't budge.

"Just after you left, Yggdrasil warned me!" Juniper says. "I have been trying to hold them off, but they are too many!"

Juniper chucks another seed bomb at a draug and it explodes at its feet, blowing its legs out from underneath it before it can jump Wyatt from behind.

Wyatt spins around and nods his thanks just as another draug charges him. He reaches back and throws his hatchet.

The blade embeds in the draug's chest armor with a solid *thunk*, and the draug slows to a stop, but it still stands. With its glowing orange eyes, it looks down at the hatchet and then looks at Wyatt, its face a permanent smile as it wrenches the hatchet from its chest. It screeches at Wyatt.

Wyatt does the smart thing and backs up.

Unsheathing a sword, the draug rushes toward him, but I won't let it.

I sprint forward and leap, landing on the draug's shoulders.

I put both hands on its rusty helmet and spin it all the way around its head, covering its eyes. When it screams, it sounds like it's screaming into a bucket. It flails blindly with me still clinging on. World's worst piggyback ride.

The draug smells like earth, and rotting meat, and mold, and I want to puke but I don't let go.

The draug grabs me by my hood, hauls me over its shoulder, and slams me, back first, into the ground.

I roll—

Flash of steel.

Pain slices through my left arm. It happens so fast, I don't have time to cry out.

The draug raises its sword again.

Like a banshee, James comes screaming out of the trees and tackles the draug to the ground. It's a tangle of limbs and swords. James kicks out and his knee connects with the draug's chin. Its head snaps back with a mighty crack as bones break.

"Oh my God!" James scrambles to his feet as the draug dies. Then he grabs my arm, hauls me to my feet, and hides behind me. "What is that?" His voice cracks.

My left arm is heavy as lead and I shake James off. Wyatt's busy fighting two draugar at once.

Before I can do anything to help him, another draug spots me and James. It hisses like a snake as it melts into the dirt, disappearing as easily as going underwater.

James grabs me again, clutching onto me so hard it hurts. "Where'd it go? What's it doing?"

Frantically, I search the ground for any sign of the draug, but I can't see it. Then James lets out a yelp exactly as a bony hand grabs my ankle.

Like water, the ground opens up under us, and the draug pulls us down.

My arms just barely slam into solid ground as the rest of my body sinks. James flails next to me, screaming, clutching the grass. His eyes are wide, terrified. "Wyatt!"

I can't talk. I pull up clumps of grass, digging my nails in, but the draug is too strong.

I open my mouth and dirt floods in.

The draug has me. It won't let go. I'm going to drown.

The only thing I can think about is my nightmare coming true.

Wyatt kills another draug, sees us, and flings himself toward us, arms out, and I grab his hand. James grabs the other.

Wyatt clenches his teeth and pulls. My arm feels like it's going to pop out of its socket.

James screams, "It's got us! It's got us!"

The ground is swallowing me up. I can't breathe. Dirt's in my nose, in my ears.

Wyatt, I try to say, but I can't.

He bares his teeth, his fingers hard around my wrist. He looks so scared. His eyes flash amber. He's slowing us down, but we're almost under. "Juniper!" he yells.

But Juniper is trapped. More draugar surround her as she shields herself with a cage of roots. She stares at us, horrified.

With a howl, a draug near Juniper drops, a knife in its neck.

Juniper yelps, clutching her staff as another knife flies past her head, landing in a draug's forehead behind her.

"Reagan!" she cries.

My sister comes out of the trees, silver armor shining, as knives appear between her outstretched hands and fly like arrows. The draugar go down in a shower of metal, howling. She summons her weapons from nothing, throwing them one after the other, each landing true.

Wyatt's grip on me never wavers. "I got you. Hold on!"

I'm running out of air. My lungs burn.

Juniper, with Reagan, finishes off the last of the draugar that surround her.

In a rush, Juniper throws a seed bomb at us and holds her hand in a claw over her head, eyes glowing green.

Next to us, roots in the shape of a fist explode out of the ground, holding the draug in its clutches. It thrashes helplessly against Juniper's magic, screaming with rage. When the draug lets us go, James and I stop sinking, but we're still trapped in the ground. Reagan runs to Wyatt and grabs us too, helping us out of the dirt, and I gasp as air rushes into my lungs, spitting and swearing.

Juniper squeezes her fist and the roots surrounding the draug snap tight, squishing the draug like a bug.

Sometimes I forget just how powerful she is.

That's the last of them. All that's left are piles of rotting armor and weapons strewn everywhere.

Everything goes quiet except for our heavy breathing.

Reagan's looking at James with pale trepidation as her armor fades. Wyatt falls back on his butt, dirt smeared on his face. Juniper scans the woods, clutching her staff.

James and I are both covered in dirt. Pain catches up with me and shoots up my arm. I stumble to a nearby tree and prop myself against it as James freaks out.

"Were those zombies? What is going on? Oh my God!" He holds his head in his hands, his hair spiking through his fingers, as he stares at the scattering of armor around us.

"Those are the creatures that attacked my village in Utgard," Juniper says, breathless. "Draugar."

Reagan pushes loose strands of her hair out of her face, still staring at James. Her valkyrie secret's out.

My left arm feels like it's on fire. When I press my hand to it, I clench my teeth and try to tough it out. Tears prick my eyes, and I hold my breath so as not to cry.

Juniper picks up one of the helmets, emotions running wild across her face. "The draugar are now in Midgard...I failed."

"It's not your fault. It's Loki," I say.

Wyatt must hear something in my voice because he furrows his brow. "Bryn, are you hurt?"

Reagan rounds on me, panicked. "What!"

"I'm fine," I say, even though I feel a warm, sticky liquid flowing through my fingers. "All good." I grab one of the draug's swords—in case they come back—and try to walk, but the world tips underneath me.

Wyatt's at my side in a second. "Let me see." I don't make a fuss as he gently takes my arm. "You're bleeding," he says.

"Oh good, I thought I was leaking."

"Not funny."

Reagan goes pale as she looks at my arm. "We don't have any more mead," she says.

Wyatt catches my eye. His are normal again. "Let's get you patched up."

24

"Ow!" It stings as Wyatt dabs at the cut in my arm.

"Sorry," he says, pausing, before pressing the alcohol swab to my skin again. It still stings but not as bad this time, and I keep holding my T-shirt sleeve up for him. We're sitting on stools in the stables, the first aid kit propped open at Wyatt's feet, and I can finally see the damage. The gash is about five inches long, but not that deep. I got lucky. The blade is awfully sharp for a piece of junk—I can tell just looking at it, lying on the floor next to my crumpled and bloody sweatshirt.

"My favorite hoodie. Ruined," I say.

Wyatt's mouth twitches into a smile but he's still focusing on what he's doing. "I can patch that up for you, too."

"Thanks.... It's weird, it's like those draugar were smart. One stopped me from summoning my armor."

"Are you sure? How would it know you're a valkyrie?"

"Yeah... it doesn't make sense."

Outside, Reagan's and James's voices carry over to us. They're shouting near the fence. I can't hear what they're saying, but if I had to take a guess, it's a long overdue conversation. Reagan holds herself tight while James presses his hands together, pleading. Neither of them look happy.

I was afraid what Reagan might think once she found out James had started helping us. It was only a matter of time, but I guess the Band-Aid had to be ripped off sooner rather than later.

Juniper mentioned she was going to Yggdrasil, which leaves me and Wyatt, alone.

Chewy snoozes in his stall, all eight legs curled up under him. Gamgee is awake, watching us over his stall door, like he's a chaperone.

"I've been meaning to ask," I say. "The name Gamgee. Like Sam, from Lord of the Rings?"

"Yeah." Wyatt tosses the bloody wipe in a bin and folds another with a pair of tweezers. "He's my favorite character."

"Wow, you are *such* a nerd."

"You say to the person helping you."

"I meant it as a compliment."

Wyatt's mouth twists into a smile, and he wipes the gash in my arm again. "And don't pretend like you're not a nerd, too. I saw your posters in your room."

I laugh. I still remember the way his arms wrapped around me when Chewy took to the sky. But somehow, with Wyatt leaning over the cut on my arm, he feels closer now than he did then. He was so scared when that draug grabbed me.

If it wasn't for him, I wouldn't be here right now. My mouth is dry and I still taste dirt. But he didn't let me go. We have a habit of saving each other, I guess.

He nudges his glasses back up his nose and leans in closer. Wyatt's eyelashes are long, and dark, and his lips are slightly pressed together as he focuses. The sharp edge of his nose catches the softness of the lamplight, and the groove of his scar looks deeper than ever.

Being this close, I can even smell him over the horses. Deodorant, and sweat, and... beeswax.

When he glances up at me, I realize I've been staring at him and tear my gaze away, pretending like I'm super interested in the patterns of the ceiling. I have to remind myself it's just lotion. It doesn't mean anything. And if Wyatt noticed me staring, he doesn't show it. I find it harder to breathe, and not because of the pain.

Outside, James and Reagan leave together, heading toward the center of the faire, no doubt continuing their shouting match along the way. If I had to guess, I don't think they're getting back together. It's one disaster after another.

The one good thing about all this is that maybe now Prima will finally believe me. It figures it would take a few monsters to make it happen.

"Do I need stitches?" I ask.

"Nah, I've seen worse. You'll be okay."

"And here I thought you were just good with animals. You seem to know what you're doing."

"Being a knight might be all pretend, but the injuries are not." The scar on his cheek twitches when he smiles.

"Like that one?" I ask, pointing to my own face. And the second I do, I know I shouldn't have, because his smile drops. "Loki?"

He looks away. "An accident."

"Horse?"

"Car."

My stomach sinks.

"My dad, he..." Wyatt shifts on his stool, trailing off. Pain darts across his face. Clearly he doesn't talk about it much.

"I didn't mean to—" I cut myself off and clamp my mouth shut. I know I talk too much, ask too many questions, never know when to stop, but I've never talked like this with anyone, especially outside my family. He has no reason to tell me, and I shouldn't have asked. "You don't have to say."

Wyatt watches me carefully before setting down the antiseptic wipe. "My dad has always been a bit of a troubled person. He's been in and out of jail my whole life. He, uh, kidnapped me when I was six."

"Are you serious?"

Wyatt nods, taping a large compress on my arm. "My mom never told my dad she was pregnant with me. They weren't together. And he never wanted kids. I was a ... *surprise*. He didn't even know until she already had me. He'd hoped the curse, or whatever, ended with him."

"He's a berserker, too?"

Wyatt nods, looking paler in the lamplight. "So when he found out about me, he took me in the night. I don't know what he planned to do with me, but he drove me out of town." A stony look comes over Wyatt's face, and he clasps his hands together so tightly, his knuckles go white. "He ran a red light and a semitruck hit our car. We rolled off the road and a piece of shrapnel or glass ..." He drags his finger above his scar. "I almost died. I should have. But I didn't. I changed.

"It was like a dream. I didn't know what was happening. I was so scared. But most of all, I was angry. And I saw my dad, out cold under the car, pinned. I remember I wanted to let him die. That this was all his fault, that he did this to me, that he's done bad things. And it would have been so easy to do nothing. But I couldn't. I lifted the car off him. Saved his life. The ambulance arrived just after I turned human again and passed out."

I can't think of anything to say. I just watch Wyatt as he stares at the lamplight for a long moment. He jolts himself out of the memory, clears his throat, and grabs a roll of gauze. "Long story short, I moved in with my uncle, my mom's brother, and my dad's been in prison, couple hours from here actually, ever since. My uncle wants to protect me, but these days I feel like I'm the one protecting him," Wyatt says, smiling despite the worry in his voice. "He took me in when I didn't have anyone else. I used to think no one could ever love me for what I was."

Neither of us speak while he starts to wrap my arm.

"Do you think it is?" I ask.

"What?"

"A curse?"

Wyatt thinks about it, then says, "No." And he finally looks me in the eye. "Not anymore."

Heat spreads over every inch of my body, and I swallow hard.

"I'm sorry," I say, "for asking, too. I didn't mean to pry."

"Don't," Wyatt says, softly. "Everything that's happened . . . I'm here now. Still alive, right? So I'm doing pretty good."

My heart might literally implode.

"My dad died before I was born," I blurt out, desperate to say anything.

"Yeah, I know. Uncle Stan's talked about him. I'm sorry," Wyatt says, sounding genuine. "But don't feel like I'm putting you on the spot."

"You shared. My turn. It's only fair."

The corner of Wyatt's mouth lifts, and that's something.

"When I was little, I made the mistake of asking if my dad was an einherjar in Valhalla, that maybe I could see him someday when I was a valkyrie. My mom looked at me and smiled, but it wasn't one of those nice smiles—but the kind that just about broke me in two. She looked like she wanted to cry, so I hugged her and promised I'd never ask about it again. Guess I never learned how to keep my mouth shut. So I'm sorry for making you talk about your dad."

"You didn't make me do anything." The tips of Wyatt's fingers brush gently against my skin, sending the hairs there on end. "Have you ever taken an einherjar to Valhalla?"

He asks it so casually without knowing the truth, and all the walls I built up inside of me come crashing down. My own smile falls sideways. I don't know how else to put it. An ice pick embeds itself in my rib cage.

Juniper is right. I should tell him. The words rush out of me before I can stop them, barely above a whisper.

"You, Wyatt. You were chosen. You were supposed to die that night the troll attacked. And I was supposed to take you."

Wyatt freezes. A dozen expressions chase one another. Confusion, shock, fear...

"Oh" is all he says after a moment.

"I'm sorry. I should have told you sooner."

He blinks a few times, and his body goes stiff. "How did you know?"

"Odin showed me a sign. That's why I was following you at the barbecue. I didn't know how or when, but I...I knew I couldn't let you die." Guilt coils tightly in my gut. "So I changed your fate."

Wyatt looks at me, steady and level, and I can't tell what he's thinking.

"That's, uh..." He clears his throat. His words sound thick. "That *sucks.*"

I shouldn't have done any of this. I jump to my feet and head for the door. "I'm so sorry. I know, Valhalla is like paradise or whatever, but I made a choice and—"

"Bryn, wait." I hear him rushing up behind me.

"I'm the worst valkyrie ever and I don't deserve—"

"Please." He grabs my hand and I whip around. We stand, inches from each other, and my face burns like it's been set on fire when our eyes meet.

I look down, and his hand is still in mine.

He looks down too, and jerks his hand back like it's electrified. The flush on his face looks as bad as mine feels.

"It's okay," he finally says. "I'm not mad. Just surprised. No offense to a god or anything, but what if *I* didn't want to go to Valhalla? Do I get any say in the matter?"

I manage to let out a strangled giggle. "I'm pretty sure 'I don't wanna' isn't in the All-Father's 'Acceptable Reasons Not to Go to Paradise' handbook."

"If there's no choice, then it doesn't sound like paradise to me." He says it so bluntly, it almost takes me aback. "You saved my life."

"I didn't give you a choice on that front either," I say, hiding behind a joke, like always.

Wyatt doesn't smile. "You know what I mean. I wouldn't be mad about you saving my life, not in a million years. So...thanks."

I scrunch my lips together. My insides turn to goo when he looks at me like that, all soft. "Don't mention it."

Wyatt gestures back to the seat. "I'm not done with you yet."

Right, I'm still actively bleeding all over the place. I sit down again and Wyatt wraps some more gauze around my arm, securing it in place.

"For real though," I say, wincing as my arm throbs. "*Don't* mention it. If my sisters find out, I'm dead meat."

"Then the secret dies with me."

When Wyatt looks up from my arm, a breath separates us. His eyes get wide all of a sudden, as if he realizes it too, and my heart jackhammers so hard, I bet he can hear it. All we have to do is close the gap, and we'd be touching.

Wyatt leans back ever so slightly—looking at me with those deep, dark brown eyes—and then, ever so slightly more, he leans toward me. Does he want to kiss me?

I can so easily picture it, pressing my lips to his. The idea is burrowing like a worm in my brain.

Kiss him, kiss him, kiss him.

I want to listen, but another part of me thinks I'm not good enough for this. How could anyone like a screwup like me? I make messes, I make trouble.

I don't want to ruin what we already have. I ruin enough as it is.

I break eye contact, and it's like breaking a spell.

Neither of us say anything. He must have come to his senses too, because Wyatt takes in a breath and starts packing up the first aid kit in silence. I have to force myself to look anywhere else but at him.

When I go to pick up my torn-up sweatshirt lying next to the draug's sword, something on the sword makes me freeze. I pick it up as Wyatt snaps the kit closed.

"What is it?" he asks.

I don't answer right away. I rub the metal cross guard with my thumb, clearing the dirt from the grooves, and tip it to the light. Carved into the metal is a looped square, a series of four loops at the corners, creating a square in the center.

I've seen this symbol before, and not just the COMMAND key on Prima's laptop.

Time's up, little valkyrie.

A wolf's voice. Ash like snow. Bladed weapons embedded in the World Tree. All of them with this exact symbol.

The symbol of Valhalla.

"The draugar," I say, my heart in my throat. "They're einherjar."

25

MY ARM THROBS IN SYNC WITH MY POUNDING HEART AS Wyatt and I run down the road, heading toward Ravenswood Castle.

"Reagan! Juniper! James!" I yell. The square is empty except for us. Dread seeps out of me like sweat.

"Maybe they went home," says Wyatt, breathless.

"Maybe."

Wyatt runs his hand through his hair, clearly thinking about one thing. "How can the draugar be einherjar? Aren't they supposed to be in Valhalla until Ragnarök?"

"Yeah. This is bad. Really, really bad!" I call everyone's name again. No answer. I feel sick.

"How can Loki control them?"

"He found a way to change the prophecy. Odin's army is his now. But it's different. They're cursed. That's why they're coming back as draugar. Wrong. It's not supposed to happen this way."

"If you had taken me to Valhalla when you were supposed to, I could have been one of those draugar," Wyatt says.

"Don't think like that. We'll figure this out." I hope I sound convincing. "Right now we need to find everyone."

"Bryn."

Wyatt's looking at the sky to the west, lit up with flashing red and blue lights.

My stomach drops, and I run.

I don't stop until I see the cop cars near the main gate. People from Ravenswood linger on the outskirts, murmuring with one another, wondering what's going on. A dozen or so North Shore police stand in small groups, hands tucked on their belts, looking bored, as a paramedic wheels a body on a stretcher.

It can't be... "No, *no no no.*"

"Bryn!"

I whip around. Reagan, James, and Juniper stand together in a huddle apart from the rest, pale and solemn in the flashing emergency lights.

Wyatt and I run over, and Reagan grabs me in a tight hug. I squeeze her so hard, she squeaks. "I thought you were..." I can barely get the words out, I'm so relieved. Next, I grab Juniper and pull her in. I can't stop shaking.

"I know!" Reagan says. "But look."

Now I can see who's on the stretcher. It's the old woman from Pagebound.

She's dead.

Her eyes are closed, cheeks sunken into her wrinkled face. She looks so small on the stretcher now. Hushed whispers follow her as the paramedics load her into the back of the ambulance.

"Heart attack, they said," says James. "Poor lady."

Juniper's hands tremble as she takes something out of her pocket. "But we found this outside the store." It's the third page.

"They killed her, didn't they?" James asks, eyes swimming with unshed tears.

The color drains from Wyatt's face and I can see misplaced guilt cross his face. All I want to do is reach out and hold his hand, but I stop myself.

I'm numb.

My brain turns to static as the ambulance drives away.

⋈

"Dad, please," James says, bracing his hands on Mr. Beaumont's desk. "You have to listen to me. Shut down Ravenswood."

I stand beside James, arms folded over my chest, but I don't say anything. I'm still reeling.

Mr. Beaumont looks tired. The clock in his office says it's well past two in the morning. He drags a hand down his face, leans back in his leather chair, and sighs deeply. He's been dealing with the police since the body was found, and now he looks even more agitated that we're keeping him awake, too.

"And why exactly should we close the gates?" he asks.

"I don't know, because someone *died*?" James says, flabbergasted.

"Lorna Birch was ninety-seven years old. She had a full and wonderful life, and unfortunately, heart attacks are not unheard of for a woman her age."

It hits me like a punch to the gut. Her name was Lorna. I didn't know that. And now she's dead.

"I just got off the phone with her next of kin," Mr. Beaumont adds. "They're flying in first thing from Toronto. There's nothing more we can do for her."

James glances at me.

After I told Reagan, Juniper, and James that the draugar are einherjar, we all agreed that we had to do something before someone else got hurt. James was sure he could convince his dad to listen, but his confidence seems to fade with every second we stand in this office.

"We should hold a memorial or something," James says. "She was one of us."

"We can't shut down the entirety of Ravenswood for a memorial. It just doesn't make fiscal sense."

"So it's about the money."

"We're a business. One person dying of a heart attack shouldn't cost us a whole day's worth of revenue. People die every day! And someday, when you take over this business after me, you'll see that, too."

James pushes off the desk and scoffs. "Unbelievable."

"The critics for *Travel Expert Magazine* will be here any day. While it's sad that a woman passed away on our property, we have to do everything in our power to make the best impression. It'll be better for everyone when we win! One person's death doesn't mean we have to risk the livelihoods of everyone else in Ravenswood."

"But Dad!" James says. "There might not be a Ravenswood if we don't close!"

Mr. Beaumont stares at James, bewildered, and then he looks at me. "What are you talking about? You are acting entirely unlike yourself—"

"Just listen!" James interrupts.

"Mr. Beaumont." My patience running thin, I step up to his desk. "All we're asking is for half a day."

Mr. Beaumont frowns at me, then at James. With a sigh, he shakes his head. "Impossible. The show must go on. End of discussion."

⋈

Outside, Reagan and Juniper stand at Yggdrasil, both of them touching the trunk. Reagan must be checking on the fjötra while Juniper is listening to the tree. Wyatt stands watch while they work and rushes over when he sees me and James.

"So?" Wyatt asks, expectantly. "Did he listen?"

James shakes his head. "Sorry. I tried. Usually that works." He glances at me defeatedly.

"We're on our own," I say.

Reagan and Juniper come up to us, both looking equally worried. "The fjötra was broken again," says Reagan. "But I fixed it. It's only temporary though. I need help later."

"But Yggdrasil is unharmed," Juniper says. Almost in response, the bells on Yggdrasil's branches chime pleasantly. "So what do we do now?" Juniper asks as we all stand in a circle.

James says, "Well, we can't stop people from coming to Ravenswood flat out."

"Will anyone even believe us if we tell them it's not safe?" asks Wyatt.

"Turns out I overestimated my persuasive abilities."

Reagan rolls her eyes. "Oh, big surprise. James Beaumont isn't as charming as he thinks."

James scoffs. "Hey, I'm not the bad guy here. Those zombie einher-dudes are. And I thought they were supposed to be the good guys!"

"They are!" Reagan says.

"Depending on whose side you're on," says Juniper.

"Not if Loki's controlling them," says Wyatt, and looks at me. "He's changing the prophecy, right? Sides don't matter anymore."

I'm going to throw up. Everything is spiraling out of control, and I'm just barely hanging on. The cut in my arm throbs and I press my hand to it. The pain is something to focus on.

"We could be asking these questions all night," says Reagan. She looks at me, worry all over her face. "Everyone go home, get some rest, take a shower. Recharge. There's nothing else we can do tonight. Loki used the last page of the book. It's safe for now. We'll meet up tomorrow. Okay?"

None of us have enough energy to say otherwise. Reagan is the voice of reason. When Reagan and Juniper turn home and James heads back to the castle, I stay behind for a moment and catch Wyatt's eye. He presses his lips together, looking grim, but he nods, encouraging me to go. He must know that I don't want to leave him.

"We'll figure this out," he says.

My head bobs, but my anxiety feels like it's crawling up my throat. "Yeah."

I follow Reagan and Juniper in silence, my mind racing. Dread sinks in. What if Mom's disappearance has something to do with Loki controlling einherjar? What if Asgard knew what was happening and she was sent to stop him? Worse, what if he did something to her? What if one of the cursed einherjar got to her?

I force myself to take a breath as we make it home.

This late, the house is dark. Reagan and Juniper don't bother being quiet as we file inside, and I'm extra careful to lock the door behind me, checking and double-checking it's secure. Though how much good it'll do us, I'm not sure.

All I want to do is fall into bed and sleep forever. I wonder if Juniper won't mind sharing it this one time. I'm so lost in thought, I nearly bump into her at the top of the stairs. She's standing in the way.

"What are you—?" I feel it, too. Something in the air sends the hair on the back of my neck on end.

I fumble for the light switch. When I flip it on, my blood goes cold. My house is totally trashed.

26

IT LOOKS LIKE A TORNADO TORE THROUGH THE HOUSE.

Kitchen chairs, toppled. The table, shoved aside. Cabinets open, hanging on hinges. Broken glass and cracked plates crunch under my feet. In the living room, lamps knocked over. Couch cushions upturned. The TV, smashed on the floor, with all of Mom's books from her bookcases.

Mom's bedroom door is wide open. Inside, her mattress is off the frame, her blankets strewn. Prima's and Reagan's, too. Their room is a mess.

"What . . . ?" Juniper starts to say, but her voice catches in her throat.

Reagan takes a few steps forward, her arms limp at her sides, speechless.

This can't be real. This can't be happening.

Butters is hiding under the sink. Juniper is closest to her and pulls her out of hiding. The cat hisses and spits, but settles in Juniper's arms, her tail still puffed out.

"We have to call Prima," Reagan says, whipping out her phone.

"She's states away by now with Muriel. What is she supposed to—"

A thump comes from Reagan and Prima's room.

Whoever did this is still here.

In a flash, Reagan and I summon our armor, and Juniper readies some acorns.

I'm the closest to their room and sprint inside.

When I turn on the light, I don't see anyone. Prima's mattress is propped against the wall, but it falls flat as a person lying on the floor pushes it off them.

"Prima!" Reagan cries.

Prima's bleeding from her lip, and a nasty bruise is already purpling at her hairline. She holds her arm to her chest and cries out when Reagan tries to touch it.

"What happened?" Reagan asks. "We thought you were with Muriel!"

"I was going to . . . I—" She puts her wrist to her lip and winces. "I came back. Muriel's dead."

"What?" Reagan gasps.

"Her son called looking for Mom." She tries to stand up, but she wobbles on shaky legs. Reagan has to help her. Her arm hangs weirdly from her shoulder.

"Sit down," Reagan says, guiding her to the bed. "Did you see who did this?"

"I don't know. It was too dark. Someone jumped me. . . ." She reaches up and touches the bruise on her forehead. "They hit me."

Reagan looks at me, panicked, but I can't move. I can't think. My blood boils.

Only one person can be responsible for this.

"Loki," says Juniper. Butters yowls and leaps from Juniper's arms, running off to hide somewhere.

"What was he doing here?" Reagan asks, looking at the torn pages of her scrapbooks scattered on the rug. She reaches for Prima's head, but Prima swats her away, saying she's fine.

"He was looking for something," I say. "He used the draugar as a distraction. Knew we wouldn't be here." Then it hits me like a brick. "Where is the book?"

"I left it upstairs...." Juniper goes white as a sheet and runs to my room. I follow close behind.

My room is a disaster, too. My posters hang off the walls, my books lie like birds with broken wings, my mattress is on the floor.

Juniper gets on her knees to look under the bed and then looks up at me. "I am sorry."

I feel violated, like someone shoved their hand into my chest and ripped something out of me. It's too much. All I can do is walk over to my mattress, set it back on the frame, and sit on it.

Loki has his spell book again.

$$\bowtie$$

It takes us most of the night to clean up the worst of the mess in the house, and even then, it can't be fixed. Nothing can be fixed. Prima's arm is in a sling, Reagan is on the verge of tears, and Juniper is despondent. Even Butters is too scared to come out of hiding.

It's clear that this wasn't some common robbery. None of Mom's jewelry was stolen. Even Prima's piggy bank full of coins she collected when she was little was left intact. Reagan wanted to call the cops, but Prima didn't know what they could do.

For once, I agree with Prima. No one can help us.

After we've swept up most of the broken glass and righted most of the furniture, I shower, eat, and even get a few hours of sleep, but nothing changes.

And Mom still isn't here.

If she were here, she would know what to do, Prima never would've gotten hurt, and the cursed einherjar wouldn't have gotten loose on Midgard. We're running out of options.

In the morning, we all eat breakfast in silence and get back to cleaning. Prima and Reagan tackle their room, Juniper and I clean up Mom's.

"I am aware it is not the time," says Juniper, "but I must find a way to contact Utgard. If Loki is sending einherjar to my realm, it will prompt full-on war."

"I know," I say as I fold Mom's quilt and put it back on her bed. Juniper presses her lips together with worry.

"I may have to return without her, but by then it may be too late—"

"I know, Juniper." I don't mean to snap, but Juniper flinches. "Sorry."

Juniper looks away. If Mom were here, she could fix everything.

Her valkyrie trunk is unopened. For whatever reason, Loki left it untouched, probably found the book before getting to it.

Resolve washes over me, and for the first time, I know what to do.

"What is it?" Juniper asks as I try to open the trunk. It's still locked, just as I left it.

I don't answer and I go upstairs and grab my lock-picking tools and come back down. Juniper doesn't stop me as I open the trunk and find everything as it was. I push aside our family photos and the raven feathers, and pull out a black velvet pouch.

The seidr kit.

"Are you sure about this?" she asks.

I slide the pouch into my hoodie pocket. "Don't tell Prima or Reagan."

⋈

It's night again before Reagan can finally convince Prima to go to the hospital to get her shoulder checked. She's stubborn, and tries to say it's not worth the cost, but even I can tell her shoulder is dislocated—if not broken. It's swollen, and she can't move her fingers. Reagan says she's impossible and calls a cab anyway, and practically shoves her out the door to go with her to the ER. That gives me all the opportunity I need to do what needs to be done.

Mom's seidr kit is heavy in my hands as I go to the stables. Juniper, Wyatt, and James are already there. Juniper had gone ahead to tell them everything, and she clutches her staff tighter when she sees me. Everyone turns toward me when I come in, all looking equally nervous.

Gamgee and Chewy watch from their stalls, but Chewy stomps his hooves. Maybe he knows what's about to happen.

"Ready?" I ask, not breaking stride.

"Are you certain you want to do this?" Juniper asks.

"I got it. Can't go back now." I hold up the bag to show proof.

James squirms when he sees it. He's still in his armor, his stage sword at his hip. "So you're going to use magic? Like, double, double toil and trouble and all that?"

"Not that kind of magic. Just a little divination. No big deal."

"Divination kind of sounds like a big deal," says James.

Wyatt looks at me, a deep crease between his eyebrows. "Are you okay? We heard what happened."

"I'm fine," I say, and try to smile.

Wyatt doesn't smile back, but he doesn't say any more about it.

"Will Reagan be cool with this?" James asks.

"I have to do this," I say. "It's our only option."

We sit in a circle in the aisle, me between Juniper and Wyatt. Having them here with me makes what I'm about to do less scary. I've done a lot of stupid things, but this might be the heavyweight champ of bad ideas.

Juniper sits with her legs crossed and her back straight. Her staff is laid in front of her neatly, like she's prepared to use it. "I am not certain we should be doing this," Juniper says.

"What are you doing exactly?" James asks, taking a seat opposite me.

"Go into a trance, maybe ask some spirits some questions, hopefully not make my blood boil. Simple enough," I say.

They give one another wary glances, but no one says anything else as I empty the bag on the floor in front of me.

James goes pale. "Are those . . . teeth?"

He's right. What I thought were tiles are pearly white teeth, a rune etched in each.

"If it makes you feel any better," I say, "I don't think they're human."

"I don't think they're animal either," Wyatt says.

"How is that better?" James asks, baffled.

My skin crawls. "Okay. Let's just get this over with."

"In my village, we have a seeress," Juniper says. "She studied for decades, honing her craft. Are you certain you know what you are doing?"

"No, but that's half the fun." No one seems to like my joke, not even me. "It's just seidr. And I'm a valkyrie. How hard can it be?"

Everyone exchanges looks again but they know it's no use trying to talk me out of it. I'm in this to find my Mom. No one else will.

"If anything bad happens, we're snapping you out of it, okay," Wyatt says. It's not a question.

I nod, stiffly. My hands shake as I scoop up the teeth and cup them in my palms.

The last time I saw Mom do this, she was humming a song. I just have to do what she did, and it'll work. I hope.

"Okay," I say, taking a deep breath. "Here we go."

I close my eyes, and start humming a song Mom used to sing to us when we were little. It's the only thing that comes to mind. A soft, haunting lullaby. I toss the runes.

When I open my eyes, no one says anything. In fact, no one moves. Time has stopped.

The teeth hang, suspended in the air in front of me.

Wyatt, James, and Juniper are as still as statues. I wave my hand over Juniper's face. She doesn't blink. James looks sick. Wyatt's hands are clenched into fists, pressed onto his knees, but he's looking straight through me with worried eyes. No sound, not even the wind.

All I can hear is my breath.

As far as I'm aware, I'm the only thing moving in the universe. So this is seidr.

Slowly, I stand up and turn around.

A gust of ice-cold wind pushes me back, and I stumble. My heel catches a ledge and I nearly fall.

I'm not in the stables. I'm in the middle of a blizzard.

Pinwheeling my arms, I drop forward and fall into a foot of snow.

I can barely keep my eyes open. Snow stings my eyes, and my tears turn to ice on my cheeks. I lift my head just enough to see the gigantic shape of a mountain looming in front of me. The wind howls, sheets of snow billow off the craggy gray-blue rocks, the cold knifes right through me. I'm on a cliff, so high up I can't see what's below. Dark gray clouds churn the sky, shielding a frenzy of silent lightning.

"Mom?" I call out, but the wind steals my voice.

Where did the seidr take me?

A dark shadow melts through the curtain of white.

A cave.

I ball my hands into fists and pin them under my armpits as I walk toward it.

I'm coming, Mom.

27

Inside the cave is barely better than outside.

The second I step into the mouth, the sounds of the blizzard melt away and the cold and dry air turns into cold and damp. My nose runs like a river and I wipe it on my sleeve as I walk deeper into the cave.

"Mom!"

All I hear is my own echo. The darkness presses on me from all sides. My arm scrapes against the cave wall. I can't see my own hand in front of my face. Using my hand as a guide, I follow the wall deeper into the mountain.

At first I think it's my eyes playing tricks on me, searching for anything in the dark, but after I blink a few times, I know it's real. Firelight glints at the end of the craggy tunnel.

I keep walking toward it. The closer I get, I can hear what sounds like the gentle crackle and hiss of flames dancing on a pile of logs. I turn around the bend, expecting to find a campfire, but instead, the world shifts again and I'm standing in someone's house.

No more cold, no more howling wind, just the gentle *tick-tick-tick* of an antique clock on a mantelpiece above a warm, cozy fireplace.

When I walked into the cave, I expected, well, more cave. Instead, I've walked into a fully furnished McMansion.

A plush couch sits in front of the fireplace. To my left is a dining room complete with a twelve-seat oak table, piled high with food and drink, like Thanksgiving. To my right is a foyer lit by a crystal chandelier, and beige carpeting lines the stairs winding up to the second floor. Outside, beyond curtains made of sheer lace, is an endless summer-green field of perfectly mowed grass, cut in diamond patterns, stretching as far as I can see.

I don't even know where to begin.

"Mom?" I call out.

I have no idea where I am, but I have to hope that the seidr has brought me to where she is. But *where* this is, is another question entirely. I'm definitely not on Midgard anymore.

At least it's warm in here.

I go to room after room: a neon-bright arcade, an in-home theater blaring a Tom Hanks movie, a whole bowling alley. The house is way bigger than I thought. But I don't see any proof that anyone actually lives here.

Even the kitchen, big and vacant as the rest of the house, is spotless. A vinyl sticker above the refrigerator says LIVE LAUGH LOVE.

"What the hell?"

I'm about to head upstairs when I spot the back of a balding head peeking above a deck chair near the in-ground swimming pool in the backyard.

I make my way outside. There's not a cloud in the sky or a tree for miles. Everything here is eerily quiet except for the gentle burbling of a fountain in the pool and a deep, nasal snoring.

In the deck chair lies a man in his sixties, fast asleep. Or at least,

I think he's asleep. He's wearing enormous sunglasses so I can't see his eyes. His skin color is a deep bronze and his hair and beard are a shocking white. He wears a humungous fur coat over his pineapple swim trunks.

"Um." I start to speak, but my voice wakes the man up so quickly, he chokes on his snore and bolts upright.

In doing so, his head rolls right off his shoulders and falls to the ground.

I'm screaming. He's screaming—or rather, his head is screaming. We're all screaming.

Startled, his body flings his suntanning panel clear across the lawn, nearly slicing my head clean off. I back up and then trip, falling into another deck chair, where I stay frozen, too shocked to move.

"What the Helheim are you doing here?!" his head shouts at me from the ground. His sunglasses have gone askew, and he looks at me with pure white eyes. "Did Kvasir let you in?"

The rest of his body fumbles to pick up his head and shoves it back on his shoulders. He lets out a grunt and his neck makes a satisfying *crack*.

"When did you get here?" He checks three Rolexes on his forearm and then squints up at the sun, as if to make sure that his watches are still working.

"Where am I?" I ask.

The man gestures around him. "My house, obviously." His accent makes him sound like he's in an old black-and-white movie, not quite British and not quite American.

I can barely get the words out. "And who are you?"

"Who am...?" The man looks somewhat flustered and offended I would even ask. "Mímir. Who else would I be? You're in my house!"

Mímir, the Aesir god of wisdom, knowledge, and memory. During the war with the Aesir, the Vanir cut off his head and sent it back to Odin, who preserved it with herbs so Mímir's wisdom wouldn't be lost forever.

"Oh come on, girl, your mouth is opening and closing like Loki's when he was a salmon."

"I'm—" I can't think of a single thing to say. I've never met a god before.

Mímir pauses and then props his sunglasses on top of his head as he leans in and inspects me with solid white eyes. It feels like I'm being looked at under an X-ray, and I mean that literally.

"Ah," he says, slowly, and straightens up, sliding his sunglasses back into place. "Brynhildr Miles Martel. Youngest valkyrie of Midgard. Born eighth of December. Incoming senior at North Shore High School. Cashier at Ravenswood Gift Shop."

"You got all that from just looking at me?"

He nods, saunters over to a tiki bar, and pours himself a shimmering drink of golden light. "Trust me, girl. Knowing everything gets old real quick." He taps a finger on the sunglasses. "Wisdom is knowing when to stop. So what does a Skuld-touched girl need from me?"

"Skuld? The Norn?"

"The youngest, and a valkyrie like yourself. How else would you have made it this far?" He gestures around us. "Even your sisters do not have her gift."

So that explains my dreams. I'm not sure if that makes me feel better or worse. I want to ask if the seeress who told Odin about Ragnarök was Skuld-touched too, but other things are more important. "My mom is missing. I'm looking for her."

"So you thought she was here. Unfortunately, Kara Martel is not in this realm."

"When's the last time you saw her?"

Mímir glances at his watches and I realize they're nothing like any watch I've seen before. They each have a dozen hands, and one even looks like a star map. "Perhaps ten days or so ago in Midgard's time? Time passes here a little differently."

It must have been around the same time she left after getting the raven-message. "What was she doing here?"

"Your mother and I are quite good friends. She's the only person who can beat me in a game of hnefatafl. Her company is most welcome."

I don't want to think about it, but I have to ask. "Are you and my mom . . . *together*?"

Mímir spits out his drink, misting a rainbow in front of him. "Of course not!"

Oh, good. For a second I thought he could be Juniper's father and I'm kind of relieved he's not. I wouldn't know how to feel about having a god as a stepdad, let alone anyone who unironically has LIVE LAUGH LOVE anywhere in their house.

Above us comes a trembling roar, like rolling thunder, that cuts through the clear blue sky. Mímir doesn't seem fazed at all by it and sips his drink.

"What is this place exactly? I was on a mountain just a second ago."

"You're in Jotunheim, at the base of one of the roots of the World Tree. Or rather, your mind is here. Your body is still in the stables with your friends."

"Jotunheim? But why does it look like a McMansion?"

"I'm the keeper of memory. Lost things find their way here. You should see the huge room of single socks. It's a mountain all on its own at this point."

"Okay, so wait. Back up. If I'm in Jotunheim, and my mom isn't here, why did seidr bring me here in the first place?"

"Seidr is a wild sleipnir. In the untrained hands, it can be unpredictable, sometimes lethal. But of course your sisters told you that. And you didn't listen."

Anger burns my cheeks. That doesn't matter. "Einherjar attacked Utgard, now they're attacking Midgard, and I need to find my mom so we can stop—"

"Ragnarök, yes," Mímir says, interrupting me. "Quite a pickle, indeed."

"That's why I had to do something. We're running out of time. I have to find my mom."

"And rather than sitting down with your sisters and hashing out a plan, here you are. Alone."

"They won't listen to me."

"How do you *know* that?" The way he says it makes my face hotter. Mímir thinks he knows everything, but he doesn't know the half of it. He doesn't know what it's like being me. I stare at Mímir for a long second before finally standing up. "They won't listen," I say again and lift my chin.

"Here's some advice, free of charge," Mímir says. "The Aesir and the Vanir were once two warring peoples who made peace, a seemingly impossible feat after so much blood had been spilled. Some thought that the war would never end. But all it took was one party to come to the table to change fate."

"Yeah, well that doesn't last forever, does it? Ragnarök comes, and everyone dies."

Mímir takes a deep breath and sets down his drink on the tiki bar. "It does not mean it's not worth doing. It's true—gods are tempestuous, and selfish, and proud, but they're also loyal and brave and they care deeply about their families. A lot can be learned from them. There's nothing more terrible than a family torn apart by petty grievances."

"I'm not the petty one."

Mímir watches me with a small, knowing smile on his face, then he throws up his hands, surrendering. "I know when to pick my battles. Listen to me or not, I've said my piece."

"Right now I only care about stopping einherjar from destroying Midgard."

"Ah yes, the einherjar. No wonder you believe Ragnarök is upon you. Odin's army is nigh unstoppable, especially with the right commander. To control einherjar takes serious firepower. That kind of magic is not to be used lightly."

"That's why I have to find my Mom so we can stop Loki."

Mímir looks at me again but I can't see his eyes behind the sunglasses to know his expression. Slowly, he walks to the deck chairs and indicates for me to sit. I do, and he sits in another. "Do you want my opinion?"

I nod. It would be stupid not to ask.

"The easiest deception is often the one we most want to believe." He sighs when I don't do anything. "What makes you think Loki is behind it?"

"Because everyone knows that Loki starts Ragnarök. Maybe it doesn't matter how he goes about it. It's how it's supposed to happen."

"Convenient how Loki always seems to be blamed when things go wrong. You of all people should know how that feels."

I blink a few times. "This is different."

"Is it? Hasn't your mother reminded you that fate is the choices we make? The same applies to us all."

"Look," I say, standing up and stepping away. "I don't have time for this. I need to find my mom. I'm not going back until I do."

Mímir sighs heavily. God or not, people do that a lot when they're around me. He smooths out his white beard and turns to look at me.

"Who am I to stop a valkyrie? Learned that the hard way. Are you certain you want to go through with this?"

"Yes."

"So be it. But it'll cost you."

"Why? Can't you *see* or whatever and tell me where she is?"

"I do not possess that kind of omniscience. Instead, you must drink from the well to see what I can't."

He points to the rippling surface of the swimming pool. There, shapes darken the bottom. I can't make out anything clearly except for a glowing golden orb, standing out from the rest.

"Your well," I say, amazed. "That's Mímisbrunnr?"

Mímir nods.

Never would I have thought a great well of sacred knowledge would look like a heavily chlorinated swimming pool.

"I can't drink that!" I say.

"It's the only way to know for certain where your mother is, in any realm. You had to know that getting my help would require sacrifice," Mímir says. "To grant omniscience, I need something from you."

"I don't have anything to give."

"It's not a material possession I need. Much like Odin's need for knowledge beyond his means, your request requires more. Equal exchange."

My breath hitches in my chest. I know the story. Odin came to Mímir asking to drink from the well and obtain knowledge of the universe, to know what he must do to prepare for Ragnarök, but it came at a cost. "You mean like my eye?"

It makes sense now. That glowing orb at the bottom of the pool. Odin cut out his own eye as an offering, desperate to know everything about his fate.

I want to find my mom, but I'm not sure I have the guts to do that.

As if sensing what I'm thinking, Mímir asks, "What are you willing to sacrifice to find your mother?"

I hate how desperate I am. I just want my family back together, I want the einherjar to go back to Valhalla, I want Ragnarök to stop. The world is coming down around me and I'm not sure what I have to give.

I clench my fists and take a breath. "What do you want?"

Mímir studies me for a long moment. He's still sitting on the deck chair, hands clasped together, elbows on his knees. He almost looks sad. "Your time."

"My . . . time. You mean, like, you want me to hang out?

"Your *time*."

"Like, a second or a day or—?"

"Years."

My mouth drops open. "Years! How many?"

"Ten."

I balk and shake my head. "No way. How about one?"

"You think one year of your short life is worth that kind of magic?"

I don't take that personally. "Three."

Mímir sighs.

"Five?"

"There is no negotiating." Mímir rises and walks toward me. "Ten years of your life. That's ten fewer holidays, fewer turns of the wheel, fewer chances to say the things you might not ever get another chance to say. All so you can find your mother."

I swallow the lump in my throat. For all I know, I could live to be a hundred, and this would mean I'd only live to be ninety. Not a bad trade. On the other hand, maybe I'm supposed to die ten years and a day from now and I'll drop dead tomorrow. Who knows what fate has in store for me? A part of me wants to say *No way, it's too risky,* but another part wants Mom back more. She would do the same for me, wouldn't she?

"Deal," I say. "Ten years of my life for me to see where Mom is."

The sky above rumbles again, rolling like an oncoming storm. But there isn't a cloud in the sky.

"What is that?" I ask.

Mímir doesn't seem to hear it. "Your fate is your choice."

My knees shake. I want to believe that I made the right call, but at the same time, I can't help but think I'm in way over my head.

Mímir holds out his arm, gesturing toward the swimming pool, and I take a deep breath as I walk to the water's edge.

"What do I do now?" I ask him.

Out of nowhere, a glass appears in his hand. It's shaped like a mead horn. When he hands it to me, he frowns, but doesn't say anything else.

That's it then. No going back.

I kneel and lean over the edge of the pool. It's strangely warm by the water, and moisture sticks to my skin like a hot, humid day. The fountain bubbles and splashes and mist swirls off the surface. When I dip the mead horn into the water, the glass turns invisible in my hand. Water from the well of knowledge . . . most overpriced drink ever.

I look at Mímir and raise my glass. "Cheers."

I think about my Mom and I put the water to my lips.

Images flood my head like a dam bursting open. I'm hurtling through space, faster than light.

The rainbow bridge, Bifröst.

The golden city of Asgard.

The massive arena of Valhalla.

Odin's throne. Empty.

Yggdrasil.

Mom.

It's dark, it's dank. Chains are wrapped around her wrists and ankles, holding her up to the trunk of the tree. Her valkyrie armor is covered in blood and dirt. But she's alive.

Slowly, she raises her head. Her face is bruised. Dried blood cakes her hair. Her eyes focus and unfocus, and then she groans, "Bryn?"

In an instant, I'm back at the pool. I'm clutching the edge of it, gasping for air.

The sky rumbles again. It's like the sky is yawning.

"Did you find her?" Mímir asks.

I nod, speechless. I can't get what I saw out of my head. "My mom, she's hurt, but she's alive. She's trapped in Valhalla. What is going on?"

"I'm rooting for you, kid, I really am," he says. He points to the bright blue sky. "I wish I could tell you more. But it seems like you're needed elsewhere."

"What?"

Without further ado, he puts his sandaled foot on my back and kicks me into the pool.

28

BUBBLES TICKLE MY SKIN AS I FALL DOWN, DOWN, DOWN, through the water. The pool is deeper than it looks from above and darkness presses in.

The roar in the sky still vibrates through me.

But all I can think about is my mom, hanging from the tree in Valhalla, trapped. She saw me, she saw me. She called my name!

I'm coming, Mom!

The darkness gets minimally brighter, like sunlight through closed eyelids.

Sound snaps in my ears like a clap of thunder.

Shouting. Heavy footsteps running.

I open my eyes.

I don't know where I am. Shapes move around me, but everything is blurry, like I'm seeing everything from the bottom of a pool.

I'm on my back. Everything is too bright, too cold except for the hands, warm and calloused, that cup my face. I smell beeswax.

Wyatt's eyes fill up my vision.

Bryn!

He sounds so far away. I want to touch him, but my arms don't work.

Bryn, can you look at me? I realize now it was his voice that I was hearing at Mímir's, slowed down in the realm shift.

I try to focus on him. His dark eyes are wide, his face pale.

"Bryn!" he gasps, relieved.

The world snaps into focus. I'm on the floor of the stable. I'm back on Midgard, back in my body. I try to speak, but I can't. My skin tingles, like my whole body fell asleep.

It was real. Everything I saw was in my head—Mímir, the pool, Mom—but it was real.

"Are you okay?" Wyatt asks.

I manage to nod, but it feels like I've been electrocuted. I try to look around, but I can barely move. That's when I hear all the noise.

Juniper shouting, James yelling, dogs barking.

Bursts of colorful light—Juniper's magic—bounce off the stable walls. What is going on?

"You had a seizure," Wyatt says. "You threw the runes and then you fell over, foaming at the mouth." He brushes my hair out of my face, and looks toward the door. "We're under attack."

All I can do is grunt and roll over to see for myself.

Juniper stands in the field, throwing seed bombs at a dozen or so frost-white dogs dashing through the night.

No, not dogs. Wolves. Ice wolves. Ancient creatures from the outer realms of Jotunheim.

Everywhere they step, the ground freezes in an instant, covered in a silvery layer of ice. Twice the size and twice as fast as regular wolves, they leap and surround her, but James holds them off as best he can with his stage sword.

He screams in our direction, "Wyatt, help!"

To me, Wyatt shouts, "Stay here! Don't move!" Then he rushes off, grabbing an axe embedded in a tree trunk near the wood pile.

With him gone, it's much colder. But some of the tingling has gone away from my fingers. I have to help. I try to stand, but my arms flop numbly against the floor. I scrape my palms to brace myself, knocking away the seidr runes as I get my feet under me and stand. My knees shake so badly, I fall sideways and lean on a stall door.

Gamgee and Chewy squeal in their stalls, rising up on their back legs and kicking. I need to close the stable doors to stop anything from getting in and hurting them.

I wobble from one stall door to another to keep myself upright. It's slow going, like I'm moving through molasses. Every part of me is heavy and dull.

So this is what giving up ten years of my life feels like.

I grab hold of one of the sliding doors and pull, but it hardly budges. I'm so weak, and tired, and it takes everything in me not to pass out on the spot.

My knees give out and I fall to the ground. Heavy paws freeze the dry grass in front of me, and I look up into the pale blue eyes of a wolf snarling at me, here for an easy kill.

Juniper throws her seeds just before it strikes. Roots burst up and wrap around the wolf like a net. It growls and thrashes, but the seed magic holds firm. Juniper closes in, brandishing her staff, a wild look in her glowing green eyes.

"Hear me!" she screams. Her words echo, and the air shimmers with power. The wolf whines and bites at the roots to chew itself free, but the air warps around it and the wolf bursts into ice.

I've never seen her magic do that before.

Juniper drags me to my feet and then helps me close the door. "Get back inside! You are in no condition to battle!" We close the first door together with a heavy bang.

"I'm getting better!" It's true. With every passing second, I'm starting to get more feeling back in my limbs, like I'm only half dead. In no time, I'll be good as new.

"But your hair!" Juniper says, helping me with the second door.

"What about my hair?"

A shout makes the both of us turn.

James is on the ground. He brandishes a sword as two wolves charge in, flanking him. At the last second, Wyatt jumps in the way, standing over him. He raises his axe.

He stops one wolf with a huge swing, and the wolf yelps into a flurry of snow, but Wyatt throws out his arm. The other wolf lunges but misses, scraping its head against his arm. Where it touches, frost creeps up his skin and he yells.

"Wyatt!" I scream.

He swings his axe, smashing the second wolf, and he holds his hurt arm to his chest, wincing. His eyes flash amber in the dark, but they go back to normal as he helps James to his feet. "I'm fine," he says. He's fighting against going berserk.

Juniper screams, "Do not let them touch you!"

"You could have said that earlier!" James barks.

Wyatt clenches his jaw and swings his axe at another wolf, shattering its ice body to pieces.

James rounds on him. "What are you waiting for? Bear time!"

"No!" Wyatt snaps. "You still need me!"

Juniper rushes in, swinging her staff. Wind kicks up under her feet and blows her hair out. She speaks, her voice low and commanding, in another language. Jotunnish.

The wolves cower, shrinking against her words, but they don't run away. They circle wide, barking and howling, as if taunting us. The kulning is too powerful. They're not running away so easily.

I try to think, but my thoughts are sluggish. They have to be weak against something, but what?

James backs up, barely blocking a wolf lunging for his arm, and screams. "What do we do?"

Juniper sweeps her staff in a huge arc, her words making the air shimmer like a mirage. She speaks Jotunnish again, saying the same thing. It almost sounds like she's pleading with them.

Wyatt and James bat away a few of the wolves, but they're closing in. Juniper's voice trembles, desperation making her hands shake.

I look around for anything we can use. My eyes land on the pickup truck Wyatt's uncle drives. In the truck bed, I see a red box that says VEHICLE EMERGENCY KIT.

I bolt for the pickup truck and jump into the bed. Flipping open the box, I find exactly what I'm looking for. A road flare.

I flip off the cap and ignite it. A big black dot appears in my vision, when the flare bursts hot and bright in my hand. This had better work.

I whip around just as a wolf dives for Juniper.

Reaching back, I throw the flare with all I have. It cartwheels through the air, landing dead center in the wolf's side. It yelps and the fire cuts right through it. The wolf disappears into a flurry of snow and the flare lands in the grass.

My victory is short-lived.

The flare catches in the dry straw, and a fire starts to spread.

The wind from the lake reaches it, and carries the flames across the field.

"The horses!" Wyatt cries.

He makes to run, but a wolf cuts him off. James grabs him back and Juniper strikes with her staff. The wolf is gone. More flee the flames reaching up toward the sky.

I stare as the fire licks across the grass, surrounding my friends. What have I done?

I jump down from the truck bed and I'm about to start running toward them when something rushes up behind me.

Without looking, I throw a punch, but a hand catches my wrist.

"Prima!"

Her arm is still in a sling, the bruise on her head purple now, but her grip around my wrist is tight. My hand goes slack. It hurts.

Reagan runs up behind Prima, panting. "Oh my God!"

Their eyes gleam with firelight, shock all over their faces.

Prima looks at me, then at the fire, and then at the wolves. She glares at me. It's like she's asking herself the same question: *What did you do?*

She lets me go and pushes me away.

Prima's spear materializes in her hand, and Reagan's knives point toward the wolves. In unison, Prima and Reagan put their hands to their pendants. Their valkyrie armor shines as it spreads over their clothes. They rush into the fight.

29

THE FIRE IS SPREADING.

Orange flames lick the sky as it rushes across the dry grass.

The ice wolves try to flee, but not before Prima and Reagan get to them. My sisters in battle is one of the most beautiful things I've ever seen.

Even injured, Prima is exceptional. Her spear is a blur as she jabs and whacks wolves. Their ice crystals glitter as they die.

Reagan summons her astral knives, flinging them with each whip of her hand, and the wolves go down one by one. Juniper helps them, holding what wolves she can with her roots while they finish the job. They work together like a cohesive unit, moving like they know one another's thoughts—it's like watching ballet dancers on a stage.

Wyatt and James rush to the rainwater basin, grabbing bucketsful to dump on the fire. The horses sense something is wrong and their screams carry on the wind.

I can't believe this is happening. It's like I'm moving underwater. I don't know who to help.

I take a step toward the stables. I'm the closest, but the wolves are still a threat. I can't get the horses out.

"Bryn!" Stan pumps his arms hard, wheeling around the stable as fast as he can toward me. He must have seen the flames from indoors. "Help me!" He puts his hands on the water pump attached to the stable.

He doesn't need to say it twice.

I help him turn the wheel and the hose whips to life like a snake. I grab the nozzle while he unrolls the hose from the wheel. Water streams out in a rush and I spray as much of the fire as I can. Wyatt and James keep throwing buckets from the other side. Steam rises up and the water hisses and sizzles on the hot, charred ground. It's going out.

Luckily, the stable is untouched.

Uncle Stan pushes open the stable door and rushes inside to deal with the panicked horses.

Wyatt wipes sweat off his brow, panting as he looks at me through the steam. Disappointment is all over his face.

He must hate me. I'd hate me.

I barely have time to lower the nozzle before Prima is on me. She yanks the hose from my hands and whips it to the ground.

"You," she growls, getting in my face, and forcing me to back up all the way to the stable wall. She's furious. "What were you thinking?"

She takes a piece of my hair and pulls it from my mess of a ponytail. Instead of dark brown, my hair is stark white. Mímir's trade.

I don't have anything to say. At least, nothing that will be good enough for her.

Her gray eyes are hard as steel as she glares at me.

But she doesn't notice when a wolf comes charging for her.

Reagan screams her name.

Prima spins around, eyes wide.

The wolf lunges, teeth first.

A bear crashes into it, giant jaws clamping around its neck, and throws it to the ground. Wyatt. He and the wolf tear at each other, but the wolf is no match. Wyatt rips it apart with his paws.

Prima backs up into me, shielding me with her body, as she watches Wyatt change back. The mist clears and Wyatt wavers and falls to his knees. James and Juniper help him stand.

Prima looks at Wyatt, breathless, and he simply nods, holding his injured arm to his chest.

Reagan comes over, eyes shining with unshed tears. "The wolves are gone."

Prima recovers from her shock and rounds on me. "You," she says again, jabbing her finger against my chest. "What did you do?" Her rage distorts the air. When I don't say anything, she grabs me by the front of my shirt and shakes me. "What did you do?"

"You used seidr, didn't you?" Reagan says, horrified.

There's no use hiding it. The white streak in my hair is proof enough.

"What did I tell you?" Prima asks, her voice shaking. "Did you not hear me? Are you really this stupid?"

I push her off. "Don't blame me, okay? I'm doing more to find Mom than you are!"

Prima shoves me hard, pushing my back against the wall. "Now all these people know our secret!" She throws her arms out toward Wyatt and James.

My anger spikes hot around my head, rattling the stable door on its tracks. "Well, if I hadn't saved Wyatt from Valhalla, you'd be dead right now!"

Everyone's faces fall.

"Saved from Valhalla?" repeats Prima.

Shit.

30

THE DRAGON'S DEN WAS JUST ABOUT TO CLOSE WHEN WE arrived, and Trudy set us up at one of the large tables inside. Reagan suggested we come here to recover. Knowing her, I think she meant it to be neutral territory, a safe place. The only sounds at this hour are the tinny music from the radio in the kitchen and the clang of pots being cleaned. The rest of the staff have gone home.

Prima doesn't say anything as she sits across from me. She's still as a statue, staring at me, with a single black coffee steaming in her hand, her other arm held tight against her chest in a sling. James rests his head on the table and Reagan sits stiff as a board between them. I'm wedged between Wyatt and Juniper. We're all too tired to speak.

Sirens resonate from outside. Clearly someone called about the fire. That I started. My stomach clenches and I shovel pancakes into my mouth. It's easier to focus on my food than look at Prima. But even a Breakfast-Fit-For-A-King special with bacon and sausage and pancakes covered in scoops of butter with a side of chocolate milkshake doesn't make me feel better. I gave up ten years of my life—might as well enjoy it now.

Juniper and Wyatt ordered heaping plates of late-night breakfast, too. Fighting has made us all hungry.

Wyatt props his head up with his fist, elbow on the table, watching the condensation on his Coke drip down the side of his glass. His arm is shiny and red, like a burn. It'll heal, but the frost left a pattern on his skin like a snowflake. There's no mead left to ease the pain.

Juniper barely touches her jalapeño poppers. She glances up at Prima every now and again, starts to say something, but stops herself.

I'm not even sure Prima is breathing. I don't know when she started drinking coffee, probably at college. I know what she's thinking, because I'm thinking it, too.

This is all my fault.

"What do you mean 'saved'?" Prima finally asks, her voice low and flat as she breaks the silence.

Both Juniper and Wyatt glance at me.

I want to lie, but there's no use hiding it anymore. I set down my fork and, finally, look up. Prima's eyes bore into me. "When the troll showed up and attacked us, it hurt him. Wyatt was supposed to go to Valhalla, but I saved him."

Her eyes dart to Wyatt, who looks ready to crawl under the table. The air feels electric.

Prima's eyes flutter and she works her jaw, chewing on the inside of her cheek. "You were called first?" she asks me. Her eyes go glassy, like she's hurt.

"That's what you care about right now?" I ask.

Prima tightens her grip on her coffee mug.

Skirts rustling, Trudy comes over, smiling wide. "How's everyone doing? Food all right? You look like you've had quite an adventure.

How was your road trip, Prima?" She refills Prima's mug of coffee, but Prima doesn't even acknowledge her.

Prima is usually the one who bends over backward to make people in customer service's job easier, just short of apologizing for existing. The fact that she doesn't even look at Trudy now means she's beyond reason.

Trudy's smile drops a little and she glances around the table as no one says anything. She gets the hint and hurries away. I remind myself to leave a generous tip.

"Do you have any idea what you've done?" Prima hisses through her teeth, barely opening her mouth. Her eyes pierce through me.

"I didn't—"

"You broke your valkyrie oath."

That's the furthest thing from my mind right now. I swirl my fork through the syrup on my plate.

Juniper's voice is soft as she speaks up. "Bryn was doing what she believed was right. We cannot fault her for that, can we?"

"She's thrown off the entire order of the universe." Prima turns back to me. "What's the one thing we're supposed to do, Bryn? One thing? Tell me."

I look at my plate and don't answer.

"I can't believe you. I literally can't believe you. But why am I not surprised you'd screw it up." Prima's shoulders drop and her fury turns on Juniper. "And you knew about this?"

Juniper goes pale, but I leap to her defense. "Juniper's got nothing to do with this."

"Reagan? Did you?" Prima asks, but Reagan looks so heartbroken, I can't meet her gaze.

"It was all me," I say.

"So then it was your idea to use Mom's seidr when I specifically told you not to?"

"Yes." I look at her solidly now. It's no one else's fault that I'm a screwup. I can at least own up to that much. "I wanted to find Mom. And I did. No thanks to you."

Prima's upper lip twitches. Her eyes dart from me, to Juniper, then to Wyatt, then back to me, lingering on the streaks of white hair framing my face. "What happened?"

"I met Mímir. He had me drink from his well to see where Mom is."

"No one can just drink from his well for nothing. What did you give him?"

"Ten years. Of my life."

Everyone at the table goes quiet.

"Oh, Bryn," says Reagan mournfully.

Prima stares at her steaming mug of coffee with a distant glare, and her face is tight and soured. "Where is she?"

"Valhalla. She's alive. But she's hurt."

Prima lets go of her coffee and drags her hand through her hair. Frustration streaks across her face, and I can see her brain working behind her wide eyes. It's almost like she's annoyed. I expected her to be overjoyed—*Great job, Bryn! You're the best!*—but instead it's like she's mad I found Mom first.

"I think Mom was trying to stop all this," I say, trying to stay focused. "The einherjar are under Loki's control. They invaded Utgard first, and Ravenswood is next. Whatever's happening, it's all connected."

"Ragnarök," Prima says.

"We can still stop it."

Prima's eyes darken. "There's only one way to fix this." She rises from the bench and moves around the table. "Wyatt, come with me. I'm taking you to Valhalla."

Wyatt's eyes go wide and I slam my fist down on the table, making the cutlery clatter. "Over my dead body."

James holds out his hand. "Whoa, hey, you can't be serious."

"Odin claimed him," says Prima.

I shield Wyatt from her. "What, you're going to kill him?"

"He belongs to Valhalla. He's the only way we can get to Asgard. Once we deliver him to Odin, we can rescue Mom. It's our duty."

It's terrifying to think that she's serious. Could she really kill a person with her own hands because a god told her to? I thought I knew my sister, but maybe I don't.

Reagan pleads with her. "Prima, slow down. Einherjar have to die in battle to go to Valhalla. How do we even know Odin still wants him?"

James stares, slack-jawed, at Wyatt.

Juniper stands and moves in front of Prima. "We won't let you hurt him."

A chill rakes down my spine as I realize the look on Prima's face is the same one I must have had when I found Wyatt in the lake and Valhalla was calling to him. Impassive. Resolute. An all-consuming compulsion for the sake of duty.

"There's another way to get to Valhalla," I say. "Mom left us raven feathers, one for each of us. They're in her trunk at home. We can use them to get to Asgard."

A darkness lifts from Prima's eyes and she blinks a few times. It's like she's snapped back to her senses.

"Um, sorry," says Trudy. I didn't hear her coming. She steps up to the table, gauging all of us with a wary expression. She must have heard us fighting. "I know it's probably a bad time but ... Wyatt?"

Wyatt looks up, surprised. "Yeah?"

"I just got off the phone." She gestures to the kitchen. "Apparently people have been trying to call you? Something about your dad." She glances around, nervous. "I'm not sure I should know this, but they said there was an incident at his prison? Some kind of . . . animal attack?"

Wyatt freezes, eyebrows up and mouth open.

Juniper and I look at each other. We're thinking the same thing: Did Wyatt's dad go berserk?

"Th-thanks, Trudy," Wyatt stammers.

"Is there anything I can do?" she asks. "Do you need a ride somewhere?"

"No. No, I can handle it."

"Okay." Trudy gives him a small, encouraging smile before she goes back to the kitchen.

No one speaks. Everyone stares at Wyatt as he stands up. He's pale and his fists are clenched at his sides.

"You okay, bro?" James asks.

Wyatt shudders out a breath and a million emotions flash across his face. "I have to go." All I want to do is touch him, but I stop myself, even when he rushes out of the Dragon's Den.

I glare at Prima before I chase after him.

"Wyatt!"

He's not too far ahead of me, but he's walking quickly. I have to catch up.

"Wyatt, wait," I say. He doesn't turn around, not until I run up and grab him by the back of his shirt, and tug.

He stops in the middle of the lane and faces me with a tight jaw and sorrowful eyes. Why is he the one who looks guilty?

"Are you okay?" I ask. "Do you want me to come with you?"

"No. You should stay here. In case Loki . . . If my dad went berserk, I need to check on him."

"But you hate him!"

Wyatt's eyes soften. "He's still my dad."

He turns to leave, but I grab his shirt again. "Wait. Before you go, I just wanted to apologize about Prima. She didn't mean—she's just scared. I won't let anything happen to you. I swear."

Wyatt draws his gaze upward, looking at the hazy orange sky drowned out by the city lights, like he's looking for stars. "It's okay."

I know he's lying. I've said everything's okay a million times and didn't mean it.

"I can figure this out. I didn't mean to make such a mess. I just want to make it all right."

"I know. I knew you were trouble the moment I first saw you." He says it with an amused smile that doesn't quite ease the pain in his eyes.

He takes my hand, and my skin comes alive at his touch. I don't want him to let go. When he looks at me with that glint in his eyes, something I can't quite name fills me up, makes me want to be reckless, to run, to fly. Why does my heart hurt so much?

"I was trying to find my Mom and I . . . I'm such a screwup."

He looks at our fingers, and rubs my knuckles with his thumb. It's crazy how the smallest touch can make me want to explode.

"You'd do anything for your family," he says. "And I have to do this for mine. My dad's correctional facility is only a few hours outside the city. I'll be back. I promise. It'll be okay," he says, giving me another smile.

He takes a step backward, and then another, still holding my hand.

"I'll be back," he says again before he lets go, turns, and runs down the lane.

31

I'm the last one to come home.

By the time I come upstairs, everyone must know I'm here, but no one looks at me. Reagan and Prima sit together on the couch, talking about what they're going to do next, while Juniper sits at the kitchen table, her hands clasped in front of her, her gaze distant.

The only one who acknowledges me is Butternut Squash, who weaves between my legs, begging for food.

I'm tired. Every muscle aches. All I want to do is collapse into bed and forget this day ever happened. But I can't. So I stand there, in the living room, my feet planted on the floor, because I don't know what else to do.

Prima speaks to me, but doesn't look at me. "So, were you ever going to tell me? About any of this?"

I huff out a laugh. "Why? It's not like you'd listen."

Prima stands up so suddenly, towering over me, I take a stumbling step back and knock into the coffee table. "Don't. You. Dare," she says, clipped, through her teeth.

"I had to do something. Unlike you!"

Prima's anger is palpable. "Unlike me?" When she laughs, it sounds more like a hiss. "Right."

Heat rises in my face. It feels an awful lot like shame, but I won't let it get to me. I punch it back down behind the dam in my chest. "Well, without me, you wouldn't know where Mom is now, would you? You wouldn't know that Valhalla's army is walking Midgard. You wouldn't know anything."

Prima's lips twitches into a snarl and I lift my chin. She looks like she wants to hit me, and I almost want her to.

Tears line her eyelashes but don't fall. "Is it fun for you? When I tell you to do something, and you do the opposite?"

"You didn't listen to me! I was telling you this whole time that something was wrong. What else was I supposed to do?"

"Not use dangerous valkyrie magic, for one!"

"I've been seeing the future and you didn't believe me. I was running out of options."

Reagan's eyebrows shoot up. "The future?"

"Mímir said I'm Skuld-touched."

Prima drags her hand over her face. "Great, that's yet one more thing I get to worry about! Lucky me!" She looks at the ceiling, shaking her head. "I don't know how to deal with you."

"Don't pretend like you care about me."

"You're my baby sister! How could you *think* that?" Prima cries. Her voice cracks when she does. "All I do is care! It's like a full-time job with you. And you throw it back in my face!"

I flinch at her words.

"Stop," Reagan says, holding out her hand. "We can fight about this later. Mom's still in trouble. How is she trapped in Valhalla? Why couldn't the ravens find her?"

Prima presses the heel of her palm to her eyes and walks away from me. Juniper still hasn't moved from the kitchen table.

"They must have been blocked somehow," I say. It's my best guess. None of this makes any sense.

"And how did those wolves get in? The fjötra hasn't been damaged since the draugar."

I shrug. I'm too tired to think.

Still with her back to me, Prima says, "Bryn. Go get the raven feathers."

Wordlessly, I do as she says. I find them exactly where I left them in Mom's trunk and bring them to her. She practically snatches them out of my hand.

"We're going to get Mom," Prima says. "She'll fix all of this."

"There's only three. One of us has to stay behind." I glance at Juniper.

"Oh, I'm sorry," says Prima, not sounding sorry at all. "By 'we,' I mean Reagan and me. You and Juniper are staying here."

"What!"

"This whole mess"—she vaguely waves toward the house and Ravenswood—"is because of you. All you do is make everything worse. All you ever do is ruin everything!"

Funny how some words can totally gut me.

The kitchen bench groans as Juniper stands, fists clenched at her sides. "Do not blame Bryn. Ragnarök is not her fault."

Prima casts a sidelong glance at her and waves her hand dismissively. "I've heard enough from the both of you. We're done here."

"All she has done is try to help, and she does not deserve to be treated this way."

"It's okay, Juniper," I say, holding out my hand. "I'm okay."

"No!" She marches toward us. "It is all my fault! I should have told you from the start, but I was afraid..."

Prima narrows her eyes. "What are you talking about?"

Juniper takes a shuddering breath and says, "Reagan, do you still possess the arm ring?"

Reagan reaches into her cardigan and pulls it out. The silver glints in the lamplight when she hands it to Juniper. "Did you figure out what it is?"

Juniper runs her thumb across the runes and takes a shaking breath as she looks at me. "Loki did not place it in Yggdrasil. I did."

"What?" I look at Prima, who stares shocked. "Why?"

"It is not meant to call monsters. It was forged by unbreakable magic. I wanted to use Yggdrasil's power to help reinforce the fjötra, make it so it could not be broken. It is made out of the same unbreakable chains that bind my father. Fenrir. The wolf."

No one speaks.

It's like I've been kicked in the chest.

Reagan rises to her feet and comes over, staring with disbelief. "You're joking...."

"What?" Prima says, barely a whisper, her face pale.

Juniper straightens her shoulders. "It was given to me when I was born. A raven feather from my mother, and an arm ring from my father. I am the daughter of Fenrir and Kara Martel."

No wonder Mom kept Juniper a secret.

Prima rounds on me. "Did you know about this?"

"What? No!" I blurt out, then look at Juniper. "Why didn't you tell us?"

"I was afraid that you would distrust me. That you would fear me."

I'm not sure that plan is working in her favor now, based on how Prima and Reagan are looking at her.

"You mean to tell me," Prima says, quietly, taking soft steps toward Juniper, "that our mother had a kid—you—with the giant wolf destined to kill Odin and destroy all the realms?"

"I do not want war. I want to protect this realm. All realms." Juniper's voice breaks. "The wolves today were scouts from Utgard. That can only mean the army has gathered. I tried to turn them back, but they would not. We must act now." She holds up the arm ring. "I must prove that I am unhurt, give them a chance to stop before it is too late."

I'm having a hard time wrapping my head around everything. How could this be real? It's like I've rounded the top of a roller coaster and now it's a straight drop down, and I have no other choice but to hold on.

"If Fenrir is your dad. Then your Amma..." I say, piecing it together. "She's Angrboda, isn't she? Loki's lover? The mother of monsters."

Juniper nods again.

Loki, our number one suspect this whole time, is actually Juniper's grandfather? This is all too much. I'm not sure what's real anymore.

Prima's eyes are flat, distant, and in the next breath a burst of light appears in Prima's hand and she levels her spear at Juniper's face, making Juniper flinch back. "You're a spy."

Juniper shrinks away from Prima's weapon. "I swear on the nine realms, I am not."

"We don't believe you," Reagan says, her knives flashing in her hand.

Not thinking, I leap in front of Juniper, shielding her. "Stop!"

Being on the other end of Prima's and Reagan's weapons makes my skin crawl, but I won't let them hurt Juniper. My sisters stare at me, their blades steadily aimed at my throat.

I sense Juniper get very still behind me, her breath quickening.

"Move, Bryn," says Prima.

"No."

"Move!"

I can tell they'll make me. Before anyone can do anything, Juniper shoves me into Reagan and throws a seed bomb at Prima.

Roots shoot out, wrapping around Prima like ropes. Before Prima falls, Juniper steals one of the raven feathers from her hand and runs.

"No!" Prima shouts as she hits the floor, arms and legs bound.

Reagan hurls a knife just as Juniper throws another bomb at her feet. The knife hits only solid roots as they weave into a thick wall between us, splitting the wood floor with a huge crack. Juniper's footsteps pound down the stairs as she runs.

By the time Reagan cuts Prima loose, Juniper is long gone with the raven feather.

"I knew she couldn't be trusted," Prima says through her teeth, getting to her feet.

"Bullshit," I spit, rounding on her. "She's been helping me figure out the kulning, and how to protect Ravenswood. Why would she be working against us?"

Prima jams her finger against her forehead. "Think, Bryn, for once in your life! Do you keep track of Juniper? Do you know where she goes when she's not with you?"

At first I don't want to think, I don't like being told what to do, but I can't help it as my mind rushes back. The troll—why was she awake when I was? The smoke bomb at the feast? The draugar attack the night of my flight with Wyatt? The old woman's death? The book, the robbery.

No, no, no! It can't be.

Prima clenches her jaw. "She was probably lying about everything."

"Why would she lie?" I ask.

"She's the enemy."

"She's our sister!"

"Prove it! A sister doesn't run!"

Without Mom, I can't prove it. All I have is Juniper's word. And all I can do is trust her. "She's running because you threatened her! She needed help, and look what we did! I'd run away, too! All you've proven so far is that you're willing to throw out any loyalty you have because you're told to."

Prima scowls and glances at Reagan. Reagan scoops up Butternut Squash and says, "Odin will have her executed. If he finds her, she'll be tried for her crime."

"What, for existing? Who gives a shit what Odin thinks?"

Both Prima and Reagan stare at me. What I've said is tantamount to blasphemy, but I don't care. After everything I've seen so far, of the gods, of draugar, of their magic hurting people, I've had enough. If Odin has a problem with it, he can take it up with me personally.

"Enemies of Odin are enemies of valkyries," Prima says, as if I don't know. "It's our job."

Well then, I guess I'm proving that I really am the worst valkyrie. "Aren't you tired of always being told what to do?"

Prima's eyes shine as she takes a step back, turns, and goes to her room. "Reagan, we're leaving. Now."

I follow her to her room. "Do you even know how to use the feather?"

"Yggdrasil's starlight. There's still time before the sun comes up." Prima takes off her sling and rolls her shoulder, wincing.

"You're hurt. You can't go."

Prima glares at me as she gets her jacket. "Reagan, make sure she doesn't follow us."

I ask, "What are you doing?"

"Something we should have done a long time ago."

Reagan looks like she's about to say something, but she holds herself back. She glances at me as if to say it's for my own good. She and Prima clasp hands, then they grab mine. The air shudders with their power as they summon a fjötra. I try to break free, but they hold me tight.

"You are not to walk through Ravenswood's gates until Mom gets home," Prima says. "Understood?"

The fjötra is cold and wet like egg yolks as it winds its way around my wrists, invisible shackles snaking up my arms and cinching closed as they set their intention. This is worse than being grounded.

"I'm sorry, Bryn," Reagan says as she walks away. "You'll be safer here."

"You can't leave me behind! You need me!"

Prima drops my arm, disappointment all over her face. "We really don't."

Behind her, Reagan puts the last raven feather on the table, looking at me briefly before looking away. She must know they only need one, that they can get Mom without me. I don't know how to change her mind. I'm more helpless than ever.

"Ready, Reagan?" Prima asks.

Reagan nods. "We'll be home soon. We promise."

32

I MUST HAVE FALLEN ASLEEP ON THE COUCH, BECAUSE I wake up curled against a pillow, still in my clothes from yesterday, as morning light pours in. Butters is crying for food. Besides that, the house is quiet and empty. The last raven feather sits on the coffee table as a reminder that this wasn't all a bad dream.

No matter how hard I try, I can't do anything right.

My insides twist as I hold my Yggdrasil pendant and think about what Prima and Reagan are doing without me, what they're accomplishing while I'm stuck here.

With Prima and Reagan off to save Mom, Juniper who-knows-where, and Wyatt with his dad, the only thing I can do is go to work.

But work doesn't distract me in the slightest. I move through my day, operating on autopilot, ringing up souvenirs for one guest after another with hardly a thought outside of wondering what is happening in Valhalla. Prima and Reagan should be finding Mom right about now, bringing her home any second.

Better them than me, I guess. They're the only ones who are capable of not screwing it up. Everything that could go wrong did, spectacularly. Practically blew up in my face like a powder keg.

One thing that Prima said still rattles around my head though. *All you do is make everything worse.*

It's true. I really am the best at being the worst.

When my lunch break finally comes, I stop by the house to check if anyone's back yet, but the only one who greets me is Butternut Squash, crying to be fed again. I cave and drop another scoop of cat food in the bowl.

With nothing else to do, I go to the one place I know I can vent.

The Dragon's Den is unusually quiet after the lunch rush ends. No one's here. But, as always, I find Trudy behind the bar, cleaning glassware and wiping down the counter.

I don't say a word as I slide onto a barstool and pillow my head in my arms.

"Nice hairdo," she says. "Did you do it yourself?"

I raise my eyes to look above my arms, and groan. Yet another reminder of what I've done.

"Uh-oh," says Trudy. "What's got you down?"

"Everything's great."

"What happened." She doesn't say it like a question, more like a spill-the-beans kind of way.

"Where to start? My mom's been at work for a while, and we couldn't reach her for a long time. Long story short, we found out where she is, so my sisters are going to get her. Without me."

"*Oof.* They left you behind?"

"They said I'd just get in the way." As I talk, Trudy pours me a pop from the tap. I don't deserve it, but I don't complain. "And it hurts because they're right."

"Where's your friend? The one with the ears?"

I wave vaguely in another direction. "Probably a whole world away."

"Well, is your mom okay at least?" Trudy asks. She slides me the drink and I take a sip.

"Yeah," I say, wiping my lips on the back of my wrist.

"That's good, right?"

"I guess. It's just all I've ever done is try to do the right thing. But I messed everything up, for real this time. It's bad."

Trudy leans on the bar, arms folded, as she watches me, her eyebrows knit in thought.

"Ah." She sucks on her teeth. "Being alone is the worst."

I try to say yeah, but my head feels too light. When I nod, it's like my skull will float away. I take another sip, trying to snap out of it, but the world tips under me.

Before I know it, I'm falling.

I slip right off the edge of the barstool and hit the floor, hard.

Everything is spinning. The edges of my vision start to go dark, and I fight to stay awake even though the idea of sleep feels pretty good right about now. What's happening?

My vision blurs, focusing and unfocusing, and the glass lies broken near my head, pop soaking into the floorboards. *Trudy?* I try to call out to her, but I can't talk. It's like my mouth is stuffed with cotton.

I roll over, and the ceiling spins like I'm on the scrambler. It's a color wheel of banners and royal crests.

Trudy appears over me, watching me without much concern at all.

"What did you do?" I try to ask, but I think it comes out more like *wha-doo-doo.* I try to get up, but my body won't work. Everything is so heavy. It's like holding the power button to force a computer to shut down, only a matter of seconds.

"It's okay, kiddo," Trudy says, her voice echoing as the dark swallows me up. "Everything is going to be okay."

⋈

The world melts back around me. It's like waking up from an afternoon nap and it takes me a second to remember where I am. For one, I know I'm not in bed.

My hands are chained above my head, and the floor is hard under my butt. I'm sitting, but I don't know where.

My eyelids feel so heavy. I force myself to open them.

Next to me, a skeleton sits on the floor, its bony arms shackled just like mine above its head, smiling its toothy grin in my direction. At first, I think it's a draug, and I scream and kick out and the skeleton falls to pieces, clattering hollowly on the hay-strewn floor. The sound itself makes me pause. When I look closer, I realize it's not a real skeleton. The bones are made of plastic, held together with wires, like a Halloween decoration.

And that's when I realize with a jolt that I'm in the Ravenswood Castle dungeon. They must have started decorating for haunted tours already. Like everything else in Ravenswood, the dungeon is authentic. The cell is lined with solid iron bars and stone, covered in sparse patches of hay and dirt. The only window I have is high above me, barred and level with the ground. A box of sunlight casts a yellow rectangle on the floor beyond my cell. I try to wiggle my fingers to slip out of the shackles, but they're tingling. I have no idea how long I've been locked up here. The skeleton may be fake, but these iron cuffs are very real.

"Help!" I try to scream, but it comes out like a croak. My throat is dry and words scrape like sandpaper, making me cough.

I try to lift the chain off the hook overhead, but I'm too low, and when I try to stand, I can't angle my legs under me. I'm trapped.

A shadow moves outside of the cell.

The first thing I see is her red hair, tied into a loose knot at the base of her neck, then the flowing white skirts of her Dragon's Den costume.

"Trudy! What the hell!"

"I told you everything was going to be okay," she says coolly.

"Full offense, but everything doesn't look okay! Let me go! Now!"

"I can't do that." She says it almost like she's sad, like she doesn't have any control over the matter, even though I see the keys dangling off her apron string. "The einherjar will be here soon."

How does she know . . . ? My head is still foggy. "If Loki is controlling you, or if you're under some spell, we can fix it! I can help you! You just have to let me go."

"I like you, Bryn. I really do. You've got a spark. That's why I'm doing this, instead of killing you."

"Excuse me, what?"

Trudy moves closer into the light. Even though this is the same Trudy I've known, she looks totally different now, but not in any physical way. A flat resolve has settled over her face, making her look stoic and dangerous. The skin on the back of my neck tightens, and I realize maybe I don't really know Trudy at all.

"It's you? You're the one behind the monsters attacking Ravenswood?"

She gestures to herself, looking quite proud. "Me."

"Let me go, Loki!"

A curious expression crosses Trudy's face. "Loki?" She almost laughs. "Why does he get all the credit for my hard work starting Ragnarök?"

My ears ring. This whole time we've been chasing after a trickster god who can look like anyone, and instead the culprit has been right under my nose.

315

I mean to say something clever, like *Aha! Of course I knew it was you all along!* Instead, what comes out is: "Huh?"

"You really aren't that bright, are you?"

That stings, and she knows it. I've only been spilling my guts out to her this whole time. Maybe I really am an idiot.

"Then if you're not Loki, who are you?"

"Really? You didn't figure it out?" Trudy smiles and sighs, like she's looking at a dumb puppy chasing its tail. "I've been waiting a long time for this," she says. From beneath her chemise, she pulls out a necklace with an Yggdrasil pendant. My necklace.

I look down at my chest and see that the pendant is gone.

"Give it back!" I snap. Somehow this makes me angrier than ever.

Trudy's laugh echoes off the walls of my cell. "This isn't yours."

I'm blinded for a second as Trudy's bartending uniform melts into bright light, turning into armor. A silver breastplate covered in runes, gleaming pauldrons, engraved braces, and a winged helm. With a great rush of air, metallic wings stretch out behind her. If I have armor, then she has capital-*A Armor*. It's breathtaking.

"Trudy. You're . . . a valkyrie?" I ask, stupidly.

"I am Thrúd of Asgard. Daughter of Thor. And *this* is your necklace." She holds it up, the Yggdrasil pendent Mom gave me glinting in the low light, before she tucks it into her armor. "From what I hear, you're still having a hard time using your magic without it."

"You . . . But . . . What?"

Thrúd huffs a sigh and her armor fades, returning to her normal self. It sounds as if I'm not reacting to her grand reveal in the way she expected. She paces back and forth in front of my cell. "Do you know how many people told me how lucky I was to be stationed in Valhalla? Being a daughter of Thor, everyone was patting me on the back, congratulating me on being handpicked by Odin himself. 'Oh,

Thrúd! You're so perfect for Valhalla! Everyone will adore you there! All the einherjar will fall in love with you! Yay, Thrúd!' Even my dad was proud, and he hardly paid me any attention."

I then realize just how much older Thrúd might be than I initially thought, how much more powerful. If she really is the daughter of a god, what else can she do? If I can keep her talking, maybe I can find a way out of this.

"And, I admit," she says, "Valhalla was good at first. Really good. But that's the thing about eternity . . . it gets boring. Fast. Every day is the same. You serve the same mead, serve the same boar, serve the same brainless, oafish einherjar every day again and again. Forever. Every mess I had to clean up, every smile I had to put on to make it through another hour, every thankless day . . . I was sick of it. It was time for something new."

"You want to start Ragnarök because you're *bored*?"

"We are valkyries! We are meant for the battlefield!"

"Pretty sure I wouldn't start Ragnarök because I hated my day job."

"It's not a day job. It's an *eternal* job. Can't clock out, can't take a break. Can't do anything—"

"Boo-hoo, cry me a river. Just quit like a normal person."

Thrúd goes still and squares up to me. She leans on the bars of the cell and watches me, a blue glow rising in her eyes. The hairs on my body stand on end, like static. She's a daughter of Thor, god of lightning. I brace for the shock, wait for the jolt to stop my heart, but the static fades, like she's only reminding me of what she can do to keep me in line. I remember this feeling. How could I forget? It was one of the best days of my life sword-fighting with Wyatt.

The rainstorm. The lightning. It wasn't a freak accident. "You tried to kill Juniper."

"I wanted my book."

"The spell book? How did . . . Why would that lady from Pagebound have it?"

"When I fought my way out of Valhalla, I was injured. I lost control of that sleipnir and dropped my book in the woods. That woman found it and kept it for herself—fortunately I had some pages with me, but by the time I figured it out, she'd already sold it to you."

"It wasn't really a heart attack, was it? It was a shock to the heart. You murdered her."

Thrúd shrugs. "She stole my stuff. And I stole it back. My einherjar were a good distraction to keep you occupied."

Distraction. Just like the smoke bomb at the feast, making Wyatt go berserk, to summon more monsters. Of course, a valkyrie would know how to make a berserker lose control. She would have been training them for a millennia in Valhalla. Why didn't I realize it before? I clench my fists despite my numb fingers. "You trashed our house. You hurt Prima."

"I never thought she would be there! Can't you see? I don't want to hurt your family! We valkyries, we're bonded by more than blood. I'll build a future where we—you, me, your sisters even—can stop waiting on the sidelines. The battlefield is where we belong! We'll build a new universe, together!"

She's nuts. No way would my family join her, never. "So the attack on Utgard, that was just the beginning for you?"

"It was a good test run. Make it look like Hel-walkers have risen, that Ragnarök had begun. And if anyone found out my draugar were really einherjar, it would be even more reason to go to war with Asgard. That half-breed giant surprised me though, I admit. I didn't think anyone could escape, so when she showed up here of all places you can imagine how surprised I was."

Thrúd's smile is cold. "But even so, attacking Utgard proves the giants are ready for Ragnarök, and wouldn't want to be caught flat-footed in the ultimate battle. The giants want war just as much as we do. It would work itself out in the end." She grins, lifting one shoulder. "Ragnarök! And Midgard is our battleground. Their hatred for each other is the perfect opportunity to get what I want."

"Oh, go fart lightning bolts."

She looks at me, her mouth not quite forming a smile, as if it's snagged on a sneer. I may have hit a nerve, and it gives me a sliver of satisfaction.

"Why couldn't you just attack the giants yourself?" I ask.

"I needed an army. I needed Odin's army. To control them, I needed his death magic, and the only way I could learn it was by drinking from Mímisbrunnr. Mímir tried to talk me out of it, but... funny how persuasive a knife to the throat can be."

"So why are they draugar?"

Thrúd paces in front of my cell. "Part of my sacrifice was that I could know Odin's magic but I wouldn't be able to remember it. I learned how to control his armies, control monsters, so I needed to record what I could before I forgot. I wrote it all down in my book. That's why the einherjar aren't quite... whole. Though I suppose I don't need them to be."

Now I remember how vague Mímir was when I saw him, how he'd said he learned the hard way not to challenge valkyries. I was so focused on finding my mom, I didn't stop to ask.

"My mom knew what you were doing. She got a raven-message before she disappeared," I say, piecing it all together.

"My sisters-in-arms were getting suspicious of me. I trusted a few of them, believing they shared my vision. One of them must have sent her a message asking for her help. By the time it reached your mother, it was already too late. I admit, your mom put up a good fight."

Anger rushes up in me again. Thinking about Thrúd hurting my mom makes my blood boil.

"Oh, don't look at me like that. She's fine! Relax! She got a few good hits in. Though I expected as much after battling my way through my sisters before her. She almost got me—would have, but for the fjötra I used to trap her. And with your sisters trying to rescue her, it's only making my plan easier, leaving Midgard exposed and defenseless. All that stands in my way is one little valkyrie." She accentuates those last three words by tapping a delicate fingernail on the bars to my cell. Somehow, coming from her, I'm smaller and more of a failure than ever.

"If you hurt my family, I swear . . ."

"Please. They're way safer in Valhalla than they would be here. I'll need more valkyries when this is done. Soon enough, they'll see that this is for the best . . . for all of us. The einherjar will rise at nightfall. Once the gods and giants fight each other to the death over this, I'll rule all the realms like they were meant to be ruled."

"There won't *be* any more realms to rule!"

"Then at least I won't be answering to anyone anymore. Not einherjar, not my sisters-in-arms, and definitely not Odin. I am a valkyrie, born for war, and I will have it. What's the point of having a huge army if you don't even use it?"

I'm so angry, I'm shaking. "What about when it's over? What about when there's no one left?"

Thrúd cocks her head to the side, like I'm an idiot who needs to have the simplest things explained to her. "There will always be an enemy to fight. And aren't valkyries the best ones to lead the charge?"

I can already picture it. Thrúd as the new god of war—endless war. I yank on the chains again, but they won't break.

"When I get out of here, I'm going to kill you," I say like it's a promise.

"There's that valkyrie rage! Almost makes me wish it didn't have to be this way. I would have liked you to be at my side in the end."

I grit my teeth and pull on the chains, but I'm not strong enough. Angry tears sting my eyes.

"I've already set the kulning. The fjötra is broken. With that giant's arm ring gone, you've made my job a lot easier, so I thank you."

"Juniper will tell Jotunheim what's happening. It won't work."

"No one can stop this war. Not you. Not the giants. Not even Odin. But I can start it. My einherjar will be here soon," she says over the sound of my chains as I try to yank them free of the wall. I've given up on trying to reason with her.

From the shadows, she shakes out an inky black cloak covered in feathers. A raven cloak, the same one all proper valkyries wear. Her face falls, and she looks at me again, sounding genuine. "I'm sorry, Bryn. I really am. I would have hoped you'd understand, but maybe when this is all over, I'll build a new afterlife, just for you."

Then, she clasps the cloak around her neck, and Thrúd vanishes in a flurry of raven feathers.

33

No matter how hard I try, the iron cuffs dig into my wrist bones and send shooting pains up my forearms. I have to get out of here. I have to warn someone.

I try to stand up. First, I wedge one of my legs underneath me and try to push off the floor. It's an odd angle, and I have to ram my back into the wall to get into a half-kneel. Sweat breaks out on my forehead. I swear as my hip pops when I wiggle my other leg under me. In one huge heave, I manage to stand up and the chain slips off the hook.

I'm still handcuffed.

I rush the bars and press my face between them. I can't see a whole lot down either side of the hall, but as far as I can tell, I'm the only one here.

I scream so loud and so long, my voice breaks. I'm running out of time. No one's coming.

Panic rises up in me and I start to pace. *Okay, Bryn. Think. Breathe. Then think. There's no time for panic. You can figure this out yourself. You're not too late.*

Of course, I'm lying. I can't even convince myself otherwise. I need help. I can't do this alone.

And I'm not alone. My eyes land on the skeleton, an idea forming. "Hello, Mr. Bones."

The wire holding the skeleton together easily slips out of the drill holes, and I twist and bend a couple wires together into a pretty convincing set of lock-picking hooks. It's not the best, but it's not the worst.

I insert the hook into the handcuff, working at such an awkward angle I have to use my teeth to hold it steady, and slide the other wire into the lock.

I work at it, slowly, diligently, despite the adrenaline making my hands shake, and then there's a satisfying little *click*.

The shackles drop with a clang to my feet and I rub feeling back into my wrists. There's no time to be relieved as I rush to the cell bars again and try to see if anyone is nearby.

"Hello!" I cry again, my voice echoing into the empty castle. Of course no one answers.

Blindly, I fumble for the lock on the other side of the door, running my finger over the keyhole. I won't be able to see what I'm doing, but I have to try.

I insert my makeshift picks into the slot, feeling my way through the pins. My hands are shaking so badly, I'm afraid I'll drop them. Adrenaline is not making things easier. Fortunately for me, I don't drop my picks. Unfortunately for me, the lock goes click, but it's not the good kind of click. My stomach drops. "No," I groan. One of the wires snapped in half, and a part of it is still stuck inside the lock, jamming it. "No, no! Stupid!"

Mrrup! A soft meow echoes down the hall.

I know that meow. "Butters!"

Sure enough, it's Butternut Squash, my lucky charm. She prances in, tail high, as if she's begging for food.

"Am I glad to see you! Get me out of here, please." I'm not sure how an orange tabby cat with no opposable thumbs is going to be useful in this situation, but hey, I have to try something. "You have to find someone like a custodian, or a locksmith, so they can take off the hinges. Midgard depends on it! I will give you so much food, you won't know what to do with it."

Butters just looks at me flatly. She sniffs the bars and then looks up at me with her wet, empty eyes.

"Come on, Butters. You gotta help me."

Mrrup! With a flick of the tail, Butters turns around and leaves.

"Butters! Come back here, you—" But Butters is gone. My luck, again, literally running out.

The sun is already setting. The einherjar—draugar—whatever, will be here soon.

I close my eyes and lean on the bars, thumping my head on the solid iron.

I should never have let my sisters go alone. I should have talked them into letting me come with them. But then I would be trapped with them right now if I had.

If they were here, Prima would no doubt tell me how I'm an idiot for trusting Thrúd, but Reagan would use her magic to get us out.

Why not try now?

I stand back and shake out my hands. What did Reagan tell me before? Focus my intention. What do I want to do? What does it look like? I roll out my shoulders and bounce on the balls of my feet. "I can do this. I can do this."

I stand in the middle of my cell and face the door. I hold my hands in front of me, hovering my palms over each other, and focus. Sweat immediately breaks out on my lower back. I imagine creating a cannonball, or a sword, or—shit, even another set of lockpicks, calling the shape of it to form between my hands.

I hold my breath, straining with the effort, and focus on the space between my hands, but I can't do it for long enough for anything to happen. I drop my hands, exhausted, and let out a groan.

Without my necklace, I'm not sure I can even use my magic.

Magic doesn't come easy to me, not like it does for my sisters. And Juniper. I wish I could tell her how sorry I am for letting it get this far. None of this was ever her fault, and I shouldn't have doubted her. I wonder if she's found a way to get back to Utgard somehow. But even then, no matter where she goes, she won't be safe. No one will.

I have to stop Ragnarök before it destroys all the realms.

I hold up my hands, close my eyes, and try again. This time I can't focus on any weapon in particular. Instead, I focus on my target. Just like shooting my arrows—Mom taught me early on not to look at the tip of the arrow, but where I was aiming. I think about Thrúd, I think about the einherjar, I think about them hurting people.

The space between my hands feels more solid somehow, but I don't dare look.

"Bryn!"

A voice jolts me and a flurry of ghostly arrows escape my hand. They go flying, missing Wyatt's ear by a hair just as he dodges out of the way.

He looks at the space where the arrows flew by and then looks back at me, stunned, but unhurt. "Close one!" he says.

"Wyatt!" I rush to the bars, completely ignoring the fact that I created a dozen arrows out of thin air, because now I'm holding Wyatt's hands. "Your dad! The animal attack!"

"I showed up and no one had any idea what I was talking about—"

"It was a lie! Trudy lied! She wanted to separate us."

"It almost worked, too!" Another person calls from down the hall, being led by Butternut Squash.

"Juniper!" She smiles at me, staff in hand, moss cloak around her shoulders just like the first time I met her. I reach out my hand and she holds it. "You're not on Utgard!"

"No! I used the raven feather and sent my arm ring back instead, a sign telling Amma I'm all right, to stand down."

"How? The stars, you can't see them from here!"

"The seed from Yggdrasil!" She shows me the empty glass vial around her neck. "It acted as a . . . what did you call it, Wyatt?"

"A battery."

"Yes! Battery. My seed magic and the ring would be enough."

"You helped?" I ask him.

Wyatt blushes. "It was kind of my idea. We ran into each other and she told me what she needed to do, and I remembered what you said about the Milky Way and Yggdrasil."

Juniper continues, "And so what does that make a seed from the tree?"

"A star," I say, amazed. I press my forehead against the bars, relieved. "I'm so glad to see you guys."

Mrrup goes Butternut Squash. She came back. I could kiss that cat a million times.

"What happened?" Juniper asks. "Why are you imprisoned?"

"Thrúd! Trudy from Dragon's Den. She's a valkyrie. A bad one. It's not Loki. She's the one behind Ragnarök."

"What?" they ask in unison.

"I'll explain on the way. Jotunheim might not be marching, but draugar still are. The lock is busted. Get me out of here."

Juniper rummages in her bag and pulls out a seed bomb. She

throws it on the stone and roots burst between the gaps in the rock, wrapping around the bars like rope.

Wyatt tells me to stay clear and I do, pressing back up against the far wall, while Juniper scoops Butternut Squash into her arms and out of the way. Wyatt's enveloped in a swirl of white mist and turns into a bear. He takes some of the roots with his giant teeth and he pulls like it's an epic game of tug-of-war. The roots creak, straining against the bars as Wyatt huffs and digs his paws in. With a grinding sound and then a terrible wrenching noise, the bars yank out of the wall and hit the other side of the dungeon.

I throw myself into the mist as Wyatt changes back and wrap my arms around him and Juniper. Wyatt wavers on his feet for a moment, dizzy, but I hold him close to me and Juniper as I bury my face against his shoulder. Wyatt tenses up, but slowly his arm wraps around my back as he relaxes. Juniper squeezes me so hard, my back cracks.

"I made a promise, didn't I?" Wyatt murmurs in my ear. Wyatt's eyes shine when he smiles, and I want to grab him by the face and kiss him, but I don't. I pull out of the hug and take a deep breath. There are bigger things happening.

While we rush out of the castle and into the faire, I fill them in on everything that's happened and Butters makes a break for Yggdrasil, clawing up the trunk and disappearing into the branches, which sway like a storm is coming. By now, the sun has set. It's only a matter of time before the draugar show up.

"People are still in Ravenswood," Wyatt says as we move through the square, full with guests. "The gates don't close for another hour."

Juniper nods. "If the draugar are coming, we need to get everyone to safety."

"I'm not sure anywhere is safe." I start thinking of what we could try. I could pull a fire alarm, make it seem like an emergency that everyone needs to evacuate. Or I could go on the comms system and make an announcement saying there's a loose animal. Or I could cause a real fire and blow something up, which would give us different problems.

"What happened to your valkyrie pendant?" Juniper asks.

"Trudy—Thrúd stole it."

Wyatt looks worried. "Without your armor, you'll be exposed."

"I don't care about that right now," I say. "What kind of valkyrie am I if I need magic armor?"

"Oh no!" Juniper cries, looking back toward the castle.

"What's wrong?"

"Yggdrasil," she says. "I hear it. It's warning us. They're coming."

"Look!" Wyatt points toward the main gate. Instead of running out of the park, people are running back in, tripping over themselves and dropping whatever they've been holding. It's a mess of souvenirs, and wooden shields, and ice-cream cones. Something is chasing them.

Nearby is the archery range, where some curious guests stop their target practice and crane their necks to see what the commotion is about. I rush in and grab a bow and a quiver of arrows, and no one even gives me a second glance as I casually steal it. I cinch the quiver tight over my shoulder and inspect the bowstring. It's old and a little frayed, but there's no time for me to go home to get my own bow. Gotta work with what I've got.

I have to rush after Wyatt and Juniper, already way ahead, and catch up near the front gate. They've had to stop, with the crowd of people fleeing toward us.

I ready an arrow, but I can't find a target. Guests look scared, some look excited, constantly looking over their shoulder wondering just why people are screaming in the distance. Some are confused. A guest asks me, based on the fact I'm still in in my gift shop surcoat, "Is this part of the Halloween show? Kind of early for a zombie parade, don't you think?"

"Yes!" I say, putting on my best smile. "This is all part of the show! The best viewing experience is actually that way though," I say, pointing in the opposite direction, toward the castle. "You better hurry, or all the seats will be taken!"

The guests hurry off, more eager to catch a sneak peak of a special event than to run for their lives. But hey, whatever works.

"This is going to be a disaster," Juniper says, clutching her staff. "There are too many people!"

"I still can't see any draugar," says Wyatt.

Dozens more guests flood in through the gates, confusion and fear rising in their eyes. More screams cut through the air. Even more people rush in, and I'm now against the gift shop. I yank Wyatt and Juniper inside with me and close the door, shutting out the shouts of panic. We need space to think, but we're not alone.

A pair of kids, siblings I think, are crying under a dragon plushie display. The girl is older, about seven or so, and the boy is around five.

"Where're your parents?" I ask.

"I don't know!" the girl says through sobs. "What's happening?"

"I don't like zombies," the boy cries.

Oddly enough, this calms me down. "Me too," I admit, "but it's going to be okay. I promise. Take your sister's hand, that's it, and— Here." I give the girl a Ravenswood dragon to hold. "This will protect you."

The little girl and her brother huddle together, ducking their heads, and clutch the plushie like it's a life jacket. Sometimes a lie can be a good lie for the sake of someone else.

"It's not safe here," Wyatt murmurs in my ear so they don't hear the edge in his voice.

"Working on it," I say.

The gift shop door bursts open, making us spin around, hands up, ready to fight—but we drop them when we see who it is. James.

"What the hell is going on?" He's breathless as he slams the door closed, locks it, and presses himself against it in pale-faced terror.

"Get out of here!" Wyatt barks.

"Draugar! They're here!" James hisses, trying to keep his voice low. He crouches down at the window, peeking through the glass. No one's outside anymore. Most people have fled.

"And more will be coming," I say. "You need to leave. Now."

"Get down!" Wyatt grabs my wrist and pulls me under a table just before draugar appear outside the window. Horned helmets, wiry beards, skeletal sneers—all of the draugar armed.

The first wave of Valhalla's army has arrived.

We crouch low, trying to stay out of sight as a draug approaches the window. From my angle, I can see James pressing himself flat against the wall, his chest rising and falling with fear. Juniper shivers next to me and I hold her hand. Wyatt's wide eyes catch mine, but neither of us dare to speak.

The draug puts a frostbitten hand to the window, the exposed bone on his fingers scraping the glass. Then, it knocks a few times, peering with glowing orange eyes into the dark gift shop. In its other hand is a gleaming axe that catches the light of the lanterns. I'm frozen, watching from beneath the table, clutching Juniper with all I have. Blood roars in my ears.

The kids hold each other, their faces buried in their arms, and they squeeze the dragon plushie so hard, it activates the voice box. "You're a treasure to me!" the dragon guffaws, breaking the silence. The kids look at the toy in horror, but they can't shut it off. They let out a small squeak of fear, but I shush them with a finger to my lips.

The draug cocks its head. Did it hear us? It stares for a long moment, its skeletal face unreadable. Then, slowly, the draug sinks down, vanishing from the window.

Shit, shit, shit.

"Did it leave?" James hisses.

As if to answer him, there comes a great *BANG* beneath our feet as what sounds like a heavy fist pounds beneath the wooden floor, trying to break through.

Then *Bang! Bang! BANG!*

More and more fists pummel like thunder and the floorboards pulse when draugar try to come up below us. We all leap to our feet, ready to run, but the floorboards hold. Any second, a hand will grab us, but so far all the draugar can do is make us feel like we're standing on a subwoofer.

Then I remember how Juniper could wrap her roots around draugar, how she could pin them down, and the realization hits me.

"Wood!" I say to Juniper. "They can't phase through wood!"

Her eyes widen when she realizes what I'm getting at.

I have an idea.

34

"WE HAVE TO GET PEOPLE TO THE CASTLE!" I SHOUT OVER the fists pounding on the floor beneath us. "It's made of stone and wood. Draugar can only phase through dirt. It's protected."

"Are you sure?" James asks.

"It is the best choice we have," says Juniper.

"And we can defend the tree at the same time," I say. "If the draugar cut it down, it's over."

Still keeping an eye on the floor as the boards bounce with each blow from a draug fist, Wyatt asks, "How are we supposed to get there?"

"And with cargo," James says. The kids hold on to him, their prince, for dear life.

"We need a distraction," I say. I'm already thinking about how I can draw attention, when Wyatt turns to James, a gleam in his eye. Whatever he says with that look, James doesn't like it.

James shakes his head and wags his finger. "No, nuh-uh. No way."

"The Chant. Oathbreaker's Vengeance. The Scratch and Rumble." I realize Wyatt's listing off choreography moves they use in their shows. "Take your pick."

"I'm not going out there with you!"

"We do this all the time," Wyatt says.

"In the arena! For an audience! This isn't pretend, Wyatt!"

Wyatt goes to the souvenir weapons hanging on the wall and tosses a sword to James, who catches it. The kids look up at James like he's their hero, and he swallows thickly. He's a coward, except when his narcissism is at stake.

"Fine!" James groans. "The Scratch and Rumble sounds good."

With his own sword in hand, Wyatt moves to the door.

Juniper takes the kids, who cheer them on.

"Meet us at the castle," I say.

Wyatt looks back at me and gives me one last nod before he and James rush out the door.

James projects his fake English accent loudly, reciting the scene I've heard so many times. "Avast, blaggard! What pray thee plan to do next before I strike thee down?"

The pounding on the floorboards stops as the draugar follow the sound of James's voice. He and Wyatt stand back-to-back, weapons raised. Slowly, a handful of draugar emerge from the dirt and stalk toward James and Wyatt. Wyatt cuts down toward the nearest draug, who deflects his sword with an axe, and another goes for James, who lets out a frightened scream and takes off running, leaving Wyatt no choice but to follow.

Together, they disappear in the opposite direction of the tree as the draugar chase them.

I wait a beat and then another, making sure the draugar are gone, before opening the door and stepping onto the empty street. It's littered with garbage.

I look back where I last saw Wyatt, but don't see or hear any sign of him. I wish I'd said something to him, as I take off running toward the castle.

When I get closer, I see more and more people, guests and staff alike, standing around confused. At the square, the kids have found their parents and cry as they get scooped up into their arms. It's still not safe for everyone to be out in the open like this.

I leap up to the wooden stage, recently rebuilt from the troll attack, and grab the microphone.

"Hear ye, hear ye! Citizens of Ravenswood!" My bad English accent booms over the speakers as I address the crowd from atop the stage. "The show is just getting started! If thou'd be so kind as to file into the castle with the nice wooden floors and giant wooden drawbridge in a calm and orderly fashion! Please, uh—prithee!"

Juniper helps guide excited guests into the castle as murmurs of curiosity fill the air. Most guests are thrilled this is a special event.

I notice, with a lurch, there is a trio of people with clipboards looking around the faire, eyebrows raised. They must be the critics for *Travel Expert Magazine*. They linger near the stone troll, making notes, before letting Juniper bring them inside.

As the last guest shuffles in, going *ooh* and *ahh*, amazed by the interior of the castle, I still can't see James or Wyatt. Juniper and I stand on the drawbridge together, scanning the streets.

"Where are you guys?" I plead. They should be here by now. I can't see anything down the firelit streets, no movements in the dark, not even draugar.

I shouldn't have let him go without me. I should have been the one to cause a distraction.

"There!" Juniper points down the market lane.

It's James, alone, charging right for us at full speed, terror all over his face. His shoulder is bleeding, red soaking through his T-shirt. Where's Wyatt?

"Wait for me!" James screams. "Wait!"

Sprinting behind him is a wave of fifty draugar. They swarm the street, rushing across the dirt so fast, closing in.

A strange shadow moves among them, huge and hulking. At first, it looks like another troll, but then I realize it's a bear.

Wyatt.

He roars and bites down on a draug, shaking his head like he's got a chew toy and throws the draug into a cluster of draugar, sending bodies flying like bowling pins. He doesn't seem to be slowed down at all by the axes and swords that slice into him. It seems to be making him angrier as draugar swarm him.

James waves his arms and screams, "Raise the bridge! Raise the bridge!" The fastest draug is almost on him.

Just before the draug can jump on James's back, I lodge an arrow in its eye and it goes down, but another is close behind.

James dives headfirst through the door past us. Juniper doesn't waste a second. Right before another draug can reach it, she summons roots to flip the lever and raise the drawbridge. James and I bar the door closed, slotting a wooden beam in place for good measure.

We left Wyatt alone out there.

As if reading my mind, James gasps, "He told me. To run." He holds his hand over his bleeding shoulder, looking pale. Wyatt's roars from outside cut right through me.

"I have to help him," I say.

"How?" Juniper asks. "I sealed the door. If I let you out, draugar can get through."

I move through the packed castle, weaving through bodies crowding in the hall.

All the tables have been pushed to the side, giving everyone enough room to mill about and chat with one another, oblivious to the danger they're in. The battle rages outside, but why would they think anything's wrong? Questions are thrown around left and right.

"Where's the brochure?"

"How long is this going to last?"

"Where's the bathroom?"

James climbs on top of one of the tables, addressing the crowd with his trademark smile, despite the fact that he's covered in his own blood.

"Good evening, everyone! If you'd be so kind as to sit tight while we get everything ready—" There's a deafening *boom* at the door that shakes the whole castle. People gasp as dust rains down from the ceiling, but the door holds. James keeps smiling. "It's an interactive experience!"

While James assures them that this is all part of the show, he convinces some bards to start playing in an effort to drown out the battle raging outside.

My plan is working so far, but how long it'll last, I'm not sure. As long as people are safe behind walls made of literally anything else other than dirt, the draugar can't get them. But Wyatt is still alone out there.

Wyatt's uncle Stan spots me through the crowd and pushes toward us, frantic. "Bryn! Where are the valkyries?"

"Wh-what? You know about—"

"Later! Where are the others?"

There's no time for me to process any of this. "It's just me," I say, as another boom shakes the door.

"And Wyatt?"

"He's still out there."

Stan looks horrified.

"I'll get him," I say. "I swear."

He sets his jaw and nods, then turns to Juniper. "How can I help?"

"Seeds! I need plants!"

"The garden." Stan pushes through the crowd, heading to the back garden, but before Juniper can follow him, I hold her back.

"I'm going to get to Wyatt, and then I'm going home. There's one raven feather left. I can use it to get to Valhalla, rescue everyone, and stop Thrúd."

"But there is a whole army standing between you and the house!"

"We can make it." Even I'm starting to wonder if I'm lying to myself. "You and James stay here with Stan. Keep him safe, for Wyatt. Get your seeds and then seal the door. Defend Yggdrasil at all costs. If anything happens to it, it's over."

Juniper nods stiffly, and then she wraps me in a hug. I squeeze her back. I want to tell her how glad I am to be her sister, but I choke on the words. I don't want that to be the last thing I say to her, a thing so sad I don't even want to think about it, so I settle on: "Bye." And head for the last exit I have.

I take the spiral staircase three at a time and barge into Mr. Beaumont's office, the tallest part of the castle, getting a three-sixty view of the faire.

Ravenswood is surrounded.

The dead swarm the streets, their war cries rising up in the air, the glow of their orange eyes unmistakable. Smoke rises from the outer edges of the faire as the draugar carve their way through, destroying everything in their path.

On the lake, sailing from the east, a hundred wooden ships carry even more. Their shields and armor glint in the moonlight. Oars push them toward shore.

The furious beat of their war drums matches the rhythm of my heart.

All of Valhalla is here.

And Wyatt is out there.

I move to the window just as a hand lashes out and grabs me by the wrist.

I raise my fist, but stop just short of punching Mr. Beaumont in the nose. He's curled up under his desk, terrified. He holds his knees to his chest, trembling, and stares at me with round eyes. "What's happening?"

"Monsters are attacking Ravenswood."

Mr. Beaumont is frozen with fear. He doesn't know how to process, even when the proof is right in front of him.

I open a window overlooking the square and lean out. The ground is swarming with draugar. Below, I spot Wyatt, his giant bear form like a tank, but he can't last forever. Foam drips from his jaws, and I can tell he's exhausted.

I picked up fewer than a dozen arrows from the archery range— hardly enough to make a dent in the draugar numbers. Even though I summoned arrows in the dungeon, I can't rely on it. There are more arrows at home, but they won't be enough against hundreds of draugar.

From up here, I can see Juniper has already encircled Yggdrasil with a tight net of vines and roots, blooming roses and wildflowers. The draugar can't break through, no matter how they hack and saw at the wall.

Obviously, I can't shoot them all. I have to think bigger.

Behind Wyatt, the sea of draugar parts as a taller, heavily armored draug approaches. The draug removes its rusting helmet, grinning with frostbitten blue lips.

The draug screams as mist envelops its body and out rises a giant, undead grizzly bear. Its face is half-rotted off, its ribs exposed, its fur mottled and gray. It roars, spittle flying everywhere.

Draug berserker? Draug berserker!

Wyatt spins around just as the zombie bear tackles him with such force, it blows back nearby draugar. They claw, bite, and punch each other, crushing anyone under them as they wrestle.

Wyatt stands on his hind legs and sinks his teeth into the draug, but the draug doesn't seem affected. It grabs Wyatt and throws him to the ground.

I have to do something.

Draugar rush the raised drawbridge, barraging it with sheer numbers, but my eyes land on the rope levering it up. Time for a physics lesson.

"What are you doing?" Mr. Beaumont asks as I put one leg through the window and sit on the ledge. I grab hold of one of the lines of Ravenswood bunting that stretch across the square and wrap it around my wrist. I hope this works.

"You said it yourself, Mr. Beaumont." I give him a smile. "The show must go on!"

From my quiver, I pull out an arrow and aim for the drawbridge rope. I draw back, breathe, and let loose. The arrow flies true.

It slices through the rope, split ends fraying as the fibers break one by one.

The rope splits even more, then the whole thing snaps.

The drawbridge groans on its hinges like a cave troll and then it begins to fall.

The draugar below only have time to look up.

WHAM—it crashes flat on top of them and the draug berserker, smashing them all to dust with such force, the whole earth rumbles.

Shaking his head, Wyatt manages to get back to his feet. Other draugar are so surprised, they stop long enough for him to pounce and tear into them with his huge paws.

Without wasting another second, I fling myself out the window. I'm falling.

My stomach lurches up as I'm weightless, and I realize how stupid I am—then the bunting line yanks hard on my wrist and I swing down to the fallen drawbridge. I let go just in time to roll to my knee on the ground.

I let loose a flurry of arrows, downing the draugar as they rush Wyatt.

Wyatt rises up on his hind legs, roaring, and he swipes the rest away. But he's exhausted. He hits another draug, but his eyes roll back and he groans. He falls.

Mist explodes around him. He's turning back.

I down one more draug with an arrow to the eye and charge into the mist, where I slam into Wyatt—on his knees, human again—dizzy and weak. Without stopping, I grab his arm and yank him to his feet. "Let's go!"

The mist gives us enough cover as we sprint away from the castle toward home. But the draugar see us and scream. Their armor clangs as they run after us, the sound getting closer and closer.

My legs and lungs burn as I sprint up the street, Wyatt beside me.

A draug leaps, attempting to tackle me from behind, but Wyatt knocks me out of the way just in time. The draug howls like nails on a chalkboard and tries to attack again, but we don't stop.

"Keep running!" I scream.

I can already see the house.

Draugar are right on us as I throw myself in through the front door, Wyatt right behind me, and we slam the door closed. Draugar throw themselves against it, rattling the frame.

"You saved me again," Wyatt says, jamming his shoulder against the door.

"Let's not keep count." I knock the coatrack off its legs and wedge it across the door. "That won't last for long. Quick!"

I run upstairs and grab the raven's feather still on the coffee table. "Bryn!"

Wyatt stands at the top of the stairs, looking down at the front door. The coatrack is almost broken in half. Draugar are coming.

I grab Wyatt's hand just as the door splinters open and draugar flood into the house, screeching in fury. We run for the attic, climbing another floor just as the draugar rush the living room.

In my room, we use my dresser and my mattress as barricades. The draugar try to smash their way through, but the door holds. Breathless, Wyatt and I stumble back. I realize we're still holding hands.

"Are you okay?" I ask. He's got some bruises and a few scrapes.

"I'm okay," he says, nodding. "Are you?"

"Yeah."

He cups his hand on the side of my face and lifts it to see me better. His eyes are bright and his hand is warm on my cheek. His fingers brush against my skin and my stomach swoops. The thump on the door must make him realize what he's doing, and he snatches his hand away. The draugar will be here any second.

I grab my bow, the one my mom made me, and my quiver hanging at the foot of my bed. Twelve more arrows. Don't fail me now.

"What's the plan?" he asks.

I hold up the raven feather. "I'm going to Valhalla."

"Do you want me to come with you?"

I strap my quiver across my back and smile. "I didn't let Valhalla have you then, I won't let it have you now."

The way he looks at me makes it hard to look away. I don't know how to process it. No one has ever looked at me like that before, and a million emotions rush through me. My first instinct is to make a joke so I don't have to acknowledge those feelings. I'm so used to keeping them nestled safely in a sealed box behind my sternum. But now it's just me and him, and a thousand draugar pounding on the door. "Bryn, I . . ." He trails off, a blush high on his sweaty cheeks.

I like it when he says my name. I like it when I make a joke and he has to hide his laugh, or when he's embarrassed, or when he's shy. And all of a sudden, like getting hit with a ten-pound brick right in the gut, I realize I like *him*. And I'm not afraid to admit it anymore.

His eyes dart between my eyes and my lips, and he holds his breath like he wants to say something more. I want to say something too, but I can't think of anything at all that would be right for the situation.

But if this is the end of the world, don't I want to kiss someone in the midst of it all?

I'm moving before I even realize it, and he's leaning in, too. His lips are soft, and warm, and he puts his hand on my cheek again, tipping my face up to his as we kiss deeply. My mind goes blank, like TV static, and I'm lost in his touch. Pretty good for our first one, and pretty good if it's our last, too.

When we pull away, I can breathe again. Wyatt's eyes flutter open. We stare at each other for a long moment, realizing what just happened.

Finally, I find my voice enough to whisper, "I . . . need a ride."

I meant to say something else, but the wires got crossed somewhere along the way. Wyatt smiles and my heart soars. But, as if on cue, I hear a familiar whinny.

I throw open the window.

"Chewy!"

The sleipnir and Wyatt's horse, Gamgee, are charging down the lane like proper warhorses. Chewy leaps and takes flight, using his eight hooves to pulverize draugar skulls from above, while Gamgee bucks and kicks from the ground. Chewy soars high into the sky, then circles around, heading right for the window, as if knowing exactly what I need to do.

"This is the second window I'm jumping out of today," I say, blushing because my lips still tingle from our kiss. I make sure the arrows are secure to my back and throw the bow over my shoulder.

Before I can jump on Chewy's saddle, Wyatt takes my hand. Somehow I know exactly what he's feeling. We might never see each other again. Neither of us say anything, we just look at each other. His hand in mine says enough. He gives me a nod and I give his hand a squeeze, before I leap out the window and onto Chewy. Wyatt climbs out onto the trellis after me.

When Chewy takes off to the sky, I look back one last time to see Wyatt and Gamgee galloping down the lane. Even from here, I can see his smile as he watches me go.

I push Chewy faster, leaning low. Prima should have really thought about her intentions more carefully when she set her fjötra. I don't plan on walking anywhere.

"To the stars, Chewy!"

My eyes water as Chewy races toward the clouds, carrying me into the dark sky, and my fingers go numb from clutching the reins so hard.

He breaches the clouds and bursts into a sea of starlight, Yggdrasil cutting like a ribbon through the sky.

I hold the raven feather toward the stars.

"Take me to Asgard!"

35

THE RAVEN'S FEATHER FILLS WITH THE LIGHT OF YGGDRASIL
and explodes in a kaleidoscope of color.

One second I'm flying high above Chicago, and the next, I'm flying
high above a strange and alien city made of glittering gold and silver.

Asgard. The realm of the gods.

But the city is dark. I don't see any fires, or lights, or anything at
all. A bright strip of stars crosses the sky to light my way, a constel-
lation I don't recognize except for the branch of Yggdrasil. Now, more
than the chill of the air raises the hairs on my skin. I lean low into
Chewy's neck as he gallops through the clouds.

"I need to get to Valhalla," I say into his ear, and Chewy snorts in
response as if he already knows.

A dark shape looms on the horizon ahead of us, and it takes my
breath away seeing it for the first time.

Valhalla.

An arena of the chosen dead.

It's exactly like Mom described, except when she said it was massive, I guess I never really understood what that meant. Golden

towers jut out of the arena, like a city on its own, surrounded by a high wall. But it too is dark, lifeless.

I squeeze Chewy's mane as he dives, and I'm lifted out of my seat slightly, tears streaking across my face from the wind. At the last second before hitting the ground, Chewy pulls up and lands as light as a feather on one of the golden bridges, leading into a door flanked by two giant statues of valkyries in full armor.

Silence. No shouts, no sounds of battle, nothing. Everything is quiet and dark. Just like the vision I had the night I met Juniper.

"I don't like this...." I say, after I dismount.

Chewy whickers and shakes his head.

"You scared, buddy?" I pat him on the chest. "Me too. But I brought you home, like I promised."

With a huff, Chewy trots past me and heads toward what looks like a small set of stables at the foot of one of the valkyrie statues. Chewy seems to call out and a couple other sleipnir trot from their stalls. They nicker to each other, and rest their heads on one another's necks. If I had to take a wild guess, I'd say this is Chewy's family.

With my bow in hand, I quietly make my way into Valhalla. It takes a while for my eyes to adjust to the dark. The first thing that hits me is the smell. Bonfire, mead, and ... blood. I hold my bow tighter, scanning for any movement in the shadows.

For all I know, Thrúd kept some einherjar behind as reinforcement. It's what I would do.

As my eyes adjust, I find myself walking in a large field surrounded by immense skyscrapers. The field is littered with swords and shields. This is where they must train.

I nearly drop my bow when I look up and see a stag walking on top of the skyscrapers. Its coat glitters like starlight. The stag stretches its neck high enough to graze on the stars of Yggdrasil above. Eik-thyrnir. It prunes the World Tree, ensuring new growth. I'm truly stunned. I've never seen anything more beautiful.

As if it senses I'm watching, Eikthyrnir looks down at me with bright starlight eyes.

"Don't mind me," I say.

Eikthyrnir takes another large stride atop a nearby skyscraper, and steps out of view, soundless despite its gargantuan size.

I don't see another creature as I walk through the city. It's as quiet as a mausoleum.

At the center of the city is a large hall, small compared to the rest of the buildings, but large enough it's like its own sports arena. Its roof is thatched with shields, and a stone wolf snarls at me above the door.

The mead hall. This is it.

As I push open the heavy door, I edge aside goblets and plates, all littered across the floor. It's a mess in here, like someone had the ultimate rager. It's dark, and I trip over something heavy that slides across the stone. Bending down to pick it up, I can see it more clearly. It's a valkyrie's helm. One of the wings on its temples is broken and my fingers come away rusty brown. Dried blood.

My stomach churns uneasily and I set down the helm.

The army of Valhalla has emptied out into Midgard. There's no one left, not even the valkyries. Except me.

I swallow a thick lump in my throat and keep walking.

Above me is the ceiling made of shields, a cloud of nebulas barely lighting the way, just like my vision. I try to keep my footsteps as quiet as possible as I walk. I use some of the stone pillars for cover, and rush between the columns of unlit braziers, staying low and quiet, and try to stay out of sight. My heartbeat echoes in my ears, making it almost impossible for me to hear anything else.

I go on for what feels like forever, until a shape appears through the mist.

Yggdrasil twinkles softly in the dim light, and the tops of its branches disappear into clouds, covering the ceiling high above. Thousands of weapons stick out of the trunk, waiting to be used by those who are worthy. It's just like my vision.

The only difference is the three figures chained to the tree.

"Mom!"

I run for her first.

Next to her, Prima and Reagan are unconscious and bloodied. A gash runs across Prima's eyebrow, and Reagan's lip is bleeding. But Mom looks the worst of them all. Just like my vision, she's covered in blood and bruises. When I reach her, I put my hands on the sides of her face to lift her head. To my relief, her skin is still warm. Her eyes flutter open, unfocused at first, but I break into a smile when her gaze lands on me.

"No," she croaks.

"It's me! It's okay. I'll get you out of here." I check on Prima and Reagan, but the both of them barely move when I shake them. Prima groans and Reagan's head lolls to the side.

"Bryn, run," Mom says, her voice stronger.

"I can't. I won't."

"You should." The voice makes me spin around, heart in my throat.

It's Thrúd, watching me with amusement. She emerges from behind the tree, her helm tucked under her arm, decked out in full armor.

"I tried to be merciful," she says. "Dying on Midgard would have been a noble death. But you can't make anything easy for anyone, can you?"

"It's over, Thrúd." I bluff. "Call off your army."

Lazily, as if she's in no rush, Thrúd walks around me, smiling.

347

She always knew I was a bad liar. "It's too late." She drops down onto Odin's throne, like she's lounging on a La-Z-Boy, and waves her hand. The unlit braziers spark to life, illuminating the hall in a fiery glow. "We are well beyond the negotiation phase."

"Where's Odin?"

"Haven't you heard?" Thrúd asks. "It's the end of the universe."

In one fluid move, I nock an arrow and let fly. The arrow aims true, straight at Thrúd's chest, but Thrúd catches it in a web of bright blue lightning. The arrow shakes and snaps in two with a zap of electricity.

Thrúd smiles. "Good. I'm done talking, too." The air shimmers around her as a dozen blades—swords, spears, knives—gleaming and solid as steel materialize around her, pointed right at me. She stands up and tosses her helm to my mom's feet, like she won't be needing it.

I stumble back as Thrúd walks toward me, arms thrown wide.

Armored wings emerge from her back and Thrúd rises into the air.

"Shall we see what a real valkyrie can do?"

36

IT'S RAINING METAL AS THRÚD THROWS BLADE AFTER BLADE, whizzing like bullets. I hide behind the tree, but Thrúd follows me.

I don't have time to look as I let loose an arrow, but she blocks it with a cluster of blades. She winks at me and laughs, lobbing more blades my way again. "You can't summon your weapons? How embarrassing!"

I leap for cover behind Odin's throne, and eat dirt as I hit the ground.

"Here, let me show you!" Thrúd calls. She throws a bolt of lightning at a column.

Pieces of it rain down on me as the column groans and sways, and I realize it's falling. Shifting rocks grumble like thunder and it tips toward me. I scramble out of the way just as the column comes crashing down, crushing Odin's throne so hard that it rattles my teeth.

I shove myself up and let off another arrow. Thrúd blocks it with a lazy hand wave. "Boring!"

Column after column she blasts to dust, and all I can do is try not to get flattened.

She's stronger than I ever imagined. This is what a real valkyrie is supposed to be. Relentless, furious, insatiable.

I have to get away from her.

"Stand and fight!" she shouts.

I dive behind an upturned table and shield my head as Thrúd lets loose a volley of blades from above, embedding themselves within the wood like target practice. One of the swords pierces straight through, coming out the other side inches from my eye.

"How ordinary of you, Bryn. Run and hide. Are you not a valkyrie?"

Everything I've tried to repress, every joke I've used to cover up whatever I was feeling, bubbles up inside of me and turns to acid. I could kill Thrúd.

I want to kill her.

It's what I was trained to do.

I was built for this. I was born for this. I am a valkyrie, a decimator of armies, of men.

But I'm hiding behind a table.

My skin tickles, and all my hair stands on end.

I dive out of cover and hit the floor just as lightning strikes the exact spot I was a second ago. My ears ring. I barely get to my feet again before Thrúd grabs my throat and punches me in the face.

Stars burst in my eyes.

I fly backward through the air and hit the floor. The room keeps spinning even after I stop. Blood fills my mouth and I spit it out. My face throbs, burning hot.

"This is how I initiate new einherjar," Thrúd says. Her voice is muffled by the ringing in my ears. "Find any weakness, and crush it."

I look up just in time to see Thrúd's greaves as she moves to kick me, but I roll out of the way and run to another table. Her laughter follows.

She's playing with me.

I don't have any magic. I don't have any armor. I'm the worst valkyrie.

Thrúd sends another bolt of lightning and breaks the table I'm hiding behind in half, sending the smoldering pieces flying clear across the hall. More columns fall, crumbling to pieces, rubble scattering the floor, making it hard for me to run.

"I feel kind of bad," she says. "And Kara trained you?"

"How about you give me my armor back for a fair fight!"

Thrúd laughs and hurls spears at me. I hide under another table, crawling on my stomach to get to the other side. I can't keep running.

I roll out and land on one knee. I take aim again but something knocks into my shoulder, sending my arrow wide.

I'm on the floor. I don't know what happened. Then—

Pain.

Hot. Blinding.

I can't breathe. I drop my bow.

I put my hand to my shoulder to get rid of whatever it is, only to find an arrow there.

Thrúd shot me. Every move is agony.

I let out a howl and kick the table, knocking it over, to take cover again.

Thrúd laughs. "Not so fun, is it?"

I can barely think. It's like my brain has short-circuited. I know I shouldn't, but I rip the arrow out, and white-hot fire rips through me when I do. I think I'm screaming, but I don't know. Blood runs down the sleeve of my chemise.

I'm going to die here.

My blood is hot and wet, drenching my clothes, and it's the only thing that matters in the universe. That's all there ever is. Pain.

I can't move my arm. Can't move my fingers. Everything hurts too much.

Thrúd's blades start to sound like rain, a steady rhythm beating against the table. She's coming for me.

Dust and ash choke the air, fires blaze. The world is crumbling around me.

I look at my mom and my sisters.

Prima's eyes drag open, and she sees me.

I can still hear her voice.

All you ever do is ruin everything.

Could I have done anything to make all of this different? Could I have done something that would have stopped this from ever happening?

Prima and I look at each other for a long second.

She's right. All I ever do is ruin everything.

Blood drips down my limp fingers and falls to the floor.

I'm not good for anything.

Thrúd starts laughing, but it sounds distant and tinny, like I'm hearing it from far away.

Thrúd doesn't care about Ravenswood, Midgard, or even Valhalla. She's destroyed most of it already. She doesn't care about anything. She would rather burn the world than save it.

I look back at Prima.

Maybe she is right. I ruin everything, too.

I peek through a hole in the table and find my target.

I have one last play, one last move, and it's the most obvious move I can make.

37

"COME OUT, BRYN!" THRÚD CALLS IN A SINGSONG VOICE. "Let's end this already. I'm bored."

I pick up Thrúd's arrow, still slick with my blood, and nock it into my bow.

Pain like fire shoots up my arm—

Black spots swarm my vision—

My hand is numb, my muscles scream for me to stop—

I bite down on my tongue to stop myself from passing out. I get to my knees and take aim.

Thrúd grins, floating toward me. She's in no rush. She's almost here.

Tears blur my eyes.

I let loose.

Thrúd doesn't even flinch as the arrow whizzes by her ear. Only her auburn hair moves in its wake as it harmlessly shoots by.

I drop my bow and it clatters to the floor. I can't hold it any longer. Everything hurts.

Thrúd's laugh echoes in the hall. "You missed!" She lands in front of me and smiles in disbelief, looking at me with something almost like disappointment. "I'm literally right here! You really are the worst."

"I didn't miss," I say, holding my shoulder.

It starts off as a groan above us, then slowly it turns into a kind of craggy growl.

Thrúd's smile drops at the sound, as she turns and looks up to see my arrow wedged in a crack in the ceiling. A weak point. Giant fissures spread like bolts from where I hit.

With all the support columns Thrúd destroyed, the ceiling starts to crumble. Pieces drop, one by one. Then, all at once, it falls.

I barely have time to duck under the table and cover my head.

The air surges and snaps with Thrúd's lightning as she tries to deflect it, but even she's not powerful enough to stop Valhalla as it crashes down on us.

Thrúd screams—

It's so loud—

All the fires go out as the ceiling turns into an avalanche of stone and wood and gold. Everything goes dark. I choke as dust fills my nose and mouth. The ceiling thunders down around me like bombs and my ears ring, even after the noise settles.

It's so quiet, I think I'm dead, but being dead can't hurt this much.

The table collapsed on top of me, but it protected me. It presses down on my back, but I'm not pinned. I cough and choke on more dust.

I'm blind. My eyes sting with ash and grit. A high-pitched whine echoes in my head. I stumble out from under the table and trip on rubble. My knees shake. I can barely stand. The world seesaws under me, and I fall before I can stay on my feet.

Valhalla is in ruins. A gaping hole in the roof spans overhead, opening up to the stars above. Yggdrasil. Seeing the ribbon of light stirs something in me and it burns hot in my gut.

I move with singular purpose. My bow lies buried under some rubble and I snatch it up just as a pile shifts and Thrúd's hand emerges.

She huffs and puffs as she hauls huge rocks off herself. She looks like she's in grayscale, covered in so much dust, except for the sheet of blood creeping down her face.

When she looks up, she stares directly down the line of my arrow.

All I have to do is let it go.

Killing her would be so easy. This whole time, she's done nothing but cause misery and lie and hurt the people I care about most.

The universe would be a better place if she wasn't in it.

Slowly, Thrúd kneels before me, her shaking hands raised above her head. Looking at her, with her messy hair and her bloody nose, and her dirt-strewn face, I can see her up close for the first time in a long time.

Dust falls around us, like snow, and all I can think about is seeing a target bright and still in the dark during a blizzard. I know what to do. It's all I ever do.

"Please," Thrúd says, her voice breaking and weak.

I want to kill her. I really do. After everything she's done to me, to my family, to my friends, my home ... The muscles in my back ache with the strain of holding the bowstring taut. All it takes is for me to drop my fingers, let the arrow do the work, let fate decide. I am a third party in Thrúd's death. It'll be so *easy*.

"Bryn." My mom's voice is strong and firm as it cuts through the din of silence. Her gray eyes capture mine.

Once the arrow leaves your hand, you can't take it back.

Those were her words that night all those years ago.

My breath hitches and I look at Thrúd again. She looks so small, and cowers in front of me as she waits for me to put an arrow through her eye.

I am an agent of fate. And I can choose.

And I can't kill her. I can't kill anyone.

Maybe I really am the worst valkyrie, and maybe that's okay.

I lower my bow. "End this. Call off your army," I say.

"I surrender," gasps Thrúd. "The only thing I do now is beg for mercy."

A breath tickles the back of my neck.

Somewhere distant, I hear bells ringing, like the ones on the tree in Ravenswood.

Something in Thrúd's eyes isn't right. Her fingers twitch.

I know those words. The words of a Black Knight.

I'm diving before I can think.

One of Thrúd's astral swords bolts from behind me at lightning speed.

With a thud, it stops deep in Thrúd's breastplate. She gasps, like she's been punched, and shock opens her face.

She heaves, trying to breathe, but she can't. Her breath rattles, thick and wet. She looks at the sword sticking out of her chest and then up at me, confused, furious, and offended.

I rush to her. Blood spills from the hole in her armor as the sword dematerializes. She coughs, and more sprays out of her mouth. I grab her shoulders just before she falls back.

"Oh," Thrúd gasps, eyes barely focused on me. "Very good."

I don't know what to do. I need to help her. She tried to trick me, but I have to help her. I need to stop the bleeding. I move to take off her armor, but she stops my hand, clutching it so hard it hurts.

Then Thrúd looks at me, and does just about the worst thing she can do: smile.

And then she dies.

38

I FREE MY MOM FIRST, USING A ROCK TO BREAK THE FJÖTRA that bind her arms and legs to the tree.

"Oh, my little valkyrie," she says, holding my face and smiling through tears. She kisses me on both cheeks, and wipes the dirt from my face. I can barely move my arm, but I don't care. I missed her so much.

Together, we free Prima and Reagan.

Everyone's arms wrap around me and we collapse into a huddle on the ground.

"I'm sorry," I say. It's what I should have said a long time ago. And I realize I'm crying. Not just crying, full-on sobbing. "I'm so sorry. For everything."

I don't care that I look like a baby, bawling my eyes out in front of my strong, capable, better-than-me family. It doesn't matter anymore.

Everyone keeps telling me it's okay, but I keep crying, like I've never cried before. I've been holding all of it in until now, and now I can't stop.

"You did so good," Prima says. She's crying, too. "I'm the one who's sorry. I was wrong. I should have listened to you."

"No, I'm sorry!" I say, ignoring the fact that Prima never admits that she's wrong. It's my turn to say it.

"We're all sorry!" Reagan cries. She's holding on to our mother like she did when she was little, pulling on Mom's armor and letting the tears streak her mascara.

Mom shushes us, and squeezes us all tight. It's so good to finally be together again, I don't even care about my shoulder. I'm not sure how long we stay huddled in one another's arms, and I've cried so hard for so long, I'm exhausted. But we're not done.

"Einherjar are attacking Ravenswood right now," I say, wiping my nose on my arm. "I don't know how much time we have left until they destroy everything."

Mom brings us all to our feet, and Prima and Reagan finally take in the state of the hall around us. When they look up through the hole in the roof, they can see the stag Eikthyrnir looking down at them, its jaw rolling as it munches on starlight.

"Bryn, what did you do?" Reagan asks.

"Valhalla is totally wrecked," Prima says.

I shrug my good shoulder. "That sounds like an Odin problem."

Prima and Reagan glance at each other.

"This way, girls!" Mom says as she runs, leading the way through the sea of rubble.

Before I follow them, I pick up my bow and what arrows I have left and look at Thrúd's body. Dangling from her armor, I spot my necklace. I yank it free. It's covered in dust, but I wipe it clean with my thumb and put it around my neck. Squeezing it tightly, I wipe my eyes and glance at Thrúd's lifeless form before running after my family.

At the sleipnir stables, my family is waiting, including Chewy, who trots over, ears perked, as if glad to see me. I press my hand on his nose and he leans into my touch. I admit, I'm glad to see him, too.

Mom leads the last of the sleipnir out, one for each of us.

"Your raven cloak won't carry us home?" Reagan asks, holding on to a spotted sleipnir's reins.

"We'll have to do this the old-fashioned way," Mom says with a twinkle in her eye.

"Think you can make another trip, Chewy?" I ask.

Chewy flutters his lips. I take that as a yes.

Mom leads the way, nudging her sleipnir into a gallop into the sky, her hair flying out behind her. I wrap Chewy's reins around my arm, securing myself to his back, and follow behind Prima and Reagan.

Mom's sleipnir kicks up storm clouds and lightning sparks under hoof and—with a crack of thunder—a rainbow stretches out ahead of us. The Bifröst, the rainbow bridge between Asgard and Midgard.

We burst through the veil between realms, riding on waves of thunder, as Chicago materializes in front of us, cast in gray morning light.

"Charge!" Mom yells. She's the most beautiful person I've ever seen as she stands in the stirrups from her saddle, her sword in her hand, raised above her head.

We dive for the water, breaking through the clouds, and Ravenswood rises to meet us. My stomach leaps into my chest as I lift off Chewy's back and hold on as hard as I can, but I'm not afraid of anything anymore. I'm home.

Mom releases a volley of blades, raining down on the undead army. They yell and howl, as her swords pierce them and slice through their skeletal bodies, and they crumble back into dirt, and the white smoke of their souls dissipates.

Prima spikes draugar, one after the other, charging her sleipnir overhead, driving the army back with a war cry.

Reagan throws her astral knives like a dancer, graceful and beautiful, and laughs with pure joy.

Without Thrúd's command, the draugar are vulnerable. The few that remain are exposed and weak as the sun rises with us.

Mom charges into the square first, letting out a high, keening shriek to make gleaming chains appear around the draugar, binding them. A fjötra. They can't escape fate.

Prima swoops in, letting her spear fly, and it soars through a handful of them in one shot. Mom calls Reagan to her side and together they ride past more draugar, launching a volley of blades that drops them like bags of flour.

I charge Chewy at a group of draugar and they fall under his hooves. My shoulder throbs like fire when I shoot more with my arrows, but I don't let it stop me. I have never felt so alive. I let fly until I have no arrows left.

"Here!" Reagan calls beside me.

She summons arrows from nothing, refilling my quiver, each one glowing with her power. I draw one and it streaks like a meteor, sending a draug's helmet flying, only for Prima to drive her spear into its head.

We lock eyes and smile.

Prima throws me one end of her spear, and we clothesline a row of draugar as our sleipnir charge on the ground. Reagan and I take turns shooting draugar as they try to regroup.

"That's it, girls!" Mom shouts, flying overhead, raining death down on the battlefield. Draugar don't stand a chance against her. Against us.

We were born for this.

I kick Chewy into gear and he hunts draugar down like the

warhorse he is, trampling them under his hooves. I take him to the sky to survey the land. There aren't many left.

Three shadows rush out of the castle. No doubt Juniper, Wyatt, and James. Their cheers are almost drowned out by the wind whipping in my ears. I guide Chewy lower, circling us back to the castle.

Before Chewy stops, I leap off his saddle and land in front of Wyatt, as Juniper and James rush into the fray.

Wyatt stares at me, breathless and flushed, but he looks unhurt.

"Hey!" I say, brightly.

The battle rages around us, but I don't care about that anymore. Not when Wyatt's here.

"Hey," Wyatt says, panting. He's filthy from the fight, and the sword in his hand is covered in dirt. He looks amazed, staring at me with relief all over his face, and then he swoops in for a hug. "You're okay!"

"*Ow, ow, ow,*" I say, and he immediately lurches back. He sees I'm hurt and hisses through his teeth.

"Sorry, sorry." He looks at me for a long moment, but a draug appears out of the ground and tries to grab us. Wyatt and I step on its head, hardly even glancing at it, because we're too busy looking at each other. The draug turns to dirt and dies once more.

I have a million things I want to say to Wyatt, but I can't seem to settle on one. Instead, I kiss him. I taste dirt, and blood, and sweat, but I don't care. My mind goes quiet and all I think about is Wyatt's lips on mine. I barely even hear Mom, Prima, and Reagan howl with bloodlust as they continue to fly overhead. His hand on the back of my head helps distract me from the throb in my shoulder. I could stay like this forever.

Wyatt and I pull back from our kiss just as the last of the draugar's unnatural screams fade into nothing, and the sun rises up over the trees.

I can't stop smiling and neither can he.

Mom, Prima, and Reagan land their sleipnir nearby as Juniper comes rushing toward me, barely stopping even when she throws herself into me, hugging me so tightly, I wheeze. "Bryn, you are incredible! Truly! Incredible!"

"She's hurt, Juniper," says Wyatt, laughing.

"Oh!" She pulls back to see the pain on my face. She frets her hand over the wound in my shoulder. "I am terrible—I can make you a poultice!"

"Juniper?" Mom dismounts from her sleipnir, looking at her with surprise.

At the sound of her voice, Juniper freezes, slowly dropping her arms from around me. She hasn't seen Mom since . . . well, probably ever. I can't imagine what's going through her mind right now.

Her lower lip trembles. "M—Mother?" Tears form in the corners of her eyes.

"Juniper, how did you . . . ?"

Juniper slowly walks to her, but stops herself just before reaching her. She holds out a hand. "Um," she says, eyes lowered. "Hello."

Mom grabs her in a tight hug and kisses her repeatedly on the forehead and cheeks. "You're here! I thought you were going to stay in Utgard forever! I can't believe it!"

Juniper's hands slowly come up around Mom's shoulders, and I can see she's smiling with relief. While Mom fusses over Juniper, Prima comes over to me.

"So she really is our half sister," I say, watching as Mom licks her thumb and cleans dirt off Juniper's cheek.

"Yeah."

"I think she would appreciate an apology, too," I say.

After everything we've been through, it's the least Prima could do, and Prima seems to know that. She chews on the inside of her cheek, looking ashamed. "Yeah," she says again. "Here." She nudges a small leather waterskin in my direction. Inside is healing mead, from Valhalla.

"How'd you get this?" I ask.

"Stole it when we were leaving."

I stare at Prima and a smile curls the corners of my mouth.

"Don't go using it all up like last time," she says.

She raises a single eyebrow at me before walking away, and I know that everything is better—not perfect, but better—between us. I'll take better any day.

I watch as she goes to Juniper, says a few words to her, and Juniper wraps her arms around her. Apparently the apology is accepted. Reagan joins in, too. Mom looks on, crying. My family is here, and that's all I've ever wanted.

The mead stitches up my shoulder and the intense throbbing turns into only a mild one. I bring some to Wyatt, who's standing by the sleipnir, staring at them with adoration. When he looks at me, my heart nearly bursts out of my chest. I'm not sure I'll ever get used to this.

Wyatt takes a swig of mead, and James comes up behind him, thumping him so hard on the back he almost spits.

"You did good," James says, bloodied, bruised, but grinning, as he throws his arm over Wyatt's shoulders.

Wyatt wipes his mouth with the back of his wrist and says, "We did good. Listen, I know what I said earlier, but you were right. We are friends. So thanks."

"Yeah, well, I've been hard on you for a while. Can you blame me for wanting to test you? But I think you've proven yourself, little cub." He claps Wyatt on the back again and steps away. "I won't be bothering you anymore."

"What?"

"And you!" he says, pointing to me. "Better watch your back. You've made some enemies in very high places after what you've done."

"Huh?"

When James smiles, a row of scars appear around his mouth. Like someone sewed his mouth shut.

"Loki?" Wyatt asks, stunned.

The scars disappear and James gives him finger-guns, winking. "Catch me later!"

Wyatt rushes toward him, but James vanishes in the blink of an eye, and a fly buzzes away from where he'd just been standing.

Wyatt stares after him, shoulders rising and falling, and he slowly turns back to me, stunned. "Did you see . . . ?"

I nod, but before I can say anything, the castle doors burst open and the guests flood out, looking dazed and confused in the new morning light. Among them are the *Travel Expert Magazine* critics, wearing baffled expressions, their clipboards still in hand.

Mr. Beaumont stumbles out with the rest of them, his perfectly coiffed hair standing on end as he takes in the ruins of Ravenswood with a mystified look about him.

Everyone stares at the battlefield, the armor of the cursed einherjar scattered everywhere, the troll statue now wearing a discarded helm on his ear, the smoldering ruins of shops and stalls, the sleipnir. Some bunting overhead falls loose and drops slowly, fluttering in the wind. Ravenswood is ruined.

There's a moment of silence. Then, the crowd bursts into a deafening cheer.

Like someone flipped a switch, Mr. Beaumont sees dollar signs. I bet we're going to have a tough time explaining this one, but I think he'll get over it soon, especially with the critics shaking his hand and congratulating him.

I share a look with my family, who are all suppressing their own laughter. Mom takes the lead and does a fancy curtsy. Juniper, Prima, and Reagan follow suit.

I hold out my hand for Wyatt. He's still looking around for Loki.

"Hey," I say, getting his attention. "You and me."

His face breaks into a smile as he puts his hand in mine, and we take a bow together.

39

ON THE LAST DAY OF THE SEASON, I BOUND DOWN THE stairs and out of the house, weaving through the line of people leading to the forge. Prima's at the register while guests look at the gleaming swords and knives she and Mom have been making together all summer.

After the house was rebuilt, Mom and Prima reopened the smith shop to welcome fanfare. Custom orders already have a huge waitlist. And Prima's been getting really good at working iron. Mom taught her how to make horseshoes, just like Dad used to.

"Aren't you supposed to be working?" Prima calls out when she sees me.

"Half day!" I say, hopping sideways. "Love you, too!"

Prima makes a face. Some things between us haven't changed.

I'm in such a rush I nearly bump into Stan as he heads toward the shop. "Easy there!" he says, smiling.

"Sorry, Mr. Evans! Need more horseshoes?"

He holds up a paper order form. "We're burning through them pretty quick." He catches Prima's eye and she comes out and takes it.

He's here almost every day, what with the sleipnir having a few extra hooves to run on. Stan's been keeping them in the stables for us until Asgard notices they're missing and asks for them back, which hopefully won't happen for a while.

When I told Mom that Stan knew about valkyries, she admitted he and my dad found out when they were all my age. It made sense then why Stan had come to Ravenswood after he found out about Wyatt's berserker abilities. He trusted her to help. Our number one house rule was broken before any of us were born. Figures.

Don't get me wrong though, I'm not mad about it. In fact I'm kind of glad we can trust other people, too.

All of us go over to the stables every weekend to play euchre.

Before I head to the gift shop, I make a pit stop to say hello to the landvaettir, dropping a handful of pennies in Yggdrasil's roots. It's becoming a daily ritual for me now. They shake the branches on the trees, and I know they're happy, too.

Cheers erupt from the arena for Wyatt's show. With Thrúd dead, no one else will be throwing any more mushroom smoke bombs making him go berserk anymore, so Wyatt decided to come back as the Black Knight. These days, the only thing he has to worry about is vengeful guests looking to empty more strawberry slushies over his head. From the square, I can hear Wyatt's voice as it carries over the speakers just before the big betrayal.

On cue, the crowd gasps and then there's thunderous applause.

Prince James is victorious once again, but the Black Knight will always return.

The real James Beaumont showed back up again a day after the battle, looking tan and confused. Apparently he'd won an all-expenses-paid vacation to a resort in Mexico, for a contest he never remembered entering, but nonetheless took advantage of it. He has no idea what happened here while he was gone. He and Reagan are still broken up, much to Reagan's relief.

It's weird knowing that the James we interacted with that whole time wasn't who we thought he was. I should have known it the moment he knew my name. At least we don't have to put up with any more of Loki's bad poetry.

I pass Reagan as she's just finishing her set on one of the smaller stages, striking a pose with a handful of knives to adoring applause. She sees me and winks, not breaking her pose. I'll miss her when she goes off to school next week. She's already picked out how she wants to decorate her dorm. I didn't know they made so much pink. Last night, Mom caught her trying to figure out how to smuggle Butternut Squash into her trunk.

Going off to school doesn't mean we stop being valkyries. In fact, we might be needed more than ever now.

All the einherjar from Valhalla are gone. Even though Thrúd's curse was broken, their spirits didn't return when we killed all the draugar. Mom tried to track them down, but it's as easy as catching ghosts. At least, they're not bothering anyone. They're just regular spirits until Odin claims them again. Wyatt isn't one of them, at least.One thing's for certain: Odin knows full well that I didn't bring Wyatt to Valhalla. But I have a hunch he can't afford to fire me, seeing as most of the valkyries are dead. He can't risk losing any more. Plus, he has bigger problems to deal with.

Folks in Asgard are trying to figure out what to do next. Most of the gods are debating if Ragnarök even happened or not and the fact that Thor's daughter tried to usurp Odin and start a universal war is a particular point of contention. Word from the ravens is that a search for the Norns has begun. I'm glad I don't have to be involved in any of those conversations, because I'm sick and tired of gods and prophecies for the foreseeable future.

According to Mom, who had to give a detailed report on the subject, Odin is furious. His army is gone. The prophecy never said that would happen. Apparently Odin had been in Jotunheim looking for Loki, thinking he was responsible for the missing einherjar, but never found him. I don't think we'll be telling Odin that Loki was the one helping us all along. Maybe Loki really did want to change his fate after all.

Lunch is always the busiest time at the park, but even more so now that it's the last full weekend of the summer season, and the food is flying off the counters. Elephant ears, beer-battered fish and chips, and deep-dish pizza. I'll never get tired of it.

Taking my usual route, I stop by the Dragon's Den to grab an apple and water. They've replaced Thrúd with a sweet college girl from Wisconsin. No one batted an eyelash when Thrúd disappeared. Most assumed that she fled during the attack.

Thinking about her hurts still. Sometimes I think I see her in a crowd, but when I look again, it's someone else. I'm not sure if it's a valkyrie thing or if I'm still struggling to process what happened in Valhalla, but one thing's for sure—I don't regret sparing her at all. I know it wasn't the valkyrie-like thing to do, but I'd try to save her again if I could, even after she tried to stab me in the back. If her ghost haunts me, I hope she knows that and it makes her furious.

The weeks after the battle in Valhalla were a blur. Most of it was spent with Mom and Juniper catching up after being separated for years. They would talk for hours on the balcony, just like we all do with Mom, and it's so normal now that Juniper gets to do it, too. I still haven't asked Mom the whole story yet, how she and Fenrir met, but I'm in no rush. Maybe she'll tell me one day when the time is right. I'm just happy to have another sister.

After learning why Juniper came to Midgard in the first place, Mom sent a raven to Utgard, asking about survivors, and Angrboda replied the next day, saying that most of the villagers had escaped to the woods. The village was destroyed, but just like Ravenswood, there is always a chance to rebuild. Angrboda was anxious to see Juniper again, but let Juniper stay for the rest of the summer.

It's hard to believe she leaves today. Don't even get me started on how much I'm going to miss her.

When I step into the gift shop, Juniper is already there waiting for me, along with an unsurprising face. They don't look up when I come in—they're so focused on each other. Quietly as I can, I flip the sign to OPEN in the window and let them have their moment.

"I made these, special for you," Danny the herbalist says as he hands her a couple of seed bombs. "Blazing star, zinnia, snapdragons. I hope you like the colors."

Juniper holds them close to her chest, beaming, then slips them into her seed pouch. "Thank you! Danny, you are too sweet."

I smile as I try not to make too much noise and pretend I'm reorganizing the coffee mug shelf.

"I wish we had more time to get to know each other this summer. Text me?"

"Text? You?" I hear the confusion in her voice and I peek over my shoulder.

"Yeah, what's your number?" Danny asks.

Juniper gives him a blank look.

"She has an international number," I say, coming to her rescue. "The fees are crazy high. How about an old-fashioned letter?"

Juniper brightens at that and claps. "Oh yes! I love letters! Write to me."

Danny smiles. "Okay, yeah. I can do that."

"I am so grateful to have a good friend like you who shares my interests!"

Danny's smile falls. "Friend?"

"Yes! Friend!" She's smiling so brightly, and so enthusiastically, I don't think she notices the heartbreak on Danny's face.

Danny swallows down any disappointment he might have and smiles again. "Okay, well, bye!"

"Goodbye!" Juniper waves as he leaves, still smiling.

When the door closes, I say, "He was flirting with you."

She turns around, eyebrows creased. "He was?"

"You didn't notice?"

"No!"

"I figured you were good at picking up on that kind of stuff, like you did with me and Wyatt."

"That is only because you two were as obvious as snowfall!"

I snort when I laugh. I guess it's different when you're on the outside looking in.

"I am not interested in romantic relationships," Juniper says. "I should have told him! Do you think he will be upset?"

"He'll get over it. You sure you don't want to stay in Ravenswood?" I ask.

"I must go back to Utgard. I need to help rebuild my village. But I will be back, I promise."

"You'd better," I say.

"You could come visit me!"

I shake my head. "I am grounded. Big-time."

"What for?"

"Would you like an itemized list?"

That makes Juniper laugh. I know my intentions were good, but I did break almost every rule in the house to save everyone's life, so I'm not too mad about the fact that I have lost all phone, computer, and television privileges for a year. No technology that isn't related to school. Mom could ground me forever and I'd be happy so long as my family was safe. I take my punishment with grace. Besides, making out with Wyatt for hours under Yggdrasil makes me forget all about stupid things like the internet.

The bell above the door chimes and Wyatt comes in, with Gamgee waiting outside. Wyatt's covered in sweat, still wearing his Black Knight armor.

"Good! I didn't miss you," he says to Juniper.

He comes to me first and plants a sweaty kiss on my forehead before going to Juniper next, holding out a paper bag. "This is for you," he says.

Juniper peeks in the bag and shrieks, "Jalapeño poppers!" He might as well have given her a bag of gold. She bounces on her feet. "You remembered!"

"Hard to forget when you react like that about jalapeño poppers," he says, grinning. "Though I'm not sure how well they'll travel. You'll probably want to eat them soon."

I already know they won't make it out of the shop. Juniper eats one immediately and melts with a sigh.

This summer hasn't been so bad. Sure, it was kind of scary, and really stressful, but it's probably the best summer I've ever had. I almost don't want Juniper to go. It would be selfish of me to make her stay.

"You have to raven-message me every day," I say, my breath

hitching. "If you miss even one day, I'm stealing Mom's cloak and I'm going to Utgard immediately."

Juniper laughs. "Do not worry. Mother invited me back for Yule, so I will have two valkyries mad at me if I do not keep my promise."

I twist my lips and nod. Wyatt glances at me. He must sense that I'm trying to keep it together and doing a lousy job about it. He tips his head toward Juniper and I don't need to be told twice.

I throw myself into Juniper's arms and bury my face in her shoulder. She hugs me back and we hold each other, neither of us willing to let go first. Just when I thought I had my whole family together, we have to split up again. This sucks.

I break the hug and turn away so I can wipe my eyes. When I gather myself and turn back around, putting on my usual smile, Mom comes in.

"Ready to go, Juniper?" she asks. She has her raven cloak draped over one arm, and she's still wearing her surcoat and chemise. "Your grandmother will have my hide if I don't have you home when I said I would. Hello there, Wyatt."

"Hi, Mrs. Martel," he says, putting on his glasses again.

Mom smiles, and then she sees me. "Bryn, are you crying?"

"What! No!" I say, my voice thick. Even I don't convince myself.

Juniper wraps me up in one last hug and says, "Thank you so much for everything. Truly. I could not ask for a better sister."

"Don't say that!" The dam breaks. I'm a sobbing mess.

Juniper lets me go and smiles at me, and I try to smile back, but it probably looks like I'm going to internally combust. Without letting the suffering drag out any longer, Juniper clips her moss cloak around her own shoulders and hefts her staff and waves goodbye. And then she and Mom are gone.

They'll be back.

I fold myself onto the counter and take a deep breath. I sense Wyatt come to my side and he leans on the counter next to me. Out of the corner of my eye, I see him watching people pass by the gift shop windows, and I'm glad he's not doing anything other than being with me.

It takes a minute for me to gather myself and I'm finally able to sigh.

"Okay," I say. "Now what?"

"Well, I'm done with my shows for the season. Now all I have to worry about is school."

I slip into an easy smile. "You ready to be North Shore High's newest senior? Fair warning, if you thought stopping Ragnarök was hard, just wait for Mrs. Hopper's homework."

"I'm used to being the new guy, so it won't be half as bad if you're around. And it's a relief not having to look over my shoulder for Loki for once. Besides, I like homework."

I scoff. "You like home— Who *are* you?" And I knock him with my elbow.

He smiles. I like making him do that. It makes me feel incredible. Almost as incredible as kissing him. "What do you say I flip that "Closed" sign over and we take Chewy for a ride for old times' sake?"

"Won't you get in trouble?"

Out the window, I spot a raven sitting on the roof of the building across the street. Another lands next to it, both of them turning their heads keenly, practically invisible to the fairegoers below.

Odin has eyes everywhere. He'll definitely be keeping a close watch on me.

I grin at Wyatt. "Only if I get caught."

ACKNOWLEDGMENTS

This book would not exist if not for the brilliant Melissa de la Cruz. You took a chance on me, and I'm forever grateful. You made all my dreams come true and I don't know how else I can thank you. Special thanks also goes to my mentor, Rebecca Johns-Trissler. It's been a long time since I've sat in your office and brought you homemade baked goods. I owe you more than cookies now.

To all the folks at Disney, you have my whole heart. My editors, Kieran Viola and Candice Snow, connected my last two brain cells together and took *Rise* to the next level. Your names should be immortalized in bards' songs, but I hope my gratitude will do in the meantime. Thank you to cover designer Phil Buchanan and illustrator Sasha Vinogradova for bringing Bryn to life. That smirk of hers brings me so much joy every time I see it. If you're holding this book, it's probably due to the tireless efforts of the marketing and sales geniuses: Holly Nagel, Danielle DiMartino, Ann Day, Crystal McCoy, Vicki Korlishin, and Marina Shults. Writing a book is a labor of love, but getting it in front of readers requires real magic. I also want to thank copyeditors Mark Amundsen and Sylvia Davis for their keen eyes and making sure Juniper doesn't love jalapeño "poopers." And to all the interns, assistants, anyone who so much as touched this book—you mean the world to me.

To my agent, Richard Abate, and assistants Hannah Carande and Martha Stevens: you were there at the very start. Thank you for your endless patience with my questions and your guidance through the chaos.

To my family: Hi, Mom and Dad! You both taught me to love stories and never to give up on my dreams. Hold fast, eh? And Joe and Mike, you made me a big sister and I don't say this enough but I love you guys.

Thank you to the Eva's Cafe writing group: Madigan and Warren, the next storytellers; Ann Marjory, for being the raddest beta reader and writing partner; Kat Keating, for being one of my dearest friends and the one who took me to my first ren fair. To Katharina Weinbrect: you are an amazing artist, writer, and the sharpest critique partner who sees what I can't. And Sarah Johnson: you are one of my oldest friends and I'm so lucky to know you. I'll write a "lazy" character for you someday.

And to the 2024-ever debut group: I'm so glad we're on this journey together. I'm so proud of us and so grateful to have met you all.

I also want to thank all booksellers, librarians, and teachers: you're literally saving lives. Education and access to books are human rights. And while *Rise* is a work of my own imagination, I relied heavily upon academics like Neil Price, Dr. Johanna Katrin Fridriksdottir, and Dr. Jackson Crawford for their expertise in all things Norse mythology and Nordic history.

Lastly but mostly, I want to thank my husband Alex: a lot of me is in this book, but so is a lot of you. I hope you never forget how amazing you are. You and me. <3

ABOUT THE AUTHOR

Freya Finch writes about myths, magic, and mischief-makers. Born and raised in Michigan, she earned her MA in writing and publishing from DePaul University in Chicago. Now she lives in the mountains of Poland, where you can find her hiking with her German shepherd or lounging at home with her husband watching their favorite movies. *Rise* is her first novel. Find her on Instagram @FreyaFinchAuthor or at her website, FreyaFinchBooks.com.